LORD OF THE MOOR

I ducked between the gypsy wagon and the small tent housing the tattooed man. I turned the corner too sharply and my foot caught on one of the ropes that secured the tent to the ground. To my chagrin, I went sprawling.

Before I could look up, hands were lifting me to my feet. Once more I came face to face with Lord Rathbone. When he drew me up, it was along the length of his sinewy body. Even through my petticoats I could feel the pressure of his legs against mine.

There was a wildness in his green eyes that startled me. His head lowered so swiftly and accurately that I had no time to think. His lips covered mine and his kiss was hard and tenacious. I knew I should pull away, but my will had fled. His kiss softened and became one of tender passion. I had never been kissed by a man in that manner, and didn't dare move lest I lose the memory of it.

When he finally pulled away, he thrust his hands into the small pockets of his breeches, his thumbs hooked over the top of them. He glared down at me and I could feel the color rush to my cheeks.

"Don't expect an apology, Miss Clarke."

LOST LADIES
OF THE
WINDSWEPT
MOOR
BEVERLY C. WARREN

ZEBRA BOOKS
KENSINGTON PUBLISHING CORP.

ZEBRA BOOKS

are published by

Kensington Publishing Corp.
475 Park Avenue South
New York, NY 10016

First printing: May, 1990

Printed in the United States of America

One

I nervously fingered the envelope I had thrust deep into the pocket of my blue merino skirt. Would my little subterfuge cost me the only prospect I had for survival?

I really hadn't done anything wrong. After all, my name is Janet Clarissa Clarke. It wasn't my fault I had the same initials as my father, Jeffrey Cullen Clarke, who was renowned as one of the foremost restorers of old paintings. Perhaps I should have signed my full name instead of just my initials.

No. I desperately needed the work and this Lord John Rathbone had implored J. C. Clarke to come to Cheviot Chase. I had every confidence in my ability to do the work with the same excellence as my late father. I prayed Lord Rathbone would give me the opportunity to display my proficiency in restoring his old paintings even though I was only nineteen and a woman. I hoped he wasn't a highly prejudiced man.

I had brought a book with me to read on the train to pass the time, but the scenery was far too enthralling for me to open the book. The train from London to Exeter made a number of stops, which gave me a chance to get off for several minutes and look around at the various stations. If I hadn't had that nagging worry at the back of my mind, the trip would have been a glorious adventure.

After steaming out of Taunton, I had to watch carefully for my stop, Honiton. I was now some one hundred and sixty miles from London, alone, and with less than a pound in my reticule, certainly not enough to take me back to London if I was not wanted at Cheviot Chase. And what would I do if I did go back to London? There was nothing there for me anymore. I pushed those questions to the back of my mind. I couldn't let myself think about them. I had to present a confident and controlled image before the Lord of Cheviot Chase.

Finally the train came to a halt at Honiton. By the time I gathered up my few belongings and left the train, my trunk had been unloaded. I stood there rather sheepishly as the several passengers who had disembarked began to drift away from the platform. I couldn't help wondering if my letter stating my time of arrival had reached Cheviot Chase.

I looked around, eyes narrowed, hoping to spy a carriage waiting for me. The train resumed its journey to Exeter and the platform was soon deserted, without a soul or a carriage in sight.

With a shrug of my shoulders, I left my trunks where they were and marched into the station house.

"Could you please tell me where I might hire a carriage to take me to Cheviot Chase?" I asked the clerk behind the ticket window.

"Cheviot Chase? Now why would a young lass such as yourself be wanting to go there?" the clerk asked.

"I have business there."

He scratched his head and looked at me as though I were mad. "'Tis not the place for a young lady. Take your business elsewhere, miss. Cheviot Chase is a sad, haunted place. Surrounded by desolate moors, it is, and creatures the likes of which are not human roam those ungodly moors. 'Tis a place to be stayed away from, if you don't mind my saying so, miss."

"It is imperative I reach Cheviot Chase before nightfall." Little did the clerk know I didn't have enough money to pay for a room for the night or food the next day.

"Well, miss, I'm afraid you won't be finding anyone out at Cheviot Chase."

For a moment I was speechless and stared at him blankly. When a pitying smile began to form on his face, I cleared my throat. "I have a letter from Lord Rathbone requesting my presence there."

"Well, now," he began with a slow shake of his head. "I know for a fact that his lordship left for London a couple of weeks ago. I heard him say he wouldn't be back for some time."

My heart started to pound heavily. Had his lordship forgotten about asking me to come to Cheviot Chase? Worse yet, had he changed his mind about having his paintings cleaned?

"Surely some of his family is there," I said in desperation.

He shook his head again. "No one, miss. He only left behind a small staff to take care of the place."

I couldn't afford to stand there and banter with the man all day. I didn't know how far Cheviot Chase was from the station and the sun was fast lowering in the sky.

"Is there someone who could take me there?"

"Well, there is a hostler in the village who has a wagon. Now he might be willing to take you. Name's Frank Sullivan. He'll do most anything for a shilling or two. I don't think you'll be finding a carriage to take you out there. Fussy lot. Don't care for the moors."

"How far is it to the village?"

"Not too far. Take the road to the right of the station. It will lead you directly to the village."

"Can I leave my trunks here?"

7

"I'll have old Matt bring them into the station for you. I'll keep an eye on them myself."

"Thank you."

As I trod the dusty road to Honiton, the hazy mass in the distance soon resolved itself into a neatly built town nestled in a splendid vale resting on the River Otter. Chimney pots and a church spire poked their way into the sky. Gables and casements shimmered coppery as the rays of the lowering sun bounced off them.

Finding Mr. Sullivan's place, I entered, which caused him to glance at me with a startled expression. When I explained my need of a ride to Cheviot Chase, his eyes narrowed with suspicion.

"Now what would you be wanting to go there for?" he asked.

I was getting tired of all the queries regarding my reasons for going there and the impatience showed in my voice. "I have my reasons. Can you take me there?"

"It'll cost you a quid," he said gruffly.

"A quid!" I was shocked and outraged. I was not about to be deprived of every shilling I had in the world. "That is scandalous! I should report you to the authorities for practicing usury, sir." He winced.

"I'll have you know Frank Sullivan is not a thief, especially when dealing with a lass as fair as yourself. But I can't do it for less than ten shillings. It is a way out through the moors and I don't like going out there when night is coming on. I'm not about to be traveling the moor at night. Eerie old place. Murderous ghosts out there, there is. Not that Frank Sullivan is a coward, mind you. But I'm not about to have my throat ripped out by the wild beasts that freely roam the moors at night. And that house!" His expression became grim.

"What is wrong with the house?" I asked.

"Strange goings-on out there, miss."

"What do you mean by strange?"

8

"Screams in the night. Lights where there should be no lights. Why, some strangers stopped there and were never seen again. I wouldn't want to be having business there. If I was you, I would think hard about going out there, miss," he warned.

I wasn't about to listen to local superstition, which was probably based on idle gossip. "Mr. Sullivan, I have no fear of wild beasts, ghosts, or anything else that might meander on the moor. I will pay you the ten shillings to take me there at once. My trunks are at the station and I would appreciate it if you would stop there first to pick them up." I was thirsty, hungry, and tired. I did not want any more delay in reaching my final destination.

He sighed heavily. "It is your ten shillings, miss."

With my trunks secured in the back of the wagon, I sat next to Mr. Sullivan on the wooden seat in front. It was a most uncomfortable ride. The wheels seemed to find every rut in the road as though they were seeking vengeance on its occupants. I had to hold on tight to the wooden slats alongside the seat to keep from bouncing out of the wagon. The horse kept a fast pace, stopping only once to let a herd of sheep pass across the road.

The irritating journey seemed interminable. Mr. Sullivan spoke little, if at all. I could sense we were getting closer to Cheviot Chase as his mouth settled in a firm, grim line. He turned the horse from the rutted lane into a crescent-shaped gravel road.

Before I knew it, Cheviot Chase was silhouetted against a muted gray sky. It was a large mansion composed of solid blocks of stone. As we drew closer, I could see the house was built in the shape of an H with a multitude of pepperpot chimneys thrusting upward. The many mullioned windows occasionally flickered golden as the sun's rays wafted over them. It certainly didn't emit a sense of foreboding. In fact, it awed me in a most pleasant way.

Mr. Sullivan drew the wagon to a halt before the wide marble steps of the portico. As I slipped down from the wagon, he already was putting my trunks on the ground. I paid him the amount agreed upon. He doffed his cap and, without a word, was back on the wagon. He quickly snapped the reins and the horse took off with uncommon speed.

I looked up at the mansion with a reverential gaze. There was no going back now, I told myself. Lifting my skirts, I ascended the marble steps to the huge oaken door. I pulled the brass chain and could hear the clang of the bell echoing inside. I waited. And waited. I finally pounded the large brass knocker in the shape of a lion's head.

The sun had dropped below the horizon and a foggy dusk was settling in. I was beginning to doubt the wisdom of arriving so late in the day. Perhaps I should have stayed in town, had dinner, and sought lodging for the night. I had a few bits of jewelry I could have sold. They weren't worth much, but they might have brought enough for a night's lodging. Perhaps the small staff at Cheviot Chase were only day laborers and had left for the day. Perhaps that was why no one was answering my knock.

I was about to trudge to the rear of the house to seek entrance when the oak door flew open to reveal a short, plump woman dressed in black with white lace collar and cuffs. She had a kindly face with extraordinary large eyes that gave her a froggy look. She smiled.

"Yes?" she asked.

"I'm Janet Clarke. I believe I am expected," I said, returning her smile.

She frowned and shook her head. "I'm sorry, miss. We are not expecting anyone."

"I have a letter from Lord Rathbone requesting my presence here," I protested when I saw she was about to close the door.

"The only person his lordship told us to expect was a man who was to come and fix some paintings. But he isn't due for weeks."

"I am that person. Lord Rathbone hired me to do restoration work on his paintings. I came as soon as I could. I'm sorry if I am inconveniencing anyone."

"His lordship didn't say anything about a woman." She eyed me suspiciously.

"Well, I am here now and can't very well trot back to London at this time of night," I said graciously. I didn't know what else to say. I could only hope she wouldn't slam the door in my face. I didn't relish the thought of spending the night on the moor.

"Well, I am not one for turning a young lass out onto the moor at night. You'd best come in. What is your name again?"

"Janet Clarke."

"I'm Mrs. Herries. Sarah Herries. I'm the housekeeper here. His lordship can decide what to do with you when he returns from London." She looked past me to the trunks squatting in the graveled driveway. "I'll have a couple of the lads bring your trunks in."

"Thank you."

I followed her into the vast marbled foyer. It was three times the size of my flat in London. I was embarrassed by my gawking, but I couldn't stop my head from swiveling around to take in the spacious and elegant rooms jutting off the foyer. The white plastered ceilings were decoratively molded and enhanced with gold gilt. I had heard about the castlelike mansions of the peerage, but had never actually seen one.

"It is beautiful. The house, I mean," I said.

"Oh, yes. Quite a lavish place. If you wish, I will give

11

you a tour in the morning."

"I'd like that very much," I said, thankful the woman was of a friendly nature. I hate to think what might have happened if the housekeeper were an unfriendly witch.

"Wait here. I'll fetch a couple of lads to tend to your trunks," said Mrs. Herries, then scurried off.

I continued to scan what I could see of the house. I became bold enough to peer into the parlorlike gallery on one side of the house, which I assumed led to the West Wing. I didn't have time to peek at the other gallery for Mrs. Herries came dashing back with two fit-looking lads.

"There are two trunks outside. Please take them up to the rooms that have been prepared for the restorer," Mrs. Herries said to the lads, who gave me a peculiar glance. She turned to me. "Follow me, Miss Clarke."

"Is there a large staff here, Mrs. Herries?" I asked as we ascended the semicircular staircase to the side of the foyer.

"Not as many as when his lordship is in residence. There are the two maids, the cook, the gardener, and a stablemaster who has a few lads working for him on a daily basis. But you will get to meet them all later." While she chatted away, I closely trailed her down a long corridor. She came to a sudden halt before a door, pushed it open, then entered. "I'm afraid the rooms aren't well suited to a young lady's needs. As I said, we were expecting a gentleman. This is your workroom." She waved her arm in a sweeping motion around the stark room. "I hope it is suitable. We didn't know what you would be needing. I'm sure his lordship will provide you with anything you might deem necessary if he decides to keep you on."

I shuddered at her last words and forced myself to say, "It will do nicely." I looked at the large, bare table and chair. A fireplace loomed to the side. Lamps and a desk made up the rest of the contents of the room. One large

12

window almost filled one wall. On either side of the window, heavy velvet drapes stood sentinel.

Mrs. Herries opened a connecting door and we entered the bedchamber. It, too, was stark. The deep red velvets and brocades did nothing to alleviate the ponderous mahogany furniture.

"I do hope you find everything satisfactory," said Mrs. Herries as the two lads came into the bedchamber from the corridor. They set one trunk on the floor then hastened away to fetch the other. "Shall I send up a maid to help you unpack?"

"That won't be necessary," I replied.

"I suspect you must be quite hungry after that long journey from London. I'll have Cook prepare a bit of supper for you. Come to the tea room at seven-thirty."

"Tea room?"

"Go down to the end of the corridor and it is the room to your right. The door will be open. We'll have a good chat then." She smiled and left me to my unpacking.

I unpinned my hat and tossed it on the bed. I would have preferred to stretch out on the bed and take a nap. The journey had indeed been a grueling one. But I couldn't afford the luxury of falling asleep when Mrs. Herries had been kind enough to offer me some food, which was more tempting than the thought of a nap. As I started to unpack, the same lads brought up my other trunk. With a quick doff of their caps, they were off. I had the feeling they thought me an oddity.

When the trunks were emptied and everything was in order, I removed my traveling clothes and poured water from the ewer into the basin. After a quick wash, I donned a plain frock. Plain? My entire wardrobe was plain and showed long and heavy usage.

I had no difficulty finding the room designated by Mrs. Herries. She was already seated, and she smiled when I took my seat opposite her at the small round table.

"I was thinking, Miss Clarke. We could change the drapes and the bedcover to make your bedchamber a little less somber if you wish," said Mrs. Herries.

"The rooms are fine as they are, Mrs. Herries. Far grander and larger than I expected." As a maid called Annie served the soup, I asked, "When is Lord Rathbone returning to Cheviot Chase?"

"Hard to say. His lordship is a bit unpredictable. He'll probably stay in London a few more weeks, then all of them will return."

"All of them?"

"Lord Rathbone, his sister and her husband, and probably Sir Percy Lewis and his daughter, Daphne. Sir Lewis is a friend of his lordship and a close neighbor. Oh, I almost forgot Robert Jackson. He is Lord Rathbone's valet. Can't abide the man, to tell you the truth. Perhaps that is why I forgot him."

"And Lady Rathbone?"

"It is because of Lady Rathbone that they all went to London. She is in a hospital there," Mrs. Herries explained.

"I hope she isn't feeling too poorly."

Mrs. Herries laughed, her face becoming cherubic and merry. Though she appeared to be mild of manner and basically good-natured, there was a glint of sternness in her large eyes. Being short of stature made her plumpness all the more obvious. Her dark hair was thoroughly streaked with gray and tightly skewered atop her head.

"If Lady Rathbone is feeling poorly, she wouldn't know it. She is quite mad, you know. When she partially burned down the East Wing, his lordship could no longer keep her here as she continually threatened to burn down all of Cheviot Chase." Mrs. Herries sighed. "Yes. Quite mad. Lord Rathbone felt it necessary to put her in a special and expensive hospital in London hoping the doctors might be able to cure her. I'm thinking he is hoping against hope."

"Are there any children?" I asked.

"Fortunately, or unfortunately, none of his wives produced any children."

"Wives?"

"I do rattle on. I probably shouldn't be babbling away to a perfect stranger, but the days get lonely with no one to talk to except Cook. The maids are too young to want to talk to an old woman. Besides one can't very well gossip with the staff. At least not in my position. Anyway, his lordship's first wife killed herself. They were very young at the time. His lordship was a lad of twenty and her a slip of a lass at seventeen. They had only been married six months when she did it. She was with child."

"How horrible! I imagine his lordship took it hard. A wife and a child."

"He was beside himself. For three years he never left the place. Worked like a common field hand. Such a tragedy. The lass left a letter stating she couldn't bear the thought of giving birth to a child. It so terrified her, she said she would rather die. We were stunned, we were. She went down to the coast and hurled herself into the rock-strewn sea. Terrible! It took him years to even look at another woman." Mrs. Herries paused to finish her soup as Annie came in with the main course—ham, boiled potatoes, carrots, and parsnips.

"How old a man is Lord Rathbone?" I asked.

She looked thoughtful as Annie took our soup plates and left. "He must be around thirty-seven now. I'm not sure." Mrs. Herries smiled sheepishly. "Once I passed my fiftieth birthday, my memory plays tricks every now and then. He is somewhere around there. Three years ago he married for the second time. In the beginning everything seemed fine, then she started acting peculiar. Little things at first. The maids weren't doing their

15

chores correctly. Cook was poisoning the food. Little things like that. Then she became destructive. Smashing dishes if she didn't like the food. Breaking vases because they weren't dusted properly. Ripping up her clothes because they no longer pleased her. She went on like that for a year or so, then really became violent. She used her hands on the maids and took a poker to his lordship. And the screaming! It would have shattered the ears of an angel. It was an awful time for everyone."

"I should think so," I said. "Is she getting any better?"

Mrs. Herries shrugged. "From what I can glean, she is kept under control. His lordship never talks about her. I think it grieves him too much."

"Why did everyone leave for London?"

"While his lordship is visiting the hospital, the others go to enjoy the diversion in London and also to shop for the latest in fashions."

"Don't they visit his wife?"

"Hardly. His lordship's sister, Clara, and her husband, Cecil, never did care for Lady Rathbone. Always quarreling with her, they were. As for the cousin, Jason Watson . . . oh dear, I forgot to mention him before. He went to London with the rest of them. Anyway, he only thinks of himself and what pleasures him. Quite a dandy, he is. Dear me, I have done a lot of talking. I haven't let you say one word. Do tell me something about yourself, Miss Clarke. Why have you come instead of the man we expected?"

"Please call me Janet. I'm not used to such formality." Mrs. Herries nodded. "The man you expected was my father. Sad to say he passed away. Unfortunately he wasn't a frugal man. The only thing of value he left me was his skill. He was one of the best restorers of paintings in all of England and much in demand. I was extremely young when he began to teach me the art of restoration. I

16

worked on old paintings without value until he saw I was becoming quite adept at it. Under his tutelage, I commenced to work on some of his clients' paintings.

"As time went on, I became as skillful as he. Then his eyesight began to fail and I took on more and more of his work. His clients never noticed the difference. When he went totally blind, I did all the work. After he died, the clients started drifting away. They had no faith in my abilities, and since I was a woman, they didn't think me capable. I advertised and Lord Rathbone replied saying the paintings were so numerous that it would be more feasible for me to come here and work. He didn't like the idea of shipping so many paintings. Naturally I was quick to seize the opportunity. It was the only way I had of making a living."

"That was a bit of luck for you," Mrs. Herries said.

"I'm not so sure. I signed my advertisement and the letter to his lordship with my initials, which are the same as my father's. I must have given him the impression that it was my father who was coming. I don't know how he will feel about having a woman do the restorations, especially considering my youth."

I was surprised how easily and quickly one's life story could be told. Perhaps it was because there was neither great tragedy nor great happiness to embellish it. I prudently refrained from mentioning how desperately I needed the work and a possible recommendation from his lordship.

"His lordship is a fair man. I think he will give you a chance. If he doesn't like your work, he'll tell you straight out. He is not the kind of man to give anyone false hopes. And your mother, Janet? You neglected to speak of her."

"My mother died shortly before I became ten years of age. She had been ill for some time. My father dominated my life, especially after mother's death," I replied.

17

"Lord Rathbone lost his mother at an early age also. It seems fate toys with his lordship when it comes to women."

"Did she die young?"

"Not her. She was too full of life to die young. She ran off with the owner of a traveling circus that came here on Fair Day. As a lad, he kept calling for her. Sad to hear. His father forbade her name to be mentioned in the house, which bewildered his lordship at the time. A difficult situation for a young boy to understand. His father was bitter and embarrassed to have his young wife run off with another man. This was a gloomy place indeed," Mrs. Herries said with a shake of her head.

"With all the tragedies in his life, Lord Rathbone must be a bitter, lonely man."

"You will have to judge for yourself, Janet. I've been too close to the family for years and my judgment is colored by a strong affection for his lordship."

"How long have you been at Cheviot Chase, Mrs. Herries?"

"Well over thirty years now. About two years before the present Lord Rathbone was born." Her eyes glazed over as though she was remembering a time long past. "There was such gaiety and carousing all those years ago. The old lord liked to entertain. I believe the merriment could be heard throughout the moors. When his wife ran away with that man, all gaiety in this house ceased. It became a gloomy place. When his lordship married his second wife, Isobel, the entertainment resumed, but only for a short while. Her slipping into madness precluded parties and the like."

Conversation continued to be animated as we discussed Cheviot Chase and London. Mrs. Herries was an unaffected person and given to jolly talk. Though the evening was entertaining and buoyed my spirits, I was glad when it was time to retire. The minute my head hit

18

the pillow, I was sound asleep.

After breakfast the next morning, Mrs. Herries, as promised, took me on a tour of the house. I was awed. Sitting parlors, drawing rooms, morning rooms, long galleries, an armory, a billiard room, and rooms that had no particular function except to exist. The furniture was exquisite, done in rich brocades or exacting tapestried material. The rugs were imported from Persia and the Orient, and there were numerous Aubussons from France. Marble and intricate inlaid woods graced most of the tables. I was duly dazzled.

"However do you manage it all, Mrs. Herries?" I asked as we savored our tea.

She smiled. "Rigid organization. It took a while, but now it is second nature to me. Besides I have the authority to hire extra help if I need it."

"Well, you have done an excellent job. Cheviot Chase is truly beautiful."

"Thank you."

"Tomorrow I would like to get started on the restorations if you could show me where they are located," I said.

"I'm sorry, my dear. I have no idea what his lordship wants restored nor where the paintings are. I think he meant to be here when you arrived, but . . ." She lifted her hands in the air in a gesture of helplessness.

"You mean I will have to wait until his lordship comes back from London? I had hoped to have one painting done so he could see how capable I was."

"I'm afraid so, Janet. Consider it a bit of a holiday. I'm sure he will be back in a week or so. You look pallid, Janet. A daily walk will put roses in your cheeks," Mrs. Herries said, eyeing me critically.

"My work keeps me indoors a great deal. In London the sun has a tendency to play hide and seek between the buildings. A walk in the fresh air would be a novelty for

19

me. Your suggestion has merit and I think I shall follow your advice."

As a steady rain prevented me from taking a walk and Mrs. Herries had duties to occupy her, I spent the next day wandering about the mansion. It was a wonderland of *objets d'art,* yet I never saw one painting. I came to the conclusion that the paintings had been put to one side in a group. I didn't think anyone would mind if I tried to locate the storage area where I might find the paintings. I desperately wanted to have one done before Lord Rathbone returned.

I combed the rooms on the main floor and found no cache of paintings. Boldness and excess energy caused me to continue my search on the upper floors. The West Wing proved to be void of the paintings. To my dismay, the East Wing was locked. I contented myself by going down to the library, choosing a book, and settling down to read.

Fortunately the next day proved fine. I walked through the gardens of Cheviot Chase, which had been designed and executed by Capability Brown in the eighteenth century. The gardens were embellished with marble statues and small classical Greek temples. An artificial lake was the home of various species of ducks and harbored several swans. Having known only the gardens of Hyde and Regent Parks, the gardens of Cheviot Chase gave me a new sense of freedom, of endless openness. Beyond the mansion's gardens lay the undulating moor, where hills and hollows stretched with brooding contemplation to the horizon.

The next day I walked the moor. It soon had me under its spell and became my favorite place for a good striding walk.

One evening, at supper, Mrs. Herries remarked on my physical improvement. "Why, Janet, I do believe those walks have made a new woman of you. Your cheeks are rosier. Your lips are a lovely crimson and the sun has brought out a reddish tint in your hair. Your brown eyes have a healthy sparkle to them."

I was flattered. I had to admit my fresh air walks had put a new spring in my step and attitude. I felt optimistic, as though all my financial troubles had dissolved.

The days slipped by pleasantly. When a heavy morning mist enveloped the land, my walk on the moor was deferred until the afternoon. Clouds continued to scud across the landscape in darkening thickness. I paid little heed to the weather. The savage beauty of the moor had mesmerized me; its serene solitude had become my opiate. The primitive and brooding quality of the moor made me feel in complete harmony with nature's bounty. But it also held an unsettling atmosphere that produced a primordial fear in me. The moor was eternal. I was not.

Suddenly I stepped back, startled by the flapping of a grouse's wings. I watched her soar and hover above me in a distressful manner. Lowering my gaze to the ground, I discovered tiny eggs in a nest of twigs. The grouse and her eggs had been so well camouflaged in the gorse and furze, I had almost stepped on them. Engrossed by my encounter with nature's handiwork, I didn't notice the thick fog creeping over the moor like a stealthy leopard.

Fingers of dampness finally assailed my nostrils and I stood. I carefully backed away from the nest, deciding it was time to return to the house. I had a good sense of direction, but a heavy fog could easily disorient one. I was about to turn and retrace my steps, but froze in place when low, menacing snarls greeted my ears. The ominous sounds rooted me to the spot as the smoky fog began to curl about my feet.

I tried to convince myself my fear was unreasonable. The noise was probably no more than the bleating of distant sheep, their sounds distorted by the rapidly increasing fog. I turned around, ready to resume my walk, when fear immobilized me once again.

Standing before me were two large, black mastiffs, their smooth coats bristling, their ears lowered, and their lips pulled back revealing strong, white, lethal teeth. Their stance was aggressive as they continued to snarl at me. I had the distinct impression that if I moved but an inch, or spoke, I would be pounced upon and torn asunder by those deep-chested, powerful beasts. I had to quell the impulse to scream. The fog was becoming markedly denser. The dogs inched forward, saliva dripping from their mouths as their snarls increased.

Two

"Romulus! Remus! Sit!" came the command of a deep voice from somewhere in the fog.

The tension in my body eased a little as the mastiffs immediately obeyed. They placidly sat on their haunches and drew their lips back over those fearsome and deadly teeth. They stared at me with all the docility of household pets. But I knew better than to approach and give their heads a pat.

My gaze shifted to the large form moving toward me from the fog. It was as if Titan were emerging from the depths of Tartarus, the gloomy, Grecian underworld. To add to the illusion, he was dressed in black with a large black cape about him. He was wide of shoulder, narrow of hip, and hatless. His features were indistinct as he remained behind the mastiffs, the fog making my perception less than keen.

"What are you doing here?" demanded the rich baritone voice.

"I was having my daily walk," I replied. I didn't like the insolence in his tone.

"In the fog?"

"There was no fog when I set out."

"Then you'd best be heading back to wherever you

23

came from lest you find yourself going around in circles as the fog thickens."

"And you, sir, had best leash your dogs lest they attack and mutilate some unsuspecting wanderer."

"That's a sharp tongue you have, lass. I pity the poor lad who might be on the receiving end on a frequent basis."

"Then be thankful I'm no concern of yours. Now if you'll kindly keep your dogs to your side, I shall leave."

"A sound decision. My dogs are quite tractable. You must have frightened them."

"*I* frightened them? Hardly, sir. The situation was quite the opposite, I assure you." I lifted my skirts, took a few side steps, then proceeded to walk past them.

"Henceforth, you'd best confine yourself to determined roads and not idly wander the moor," he called after me.

I neither turned around nor spoke, but my cheeks flushed hot with anger and agitation. The man had disconcerted me. He had made me feel like a silly schoolgirl being chastised by the schoolmaster. I decided to dislike him, whoever he was.

Though visibility was murky, I managed to find my way to the rear gardens of Cheviot Chase, which were half enclosed by a privet hedge. Not wanting to summon Mrs. Herries from her chores, I entered the house through the servants' entrance.

I was surprised to find three scullery maids hopping about in the kitchen. Usually there was only one.

"I see you have extra help today, Cook," I said cheerily, thankful to have reached the mansion without further incident.

"Aye," replied Cook, bustling about the warm kitchen, droplets of perspiration beading on her forehead. She stopped to wipe her hands on her apron and looked at me. "You look as if you've taken a chill, Miss Clarke.

Would you be liking a cup of hot tea now?"

"It would be much appreciated," I replied, taking a seat at the kitchen table as she nodded to one of the scullery maids to fetch my tea. "You seem unusually busy. Any special reason?"

"Aye. They've all come back. And without giving me an inch of notice. Six extra mouths to feed and me just knowing about it. It's enough to try the patience of a saint, it is. I'll have to be working while we do our talking, if you don't mind."

"Not at all." I put some cream and sugar in the tea then stirred it. Cook's remarks puzzled me. According to Mrs. Herries, only four people lived at Cheviot Chase. Who were the other two? I wondered idly, then asked aloud, "I thought Lord Rathbone, his sister and her husband, and a cousin lived here. Who are the other two?"

"Sir Lewis and his daughter will be staying here a few days. Although older, Sir Lewis is a good friend of Lord Rathbone. He owns the nearby estate," explained Cook.

"I hoped I would find you here, Janet," said Mrs. Herries as she came into the kitchen. "Lord Rathbone returned this afternoon along with the others, which means we won't be having our meals in the tea room. We'll be having them here in the kitchen with the rest of the staff. It eases the burden of the maids having to serve the meals."

"With the exception of Mr. Jackson," added Cook airily. "Too good for the likes of us, he is. He has to have his meal brought up to his sitting parlor, he does."

Mrs. Herries looked at Cook with a weary, yet patient eye before she turned her attention back to me. "I hope you don't mind eating in the kitchen, Janet."

"No, I don't mind. In fact I'll be much more comfortable in the kitchen. I'm not used to being waited on."

Having supper with the servants was a novel experience. There seemed to be many more now that the master of the house had returned. Conversation was lively, especially between two of the upstairs maids, Jane Ward and Agnes Read. Jane Ward was Mrs. Clara Whitney's maid and Agnes Read was personal maid to Daphne Lewis. During the early part of the meal, they amused everyone with tales of their adventures in London. As the meal progressed, they began to talk of their respective mistresses.

"Miss Lewis was divine in a green silk and velvet gown when they went to the ballet at Covent Garden," said Agnes Read. "Why, the green of the gown matched her eyes perfectly. I did her beautiful blond hair in the latest fashion. Naturally she wore her emeralds."

"Well, I can tell you it didn't make Mrs. Whitney any too happy," said Jane Ward.

"What do you mean?" asked Agnes, a frown on her face.

"The way Miss Lewis carried on over Lord Rathbone. She railed about it all the time I was undressing her, saying Miss Lewis behaved like a wanton when it came to her brother. And him still a married man," said Jane.

"You certainly can't call his a marriage, what with his wife in the hospital all these years. I understand she's no better and never will be. A hopeless madwoman. Besides, Lord Rathbone has a mind of his own. If he didn't like Miss Lewis's attentions, he'd put a stop to them. You have to admit that she is a beautiful young woman," declared Agnes.

"Very," agreed Jane.

"Oh, I've seen her," said one of the parlor maids. "A lovely heart-shaped face, a delicate bow mouth, a small upturned nose. And her skin is so fine and white. She's like a fragile doll."

"Humph!" grumbled Cook. "Never had to do a day's

work in her life, I fancy."

"Now, now," admonished Mrs. Herries. "We mustn't be gossiping about the people upstairs."

"Has Lord Rathbone been informed of my presence, Mrs. Herries?" I asked. "I'm anxious to start on the restorations."

"I told him you were here, Janet. You are to present yourself in the library at nine sharp tomorrow morning," said Mrs. Herries.

I rose early for I wanted to take extra care with my toilette. I donned a light brown day frock whose only suggestion of femininity was a small, ecru-colored lace collar. A small gold watch was pinned to my bodice, which I hoped made me appear businesslike. I stared out the window and checked my watch every few minutes. I had been taught to be prompt at all times.

At the appropriate time, I left my bedchamber and went downstairs. To my dismay, I was a few minutes early so I stood outside the library door hoping no one would see me acting so foolish. The fine hand of my watch seemed to creep with the speed of a snail. When it finally reached the hour, I took a deep breath and rapped lightly on the door. A familiar voice called for me to enter. A sinking feeling clutched at my stomach as I prayed it wasn't the man with the dogs on the moor. But the voice was unmistakable.

He was standing at the window, his back toward me. His hands were behind him, one slapping rhythmically into the other. My worst fears were realized.

"I do believe I have been deceived, Miss Clarke, and I detest deception, especially in a woman. Your letter led me to believe that the notable Jeffrey Clarke was coming to Cheviot Chase to work on my paintings. I find your deceit quite presumptuous and therefore must dispense

27

with your services. You are free to leave immediately. And be so kind as to tell your father I shall let it be known that he took part in this duplicity. Good day, Miss Clarke."

I was not about to be dismissed with my integrity, or my late father's, in question. "My legal name is Janet Clarissa Clarke and it is perfectly correct for me to sign my name with my own initials. I am as expert as my father was at restoring paintings. If you had been as astute as those of your class are supposed to be, you would have known my father had died some time ago. I have been carrying on his work ever since. I'm sorry if you feel I have played false with you."

He spun around, his hands coming to rest on the high back of the great leather chair behind the desk. A slow, arrogant smile stole across his face as he studied me.

I defiantly glared back at him, keenly aware of the good looks his saturnine face presented. And his eyes! They were cat green and luminous with a dangerous power. Thick, black eyebrows winged above those hypnotic eyes. His nose was high and straight, his lips wide in a strong, sensitive jaw. His jaw was accented by a small cleft in his chin. He moved from behind the chair to come and lean against the front of the desk, his arms folded across his chest. It was then I became conscious of his lean, rugged physique, which seemed to fill the room with a dynamic energy.

"So you are the sharp-tongued maiden of the moor. I see you still have that caustic tongue," he finally said.

"You do not seem to lack for scathing words yourself, Lord Rathbone. Why should the fact that I'm my father's daughter make you doubt my capabilities?"

"I never said it did. It was your underhanded method in your advertisement. I should have realized that someone of your father's reputation wouldn't have to advertise. By the way, I'm sorry to learn he has passed on."

"He died some two years ago. I've tried to carry on where he left off. Youth and being a woman caused some to doubt my ability. I felt I had to prove myself. I thought you might give me a chance. To dismiss me without giving me the chance to demonstrate my skills is the height of prejudice on your part. I guess peerage is blind when it comes to acknowledging that the world does progress and women are progressing with it. Some of us can and will stand on our own two feet. I'm sorry if I have caused you any inconvenience. I shall leave at once."

"Well, well, a temper too. I wasn't aware your father had passed on. Do you really think I'm a blind, prejudiced man, Miss Clarke?" he said, the smile still on his face.

"I don't know you all that well, sir. I couldn't possibly make a definitive judgment."

"We must rectify that, mustn't we? I shall let you have a go at the paintings, Miss Clarke. If your work proves to be unsatisfactory to me, I shall give you one month's wages for your trouble, then promptly dismiss you. Is it a bargain?"

"Yes," I said, perhaps too quickly.

"You're quite sure of yourself, aren't you?"

"Quite. I'm good at what I do if not one of the best," I declared with a certain amount of pride.

"Along with a sharp tongue and a temper, you lack a sense of modesty, I see."

I blushed, which seemed to amuse him further. "If I don't have faith in myself, who will? I would like to get started as soon as possible. I would have started immediately upon my arrival here, but Mrs. Herries didn't know where the paintings were kept."

"They are in the East Wing. Only I have the keys to that section of the house. I shall escort you there. Select those paintings which you wish to start with and I shall have a servant bring them to your workroom. Have you brought your materials with you?"

"Certainly."

"Shall we go along then? I have no wish to delay this business. I shall be able to tell when you have finished with a quarter section of a painting whether or not I will continue with your services. Does that sound fair to you, Miss Clarke?"

"Perfectly."

"Come along then."

I trailed out of the library after him. He strode across the foyer to the middle gallery and commenced the long walk to the East Wing. I was falling behind as his stride lengthened. Suddenly he stopped and turned.

"Are you coming, Miss Clarke?" There was a touch of impatience in his voice.

"My legs aren't as long as yours, Lord Rathbone," I replied, catching up to him.

His eyebrows rose while an engaging smile curved his lips. "Are you a precursor of the modern woman, Miss Clarke?"

"I don't know what you mean, sir."

"I thought it was forbidden for a young woman to mention any part of her anatomy in the presence of a gentleman. I'm sure our good Queen Victoria would gasp at your blatant reference to legs," he said with some amusement.

"Have I offended your gentlemanly sensibilities, sir?" There was an unintentional note of sarcasm in my voice. The man had a way of vexing me. There was an arrogance in his manner that seemed pointedly directed toward me.

"My sensibilities were dulled a long time ago, Miss Clarke. It would take more than your sharp tongue to stir any life into them."

When we came to the end of the long gallery, huge doors, which led to the perpendicular East Wing, faced us. Lord Rathbone reached into his pocket and produced a large iron key. As he opened the doors, an acrid smell caused my nostrils to flare.

30

"I'm afraid this section of the house has been closed for some time. This wing is only used for storage now," he explained as he led the way in.

Cobwebs and dust gave the place an aura of foreboding. I felt as though I had left the real world to enter a realm where only phantoms and illusions lived in easy comfort. In my imagination I envisioned what the wing must be like in the dark of night, especially with the distinct odor of burnt wood and cloth. I shuddered and lengthened my stride to keep up with Lord Rathbone. He stopped before another door and, using another key, opened it.

The room contained a multitude of paintings and diverse *objets d'art*. I walked around, browsing through the paintings.

"They look as if they have been here for some time. Was there any particular reason for storing them away, sir?" I asked.

"You are here to restore the paintings, Miss Clarke, not to question my motives."

"You're quite right, Lord Rathbone. My curiosity overwhelms me at times and I forget my place."

"Do you see anything that captures your fancy?"

"Under the circumstances, I would prefer if you selected a painting which, in your opinion, is in the most deplorable state. I wouldn't want you to think I chose an easy piece to work on. And I see no reason to move a number of paintings to the workroom when I may not meet your criteria," I replied.

"A sensible suggestion, Miss Clarke." He went through the paintings, selected one, and studied it for several minutes. "I think this will do nicely. If you're as good as you claim and this is restored to its original beauty, you may contend with the rest of them. Seeing we have decided on one painting, we shall dispense with a servant bringing it to your room. I shall carry it there myself."

"You needn't bother, Lord Rathbone. I can carry it."

I reached out for the painting.

"You know, Miss Clarke, you have an absolute penchant for trying to thwart me. Or do you find my company not to your liking?"

"I was trying to be helpful. You must have more important things to do than to carry a painting to the workroom at the other end of the house."

"As you will eventually learn, this is my house and I do what I please in it." Without another word he marched out of the room, locking the door behind him.

Following after him, I thrust my hands into the pockets of my skirt. Anger gnawed at me as I wondered how long I could endure his churlish manner. He had to pause at the great doors to the East Wing until I had caught up and slipped through them. He leaned the painting against the wall while he carefully shut and locked them. No words passed between us on the trek back to the other side of the huge mansion.

I opened the door to the workroom. He stalked in ahead of me and put the painting on the table. I was about to thank him, but he turned on his heel and headed for the door. I said nothing. I saw the door closing and directed my attention to the painting. I had barely scanned it when the door was flung open and Lord Rathbone spoke.

"Miss Clarke, I will expect you at our dinner table this evening. Be in the drawing room shortly before eight. We dine at eight o'clock sharp."

He closed the door before I could say a word. I wanted to decline his offer. He had an unsettling effect on me and I wanted to avoid him as much as I could. Besides, dinner in the main dining room would entail the wearing of a suitable gown. I had no such item in my wardrobe and Lord Rathbone must have been aware of that fact. Was he trying to humiliate me for my supposed brashness? I certainly wouldn't fit in with those people. The kitchen was my proper place.

I decided to put the man out of my mind and examine the painting. The quicker I went to work, the sooner I'd know my fate. I prayed he was the fair man Mrs. Herries said he was and would admit I had done a good job.

The painting was indeed a challenge. It was old, in poor condition, and had a smoky odor to it. I examined the back to see if relining was necessary. Fortunately it was not.

I had set the table next to the window, where a strong north light gave me better discernment of color. I had already placed my materials on the table. I donned my large linen smock then started to place my bottles of mineral spirits, castor oil, and other paraphernalia in essential order. I removed the painting from its frame and put the frame aside. As I placed the painting on the table, I glanced out the window and saw Lord Rathbone, with his two black mastiffs, heading toward the moor.

His stride was sure and purposeful. He held himself erect, the wind whipping his hair into a black halo. His broad shoulders were square, his hands shoved deep into his pants pockets. He had the tread of a man who was prepared to do battle with life every waking moment.

It was then I remembered something incongruous about the man. When he had reached for the painting, I had seen that his hands were not the soft, carefully groomed hands of a peer of the realm. They were large, broad, callused hands as if they had known hard labor for a long time. Though he was clothed, my trained eye detected the formidable physique of the man. Hard sinews gained from arduous toil, not at all the flaccid muscles of a leisurely life. I began to wonder just who this Lord Rathbone really was.

As I was descending the servants' staircase to the

kitchen, one of the parlor maids stopped me. She informed me I was to take lunch with Mrs. Herries in her sitting parlor. With a shrug, I went back up the stairs.

"I thought we would be taking our meals in the kitchen, Mrs. Herries," I said as I sat down at the small round table.

"Cook is in a foul mood. Mrs. Whitney gave her the menus for the week. Then Miss Lewis told one of the maids what she preferred for dinner. Cook had to ask Mr. Jackson, his lordship's valet, whose menu should she prepare. She thoroughly dislikes having to ask Mr. Jackson anything. He always acts as though he was the lord of the manor and doing a favor by even speaking to her. But then he acts like that with everyone. Have you met him yet, Janet?"

"No. The only one I've met is Lord Rathbone."

"I thought it best we have our dinner here out of Cook's way. If she's still of a mood, we'll have our supper here too."

"I've been requested to dine with Lord Rathbone. It seemed more of a command than a request," I said.

"Oh? In the main dining room?" Mrs. Herries's eyebrows arched over her great eyes. "Well, I must say that sounds like his lordship. Always doing the unexpected. To be honest, I'm surprised you're still here, Janet. I was sure he'd send you packing when he found out you are a woman, a very young one at that."

"Actually, I've been put on probation. I am to restore a painting and if it pleases him I am to do the rest."

"Did he take you to the East Wing?"

"Yes. A gloomy place. It had a peculiar odor."

"That's from the burning," said Mrs. Herries.

"Burning?"

"When his lordship married his second wife, they made their apartment in the East Wing. As time went on and her mental condition deteriorated, she set fire to her bedchamber and morning room. His lordship managed to get her out, much against her vociferous protests. Fortunately we managed to put the fire out before it spread to other parts of the manor and did irreparable damage.

"Oh, I'll never forget that night!" Mrs. Herries continued. "Lady Rathbone was a wild woman. His lordship had to tie her down and have someone sit with her. The next day he and Mr. Jackson took her to London in a closed carriage. He didn't dare use the train for fear she'd hurt herself or some innocent bystander."

"Does Lord Rathbone walk the moors frequently? I met him the other day with his two dogs. I have to admit those dogs frightened me. They are so huge."

"The dogs are very protective of his lordship. Even Mr. Jackson is afraid of them." Mrs. Herries smiled. "I think Lord Rathbone finds solace of a sort walking the moors. He's been doing it for years and years."

After lunch, Mrs. Herries returned to her duties while I took my constitutional walk on the moors.

The smell of salty air became more pungent as I walked in a southerly direction. Gulls became more prevalent as they circled overhead, raucously screeching their private vocabulary. My pace quickened as the sound of the sea reached my ears.

To see the ocean for the first time evokes an emotion that defies words. I stood there and stared without regard for time. Green-blue water with white-tipped crests rolling in constant cadence toward the shore enchanted me. It sparkled and shimmered with a life of its own. It dispelled the vision of the Thames River, that mottled brown water sluggishly moving toward the sea with its fetid stench.

Before my eyes the turbulent water was clear and in my lungs was the sweet air of the preindustrial era. So lost in this newly found wonder, I barely noticed I was standing on a high chalk cliff.

At that moment I realized I never wanted to go back to London again. I marched back to Cheviot Chase determined to prove my abilities in restoration.

With the painting flat on the table, I dipped a wad of cotton into the dish of mineral spirits, squeezed out the excess, and began to clean the surface grime from a corner of the painting. To my surprise the painting didn't appear to have extensive damage. The surface grime had not seeped into the varnish, which meant I did not have to strip the painting. Though the varnish had webby fissures, it had enough clarity to let the vibrancy of the paint come through. The small fissures could be eradicated with castor oil and a solvent. The task was going to be an exceptionally easy one and would produce excellent results.

I wondered if Lord Rathbone realized the simplicity of restoring this particular painting. I thought he would have chosen the most difficult painting to restore, not the easiest. I was beginning to think he truly wanted me to stay on when I remembered he had chosen the painting haphazardly from the pile. I could only conclude he had no knowledge of paintings. A piece of luck for me.

I became so absorbed in my task that time slipped by. The fading light caused me to glance at the clock on the mantel. There was precious little time for me to clean up, make a toilette, and get dressed for my debut at dinner.

Despite my anxiety, everything went smoothly until I had to choose a frock. They were all plain, nothing the least bit festive nor colorful about them. No bustles, no kilted flounces, or anything that would hint at being fashionable. The only frock that could be deemed suitable was my Sunday best. Plain of bodice with a slightly scooped neck and not too full of skirt, it was made of a lightweight velvet which was tan in color. White lace around the neck and at the end of close-fitting sleeves was the only pretense at decoration. I plaited my long, brown hair and coiled it in a chignon that started high on the back of my head to loop down to the nape of my neck. It was the best I could do. I pinched my cheeks and left for the downstairs drawing room.

Voices and a smattering of laughter emanated from the drawing room, whose doors were open to the foyer. I stood to one side outside the drawing room while I forced myself to regain a certain amount of composure.

I swallowed hard, took a deep breath, then entered the drawing room, my head held high.

Three

I stood at the entrance to the drawing room for several minutes without attracting attention. Though my common sense told me to flee, stubbornness rooted my feet to the floor. Suddenly Lord Rathbone's gaze lifted from his beauteous companion on the settee, his eyes boring into mine.

He rose and came toward me with a smile, not a warm and friendly one, but a cynical smile. I didn't want to admit it, but he looked extraordinarily handsome in his formal dinner attire. His cat green eyes slowly looked me over and the wide-lipped smile remained on his sharp-boned face.

Introductions were brief. With a wave of his hand, Lord Rathbone indicated for me to be seated and the previous conversation resumed. If I had feared being deluged with technical questions on restoration, or being stared at like a freak, or gaped at, that fear was quickly dispelled. I was paid no more attention than a vase on a table. In a way I was thankful. It gave me an opportunity to study the major occupants of Cheviot Chase.

Clara Whitney, Lord Rathbone's sister, bore little, if any, resemblance to her brother. Her auburn hair complemented her blue eyes. She was an attractive woman whom I judged to be a few years younger than her brother, perhaps in her early thirties. Her dinner gown was of dark blue taffeta with white vertical stripes which helped to mask her rather full figure.

Her husband, Cecil Whitney, was a tall, lean man whose long arms and legs gave him an awkward appearance. He sported a trim moustache and wire-rimmed glasses. A small mouth graced a pleasant, but plain face.

The cousin, Jason Watson, looked to be several years older than I. His dark blond hair was combed straight back. He was a stocky man of medium height with a high-bridged nose that flared out above full lips. High cheekbones perched under small, gray eyes. He certainly wasn't handsome, but there was a compelling attractiveness about him. His dress was flamboyantly fashionable.

Lord Rathbone's neighbor, Sir Percy Lewis, was a tall imposing man. His predominant features were a long, wide chin and a large bulbous nose. Wiry gray hair fringed around his bald pate while thick muttonchop whiskers flounced along his jawbone, leaving his chin clean shaven.

And then there was Miss Daphne Lewis, Sir Percy's daughter, a beautiful, fragile-looking woman whom I deemed to be in her middle twenties. Her mass of blond hair was looped in the latest fashion to a chignon at the back of her head. The depth of the chignon was well over six inches. Though it matched the color of her own hair perfectly, I was sure the effect was achieved with the assistance of a hairpiece, a most popular adornment of the day. Around her long, slender neck was a four-stranded choker made of unusually large pearls. Her face was thin with the delicate features of a Dresden doll. Her colorful gown of cherry red taffeta made me feel even dowdier.

But this paragon of beauty shattered her exquisite

appearance when she spoke. Her high-pitched voice had an irritating quality as if her vocal cords were emulating the squeal of a train's iron wheels as they braked against iron rails.

The casual, erratic conversation was lighthearted, almost merry, and completely excluded me. I sat as though I were a disembodied soul watching a static tableau in a diorama. The more I studied it, the more I thought something was drastically wrong. It was too perfect. I sensed a deep-rooted tension between the characters in the tableau, a distinct energy of discontent, perhaps enmity. The longer I sat there, the uneasier I became, and I dreaded sitting through a meal with these people.

I shifted in my seat and was about to rise and excuse myself when Lord Rathbone's head turned and he glared a warning at me. The man was uncanny. I felt as though he could read my mind. I was about to defy him and rise anyway when a liveried man stood in the door frame of the drawing room and announced dinner. Not having seen the man before, I assumed he was the infamous Robert Jackson.

The ladies rose. Miss Lewis immediately laid claim to Lord Rathbone's arm while Mrs. Whitney snaked her arm through her husband's. Sir Lewis and Jason Watson, deep in a discussion of Gladstone's liberal policies, especially where the Irish were concerned, walked together. I was left to trail behind alone.

"It is so good of you, John, to have Father and me stay at Cheviot Chase while Foxhill is being refurbished," said Daphne Lewis once we were seated and the maids began serving dinner.

"It is my pleasure to accommodate you," replied Lord Rathbone.

"Your beauty lights up this house like a thousand crystal chandeliers, Daphne," said Jason Watson.

"Are you always so gallant, Jason?" Daphne asked coyly.

Clara Whitney snickered. "Gallant? Why, our Jason is a master at turning simple words into extravagant flattery."

"My dear Clara, do I detect a note of sarcasm in your voice?" asked Jason, his lips curved in a smile, his eyes cold with contempt. "Or is your ego pinched because your beauty is only a candle compared to Daphne's, a flickering one at that."

"You can be positively beastly at times, Jason," declared Clara Whitney. "I do believe there is a basic flaw in your nature. I'll never know why my brother tolerates your presence here."

"Clara, this is not the place to air our family differences," said Cecil Whitney.

"John, do you think Gladstone will get Irish Land Reform through Parliament?" asked Sir Lewis a little too loudly in an attempt to change the current topic of conversation.

Lord Rathbone smiled. There was a devilish glint in his eyes when he asked, "What do you think about Gladstone's sway over Parliament, Miss Clarke?"

With raised eyebrows, all eyes came to rest on me. I glanced at each face in turn, then cast a stony glare at Lord Rathbone for putting me in an awkward position. Nevertheless, I replied, "Though he is not a particular favorite with Her Majesty, I do believe Gladstone will exert enough influence on Parliament to enact the legislation."

The ladies gave me haughty glances then went back to their dinners. Cecil Whitney stared at me as though he had no idea what was said. Jason Watson had a smirk on his face as he picked at his food with bored indifference. Only Sir Lewis expressed astonishment, his bushy gray eyebrows arching into his forehead as though the fact

41

that I could speak overwhelmed him.

"My dear young lady, what would a woman of the working class know about politics?" asked Sir Lewis.

"More than you think. I am able to read newspapers," I replied, shifting my gaze to Lord Rathbone, who was obviously amused by the scene. I had the feeling my presence at the dinner table was solely for his divertisement.

"Hmph!" was Sir Lewis's only comment before he concentrated on his dinner.

"Are we going riding in the morning, John?" asked Daphne, breaking the sudden silence at the table.

"If you wish, Daphne."

"I'll go with you," said Jason.

"Percy?" queried Lord John Rathbone.

"I intend to see how things are progressing at Foxhill Manor. If you're riding that way, I'll start off with you."

"Why don't we all ride to Foxhill?" suggested Jason.

"Oh, must we, John? It's so dull watching workmen plodding about. And their talk is positively crude," moaned Daphne.

"I should think you'd want to see how your manor is progressing, Daphne," said Lord Rathbone.

"I'd rather see it when it is finished and all the workmen have gone."

"Does anyone mind if I join the ride tomorrow?" asked Clara Whitney, causing Daphne to pout.

"Of course not," said Lord Rathbone. "The more the merrier. What about you, Cecil? Care to come along?"

"Not this time, John. I have a tremendous amount of paperwork to do. I'm afraid I'll be cooped up in the library for the entire day," said Cecil Whitney.

"Still working on your history of the Romans in early Britain?" asked Sir Percy.

"Yes. A devilish amount of research," replied Cecil.

"Silly waste of time," commented Jason Watson.

"I agree with you for once, Jason," said Clara Whitney. "He spends all his time poring through old books to the neglect of everything else."

"There aren't too many definitive studies of the Romans in Britain," Cecil defended.

"Who cares?" said his wife.

Cecil cast a scathing glance at his wife with a glint akin to hatred.

To my relief, the meal was over. Clara Whitney rose. "We'll adjourn to the drawing room while you gentlemen have your brandy and cigars."

I rose and followed the two women out of the dining room. But when they continued across the foyer, I turned and went up the main staircase. Apparently they took no notice of my departure. I had no wish to further my discomfort nor prolong their obvious displeasure by my company. Lord Rathbone had only requested my presence at dinner. He said nothing about my socializing after dinner.

Seeing a shaft of light spilling from under Mrs. Herries's door, I knocked softly.

"Come in."

"Am I disturbing you, Mrs. Herries?" I asked, entering her small sitting parlor.

"Not at all, Janet. I was hoping you'd stop in and tell me about the dinner this evening. My, but you do look fetching. That's a pretty frock."

"Thank you."

"How was your dinner? And do sit down."

"The food was excellent."

"I take it the company was not." Mrs. Herries smiled.

"I did feel out of place. And I think my presence made everyone else uncomfortable."

She shook her head. "I can't imagine why his lordship made such a request of you. It's unlike him to be inconsiderate. He knows his sister is very class conscious, not to mention Sir Lewis and his daughter. Miss Lewis deplores the company of those she considers beneath her station in life. I hear she treats the servants at Foxhill like so much mud underneath her feet."

"She is a very beautiful woman," I said.

"That she is . . . that she is. But I daresay it doesn't extend to her character and disposition."

"I learned Mr. Whitney is writing a history about the Romans in Britain. Sounds like quite an undertaking."

Mrs. Herries twittered a laugh or two. "He's been writing that history ever since he married his lordship's sister."

"How long have they been married?"

"Over ten years now, I think. When they returned from their honeymoon, they moved in with his lordship. It was about six months after that Mr. Whitney began writing his history."

"He must be a very thorough and dedicated man," I said.

"More likely he tries to keep out of his lordship's and wife's way. Not a very ambitious man. I don't know what he'd do if he ever had to work for a living. A schoolmaster, I suppose. That wouldn't set too well with his wife, not that she's ecstatic with her life and him now."

"Oh? Is there trouble there?" I asked, remembering the sharp words and tense atmosphere at the table.

"Well, I guess it's no secret. Their quarreling echoes through the house and is common knowledge among the servants."

"His lordship and Mr. Whitney?" I couldn't imagine Lord Rathbone engaging in a shouting match with anyone. He appeared to be a man totally in control of himself. He seemed like one capable of harnessing his temper to present outward calm.

"Gracious no. Mr. and Mrs. Whitney. She deplores him burying himself in books all the time, refusing to travel and socialize when she wishes. She prefers the excitement of London or Paris. Hates being stuck out here in the middle of the moor. Perhaps if there had been children, she wouldn't be so restless."

"And his lordship? Does he mind them living here?" I asked.

"I don't think so," said Mrs. Herries. "But he does resent the quarreling. Though his sister will plead with him, he refuses to take sides. Yet it must be lonely for the poor woman. What did you think of Mr. Jason?"

"Nice-looking young man. He did pass some bitter words with Mrs. Whitney though."

"They were more than friendly about two years ago. Then something happened—I don't know what—that caused them to be at each other's throats over the littlest things. I'm afraid you've stepped into a troubled and unhappy household, Janet."

The next morning as I prepared my cleaning solvents, I glanced out the window to see the parade of horseback riders as they pranced off the grounds toward the main road. The women wore riding habits I had seen on display in London's finest shops. Although I tried to study them individually, I found my gaze returning again and again to Lord Rathbone. His back was rigid and he was the only one hatless. I watched until they were out of sight, then commenced to work.

It had become habit to take a walk after lunch. It helped to clear my head of the odor of the solvents I had to use. As usual, I headed for the moor. I knew I didn't have to fear a sudden appearance of the mastiffs as Lord Rathbone and his party were still on their riding expedition.

With brisk strides, I walked through the gorse and over the undulating earth. Reaching the crest of a hill which boasted a scraggly privet hedge, I went through a small opening and, from an excellent vantage point, was greeted with a wondrous view. Rolling fields stretched out before me like a lumpy carpet nature had forgotten. Sheep placidly grazed in the distance. It was a pastoral scene that could have taken place in any century. Then I spied it.

A figure was crouched low in the ground below me. Though I couldn't see the man's face, there was something familiar about him. He seemed to be digging in the earth with a fevered concentration. Suddenly he stood, both hands going to the small of his back as he stretched backward. Feeling like an intruder, I ducked behind the sparse hedge, but not before I had a glimpse of his face. It was Cecil Whitney.

I stood behind the hedge wondering why he was digging when he'd claimed he would be in the library all day doing research. When I peered through the hedge, he was once again crouched down but this time he was filling in the hole he had dug. I was curious as to what he could be burying in that forlorn spot. He stood and looked around as though he had to preserve his secret. Not wanting him to discover me there, I sped down the hill and back to Cheviot Chase.

Though I worked on the painting with professional accuracy, my thoughts dwelled on Cecil Whitney and his peculiar behavior in the field. What could he possibly have been burying? Though curious, I had no intention of mentioning the incident to anyone, not even Mrs. Herries.

I worked diligently even when the sun started lowering in the sky. Suddenly I sensed I was not alone, though I had neither heard a door open nor anyone enter. I turned around and gasped, my splayed hand rushing to my bosom.

"Lord Rathbone!" I cried. He was a few feet behind me.

"I see you've almost finished a quarter of the painting. Fine work."

"Thank you. You picked out an uncomplicated painting for restoration. It only needed a good cleaning." I dropped my hand to my side and assumed a stance of composure, but my heart was still pumping erratically. He was staring down into my face with those enigmatic green eyes and standing close to me, too close. I took a step backward.

"I hope I didn't frighten you." His voice was deep and mellifluous.

"Not frighten. But you did startle me. I didn't hear you come in. It would have been more fitting if you had knocked, sir."

"You do have a tendency to reprimand me, Miss Clarke. But perhaps you are right this time. I was afraid any pounding on the door would disrupt your work. You need not fear I would enter your bedchamber so unceremoniously."

"I should hope not," I replied quickly and firmly. The thought of his entering my bedchamber, especially at night, sent a shiver through me. When I saw the amusement in his eyes, I knew I had spoken too sharply. I would have to learn to control my stinging, blunt manner toward him.

"I suspect you have no great liking for me, Miss Clarke. Is that why you disappeared right after dinner last night?"

"No. Surely you must have felt the uneasiness my presence at the dinner table caused everyone. Lowly employees do not sit at their employer's dinner table," I replied.

"I wasn't under the impression you considered yourself lowly, Miss Clarke. Do you?"

"*I* do not, Lord Rathbone. But I believe others at the table held that opinion, especially when I was not suitably dressed for the occasion."

47

"I would never take you for a person to be concerned with the outward material aspects of life," he said.

"My manner of dress seemed perfectly adequate to me. However, it was obvious your guests did not feel the same way. I could sense their discomfiture."

"It is my house and my guests will have to endure my whims and fancies. And I fancied you at my dinner table."

"Why? Am I a *divertissement* to be discussed after dinner? A topic for the amusement of your guests? Or your private amusement?" He had an annoying way of pulling my temper to the surface.

He smiled. It was beguiling. "You shall be at dinner tonight, won't you, Miss Clarke?" he said in a tone more demanding than questioning.

"I must decline your generous offer, Lord Rathbone."

"Any appropriate reason?"

"Yes. I will embarrass neither myself nor your guests by my unfitting attire. Though you may not realize it, I do have a sense of vanity. I feel quite drab in the presence of beautifully gowned ladies. As a man, you may find that difficult to comprehend. I would appreciate your not insisting I attend."

He put his hands on my shoulders. There was a softness to his touch. "Do you sew, Miss Clarke?"

His question took me by surprise. I stared at him wide-eyed as though I had lost all comprehension of the English language.

"Come, come, Miss Clarke. It is a simple question. Surely you can answer yes or no."

"Yes," I blurted out, still bewildered by the question. Was I now to be a seamstress to the ladies of the house?

"Come along," he said, cupping my elbow.

"My smock! I must take it off," I exclaimed.

"Nonsense." His grip on my elbow tightened and I was soon trotting alongside him down the hall.

He ushered me down one corridor after another like one who had traveled that maze for a lifetime. He stopped before a door and a peculiar expression covered his face. He released my elbow, put his hand on the knob, and seemed to hesitate. A pained, tortured look contorted his handsome, sharp-boned profile and a vein at his temple began to throb. With a sharp intake of breath, his chest swelled and his shoulders broadened. He turned the knob and thrust the door open. Marching toward a wall where several large wardrobes stood, he went to each one and pulled the doors open.

He waved his hand over the open wardrobes, then turned to me. "Gowns for every occasion, Miss Clarke. I'm sure they are too large for you and are quite out of date, but if you can wield a needle, you can have all the gowns you need."

"Are you suggesting I take one of these gowns?" I was stunned.

"One of them? All of them, Miss Clarke. And I'm not suggesting anything. I am insisting you take what you will and redesign them. As you can see, the material is of excellent quality and hardly used," declared Lord Rathbone.

"I couldn't. They must belong to someone." Why was he offering these clothes to me?

"They belong to my wife, who has no use for them where she is. She'll never use them again."

"I'm sorry about your wife, Lord Rathbone."

"I don't need your sympathy, Miss Clarke."

"I couldn't possibly wear your wife's clothes, sir. It wouldn't be proper. I should think you wouldn't want a constant reminder of her. And what if she should recover and need her gowns?"

"If by some miracle she should recover, she is the type of woman who would require an entirely new wardrobe in the latest fashion. These gowns would be thrown out or given to the church. They are of no use to anyone with the possible exception of you, Miss Clarke. I should think it would be to your advantage."

"I'm sorry, but—"

"If you won't select what you would like, then I shall have to choose for you."

I shoved my hands deep into the pockets of my smock. "This is ridiculous, Lord Rathbone. I neither want nor need elaborate gowns." I turned on my heel and left.

I was so flooded with indignation at Lord Rathbone's presumption, I lost my way in the labyrinth of halls and corridors. My only hope was a window where I could view the courtyard and orient myself. As I began to think my situation was hopeless, a shaft of light fell across the carpeted hall. A window!

I quickened my step and, reaching the window, peered out. Below me a lovely courtyard nestled between the East and West Wings. It was a replica of a French formal garden, everything trimmed and neatly arranged in squares, triangles, circles, and oblongs, with a marble fountain in the center. I hadn't noticed it before and promised myself I would examine the courtyard at close hand before too long.

I lifted my gaze to the windows of the East Wing directly across from me. My eyes narrowed to make sure my perception was correct. A figure in flowing white robes glided by one window then another, then another before disappearing from view. Who could be in the East Wing? Mrs. Herries had said it had been closed since the fire and Lord Rathbone was the only one who had a key to it. I watched for several minutes but the apparition did not appear again.

I finally made it back to my rooms. It was too late to work on the painting. I removed my smock and hung it on a clothes tree in the corner of the workroom. As it was almost teatime—which I usually spent with Mrs.

Herries—I went into my bedchamber to have a wash. My mouth fell agape when I entered. A myriad of gaily colored gowns and frocks had been dumped on the bed. Lord Rathbone was not only presumptuous, but arrogant in his thinking I would be delighted with his demented wife's old clothes.

I marched out of the bedchamber down the hall to Mrs. Herries's sitting parlor, knocked on the door, and when she opened it, I explained what had transpired. She came back to my room, and lifting each gown gingerly, she studied them.

"I remember most of these," said Mrs. Herries. "Lady Isobel seldom wore any gown twice. Such a shame. I gather his lordship took you to the room where everything of hers is stored. He despises going into that room. Too many memories. He must have really wanted you to have them to take you in there. The material is exquisite and in fine condition. It would be a shame to throw them away, Janet. I'm sure we can make them into entirely different gowns and frocks. Lady Isobel was much larger than you," said Mrs. Herries as she gazed at an emerald green satin gown rippling with a pale green tulle.

"I would feel like an usurper wearing Lady Rathbone's clothes. I would never be comfortable in them," I declared.

"I've a fair hand with a needle, Janet. Try to think of them as new bolts of cloth. We can take out all the seams and have fresh material to work with. I have some magazines showing the latest fashions in London. I'm sure between the two of us we can create entirely new gowns and no one will be the wiser for it."

She made sense and it eased my conscience somewhat. "But you have so much to do, Mrs. Herries. I certainly couldn't impose on what precious little time you have to yourself."

"Nonsense, my dear. I'm quite bored with knitting or reading every evening. This would be a challenge for me. An exciting one, I might add. Now, let's go back to my parlor and have our tea and biscuits. We can go through the magazines and select the styles you care for best. Oh, I do want to do something with this green satin." Her eyes sparkled with anticipation.

As she suggested, we pored over the fashions pictured in the numerous magazines while we had our tea. We were interrupted by a sharp rap on the door of Mrs. Herries's sitting parlor.

"Now who could that be?" she asked as she ambled to the door and opened it. "Mr. Jackson! Is something amiss?"

"I understand Miss Clarke is having tea with you."

"Yes, she is."

"May I speak with her?"

"Of course. Do come in."

With back stiff, Mr. Jackson walked into the sitting parlor. He was so rigid I had the feeling a strong wind would not crumple him, but would cause him to fall to the ground like an iron rod. He looked directly at me and did not try to mask the obvious and intense dislike he had for me.

"Miss Clarke, his lordship wishes me to remind you of your required presence at dinner tonight," he said.

"You may tell his lordship I will appear at his dinner table when I have something suitable to wear. That is if he still wants me there."

"Yes, miss." He turned and left the room.

"His lordship isn't going to like having his wishes thwarted. He's used to getting his own way," said Mrs. Herries, resuming her seat at the table.

"This time he doesn't have a choice. He knows how I feel about sitting down at his dinner table with the other ladies properly dressed and me looking like the chimney

52

sweep's daughter. I will not be humiliated like that again."

"But it will take several days for us to fashion a gown for you."

"Then he will have to wait. Perhaps he will change his mind by then."

Mrs. Herries smiled and shook her head. "He is not a very patient man, Janet."

"I came here to restore paintings, not to socialize with his lordship and his guests. If he doesn't like my attitude, he can send me packing." It was not a thought I wanted to entertain. But neither did I care to be tyrannically ordered about. "By the way, Mrs. Herries, I saw someone walking about the rear part of the East Wing today."

A startled expression wrinkled Mrs. Herries's face. "That can't be, Janet."

"I wasn't imagining it."

"It's quite impossible for anyone to be in that section of the East Wing. It is always locked and no one but his lordship has the key. I do believe all the doors and windows are boarded up. A breeze probably stirred some of the curtains and gave the impression someone was there."

"It was definitely a human being walking about in a large white robe," I insisted.

"Well, I wouldn't repeat that story to anyone, especially the servants. They are quite superstitious and their gossiping tends to embellish stories. If they heard you saw someone in the rear of the East Wing, they'd soon have the East Wing bubbling over with ghosts and goblins," said Mrs. Herries.

"It shall stay between the two of us, I assure you." There was a short lull in our conversation as we resumed thumbing through the magazines. As Mrs. Herries put her magazine down and prepared to resume her duties downstairs, I rose and asked, "May I take these

53

magazines to my room? I would like to match the material to certain fashions."

"Of course, Janet."

I started toward the door, magazines in hand, then turned. "Mr. Jackson doesn't seem to like me. Can you think of any reason why, Mrs. Herries?"

"Do call me Sarah, Janet. Regarding Mr. Jackson, I wouldn't let his attitude bother you. He is a solitary man who doesn't seem to care for anyone except his lordship. He refuses to have anything to do with the staff and begrudgingly speaks to me. And then only when he deems it necessary. No. Don't concern yourself with Mr. Jackson, Janet," said Sarah with a warm, reassuring smile.

As the wardrobe in my bedchamber contained only my three frocks, there was plenty of room for the clothes Lord Rathbone had dumped on my bed. I put them away with the exception of the green gown. After dinner that night Sarah and I began the tedious job of taking the green gown apart seam by seam.

The days passed and a routine developed. Breakfast, work, lunch, a walk, work, tea, the tearing apart of the gown, dinner, then sewing with Sarah.

Taking my meals with Sarah, I seldom saw members of the family or the guests at Cheviot Chase. On occasion I would see his lordship strike out for the moors with his dogs in the early part of the mornings.

In a way, I dreaded the completion of the green satin gown. It meant having dinner downstairs. I was perfectly content to have my meals with Sarah. My absence from the dinner table brought no response from Lord Rathbone as I had feared it might. With luck, he might have forgotten all about it and I wouldn't have to endure those wretched dinners in the main dining room.

The day came when I had completed work on the painting. Oddly enough the green gown was also completed. Though it wasn't a chore I relished, I had to seek out Lord Rathbone to apprise him of the finished restoration. I would not bring up the matter of the gown.

In the morning I went downstairs, where I encountered Mr. Jackson entering the foyer.

"Excuse me, Mr. Jackson, could you please tell me where I might find his lordship?" I asked.

"He is in the library and under no circumstances must he be disturbed," he replied in his usual haughty manner, his lips compressing with disdain.

"I'll only be a minute. Surely he can spare one minute."

"I said he cannot be disturbed, Miss Clarke. Whatever it is, it will have to wait."

Our heads turned when the library door opened then slammed shut.

"What the devil is going on out here?" demanded Lord Rathbone, striding toward Mr. Jackson and me. His mood was black as he frowned at us.

"I was telling Miss Clarke you were not to be disturbed, milord, and she became obdurate."

"What is so important, Miss Clarke?" asked Lord Rathbone, his green eyes smoldering with contained anger.

"I wanted you to know the painting is finished and ready for your inspection." I resented Mr. Jackson's characterizing me as stubbornly persistent when I was about to return to my rooms without another word.

Lord Rathbone sighed. His tone softened. "It's all right, Robert. I'll see what Miss Clarke has accomplished."

"If I am interrupting you, it can wait until later, sir," I said, even though I was anxious to learn whether I would be allowed to continue the work.

"Nonsense. I could use a rest from the tedium of . . .

business. I'll take care of this, Robert. You may leave," said Lord Rathbone.

"Very well, milord."

As he left, Mr. Jackson gave me an imperious and scathing glance which his lordship failed to notice.

"Well, Miss Clarke, shall we have a look at that painting?"

I nodded. This time he waved his hand for me to precede him out the door.

"It wasn't a stringent test of my abilities, Lord Rathbone. The painting only required a good cleaning. There was no actual restoration involved," I ventured as we walked along the upstairs corridor.

"No matter. Even cleaning a painting takes a certain amount of skill. I believe I'll be able to make a judgment from what you have to show me," said Lord Rathbone, lessening his stride in order to walk by my side.

Reaching the door of the workroom, he opened it and waved me inside as he partially stood in the door frame. Passing him in the small remaining space, my body brushed against his. The sensation caused my flesh to ripple. Though I didn't want to admit it, the sensation was a pleasant one. My hand trembled slightly when I handed the painting to him, not from fear of losing the work, but from his close presence.

He took the painting and held it to the light. I couldn't read the expression on his face, which caused me to hold my breath. He put the painting back down on the table.

"I'm pleased with what I see, Miss Clarke. You appear to have the same skills your father was noted for. You may work on the rest of the paintings. I shall have them brought down here. It will be easier than getting one painting at a time. Is that all you wish to see me about, Miss Clarke?"

"Yes. And thank you, Lord Rathbone. Your confidence in my abilities won't be misplaced." Relief washed over me as I watched him head toward the door. I had the job and he had forgotten about dinner.

As his hand touched the knob, he turned. "By the way, Miss Clarke, Mrs. Herries has informed me you now have a suitable gown in which to attend dinner. I expect you to come and dine with me tonight. If you do not appear, I shall have them hold dinner and fetch you personally. Have I made myself clear?"

"You have, Lord Rathbone. But I fail to understand your reasons for such an inappropriate request."

"You don't have to understand my reasons, Miss Clarke. Put it down to a fancy of mine."

"Then I am to be discomfited due to a fancy of yours?" I countered.

"You are a very argumentative young woman, Miss Clarke. If you feel any discomfort, it is of your own making."

"And your guests? Have you thought of the awkwardness it causes them?"

He smiled. "My guests are my concern, not yours, Miss Clarke. Dinner tonight." He shut the door behind him, preventing any response I may have had.

True to his word, within two hours servants had brought all the paintings into my workroom. They stacked the paintings against the walls. I spent the rest of the day sorting the paintings into stacks. Those that needed only a cleaning. Those that needed some restoration. And those that required extensive work. I soon realized I would need additional materials as a number of the paintings required relining.

I happily related the news to Sarah as we ate our lunch. She was more enthused by the knowledge I was to make a command appearance at dinner. She was so excited I couldn't refuse her offer to help me dress for the occasion.

After lunch the bright morning sun gave way to

scudding clouds. One could almost smell the rain in the air. I felt it prudent not to take my usual walk on the moor. I decided it would be a good time to explore the formal garden that rested between the rear wings of Cheviot Chase. As always, I used the servants' staircase to exit or enter the house.

I strolled along the white pebbled paths, admiring the symmetry of the various garden beds. Nestled among a few of the beds were budding tulips. The leafing of roses was occurring in other beds. I could envision the riot of colors that would burst forth in spring and summer. All the paths led to the center fountain, radiating like spokes of a wheel. Three angels formed the top of the fountain. The marble trumpets that sat between their puffed marble cheeks spewed water into a wide basin at the foot. I trailed my fingers over the water, causing ripples to circle around the fountain.

The clouds thickened and darkened. Not wanting to go inside right away, I spied a bench near the entrance to the West Wing. Most commodious, I thought, and proceeded to make my way there. When the skies did pour forth their tears, I would have quick access to shelter.

I sat down on the cold marble. Though the garden was beautiful and expertly arranged, there was an intangible sterility about it. It lacked the wild abandon and elusive beauty of the moor. It came to mind that Lord Rathbone was very much like the moor—unpredictable and moody. But I suppose the women in his life colored his character.

I looked around. Even though there was a large staff and a number of people in residence, the mansion appeared desolate and empty, devoid of warmth and welcome. I thought of my small flat in London which I had shared with my father. Feeling an attack of homesickness coming on, I decided to go back into the house and work on the paintings.

I stood and, for some unknown reason, looked up at

the East Wing. The specter in white stood brazenly looking down at me with a puzzled expression. As I returned that gaze, the expression of the barely discernible specter became one of terror and the image fled.

I knew I could never put my curiosity to rest until I had searched the East Wing and found this reluctant spirit. But how does one go through locked doors without a key?

Four

"Do hold still, Janet," urged Sarah Herries. "I'll admit my eyes are large but they aren't as keen as they used to be and these hooks are very tiny."

"We should have used the larger hooks." I didn't want to, but I had to admit I was nervous. The gown had come out much better than I had hoped. It was exquisite and fashionable with its low-cut, off-the-shoulder neckline. A full skirt was graced by an overskirt of tulle, which was drawn up at the sides and swung to the back where it formed a bustle. Ruffled green satin puffs of material rested just below my shoulders. I felt transformed, especially with my long brown hair piled high on the top of my head to cascade down the back of my head in a thickly coiled chignon.

"If we had used the larger hooks, they would have shown. There . . . that's the last one," said Sarah. "Let me see you."

I stepped forward and slowly turned for her approval. "I feel like Cinderella about to attend her first ball. Do I look all right, Sarah?"

"Absolutely beautiful. I hardly recognize you. That shade of green is perfect for your coloring. Now all we need is a diamond and emerald necklace."

60

I laughed. "And perhaps a diamond tiara."

"That would be nice," she replied seriously. "Tonight I'm going to start on the peach silk. You have it all torn apart, haven't you?"

"Yes, but I don't want you spending all your evenings working on gowns for me."

"I enjoy it. It's an exciting challenge. Now that we have your size well noted, the gowns and frocks can be made up faster."

I looked at the clock on the mantel and sighed. "Well, I suppose this Daniel had better face the lions in the den now. I certainly don't want his lordship coming after me."

"Keep your ears tuned, Janet. I want to hear all the comments that might be made about the gown."

I nodded and kissed the older woman on the cheek. "Wish me luck, Sarah."

Reaching the top of the main staircase, I took a deep breath and began my descent. I was halfway down when Lord Rathbone came storming out of the drawing room. He looked up and stared at me. For a fleeting second there was wonderment on his face. But it quickly hardened into a scowl and the vein at his temple throbbed. His eyes appeared deeply troubled. I wondered if he recognized the material of the gown and envisioned his mad wife.

"I was about to see what was keeping you," he said when I reached the bottom step.

"I believe I am punctual, sir," I replied, hurt by his lack of a comment on my appearance. As we stared at each other in silent battle, the others began to emerge from the drawing room on their way to the dining room.

"Well, well. Is this our Miss Clarke?" asked Jason Watson, coming up to me with a wide smile on his face. He took my hand and kissed the air above it. "Our little wren has turned into a glorious peacock. Most charming."

"Thank you," I said.

With raised eyebrows, Sir Lewis looked me up and down as though trying to remember where he had seen me before. Daphne Lewis desperately tried to ignore me as she went to Lord Rathbone's side and pushed her hand through his arm. Mrs. Whitney glared at Jason while her husband was preoccupied with notions known only to him.

"May I escort you into the dining room, Miss Clarke?" asked Jason, already pulling my hand through his arm.

"I'd be delighted, Mr. Watson."

"You must call me Jason. So much friendlier, don't you think? And if it is not too bold of me, may I know your Christian name?"

"Janet."

"Will you be so kind as to permit me to use it?"

"If you wish."

Once everyone was seated at the table, dinner was served with Mr. Jackson hovering in the background. My new image seemed to have heightened his disdain for me. But this time I was not ignored at the table. I was amazed how the outward appearance of a person could alter opinion. Underneath the gown I was still me.

"Did you bring that gown with you from London, Miss Clarke?" asked Clara Whitney as the soup dishes were being cleared away.

"No, Mrs. Whitney. Mrs. Herries and I refashioned it from some old material," I replied.

"Quite charming and fashionable. It makes you look entirely different. Very becoming."

"Thank you, Mrs. Whitney."

"You are an artist, aren't you?" asked Jason.

"After a fashion, I suppose. Actually I reconstruct old and damaged paintings. Some instances call for repainting," I explained.

"I would like to see you work sometime. Would that be possible?" asked Jason.

"I'm sure Miss Clarke has neither the time nor inclination to indulge your whims, Jason," said Lord Rathbone.

"On the contrary, Lord Rathbone. I delight in fulfilling other people's whims or fancy." I smiled but there was a definite edge of sarcasm in my voice.

With his eyes half lidded, he stared at me steadily. "Wouldn't someone gazing over your shoulder impede your work? After all, I wouldn't want to make the restoration of my paltry art collection your life's work."

"Hardly, Lord Rathbone." I was seething inside. He could use me to indulge his whims or fancies but wouldn't tolerate my agreeing to indulge anyone else's whims. The man baffled me. I was glad to hear the twittery voice of Daphne Lewis.

"John, if it's a nice day tomorrow, couldn't we go on a picnic and perhaps stroll the beach? I haven't been on a picnic in ever so long," mewled Daphne.

"My dear Daphne, you do think of the drollest ways to idle a day away," said Jason.

"Nobody requested your presence, Jason," said Daphne.

"I think it is a delightful idea," said Clara Whitney. "Don't you, Cecil?"

"Hmm?" responded her husband absently.

"I don't know why I bother talking to you," cried Clara Whitney. "You never listen to a word I say. All you can think of is your silly old history. You know as well as I do you'll never write that book. You just want to idle your time away in the least exerting manner. Who cares about the Romans in England? They're long dead now and we're the living. You never think about my needs and wants. Nor anyone else's for that matter. I'll never know how my brother has put up with your lack of responsibility all these years. You try the patience of a saint, Cecil."

Cecil Whitney reddened. Murderous fury gleamed in his eyes, which he kept focused on his plate. He said nothing and I felt embarrassed for him. I hoped Lord Rathbone would say something to defend Mr. Whitney, at least a word or two to ease the tension in the room. But he said nothing.

"My dear Clara, you do have an acute knack for subtlety," said Jason. "Have you ever thought of becoming a barrister? If not completely persuasive, you are quite vociferous."

"You're a boor, Jason. I'm surprised I never realized it sooner," said Clara Whitney.

Sir Lewis cleared his throat. "John, what do you think will happen in Europe? Do you think there'll be war?" His voice boomed and deflected the bickering at the table.

"By listening to the ultra-imperialists and seeking assurances from old William of Prussia not to have his kinsmen sit on the Spanish throne, Napoleon the Third is playing right into Bismarck's hands. If Bismarck has his way, there'll be war. A war with France would consolidate the German States like nothing else and Bismarck knows it."

"Do you think Prussia could win the war?" asked Sir Lewis.

"With Bismarck as Chancellor, there's no doubt about it. I think he will live to see a united German Empire and then the face of Europe will alter the course of history," replied Lord Rathbone.

I looked at Daphne. She was dreamily gazing at Lord Rathbone. She seemed detached from everyone at the dinner table. She had a reverent expression on her face, yet her blue eyes glittered cold and hard, giving me the impression she was incapable of true emotion. Not only did she look like a China doll, I suspected she had all the passion of that inanimate object.

And there was something odd about the squabbling

between Clara Whitney and Jason Watson. Their voices suggested deep hatred born of a sudden bitterness. I felt some sympathy for Clara Whitney. Her husband did appear insipid. If he did ignore her as much as she claimed, her life must be lonely indeed.

I was so busy making suppositions about everyone at the table, I never noticed the furtive glances Jason was casting my way. When I shifted my gaze to look at him, I learned he was blatantly staring at me. He smiled. I returned a fleeting smile then tended to the food on my plate.

Clara Whitney was the first to rise from the table. "We shall leave you to your brandy and cigars, gentlemen," she said.

The men were on their feet before either Daphne or I stood.

"Robert," said Lord Rathbone, addressing his man-servant even though his gaze rested on me. "Make sure the *three* ladies are served their tea promptly in the drawing room."

There was no mistaking the threat in his eyes. His tone commanded my presence when the men came to join the ladies.

When seated, Clara Whitney poured the promptly served tea. She handed me a cup with complete indifference.

"I do declare, Daphne, that Cecil is becoming as insane as Isobel. He is positively obsessed with his ancient Romans. And Jason! He is more impossible than ever," lamented Clara.

"Did you go to see Isobel when we were in London?" asked Daphne in that scratchy, twittery voice of hers.

"No. John went to the hospital alone. I visited friends and did some shopping. Needless to say, Cecil spent his time among the musty tomes in the University of London's library. As for Jason, well, one never knows where he's off to half the time," replied Clara.

"Did John say whether she was better or worse?" asked Daphne.

Clara hesitated, then frowned. "Come to think of it, he didn't mention his visit to her at all. I remember questioning him once or twice about it, but I don't think he ever gave me a direct answer. Probably wants to forget. I remember the last time he saw her, she became quite violent, saying he was the devil trying to snatch her and bring her to his netherland. Isn't that absolutely ridiculous? The one time I did go with John to see Isobel, she had no idea who he was, nor did she recognize me. An utter waste of time. I don't know why my brother bothers to go to see her at all. It only brings him more grief."

"Poor woman. How long do you think she will continue on like that?"

"Mad?" asked Clara of Daphne.

"No. I mean . . . well, doesn't insanity do something to shorten one's life?" asked Daphne.

Though her tone resounded with sympathy, there was a glimmer in Daphne's eyes. I had the distinct impression she fancied herself the next Lady Rathbone. I silently wished her luck. My impression of Lord Rathbone's character was not a favorable one. He was imperious, brooding, and overbearing. If she hoped to change or tame him, I feared she would be greatly disappointed. He possessed a will of iron no woman could break. Clara's voice roused me from my mental musings.

"I wouldn't know. Miss Clarke, would you know anything about insanity?"

"From what I have gleaned in London, all I know is that it can take different forms. I very much doubt if it shortens one's life unless it is the kind of insanity where one tries to do oneself in."

For the first time, Daphne looked directly at me. "You mean one can live like that for a long time?"

Clara replied for me. "I daresay Isobel will outlive us all. She is well tended to in that hospital. Properly nourished and exercised, she could go on forever. Poor John. He did so want an heir."

"Oh." Daphne's delicate features curled in a moue which, oddly enough, made her beauty almost grotesque, like some eerie mask at an All Hallow's Eve ball.

When their talk turned to gossip, my thoughts curled in on themselves, convoluting in my brain until one primary thought emerged—getting into the locked section of the East Wing.

The Whitneys and Jason Watson lived in the front part of the East Wing. Lord Rathbone and his guests occupied rooms in the front part of the West Wing. Mrs. Herries and I had our rooms in the rear part of the West Wing. After my walk on the moor, I would casually stroll around the periphery of the back ell of the East Wing to find an alternate entrance. As I calculated the time it would take me, the gentlemen entered.

John Rathbone's eyes quickly captured mine. A superior smile lifted his lips. He had triumphed and he wanted me to know it.

"I trust your tea was enjoyable, Miss Clarke," said Lord Rathbone.

"Quite pleasant." I smiled. If he wanted a battle of wills, I would give him one.

A smirk began to form on his lips, but before it could materialize, Daphne urged him to sit with her. She flashed her dazzling white teeth at him as she told him how marvelous it was of him to put them up while Foxhill was being refurbished. Though no words passed between them, Cecil Whitney sat next to his wife. Sir Lewis picked up a newspaper and cracked its pages as he began to read it. Jason stood by the fireplace not too far from where I was seated.

"Tell me, Janet, have you ever restored a famous

painting?" asked Jason.

"Two or three of note, but not one that was world famous. For the most part, the paintings were of family members of past generations," I replied.

"And what were those notable paintings?"

"A portrait of Ben Jonson by Sir Joshua Reynolds and a portrait of Joseph Addison by Sir Godfrey Kneller. The oldest painting I ever restored was a portrait of the Earl of Arundel painted in 1618 by Daniel Mytens."

"No European masters?"

"I'm afraid not." I found his steady and intense gaze disquieting.

"I have persuaded our dear Daphne to play the piano for our entertainment," said Lord Rathbone in a stentorian voice. "Shall we adjourn to the ballroom, ladies and gentlemen?"

As we settled down in the ballroom, I was seated between Cecil Whitney and Jason. Lord Rathbone stood by the piano so he could turn the music pages for Daphne.

I had expected an accomplished pianist, but Daphne was far from that. My father was a devotee of the classics and imbued me with a love for good music. Daphne displayed no such proficiency at the piano. Her playing was mechanical. By the end of the first piece, I came to the conclusion she was tone deaf. But she did look beautiful sitting there. Every time she stumbled over a passage, she would giggle, look up at Lord Rathbone, and flutter her eyelashes. It made me wince inside. I soon lost interest in the cozy musicale.

My eyes strayed to Cecil Whitney's lap, where his hands clenched and unclenched. I stole a sidelong glance at his face. A vein throbbed in his neck, and from the flaring of his nostrils, I could tell his breathing was becoming rapid. I tried to mask my alarm. I was sure the man was going to become apoplectic. His eyes were closed, his body rigid, his face reddening. I was certain he would collapse any minute. But I didn't dare bring it to anyone's attention, lest this behavior was normal for him. I would only wind up making a fool of myself.

My concern for Cecil Whitney was sharply diverted when I felt, through all my petticoats, a knee pressing against my thigh. I indignantly glared at Jason, but he was staring straight ahead as though caught in rapture by the music. I moved my leg and fervently prayed Daphne's fingers would drop off, making it impossible for her to continue.

When Sir Lewis's snoring became louder and more rhythmic than Daphne's musical efforts, she stopped and gave Lord Rathbone an apologetic smile that dripped with sweetness.

"I think Percy has initiated the thought of retiring," said Lord Rathbone.

Clara Whitney stood and gave her husband a jab with her elbow. "It's been a long day and we do have the picnic tomorrow." When Cecil continued to sit there, she put her hand on his shoulder and roughly shook him. "Come along, Cecil. The recital is over."

His eyes opened and he appeared to be quite normal. He rose and docilely followed his wife out of the ballroom.

While Daphne roused her father, Jason jumped to his feet to hold my chair.

"Horrible, wasn't it?" he whispered in my ear, a smile on his face. "I think John delights in torturing people. He knows we detest having to sit through one of Daphne's debacles. The woman should shun all musical endeavors with the earnestness of one avoiding the plague."

I made no comment. I was too mindful of Lord Rathbone's gaze on me. Besides giving me a look of consternation, his eyes seemed to be flashing me a warning. Or was it a challenge? He so distraced me, I never realized Jason was pulling my hand through the crook of his arm and leading me from the ornate ball-room.

As Jason steered me up the grand staircase and toward the West Wing, I said, "Mr. Whitney didn't look well during the recital. Is he ill?"

"Cecil is quite sick. Sick of Clara. Sick of John. And I daresay he's sick of me, although I do my best to avoid the fellow. I think he shuts his ears when Daphne plays and probably starts thinking about his life here. I guess you noticed how fast he breathes and how red he becomes. I've noticed it too. Many times. It seems to occur whenever he has time to himself and thinks."

"If he is so unhappy, why does he stay here?"

Jason shrugged. "It certainly isn't because he has any great love for Clara. And John's manner irritates him, especially John's attitude regarding the moor."

"Oh? What attitude?"

"John has a tendency to view the moor as his private domain. His thinking place, he calls it. One time he caught Cecil heading for the moor with a shovel. He didn't approve and told Cecil not to be mucking about on the moors. Cecil didn't like it and has resented John ever since."

"Doesn't he have enough means of support to leave here?" My curiosity was smothering my sense of propriety regarding gossip.

"A small annuity. Not enough to maintain this style of living, but enough to keep him from starving. Now me, I'm not that fortunate. I haven't a sou to my name. I rely on John's generosity for the little things that make life tolerable. I often think about working for a living, but I immediately lay myself down until the notion goes away. Though I envy your independence, I couldn't abide actually having to work."

"When you enjoy your work, the money is merely an

added inducement," I said.

"Ah . . . I see we're at your door. I was serious when I said I wanted to watch you work sometime."

"Lord Rathbone wasn't very encouraging on that point."

"Don't pay any attention to John. He's been in a foul mood of late. I promise not to disturb you. Just quietly observe."

"Morning would be the best time."

"I shall remember that. Good night, dear lady." He turned and walked down the corridor to the East Wing.

As I opened my door, I spied Sarah scurrying down the hall toward me. With an anxious smile, she entered my room with me, questions bubbling forth regarding how the gown was received. It was pleasant talking to Sarah and we chatted away for an hour or more.

Before sleep clamped down on me like a falcon's talons on prey, I thought about Jason Watson. Though he was courteous and friendly toward me, he elicited a warning in me. I knew it was irrational of me to suspect him of anything—he seemed innocuous enough—yet I couldn't shake the notion there was more to Jason Watson than met the eye. If I felt it necessary to be wary of anyone, it should be Mr. Jackson or Lord Rathbone himself.

Mr. Jackson made no secret of the disdain he felt for me. But then Mr. Jackson seemed to hold most people in contempt. On the other hand, Lord Rathbone displayed neither disdain nor contempt. Though he didn't appear to be hostile, there was an undercurrent that seethed within him whenever we met. Those cat green eyes of his bore into mine with enigmatic alarm.

As I worked over my table, my attention was drawn to the window. It was midmorning and the Whitneys and

71

the Lewises were seated in a large barouche while Lord Rathbone and Jason Watson rode horses alongside the vehicle. With the exception of Lord Rathbone, everyone seemed in high spirits, laughing and chatting among themselves. I returned my attention to my work.

After lunch with Sarah, whose bright nature always lifted my spirits, I went for a short walk on the moor, planning to return earlier than usual to explore the outer perimeter of the rear East Wing.

Reaching the pinnacle of one of the rolling knolls, I stood and breathed deeply of the salt-tinged air. The melancholy land stretched under my feet and before my eyes in timeless desolation. For all its solitary dreariness, there was a peace about the moor, a peace that would soon stir to the awakening furze and gorse.

I lifted my face to the sun's rays and stared at the sky, its blue canopy shrouding the land. At that moment I understood Lord Rathbone's selfish possession of the moor. It filled one with reverence and awe. A place where private thoughts could frolic freely and mingle with the very roots of life. The strident call of a stray gull brought a halt to my musings. I directed my feet back to Cheviot Chase.

I felt there was little chance of anyone noticing my survey of the East Wing. Jason and the Whitneys were gone for the day and the servants would have completed their chores in both wings. They would be concentrating on the galleries and main part of the house.

I tramped slowly around the rear facade, looking for an outside entrance. I discovered two doors, but to my dismay, they were firmly locked. Pushing my way through the shrubbery huddled against the wall that faced the moor, I spied a broad stone sill of a window. A need to peer inside swept over me. I reached up but the sill was just beyond my fingertips.

An unladylike thought came into my head and I glanced around to make sure I wasn't being observed. I bent my knees then gave a good leap upward. My hands caught the sill and I was able to pull myself up enough to have my forearms rest on the sill. I peered in to see an elaborate sitting parlor. Over the fireplace mantel, a large full-length portrait of a woman glimmered from the reflecting rays of the sun. Owing to the unruly play of light, I couldn't make out the features of the woman and that added to my curiosity.

My arms were getting tired. Using my foot, I searched for a niche where my feet could rest and help support my strained body. I moved it over the stone surface of the building but could not find a toehold. Suddenly my foot went into a void. I dropped back to the ground.

I crouched down to learn the void was a small indented window which the shrubbery had hidden. It had the appearance of being locked. I stretched out my hand to try to push it and to my astonishment it moved. I increased the pressure of my hand. Though emitting an ear-wrenching squeal, the window opened all the way.

I should have debated the propriety of what I was about to embark on, but my mind never considered an alternative. As though propelled by an unknown and unseen force within me, I stuck my head through the window; the rest of my body followed. As though to abet my intrusion, a table rested under the window, facilitating my entrance.

Though murky and damp, the area appeared to have been a small kitchen and laundry with additional servants' quarters. I gingerly made my way through to a staircase that rested in the distance.

As I mounted the stairs, excitement swelled within me, the kind of excitement that an explorer must experience when finding a new island or continent. When I saw the door at the top of the stairs, my hopes fell like a boulder from a parapet. Lord Rathbone was not a careless man. The door would surely be locked. With a sigh of thwarted desire, I placed my hand on the knob expecting solid resistance. To my surprise and glee, it turned under my hand. I stealthily pushed it open.

I was in a corridor where red damask covered the walls above the dark wainscoting. Besides the vague sooty smell of smoke that wafted through the area, there was a fetid odor that occasionally assailed my nostrils.

The doors off the hall opened easily. I looked into each room to discover sitting parlors, a library, a game room, and a breakfast room. They were similar to those in the West Wing, but with a striking difference. The colors were horribly garish.

Bright purples dashed their way across the rooms as though in flight from the apple green while gaudy yellows flaunted their defiance of the surroundings. In some rooms a glaring red gave the scene a blood-spattered look. All the rooms on that floor seemed to suggest a color-blind artist had wielded his brush in a mad frenzy. I had to get out of there before I lost my sense of color values, a necessary perception for my work. I searched for a staircase to the next floor. It was on the floor above this one that I had seen the figure in white.

Finding the carpeted staircase, I began the climb upward. With each step the acrid smell of stale smoke increased as did the putrid stench. I had expected the sooty odor, knowing a fire had devoured a few of the rooms on that floor. But the foul smell baffled me and caused some apprehension as it seemed to have the aroma of rotting flesh. Reason told me to turn back. But my inquiring mind smothered reason and I plunged ahead.

Completing my climb, I was at the head of a long corridor, almost identical to the floor below. But on my right was an open oblong room that stretched the width of the ell. It was a lavish sitting parlor with gold gilt trying to sparkle on the ceiling through a crust of soot. It spilled down the ornate plastered walls and must have been quite beautiful before the fire. The predominant color was royal blue. Subtle shades of blue mingled with crimson and pink with a startling effect. Although it jolted my sensibilities slightly, the room wasn't as color wrenching as the others on the floor below. I started down the corridor and began to open the unlocked doors.

Room after room was bare, completely devoid of furniture and trappings. The absence of anything that pointed to human habitation made the rooms appear stark and huge. I felt terribly alone as though I had wandered into a dream that was beginning to become a nightmare. The palms of my hands became clammy as I placed one of them on a doorknob and turned it.

The world of color vanished, leaving in its wake a pitted black scene where varying shades of gray made the charred parts all the more inky. The stench was unbearable. I had to take my lavender-scented handkerchief from my pocket and hold it over my nose and mouth to keep the contents of my stomach intact. Then I saw the reason for the malodorous stench of the room.

In the middle of the floor were half-plucked dead chickens. Ugly brown rats were skewered on a fireplace poker. Remnants of moldy cheese and bread lay scattered about while rotting fruit was dispersed like billiard balls through the burned-out room. Though barely recognizable, the room had been a bedchamber of generous proportions. Two charred posts of a four-poster bed remained upright in proud defiance as the rest of it angled down to the sooty threads of a carpet.

My eyes fastened on what lay between the charred bed slats. Fresh fruit and a fresh load of bread. My figure in white was no specter, but a living being who had to eat. Someone was using this section of the East Wing as a refuge, a place of hiding. But why this charred, stinking disaster of a room when others, though in need of cleaning, were far more habitable? I wondered if Lord Rathbone knew someone was using his East Wing in so bizarre a manner. I closed the door then raced back to the staircase and went down.

I thought it would be more prudent to leave by a door rather than stuff myself through that small basement window. Finding a door, I slid the bolt, turned the knob, and yanked. Nothing. I tried again with both hands on the knob. The door would not budge. After closer inspection I found the door was nailed shut from the inside.

Dismayed, I went to one of the large windows, hoping to leap out as the ground was not too far below. All the windows were nailed shut from the inside. I had no recourse but to leave the way I had come in.

As I headed down the corridor to the stairs that would lead me to the floor below, I remembered the portrait I had seen when I'd peered through the window. It was in a room farther down the corridor, a room I hadn't gone into.

The door was open. As I stood on the threshold, the portrait hung on the opposite wall. A beautiful dark-eyed woman with long raven hair blankly stared down at me with an imperious air. It was a full-length portrait of a woman standing in a red velvet gown, her hand resting on the back of a chair. Intuition told me it was a portrait of Lord Rathbone's second wife, Lady Isobel.

I stood there fascinated, wondering what had made her go mad. There was no hint of impending madness in the portrait. Had the artist neglected to paint the approaching insanity? Even if he had, she was still a remarkably handsome woman. I stood there a few minutes longer, then headed for my ignominious exit.

I clambered up on the table then propped the window open with a stick I had found on the floor near the table.

With forearms firmly on the ground outside the window, I poked my head out. Inching my arms forward, I slowly began to drag my body out. I succeeded in being halfway out when I saw a pair of shiny black boots striding toward me. I froze.

section of the house and I thought the person might be trapped. I wanted to offer any assistance if this window seems to be the only means of exit, but circumstances—

Five

My vision slowly inched upward to see arms akimbo and the stern face of Lord Rathbone towering over me. In my embarrassment I wanted to slip back into the dingy basement, cover myself with debris, and disappear from the face of the earth. I lowered my eyes to the ground. I couldn't bear the sardonic humor glinting in those green eyes.

Hands came down and gripped under my arms. In one swoop, I was pulled from the window and set upon my feet, the hands remaining in place. I knew this was the end and I would be sent packing. But I was too consumed by shame and foolish stupidity to dwell on my uncertain future. My head was shouting "curiosity killed the cat." Well, I thought, there is nothing to do but brazen it out. With a feigned air of defiance, I lifted my head and let my eyes lock with his.

He peered down at me with one dark eyebrow raised arrogantly. "Are you practicing the art of thievery, Miss Clarke? Or do you have a predilection for snooping about in places that are no concern of yours?"

I found his proximity usettling, but I managed to control the nervousness that was invading my body. "Neither, Lord Rathbone. I had seen someone in this

78

section of the house and I thought the person might be trapped. I wanted to offer my assistance. This window seems to be the only means of exit and entrance."

He threw his head back and the air echoed with his deep resonant laughter. When his amusement faded, his expression turned austere again. "Assistance indeed! I should think with your intelligence, Miss Clarke, you could offer a more plausible excuse. What was your real intention for sneaking into the East Wing?"

"I told you, sir. I have seen someone prowling about in there. I believe whoever it is is making their home in there. Stale and decaying food was strewn about the burned-out bedchamber along with fresh food," I declared.

A wan smile played about his lips, his hands suddenly dropping to his sides. Though his face was placid, not revealing a hint of emotion, there was a flicker in his eyes that betrayed a concern as though he knew I was telling the truth. A twinge of triumph skittered through me, but it was short-lived.

"I had heard artists have unbridled imaginations. I suggest you confine your imagination to the work I hired you for. Regarding Cheviot Chase, what does or does not go on here is my concern, not yours, Miss Clarke."

"Then you don't believe me?" I asked.

"Perhaps it would be best if you took your evening meal in your room tonight. I wouldn't want you upsetting my guests with fanciful tales gleaned from your imagination," stated Lord Rathbone.

"As you wish, Lord Rathbone." I could see there was no point in continuing the subject. His mind was set and any further discussion would be futile. I made a move to leave and he stepped aside. I had walked a few steps when he grabbed my wrist.

"Miss Clarke, may I recommend you take your walks anywhere but on the moor. The place is not suitable for one walking alone."

"Am I to be denied that pleasure, Lord Rathbone? Is the moor only for your contemplative walks?" I asked a bit too brusquely.

"I made the suggestion for your own safety. A walk along the path to the sea cliffs might prove more beneficial."

"Then I am not denied access to the moor?"

"You may deem me a tyrant, Miss Clarke, but I assure you I am not. If you wish to walk on the moor, you may, but at your own peril. I will not be held responsible if anything happens to you there."

"Is that a threat, sir?"

"You are a most exasperating young woman, Miss Clarke. I try to think of your welfare and you condemn me for it."

He was right. I was being unusually cantankerous. Why did he rile me so? A wave of contrition swept over me. "I am sorry, sir. I shouldn't take my embarrassment at being caught in so ungainly a situation out on you. My manners have been deplorable. I apologize, Lord Rathbone."

He looked at me thoughtfully. "Perhaps your youth cries out for some diversion. Cheviot Chase can have a stifling effect on youthful exuberance. Do you ride, Miss Clarke?"

"A horse?"

"Yes."

"I'm afraid not, sir. I was born and brought up in London. Promenading a horse on Rotten Row is not an amusement for working-class ladies," I replied.

"Then a trap will have to do. After lunch tomorrow I will take you into Dorchester. Perhaps you have a touch of homesickness and the sights of a city might relieve your melancholia," said Lord Rathbone.

"I appreciate the thought, sir, but I assure you I am

not afflicted with homesickness. I find Cheviot Chase a most pleasant place and feel quite at home here."

"Nonetheless, I expect to find you suitably dressed for the outing tomorrow afternoon. I'm sure there must be a trinket or two you would like to purchase."

"Well, I do need certain materials to continue with the restoration work. I couldn't bring everything with me. And I really had to see the paintings to know what would be required," I said.

"Good. Our trip will have a definite purpose to it. Till tomorrow, Miss Clarke."

"Good day, Lord Rathbone." Without a backward glance I headed for the rear entrance to the West Wing. As I walked away, I had the sensation he was staring at the back of my head.

Ascending the servants' staircase, I ran into Sarah Herries coming down. Her mouth fell agape when she saw me.

"Good gracious! Whatever happened to you, Janet? You look as though you fell into a dustbin," said Sarah.

"I'll tell you all about it at supper."

"Aren't you eating with his lordship this evening?"

"No. He thinks I should take a rest." I smiled and patted her arm.

Sarah shook her head and watched me climb the rest of the stairs before she continued her downward journey.

Once in my bedchamber, I rushed to the mirror and gasped. I was a sight to behold. My hair was askew with tendrils fluttering about my grimy, sooty face. My chagrin increased when I thought about Lord Rathbone seeing me in such a state. What must he have thought of me? I pushed some of the loose tendrils back then looked at my dirty hand. There was nothing I could do to erase the incident so I smiled. At least I hadn't been sacked. A thorough wash was in order.

The supper trays were emptied onto a small round

table in Sarah Herries's sitting parlor. We sat down and began to eat. Sarah was a patient woman and asked no questions. I knew she would wait until I was ready to talk. At the moment I was more intent on eating supper while it was still warm. Our meal finished, we sat before the fire and sipped our tea.

I told her of my foolhardy excursion into the East Wing and what I had discovered there. I also mentioned the encounter with his lordship.

"Oh, my dear Janet. I'm surprised he didn't give you the sack on the spot. He is a very stern taskmaster. You were lucky he was of a mood to keep you on," claimed Sarah.

"At the time I was sure he would let me go. I'd appreciate it if all this stayed between us. I wouldn't want it bandied about among the staff."

"I would never tell the staff. They have enough to gossip about. Too much for the likes of me." As Sarah sipped her tea, her brow creased in a frown. "Do you really think someone is using the East Wing as a refuge?"

"It seems that way, at least to me. But I can't understand why they would use the burned-out rooms when there are other rooms that were untouched by the fire. It doesn't make any sense."

"I should say not," agreed Sarah.

"Lord Rathbone insists it is all in my imagination. Really, Sarah, I am not the type of person who sees things that aren't there."

"Of course you're not, my dear. But then everyone exaggerates at one time or another. That doesn't mean I doubt you, Janet. But that food could have been taken there by rats or cats or even his lordship's dogs. It is my guess only an animal would prefer a destroyed room. Perhaps the creature would feel more comfortable there."

I shrugged. "It's a possibility. But how would you

account for the figure I saw moving from room to room in the East Wing?"

"A stray breeze moving curtains could play tricks on one's eyes. Why, one of the maids became hysterical claiming she saw a ghost in the East Wing. Nothing would do until Mr. Jackson went to the East Wing and personally searched it out. Of course there was no one there."

"I thought Lord Rathbone was the only one who had a key to the East Wing," I said.

"Mr. Jackson is the only other person who has a key. Mine and the others were taken away after the fire," said Sarah. "Don't go fretting yourself about the East Wing. We've all learned to pay no heed to it."

"Why doesn't his lordship have it cleaned up and redone?"

"I suspect he will someday."

"I should think the East Wing would have more priority than having the paintings restored," I said, speaking my thoughts aloud.

"Who knows how his lordship's mind works." Sarah rose and collected the tray.

"I'll do that," I said, and began to load the tray with our empty dishes.

Sarah picked up the gown she was working on and sat down in a cushioned chair. "I think this peach gown will be the prettiest of all."

"I might have no need for it."

"It doesn't matter. I like working on them," said Sarah.

"I'll take the tray down to the kitchen and then come back and help you."

I started work early the next morning. Wanting to justify Lord Rathbone's faith in my work, I took extraordinary care on each painting. I had stacked the paintings into three groups. Those that only needed cleaning. Those which would need cleaning and some surface restoration. And those that required extensive work along with new linings. I had started with those that only needed cleaning. I was so absorbed in the delicate daubing of the surface that I jumped a little at the sound of heavy rapping on my door.

"Come in," I called as I turned to face the door.

The head of Jason Watson poked in. "I hope I'm not disturbing you. You did say to come in the morning."

"Not at all. Do come in, Mr. Watson."

"Jason, remember?" He closed the door and came to stand behind me. "How long have you been working on this painting?"

"About three days."

"And that's all you've done?" he asked with genuine surprise.

"It's a slow process," I said with a smile.

"I guess so. But then I know nothing about it." His attention strayed to the framed canvases stacked against the wall. He began to look through them. "Ugly old things. I'll never understand why John is bothering with them. Frankly I wouldn't give you a farthing for any of them. I wonder if any of them have some real value. Can you judge their worth, Janet? In pounds, that is."

"To a fair degree. But some would only have value to their owners," I replied.

"If there are valuable ones here, aren't you afraid someone might pinch one? Especially the way they are lying about in an open room."

"Not really. I believe Lord Rathbone has a detailed list of what is here. I also did a complete inventory and checked it against his list," I replied.

"Still, you should keep this door locked," urged Jason.

"I do when I'm not in here even though I don't think

anyone in the house would steal one."

He walked back to stand behind me again as I continued my work. "I missed you at dinner last night. Weren't you feeling well?"

"Something like that," I replied. Evidently Lord Rathbone hadn't mentioned yesterday's escapade to anyone.

"Well, you didn't miss anything. Daphne persisted in casting moon eyes at John. Sir Lewis continued his pompous political rhetoric. Clara persevered in harassing poor Cecil. Of course, I was my usual model of decorum and wit, which was totally lost on everyone. It seems you are the only one who appreciates my droll comments. You will be coming to dinner tonight, won't you?"

"I'm not sure."

"Do come and rescue me from complete ennui." For several minutes, he peered down in silence at the painting I was working on, then asked, "Aren't you afraid of ruining the paint with all those chemicals?"

"That's why it goes so slowly. Painstaking delicacy is a must," I replied, a little surprised at his interest.

"It looks like grim and tedious work."

"Nothing is grim and tedious when you enjoy doing it."

"Why are the paintings stacked in groups along the wall?"

I explained my reasons.

"Why have you left the most difficult till last? I should think you'd do those first when your energies and concentration are at their keenest. The hard part would be out of the way and the rest should be like frosting on a cake," said Jason.

"The more difficult the restoration, the slower the progress. I've found that people like to see results rather quickly. When they see a number of paintings aglow with vibrant color, they are more willing to wait for the more difficult ones to be completed. My father always used to tell me, 'Give the people a taste for the possibilities restoration offers, and it will develop into a patient hunger,'" I informed him.

"I'm afraid it would never work for me." He flipped a watch from a pocket of his elaborately brocaded vest, clicked it open, and peered at the time. "Well, they'll be expecting me for lunch. I really must fly. It has been quite enlightening watching you at work, Janet. I hope you'll let me come again, especially when you get to the harder restorations. I would like to see for myself the difficulty involved. Promise me you'll let me know when you start them."

"I promise," I said, amused by his insistence.

"Ta-ta, for now."

When he left, the scent of him lingered in the room. He must have indulged in a lavish sprinkling of lavender water, I thought.

Though he seemed to be a personable young man, I had my reservations about Jason Watson. If I had been beautiful, I could better understand his attentions toward me. But I was plain and somewhat introverted. It was obvious his interest in my work was a sham. So why the attention?

His dress and manner indicated a man who was very class conscious and harbored a dislike for the bourgeois. With the exception of Lord Rathbone, the others in the house made no secret of their contempt for me. Was it an act of defiance on Jason's part? Did he find it titillating to flick his finger at social mores? I had no answer. Still, something about him disturbed me.

After a pleasant lunch with Sarah, I made the necessary toilette and changed my frock for the trip to the city with Lord Rathbone. I must admit the prospect excited me. But I couldn't discern whether it was the trip to the city or the thought of being alone with his lordship. The man stirred something in me, something I could not put a name to.

I stood in the foyer waiting for his lordship to make his appearance. I had a list of the necessities tucked in my reticule. I didn't want to try his patience while I scanned every article hoping to remember what I needed. Somewhere in the back of my mind, I thought if I was quick enough at the store, it would leave more time for a tour of the city with his lordship.

Clara Whitney and Daphne Lewis came bouncing down the main staircase, conversing animatedly. They paid as much attention to me as they would a marble statue resting in a recessed niche. Mr. Jackson opened the door for them and they passed outside without missing a step.

Lord Rathbone was late. It was fifteen minutes past the appointed hour before he came into the foyer. With the exception of a white shirt, he was dressed in black and, as usual, was hatless. Though somber, he exuded forceful masculinity. A shiver of a smile flickered on his lips when our eyes met, but it never fully formed.

"I am late. Please accept my apologies, Miss Clarke," he said, cupping my elbow and steering toward the door. "I'm afraid there has been a slight change in my original plans."

Mr. Jackson opened the door. I couldn't stop my body from tensing when I saw the regal barouche, replete with driver and footman, waiting at the bottom of the marble steps. I tried to keep my expression placid at the sight of Daphne and Clara sitting on the back seat.

The trip to Dorchester was not going to be what I had imagined. I sat across from Clara and would be riding backward. Lord Rathbone took the seat opposite Daphne. Both Clara and Daphne had frilly parasols that matched their elaborate day frocks. Daphne in pink, Clara in blue.

I wore my best day frock of cocoa brown. As for a parasol, I had never owned one. I felt like someone's old, drab governess. I wondered if it was Lord Rathbone's idea of revenge for catching me sneaking out of the East Wing.

"I'm ever so glad we learned you were going to Dorchester, John," bubbled Daphne, her eyelashes blinking rapidly, a mannerism I assumed she thought seductive. "Cheviot Chase is a lovely estate, but you have to admit it is quite dull. Of course Dorchester isn't London, but it is better than the village. When will you be going to London again to see Isobel?"

"I'm not sure." His smile was indulgent and fleeting.

"I meant to ask you before, John. Do the doctors hold any hope for Isobel's recovery?" asked Clara.

Daphne suddenly sat erect, her eyes wide in anticipation of a negative answer. I wondered if his lordship was aware of Daphne's more than passing interest in him. He had to know. He was an astute man and Daphne was much too obvious in her fawning attentions for him not to notice.

Their conversation turned to parties, social gatherings, and people, none of which I found interesting. I contented myself with viewing the scenery. Lord Rathbone also was gazing out of the barouche, but I sensed he was preoccupied and wasn't seeing the panorama before him.

In Dorchester I was let off at the stationers, the carriage and passengers proceeding on. The proprietor was accommodating. Though he couldn't fill my entire list, he assured me he would order the items from London and have them sent to him by train.

While the proprietor stood behind the counter wrapping the art materials, my heart began to pound erratically. I had forgotten all about money. I had meant

88

to ask Lord Rathbone for some money to pay for the materials, but the sight of Clara and Daphne in the carriage had erased all thoughts of money from my mind.

There was nothing I could do but ask the proprietor to hold the packages until I could reach Lord Rathbone. Dorchester wasn't that large and I hoped I could find him quickly. The proprietor agreed. After all it was a large order and meant money in his pocket.

I almost ran from the shop. As I darted out the door onto the street, I ran into a rock-hard body. I mumbled some excuse and began to circle around him without even a glance. A strong hand caught my wrist.

"You seem in a hurry, Miss Clarke. Are there demons in that shop?"

I looked up to see the handsome face of Lord Rathbone, a full-blown smile on his face, merriment in his catlike eyes.

"Oh, thank goodness you're here. I was about to seek you out. I have—"

"No money," he said, completing my sentence. "I realized that shortly after we left you off. But I had to see the ladies to the dressmaker's shop. I walked back so they could have the carriage to put their parcels in. I also realize you've been at Cheviot Chase a little over a month without receiving wages of any kind. I'll rectify that shortly. But first we'll take care of your purchases at the stationery. Come along."

He pulled my hand through his crooked arm. I was embarrassed for him. So elegant and formidable a man to be seen with a mousy, plain creature like me.

Inside the shop, he told the proprietor, "Send the bill to Cheviot Chase. We'll pick up the packages before leaving town."

The proprietor's eyes narrowed with recognition. "Yes, Lord Rathbone. Whatever you wish. And the items being sent from London?"

Lord Rathbone looked down at me, one eyebrow raised quizzically. I quickly explained.

"I see," said Lord Rathbone before turning to the proprietor. "The minute they arrive, have them sent to Cheviot Chase."

"Yes, milord."

Outside in the street, I thanked him for resolving the matter with dispatch.

"I can't very well expect you to work without materials. Are you having any difficulties with the paintings?" asked Lord Rathbone.

"No. The work is going smoothly. I will be happy to show you the paintings whenever you wish." I stood there expecting him to take his leave any second. But he stood still, gazing about with an abstract expression.

"Ah! There's the tea shop. Can I persuade you to have a cup of tea with me, Miss Clarke? They have delightful pastries there."

I must have looked utterly foolish standing there, my eyes wide, my mouth agape. Me having a private tea with a lord. I could picture Daphne Lewis gasping with horror at the thought of it. Once the initial shock was over, I spoke.

"I'm sorry, Lord Rathbone. It wouldn't be proper and might lower your social standing in the community."

He laughed. It was a pleasant sound that caused several people to glance our way. "My dear Miss Clarke, my social standing in the county of Dorset couldn't be any lower. Didn't Mrs. Herries tell you I am thought of as some sort of demon who drives his wives crazy?"

Bewildered, I shook my head.

"I can't really blame you for not wanting to be seen with me. My reputation is not the highest. I understand your position, Miss Clarke. I will have my tea alone." A glint came into his eyes that seemed to challenge me.

"On second thought, tea would be nice about now,

Lord Rathbone." I wasn't sure if I was rising to the challenge or thrilled at the thought of having tea alone with him. How I wished he was not a peer of the land.

Again he pulled my hand through his arm and we walked to the tea shop.

The table was small and round, topped with marble. The chairs had wire backs with caned seats. The waitress's eyes kept darting to Lord Rathbone with a mixture of curiosity and apprehension. She was soon back with a pot of tea, cups, saucers, cream, and sugar. She scooted away and returned with a three-tiered tray on which rested a variety of cream cakes and pastries. I couldn't resist them, especially the ones with chocolate on them.

"Do you like them?" he asked.

"They are delicious."

"Then we'll take a box of them back for you and Mrs. Herries to munch on," he declared.

"Please don't go to any trouble."

"Nonsense. Don't eat too many now. I expect you to come to dinner tonight."

"Really, sir. I don't think I should be at your table. As I said before, I make your guests uncomfortable, and if I may be frank, I am uncomfortable also."

"You'll get used to it. I don't care how my guests feel about it."

"Do you find my discomfort amusing?"

"Why should you think that?"

"You always seem to have an air of cynical amusement at the dinner table."

"Do I now? I wasn't aware of it. You're a very forthright young woman, Miss Clarke. Not many people would address their employer with such honesty."

"I am not good at masking my feelings and always had the audacity to speak my mind. I hope I have not offended you, sir."

91

"Your honesty is quite refreshing, I assure you." He paused a moment, then asked, "Do you think I am an instrument of the devil whose sole purpose is to drive his wives mad?"

Again there was that glint of challenge in his eyes, but I also detected a trace of sadness behind that challenge.

"I can hardly be expected to judge a person I know so little about and for so brief a time."

"Tactfully put, Miss Clarke." He drained the tea from his cup then stared at me. "Do I frighten you, Miss Clarke?"

"No." My answer came quickly and naturally.

"I hope I never do."

"Shouldn't we be getting back to the carriage? I don't think Mrs. Whitney and Miss Lewis would like to be kept waiting," I said.

"Between the milliner's and the dressmaker's they'll consume the afternoon. It's a pity they learned of our little jaunt to Dorchester. Once they knew about it, I couldn't dissuade them from coming along. I had hoped to show you some of Dorset's lovely countryside. But no matter. Perhaps another time. Thank goodnes I had neglected to give you any money. It was a good excuse to come to your financial aid and leave them to their shopping," said Lord Rathbone.

"If I'm not being too bold, may I ask how Lady Rathbone is faring?"

"It is a mite bold of you, Miss Clarke, but that is what I find so charming about you. As for Lady Rathbone, she is doing as well as can be expected. I doubt if she'll ever be truly well and normal again though."

"I'm sorry."

"Is your workshop adequate?"

His question put an effective end to the topic of Lady Rathbone. Though he tried to maintain a placid expression, I could see anger and resentment in his eyes, a reaction I hadn't expected. Pity or sadness would have been more appropriate, I thought.

"The room is quite adequate. Mr. Watson visited the workshop this morning to watch me work. I assume that is permissible."

"If it doesn't disturb you, I have no objection. But don't let him monopolize your time. Jason is a wastrel. He thinks nothing of infringing on other people. Don't let him squander your working hours with his self-indulgence," warned Lord Rathbone.

"I shall be most circumspect, Lord Rathbone."

"This has been a pleasant little visit, Miss Clarke. If you find you are lacking something or your accommodations aren't quite right, do feel free to call on me. Now, if you are finished, we'll go. I do have to put some sort of monetary limit on my sister. She has a tendency to be unmindful of the money she is spending." Outside, he stopped me as I began to make my way down the street toward the carriage, the promised box of pastries in my hand. "Miss Clarke, here are two pounds, a small advance for your work."

"It is too much, sir," I protested as he proffered me the money.

"Nonsense. Take it." He shoved the money into my reticule. "You still have some time to do a little personal shopping if you wish. We'll meet back at the carriage in just under an hour."

Before I could protest further, he strode away. I stood staring after him. Doubts began to assail my mind. Why had he taken me to tea? What was his purpose?

I don't know why I was so suspicious of his motives. Perhaps it was that peculiar gleam in his eyes that unsettled me. Another question that nagged at me was the idea if he was viewed as a person who drove his wives mad, why was Daphne Lewis so intent in pursuing him?

As he disappeared into a tobacconist's shop, my heart

whispered the answer to me. He was a handsome man who exuded elegance, charm, and a masculinity that couldn't be denied. In the light of all these attributes, it was easy to understand Daphne's infatuation with him. I had to push him out of my mind before he claimed an inexorable hold on my own heart.

I went to the shop that offered sundry items to purchase some lavender water for myself. I was afraid the odor of my cleaning solvents might cling to me at the dinner table even though I always performed a careful toilette. The lavender water would give me great self-confidence.

When I arrived at the carriage, only the driver and footman were present. With the footman's assistance, I entered the carriage, my box of pastries comfortably sitting in my lap. Though it seemed like ages, only minutes passed before I saw Lord Rathbone strolling toward the carriage, a lady draped on each arm. A young boy trotted behind them loaded with packages.

Much fuss was made to securing the many packages on the carriage before Clara and Daphne came into the vehicle, seating themselves, as before, parasols up. I could have been an unadorned pillow for all the notice they paid to me. What did surprise me was Lord Rathbone's silent indifference. I found it difficult to believe this was the same man who had chatted so amiably over tea.

Jason Watson escorted me into dinner in a most attentive manner. Though it was flattering, I couldn't help wondering what his true aim was. I certainly wasn't rich nor was I any great beauty—attributes which Jason would demand in a woman.

At dinner I did more listening than talking. Clara was busy trying to convince her brother to give a large soiree.

Daphne seconded the appeal with more than normal enthusiasm, her delicate, tiny, retroussé nose crinkling in a puerile way. I suppose she thought the affectation made her adorable. I thought it made her look comic. Sir Lewis occasionally ventured a discourse on the agrarian outrages occurring in County Mayo, Ireland. I was interested in hearing more about Ireland, but the ladies soon dominated the conversation again.

By the time we entered the drawing room, the impending ball had become a fact. Knowing I'd be ignored as Clara and Daphne made their plans for the upcoming ball, I took a seat in a far corner and amused myself with the latest copy of *Punch*.

When the gentlemen entered, they were quickly drawn into the web of Clara and Daphne's conversation, which apprised them, in detail, of their plans. I continued my perusal of *Punch*. Occasionally I felt eyes burning their way across the room at me. Whenever I lifted my gaze, I would catch the blatant stare of Lord Rathbone. When our eyes met, he would flicker an enigmatic smile then glance away. I was sure Jason caught those surreptitious glances. Though it was a scene that was probably taking place in the drawing rooms of numerous estates, I sensed an undercurrent in this drawing room. An unpleasant and macabre one.

Though he was present in body, Cecil Whitney's mind and spirit were not in the room. I wondered if he was contemplating the early Roman conquerors. Sir Lewis pulled at his mutton chops as if to keep himself awake. Jason had a preoccupied look as though he was trying to work out a complicated scheme. For all appearances, Lord Rathbone seemed rapt with his sister's and Daphne's plans for the ball. But I could detect a distant look in his eyes, a tortured look.

*   *   *

At lunch the next day, I told Sarah Herries of the impending ball to be held at Cheviot Chase. Her reaction surprised me.

"Glory be! I never thought his lordship would do such a thing," she exclaimed.

"Why not?" I asked.

"Well, for one thing, his wife being in the hospital, her condition uncertain. He'll only start those malicious rumors again."

"What rumors?"

"That he drove both his wives insane. That he's the devil incarnate with a predilection for destroying all women who take his fancy. Gossip has died down somewhat now, but a ball would only start it all up again. And having Miss Lewis in the house and the way she fawns over him . . . well, it doesn't bode well for his lordship," declared Sarah. "I don't like it. I don't like it at all. Mark my words, Janet. It will only lead to more tragedy for his lordship. A fancy ball indeed!"

I thought Sarah was exaggerating. What harm could a ball do? People will always gossip. But collective memories are short, especially when a new tidbit struck their fancy. If there was any talk about the ball, I was sure it would soon fade.

As was my custom, I went for my usual stroll after lunch. It was a fine spring day and I was looking forward to the fresh air. When I came to the end of the formal garden, two paths stretched before me. One led to the moor, the other to the chalk cliffs. Perhaps it was out of obstinacy that I took the path to the moor. Or was it a wish for a possible encounter with Lord Rathbone?

Field flowers were beginning to bud while others already nodded their colorful blooms to the breeze. Though it was an empty and desolate place, I never felt alone on the moor. I had the bounty of nature to keep me company. I felt more alone in the drawing room of

Cheviot Chase even though I was in the company of people.

As I gazed at the primordial and savage beauty of the moor, my eyes spotted a clump of brown fur nestled in the gorse. I cautiously crept closer and studied it. It hadn't moved. Finding a small, but sturdy twig, I gave it a gentle poke, expecting the creature to flee. But it didn't move. It only took an instant for me to discover there was no flesh to the fur. It was an empty pelt. I maneuvered the twig under the pelt and held it aloft. The sight caused me to shudder, but curiosity kept me from flinging it aside.

It had been a rabbit, a fairly large one. Head, ears, and skin remained. Slits down the underbelly, along the front and hind legs were jagged, but exact. The body had been completely removed. This was no attack by dogs or predatory birds. There was something very precise about the way it was skinned. I scrutinized the pelt closely for a sign of a bullet hole or tears in the pelt to indicate a trap. Nothing. Puzzled, I lowered the pelt to the ground and stared at it.

While thus engaged, everything flashed white before total darkness enveloped me as I sank to the ground.

Six

My head pounded like a thousand drums and the skirl of high-pitched bagpipes seemed to reverberate in my brain. I wanted to open my eyes, but the very thought of it increased the pain.

As though they came from empty chambers, I heard the voices of a man and a woman. The words they spoke sounded as if they came from a distance, yet I could understand them. The woman's voice was vaguely familiar, but not the man's.

"I worry about a concussion. That was a pretty nasty blow she took to the head," said the male voice.

"Do you think there might be permanent damage?" asked the anxious voice of the woman.

"Hard to say. She could go into a coma, have amnesia, or some physical impairment. We still know very little about the brain's function or how a blow to the head might affect the brain. At least the skull's intact. No dents or breakage."

"Oh, dear me," moaned the woman.

"Now, now, Mrs. Herries. You must not go expecting the worst all the time. She's young, healthy, and strong. I'm sure she'll come through it none the worse for wear," soothed the man.

No worse for wear, I thought. My throbbing head wasn't on his shoulders. No one was hammering an anvil inside his head. I now knew the woman was Sarah. But the man's voice was still unfamiliar. Certainly it was no male voice I had ever heard at Cheviot Chase.

Like the ponderous raising of Tower Bridge, my leaden eyelids opened enough for me to squint. I recognized the surroundings as my bedchamber. The figures in the middle were still hazy and indistinct. With great effort spurred by curiosity, I forced my eyelids to open wider. But with my head on the pillow, the angle was all wrong. I couldn't get a clear view of the man.

Lifting my head from the pillow was akin to lifting the entire city of London with one hand. But I managed to sit up and prop myself on my elbows. The pain caused my head to spin with such rapidity I thought it would fly from my neck, bounce off the bed, and roll across the floor. I gently replaced my head on the pillow. A groan echoed through the room. I think it was me.

With eyes still open, I watched the pudgy Sarah waddle to the side of the bed. But the man was swifter. He came to the side of the bed and peered over me, his warm hand covering my forehead.

"Can you hear me, Miss Clarke?" asked the man.

I almost nodded my head, which would have been a disaster. I was sure it would crack open. Instead I murmured a weak, "Yes. Who are you?"

"I'm Dr. Young. Dr. Brian Young," he replied.

"How do you feel, Janet?" asked Sarah, her hands twisting a handkerchief as though she was wringing a chicken's neck.

"Awful."

"Couldn't you give her some headache powders, Doctor?" Sarah said, turning to the man.

"In a case like this, I prefer to give the patient nothing until we are sure her mental and physical faculties are sound. Can you live with the headache for a while, Miss Clarke?" he asked.

"I suppose so. What happened?"

"You tell us," the doctor said with a smile.

He had a winning smile. I judged him to be about six or seven years older than I and of medium height. Brown hair curled over his head. I guess one could say he was handsome, but in a very ordinary way. His smile was reflected in his hazel eyes.

"All I know is I was walking on the moor, stopped to look at something on the ground, then a piercing pain in my head before all went black. Next thing I know I'm here with you and Mrs. Herries. How did I get here?"

Sarah answered. "His lordship found you crumpled on the ground. He carried you up to your bedchamber then sent one of the footmen to fetch the doctor. You've had us all worried, you have. Did someone hit you on the head? The doctor says you have a lump on your head as big as a golf ball."

"Someone must have. There were no trees where I was standing so a loose branch couldn't have fallen on my head."

"Did you see who it was, Janet?" asked Sarah.

"No. I saw no one."

"I think that's enough talk for now," interrupted Dr. Young. "Too much will exacerbate your headache, Miss Clarke." He turned to Sarah. "I think a light supper would be in order. A broth of some sort. And tea with an infusion of the herb rosemary. In the morning, a poached egg and toast or porridge along with the herbal rosemary tea."

Sarah nodded solemnly.

"Are you saying I must stay in bed, Doctor?" I asked.

"I most certainly am," he replied with his charming smile.

"Why? And for how long?" I asked.

"To make sure you heal properly. You might be subject to some dizziness and I wouldn't want you falling down, perhaps hitting your head again. I'll come and see you the day after tomorrow. If all goes well, I may consent to your getting out of bed. You may be bothered with headaches for several days. They'll dissipate with time, unless you are given to frequent headaches. Are you, Miss Clarke?"

"No. Never had one before."

"Good. I'm sure you'll be yourself shortly. I'll see you in a few days."

"I'll see you to the door, Doctor," said Sarah before turning to me. "Would you like me to come back and read to you, Janet?"

"No, thank you."

"Then I'll be up later with your supper."

I thanked God they closed the door softly as they left. At this point I knew a loud noise would split my head open.

As I drifted in and out of a gauzy sleep, my brain settled on the questions "who" and "why" would someone want to knock me out. Had finding the rabbit's pelt something to do with it? Lord Rathbone had warned me to stay off the moor. Would he have attacked me just to prove a point? No. I couldn't and wouldn't accept that. He was not the sort of man to go about bashing women on the head. More likely he would have chastised me verbally, but never physically. I could think of no one at Cheviot Chase who would have a reason to harm me. With the exception of Jason, they simply ignored me.

It was dusk when Sarah brought a tray with a bowl of beef broth and a pot of the herbal tea. Putting my supper tray down on a chair, she lighted the oil lamp on the table next to my bed. She helped me to sit up then fluffed the pillows behind my back.

While I was lying down, I believed myself to be

101

famished. Upon sitting upright, my head throbbed painfully and appetite vanished. Sarah retrieved the tray, flicked the legs down, then placed it across my lap.

"Do you want me to spoon the broth to you, Janet?" asked Sarah.

"It's my head that hurts. My hands and arms still function. But thank you anyway, Sarah. At least I'm saved from the boredom of the after-dinner ritual in the drawing room. I confess I much prefer to dine with you in your sitting parlor."

"What do they talk about after dinner?"

"Themselves mostly. Except his lordship. He barely talks at all." The broth tasted good.

"Well, the whole staff is talking about what happened to you on the moor. Not Mr. Jackson though. He's too high and mighty to indulge in our idle conversations." Her tone was filled with rancor whenever she mentioned Mr. Jackson's name.

"Does anyone on the staff have a theory about what happened?"

"Some say it is the demons on the moor. Some think you stumbled and hit your head on a rock, then made up the story of an assailant to hide your clumsiness," replied Sarah.

I tried to smile but it hurt. "You believe me, don't you, Sarah?"

"Of course, my dear. You are certainly not the clumsy type. Besides I don't think you're given to making up stories. If you had fallen down, you would have said so."

"Any other theories?"

"Gypsies, poachers, mendicants—any of those roaming about the moor set upon you thinking you might have had some money on you."

"Do those people really wander about on the moor?"

"I've seen gypsies with their gaily painted wagons with my own eyes. Not too often though. Out of fear, poachers have a great respect for his lordship. They seldom set foot on his lands. As for beggars, I do believe they are afraid of the moor. They frequent the villages rather than the countryside and stay on the main road from village to village."

"Do you think it might have been a gypsy out to rob me, Sarah?"

She paused and looked thoughtful. "I really don't think so. Gypsies are not the ones for bashing people about. They'd rather flimflam you out of your money. Is your head any better?"

"This tea seems to help. The piercing pain seems to be reducing itself to a throbbing ache. I suspect I shall be fine by tomorrow."

"Well, I'm going to see that you remain in bed tomorrow as the doctor ordered."

Sarah took the tray away and was back shortly with the peach gown, which she worked on as she sat by my bed and chatted. She had a way of making roses out of the peach-colored satin strips that fascinated me. The evening passed swiftly and pleasantly.

When Sarah had gone, I left the oil lamp burning as I snuggled down into bed. I was sure I'd sleep soundly. I was wrong. The sleep that did come was more of a fitful doze.

During one of my semiconscious states, I had the eerie feeling I was not alone in the room. I began to wonder if the blow on the head had enhanced or stimulated my powers of imagination. I was afraid to open my eyes and see what might be in my room. But I was even more frightened at the prospect of seeing nothing. It might mean the blow *had* affected my mind. I opened my eyes and rolled onto my back. What I saw startled more than frightened me.

Towering at the foot of my bed was the imposing form of Lord John Rathbone, his hands braced on the tall bedposts. His white, ruffled shirt was open to the waist, exposing the thick mat of black hair spreading across his broad chest, hair as black as his trousers. His presence and potent masculinity left me speechless. Without a thought about my aching head, I sat up, ignoring the jolt of pain and clutching the bedcover to my chin.

"I didn't mean to wake you, Miss Clarke. My apologies," he said without ever changing his stance.

"What are you doing here?"

"Although the doctor assured me you were all right, I had to see for myself," he explained.

"Why at this time of night?" The man puzzled me. It was close to midnight. Why now? Why not shortly after dinner?

"I had to attend to some unexpected business. This was my first opportunity. You really should keep your door locked, Miss Clarke."

"I usually do. It slipped my mind tonight." This was strange. Holding a normal conversation with a man in the middle of the night, alone with him in my bedchamber. But there was something strange about Cheviot Chase and its main occupants. "I understand you were the one who found me on the moor and brought me here. I wish to thank you."

"No need. I certainly couldn't leave you lying on the moor. I warned you about going there alone. I hope you'll take that warning more seriously now."

The cleft in his chin seemed more prominent in the amber light of the oil lamp. His handsome, roguish face had a Mephistophelian appearance; yet his Satanic mien held no terror for me. Those green eyes harbored a sadness that made my heart and soul want to reach out to him. When I didn't respond, he continued.

"I feel responsible for you, Miss Clarke. If you persist in walking the moor, I suggest, in the future, you do not do so alone."

"There seems to be a rumor among the staff that I

104

made up the story of an attacker. They feel I stumbled and hit my head on a rock. As you were the one who found me, could you tell me if my head was lying on a rock, or if there was a rock nearby?"

"I didn't particularly notice at the time. But I know the area quite well. There are very few, if any, rocks there. It is peaty land of coarse soil and poor drainage. If it is any consolation, I believe your story. Stumbling and falling in that area wouldn't even produce a bruise. The doctor said you had quite a lump on your head. Someone did indeed hit you on the head. Don't put stock in gossip among the servants. If it will ease your mind, I will accompany you to the spot when you are up to it."

"I wouldn't dream of imposing on you, sir. You've done enough for me already. I'm here to work, not to become a nuisance to you."

"I'd hardly call you a nuisance, Miss Clarke. Mishaps will occur. And there is no hard-and-fast date by which you must complete your restoration work. I am not a slave driver."

"I appreciate your indulgence, Lord Rathbone. By the way, did you happen to see the pelt of a rabbit near the spot where you found me?"

"As I said before, I didn't pay much attention to the area. I was most anxious to get you back to the house as soon as I could and send someone for the doctor. What about a rabbit's pelt?"

"Nothing really. It's of no importance." I yawned. The act caused a tremor of pain to shoot through my head.

"I've disturbed you far too long," claimed Lord Rathbone. "I will take my leave now that I know your mental faculties haven't been impaired. If there is anything you want or need, don't hesitate to tell Mrs. Herries. Good night, Miss Clarke."

"Good night, Lord Rathbone." My voice was a whisper.

However improper the encounter with Lord Rathbone

in my bedchamber, I didn't want him to leave. Not only did I enjoy his company, I craved it. I lay back down on the bed and tried to erase him from my mind. Social class is a strong barrier. I couldn't let myself entertain the notion that there could be anything more than an employee-employer relationship between Lord Rathbone and me. But I could dream about him sweeping me off my feet like a prince in a fairy tale.

The dawn came with the promise of stark and uncompromising weather. The residue of a dull ache still played about in my head but I could function. I felt the back of my head and discovered a fair-sized lump. With a shrug, I swung my legs over the side of the bed and stood. Assured I was physically sound, I sat back down on the bed. I was in that position when Sarah entered with my breakfast tray. She also brought several magazines and the latest copy of the *Times*.

Famished, I ate all the food then put the tray outside my door, knowing a maid would retrieve it. I idled away the rest of the morning by perusing the magazines Sarah had brought me.

After lunch I could no longer abide lying in bed like a lump. I got up, put a robe on over my nightdress, and went to stand by the window. Every so often the soft drizzle would give way to a heavy sheeting of rain. In London I took wet days for granted. At Cheviot Chase the rain seemed to cast a dreary pall over the entire world. It made me restless.

Realizing how stupid it was to stand and stare out the window at a gloomy day, I got dressed, put on my smock, and went into my workroom.

I went to the table where the painting I was working on rested. The light was too poor to resume cleaning it. I decided to save some time by removing all the canvases from their frames. Perhaps I would have time to clean some of the frames, a task which didn't require a strong, brilliant light.

After removing the frames from those paintings needing only to be cleaned, I went to the next group, those that would need more than just a cleaning. One by one I stacked the frames against the opposite wall, which was devoid of furniture.

After completing the task, I was about to move on to the final group, consisting of severely damaged paintings, when I sensed something was radically wrong. I went back to the pile I had just finished and counted the canvases. One was missing!

I dashed to the desk, opened the middle drawer, and took out the notebook in which I had a complete inventory of the paintings. Checking my list, I found the painting to be an ordinary still life. I remembered it was nothing exceptional and, in my opinion, sloppily executed. I didn't deem it a valuable painting. Still, I was responsible for it.

I carefully checked the rest of the paintings against the inventory list. To my relief, they were all accounted for. I went back to the stacked paintings and viewed each one separately, thinking I might have slipped the still life into the wrong pile. I hadn't.

I was confronted with the decision whether or not to tell Lord Rathbone. There was really no decision. I knew I had to tell him even if the painting was of little value. I went downstairs.

Reaching the foyer, I looked around. I had no idea where his lordship might be. I couldn't very well go barging into every room looking for him. It was unusually quiet downstairs as though the entire floor had been deserted. I caught my lower lip between my teeth and stood there pensively. I finally came to the conclusion to leave him a message to see me. I started back up the stairs to search for Sarah.

As my foot rested on the second riser, the massive front door opened. I half turned to see Lord Rathbone striding in. With a spin of his wrist, he flicked the damp cape off his body then removed his top hat, tossing both of them onto a marble-topped table. He looked up and saw me. One dark eyebrow rose curiously.

"Miss Clarke, what are you doing up and about?" His voice took on a sonorous quality in the empty marble foyer.

"I must talk to you, Lord Rathbone." I went back down the few steps and walked toward him.

"Should you be out of bed?"

"I see no reason why not, sir."

His eyes traveled from my head to my toes then back up again. "Are you really well enough to work?"

Suddenly I realized I had forgotten to remove my paint-daubed smock. I flushed. "I'm sorry, Lord Rathbone. I should have changed before coming downstairs."

"No matter. Come into the drawing room. I am in need of a warming brandy." With long strides, he stalked into the drawing room, went to the sideboard, and poured himself a snifter of brandy. "Care for some sherry, Miss Clarke?"

"No, thank you."

"How is that head of yours?"

"Functioning normally, I'm happy to say. A slight ache now and then," I replied.

He lowered himself into a large chair before the fire. "Do stop standing there like an avenging angel, Miss Clarke. Sit down and tell me what is so urgent that it caused you to leave your sick bed."

"I am not sick," I said, taking the chair opposite him. I sat on the edge of it, my hands primly folded in my lap. "What I have to tell you is somewhat disturbing, Lord Rathbone."

"Then out with it." He swirled the brandy in the clear crystal glass then took a swallow.

"One of the paintings is missing." His green eyes locked with mine, but he said nothing. I plunged on. "It isn't a very valuable painting. In fact, I thnk it is one of the poorest in your collection. I can't imagine why anyone would take it."

He slumped down in the chair, his long, muscular legs stretching out before him. "So?"

"Well, sir, I wanted to apprise you of the loss."

"If, as you say, the painting is of little value, why should you concern yourself about it?"

"The paintings were placed in my care, making me responsible for their custody."

The manner in which he studied me was disconcerting. I felt a heat rising in me and prayed I wouldn't blush. To my relief his eyes lowered to the brandy in his glass.

"Do not let it concern you, Miss Clarke. I shall have Jackson look around discreetly. Do you think your ghost in the East Wing might have taken it?" His smile was devilish.

I stood abruptly. "I do not wish to be mocked, Lord Rathbone." I headed for the door.

"Miss Clarke . . ." he called. I turned to face him. "Will you be at dinner tonight?"

"I'm afraid the excitement and conversation would only serve to augment my headache, sir." I left and spent the rest of the afternoon cleaning frames.

"You seem fully recovered, Janet," said Sarah as we ate supper in her sitting parlor. "Does your head hurt at all?"

"Occasionally, especially when I try to concentrate on anything for too long a period. Otherwise, I do believe it is normal."

"The doctor will be pleased."

"Is he from Dorchester?"

"Oh my, no. He lives in the nearby village and serves the surrounding area. Nice young man. Came here about three years ago and took over old Jeremiah Cash's practice. We had been without a doctor for almost a year."

"Did he attend Lady Rathbone?"

"That he did. In the beginning anyway. After a number f visits, he told his lordship that he was not qualified to attend Lady Rathbone and suggested his lordship take her to a specialist in London."

"And did his lordship take her to London?" I asked.

"Once or twice. The trips seemed to exacerbate her condition. After the fire, he realized he could no longer control her and put her in that private hospital in London. So sad. She was a beautiful woman," remarked Sarah with a rueful shake of her head.

"Was? I thought she was still alive."

"Oh, she is indeed. What I meant was as her mental state deteriorated so did her beauty. She no longer took care of herself. Eating became sporadic, alternating between starving herself then gorging on anything and everything. Poor Lord Rathbone was beside himself. He didn't want to put her in that hospital, but he soon realized he had no choice. He's had a tragic life, he has."

I said nothing but silently vowed not to be so truculent with him. He had enough troubles to bear without my being belligerent every time I spoke to him.

"The peach gown is coming along nicely," said Sarah as we finished our tea. "If you're up to it, I think between the two of us we can finish it this evening. I'm anxious to start on the blue silk organza."

It was fairly late when I started back to my

bedchamber. I made a slight detour to the window that overlooked the courtyard to see if it was still raining. At least that was the excuse I gave myself. I was really driven by an intuitive notion to view the East Wing.

I brushed the curtains aside and peered out. The rain had dwindled to a soft mist, which was beginning to give way to a creeping fog. I looked across the courtyard. My instincts proved to be correct.

In the room I presumed to be the burned bedchamber was a glimmering halo of lamplight. It didn't move but trembled its way across the courtyard to where I was standing.

This was no ghost. Why would a ghost need the light of an oil lamp? But I could not discern any human figure moving about over there. I was sure someone was using the abandoned East Wing as a shelter. Though my inquisitive nature urged me to dash over there, I lacked the courage to explore the wing in the dead of night. I stared for a while then padded to my bedchamber.

I was washed and dressed when Annie, one of the maids, brought my breakfast tray to my room.

"From now on, Annie, I will be taking my breakfast with Mrs. Herries. There'll be no need for you to make up a separate tray."

"Aye, miss." She bobbed a curtsy.

I could see she was exceptionally edgy. Annie always did seem a bit flighty to me. But this was something different. Her eyes darted about nervously. Her mouth was set in a grim line and a frown would wave across her brow every now and then. And there was a tension in her young, supple body that made her movements stiff and awkward.

"Is there something bothering you, Annie?" I asked.

"Why, no, miss." Her eyes widened. She had the

111

appearance of a startled sparrow about to take flight.

"Annie, I know something is bothering you. Why don't you tell me? Perhaps I can help."

She looked around the room as though a particular article would tell her what to do. "Well, miss, you must promise not to tell Cook or Mrs. Herries. They wouldn't be liking it."

"I promise, Annie."

"Please don't think I'm daft, miss," she began then lowered her voice to a conspiratorial tone. "But I saw the ghost of the East Wing last night."

"Did you actually see the ghost?" I asked, my interest sparked.

"Well, no. Only the light he was carrying," she replied.

"Did the light move?"

"Aye. It did. From window to window. Now you won't be telling anyone I told you, will you? Cook frowns on any talk about ghosts at Cheviot Chase."

"I won't tell a soul, Annie. And don't you worry about ghosts. Whatever it is, it never leaves the East Wing," I said, hoping to assuage her fears.

"I never thought of that. Thank you, miss."

My words must have done some good. When she left, she had a smile on her face.

I had finished my tea and was about to put my tray outside when a sharp knock echoed on my door. I set the tray on the bureau then opened the door.

"Dr. Young!" I had forgotten he was to call in on me this morning.

"Well, I see you're in fine fettle this morning," he said, entering my bedchamber. "How is the head? Any pain?"

"No. I believe I have survived the incident intact."

"Please sit down," he said, waving a directional hand toward a chair. I complied and his gentle hands began probing my head.

"Ouch!" I cried.

"Sorry. Still tender there?" His hands dropped to his sides.

"Yes. Very tender."

"The bump has gone down considerably. I suspect the spot will be sore for several days. Any headaches?"

"On occasion."

"Are they severe?"

"No. Only a dull ache once in a while."

"I'm sure they'll disappear in a day or so. You seem to have an excellent constitution."

"What you really mean is I have a hard head." We laughed.

"Well, I can see you have no further need of my services. If at any time you get a severe headache, do not hesitate to send for me or visit me in the village."

He picked up his bag. I stood and retrieved the tray from the bureau. He gave me a smile and a nod as he walked out the door. He went down the corridor while I stooped to place the tray on the floor to the side of the door. Before I rose, I spied shiny black shoes coming toward me. I stood to face Dr. Young once again.

"They are having a spring fair in the village this coming weekend. If I'm not being too bold, I'd like to take you, Miss Clarke," he said, his smile revealing even, white teeth under his trim dark-haired mustache.

"But your family."

"I have no family here, Miss Clarke. I am a bachelor. Please say you'll go. I'm sure you would enjoy it. I'll pick you up Saturday morning around ten if that is all right with you."

"It sounds most pleasant, Dr. Young. I'd be delighted to go with you."

I closed the door behind me and leaned on it with a dreamy expression on my face. Vague romantic thoughts floated in my head like willowy dandelion seed puffs in a breeze. It would be so nice to be in love again. The last time I thought I was in love I was ten and he was my schoolmaster. I'll never forget how much sorrow I felt when my father took me out of school.

I sighed deeply and pushed myself from the door. I would have to work doubly hard if I were to take all day Saturday off. I wondered if Lord Rathbone would object to my going to the village fair, not that I cared. I had worked diligently and had put in more hours than most restorers would have. Besides, didn't he say I needed some divertissement?

I went into the workroom, sat at the table, and without looking, reached for a wad of cotton. When my fingers bounced on an empty spot, I looked up. My solvents, oils, and cotton were not in their usual places. I always kept them in a certain order so I wouldn't have to go searching for them. Their positions were completely out of order. Someone had moved them. But the painting I had been working on hadn't been touched. Puzzled, I sat there for several seconds. Perhaps another painting was missing. I got up to check.

I flipped through the canvases. To my amazement, the missing still life was back!

Seven

I shook my head in despair and bewilderment. Perhaps
Mr. Jackson had found it and stacked it against the wall
without mentioning it to anyone. I picked it up and
examined it closely. There seemed to be no damage or
change in the painting. With a shrug, I put it back down,
went to my table, and after putting my materials back in
familiar order, went to work again.

I had no idea what the other occupants of the house did
to occupy their time. I assumed Cecil Whitney worked on
his history tome. I knew the Lewises occasionally went to
Foxhill to inspect the renovations there with Clara
Whitney tagging along once in a while. I had no
conception of what Jason did with his time. And with the
exception of Lord Rathbone, they all slept late. In the
early morning hours I usually saw his lordship walking
toward the moor with his dogs.

For a reason that was a total mystery to me, I would
anxiously wait at the window for his appearance. On
those days he did not follow this routine, I would feel
utterly deprived.

After lunch I decided to take advantage of the lovely
spring day and resume my habit of taking an early
afternoon walk.

I strolled down to the end of the garden to the lane that offered two paths. Common sense told me not to go to the moor, but inquisitiveness smothered common sense and I took the path to the moor. I had to see the spot where I was struck down.

My gait was brisk and invigorating. I was quite optimistic about finding the exact spot. And find it I did, though it took me some time. Lord Rathbone was right. There were no rocks in the area. Smooth and reedy grasses covered the soft and warm spring soil.

The rabbit pelt was gone but I spied the twig I had used buried in the fast-growing grasses. I picked the twig up and went to a group of broad-leafed bushes. Squatting down on my haunches, I thrust the twig under the bushes to see if some animal had dragged the pelt under there.

The heavy tread of footsteps startled me. I froze, wondering if my assailant had returned to the scene of the crime. But the footsteps were in front of me, not behind me. And whoever it was was making no secret of his approach. Keeping my squatting position, I peeked around the shrubbery to see black, mud-encrusted boots striding past me. My eyes traveled upward to behold the lord of the moor himself. He was wearing black breeches and a heavy black sweater whose collar rose high on his neck. He was holding his arm, his face hidden from me. Not knowing what I should do, I did feel obliged to offer assistance. I stood and called, "Lord Rathbone."

He spun around, a look of alarm on his face. "Miss Clarke! What the devil are you doing here?"

I was stunned by his appearance. He looked as though he had just fought his way out of a thorny blackberry bush. There were tears in his sweater and his breeches were mud-splattered. Numerous scratches covered his bare hands and a few trickled across his face.

"Well? Answer me. Don't stand there like a moon-struck cow." His voice was loud and demanding. A venomous gleam flashed in his green eyes. He released what appeared to be an injured arm.

"Can I do anything to help you, sir?" I finally found my voice.

"Yes. Tell me what you are doing out on the moor alone?"

"I came to examine for myself the spot where I was struck down. I thought there might be some clue as to who did it."

"Clue? The moor leaves no clues. I thought I told you never to come here alone."

"I was cautious, sir."

His gaze shifted to my hand. I was still holding the twig. "I suppose you thought you could hold off an army with that." He nodded toward the twig.

I looked at the twig, then dropped it. "What happened, Lord Rathbone? Are you hurt?"

"One of the dogs ran away from me. I chased him and fell. Nothing to concern yourself about, Miss Clarke."

I accepted his explanation, but I didn't believe it. I've seen the man with those dogs. He had complete control over them. Why was he lying to me?

"I think you'd best walk back to the house with me. There are things on this moor that no human being should have to deal with," he declared bitterly.

"Ghosts?" I asked. He eased his gait and I fell in step with him.

"I wouldn't take you for a believer in ghosts, Miss Clarke. I consider you far too practical."

"I don't believe in them. One of the maids is quite fearful of the ghost that stalks the East Wing."

"Rubbish! Ignorant wenches who have nothing better to do than conjure up titillating gossip."

"She claims she saw a light moving from room to room," I said.

"Nonsense."

"I'm afraid not, Lord Rathbone. I saw it too. And I'm not given to idle fancies."

He shrugged. The act caused him to wince in pain. "Jackson might have been the source of that light. He periodically inspects the East Wing."

Silence reigned as we walked. I knew he was using Mr. Jackson as an excuse to avoid the topic. I was the one to break the lull. "By the way, the missing painting has been returned."

Never breaking his stride, he glanced down at me, one eyebrow arching. "Canvases that stroll about whenever the mood takes them? Really, Miss Clarke, I'm sure you can do better than that."

I skittered in front of him, put my hands on my hips, and tried to look belligerent. "Are you questioning my veracity, Lord Rathbone?"

A wide smile caused deep furrows to crease around his lips, but a sad weariness lingered in his eyes, those green hypnotic eyes. "You are a very provocative woman, Miss Clarke. I only hope your work is as reliable as your passionate nature."

"I wasn't aware I was displaying a temper, sir," I said rather softly, knowing I had been too brusque in my manner. "I consider my work equal to any expert in the field."

"I'm sure it is, Miss Clarke."

"Where are your dogs?" I asked pleasantly, hoping to atone for my previous outburst.

"Probably back at the stables. Seeing you've recovered enough to go gadding about on the moor, I think it would be appropriate if you resumed taking your evening meals in the main dining room, Miss Clarke."

"If I must."

"You don't sound very pleased."

"I'm not and you know it. We've been through this before, Lord Rathbone."

"So we have. So we have. Ah! We're at the back gardens. I shall leave you here, Miss Clarke. Do try to pay more heed to my warning about the moor. Good day to you, Miss Clarke."

He turned and walked away without a backward glance.

As I turned to descend the main staircase, wearing my new peach gown, I saw the tail end of the company trooping into the dining room and Lord Rathbone racing up the stairs toward me, a scowl on his face.

He stopped short when I came into view. The scowl melted into an expression of astonishment mingled with unabashed admiration. I was flattered and smiled warmly at him.

"You are late, Miss Clarke," he said softly, his voice almost caressing.

"My apologies. I worked later than I had intended." I continued down the stairs until I was abreast of him. He offered me a crooked arm, which I took with a trembling hand.

All eyes turned to view us as we entered the dining room. Jason rose with an odd twinkle in his eyes. Cecil Whitney's glance was marked by indifference while Clara Whitney seemed far more interested in my peach gown than anything else. Daphne's eyes glimmered with intense jealousy, her small mouth resembling that of a fish as she pouted. But it was her father's expression that puzzled me. His heavy-lidded eyes exuded disdain. I suppose the sight of a plain working girl on the arm of a peer of the realm went against his rigid rules of polite society. Lord Rathbone held my chair as I took my place at the table. Once we were seated, the meal commenced.

"How is the book coming, Cecil?" asked Sir Percy Lewis as the soup dishes were being cleared away.

"Slow. It requires a good deal of research, you know."

"When do you expect to finish it?" asked Sir Percy.

"A few more years."

"Hmph! A few years indeed!" exclaimed Clara Whitney. "He'll be working on it until he gasps his last breath. It's nothing more than an excuse for sheer laziness. Has anyone ever seen any pages of this fabulous, but elusive, manuscript?" The response was silence. "I thought so. After ten years of enduring his talk about the history of the Romans in Britain, I should think we'd be entitled to see a page or two. Should we not, Cecil?"

"In time, my dear, in time."

"I say it doesn't exist," declared Clara.

"How are the renovations coming at Foxhill Manor, Sir Percy?" asked Lord Rathbone as Mr. Jackson offered the tray of roast beef to everyone.

"Coming along nicely, John. But the cost seems to be rising at a disproportionate rate. Unforeseen repairs and snags. Devilish business!" said Sir Percy.

"Would you like me to go over the various work contracts for you?" asked Lord Rathbone.

"No. That won't be necessary. I keep a close eye on everything," said Sir Percy, a little too quickly, I thought.

As I forked some of the roast beef onto my plate, my glance happened to fall on Daphne. She was gazing at Lord Rathbone with adoring stupidity. There was a dullness in her eyes that baffled me at times. I suddenly realized what that dullness was—total unintelligence. Her thoughts were incapable of going beyond her own well-being and comfort.

"Have you decided on a date for the ball, John?" asked Daphne.

"Not yet. Perhaps in a month or so."

"A month?" exclaimed Clara. "Daphne and I were hoping it would take place sooner than that."

"I have a good deal of business to attend to before I can think about setting a date. If you and Daphne find life dreary here, I suggest you spend several weeks at the townhouse in London," said Lord Rathbone.

Daphne stared at him wide-eyed. Her eyes flickered over me before returning to Lord Rathbone. "I just adore Cheviot Chase. I hope you are not going to banish us to London, John." Her eyelashes fluttered like the wings of a hummingbird.

"It was only a suggestion, Daphne. I realize how dull life here must be for you," said Lord Rathbone.

"That's a smashing gown you have on, Janet," commented Jason, causing Sir Percy, Daphne, and Clara to look at him as though he were a bug that needed squashing.

"It's most becoming, Miss Clarke," added Lord Rathbone.

"Thank you," I said. "Mrs. Herries is a positive wizard with a needle and thread."

"I didn't know I had such a talented seamstress under my roof," said Lord Rathbone.

"That reminds me, John. Perhaps Daphne and I will go to London for a spell. We'll have to have new gowns made for the ball," said Clara, capturing Daphne's complete attention.

"That's right," agreed Daphne with enthusiasm. "I'd forgotten all about a new gown. Not only will I need a new gown, but dancing slippers, gloves, a cape—oh, there are so many things I'll need for the ball."

Lord Rathbone had a triumphant smile while Sir Percy frowned. Cecil Whitney seemed relieved that he was no longer the center of conversation.

I dreaded the after-dinner tête-à-tête held in the drawing room. Instead of the expected boredom, however, the evening passed pleasantly as Jason questioned me with sincere interest regarding the restoration of paintings. We concluded the evening with a game of draughts, a game I had learned from my father.

The day of the fair arrived. Lord Rathbone rode out on his stallion early that morning. I had no idea what the others in the house had planned for the day and I didn't care. I was looking forward to a day of relaxation with Dr. Brian Young.

Dressed in my best day frock and bonnet, I waited on the portico of the house. The morning promised a clear and bright spring day. I didn't have to wait long. Dr. Young was a prompt man. He assisted me into the trap and we were on our way.

"A splendid day for a fair," said Dr. Young. "I hear there will be a traveling circus to add to the festivities."

"I haven't been to a circus since I was a little girl," I said, excited by the prospect of something different.

"I must say you look charming this morning, Miss Clarke."

"Thank you."

"Any remnants of pain from that blow on the head?"

"Not a twinge. I seem to have recovered fully."

"Good." He turned and gave me a brief smile before the road commanded his attention again. Traffic began to increase as we came closer to the village. "How do you like life at Cheviot Chase? It certainly is a formidable mansion."

"I spend most of my time working on the paintings. After my initial awe upon seeing the house, I hardly notice my surroundings now. But I never cease to marvel at the wonders of the moor and the chalk cliffs. Spending my entire life in the city, I find the sea most fascinating. So vast. An endless watery horizon. And the moor. I never knew there were so many different kinds of wild flowers and species of birds. London gives no hint of the savage beauty of nature in the raw."

The road soon became clogged with wagons, carts, traps, and other vehicles. Cries of impatient children filled the air as parents tried to quiet them. Men were shouting at their horses or other vehicles in coarse language as they inched toward the open, grassy field where the tops of colorful tents could be seen. Dr. Young proved himself to be a most patient man.

He finally maneuvered the trap into the field, looped the reins over a rope that had been tied between two trees, then came to help me down. I took his proffered arm and we strolled along, edging closer to the numerous tents.

We passed makeshift corrals where spring lambs nestled against their mothers. Fancy hens and cocks were displayed in cages. Piglets and calves had their own separate stalls. Yearling horses were being groomed for an auction to be held in the afternoon. Dr. Young indulged my passion for stopping at each show of animals. Though I had frequently visited the London Zoo, these animals seemed realer than the zoo's exotic exhibits.

A row of vibrant, multicolored, striped tents stood parallel to a row of covered stalls. There was a large space between them to accommodate the ever-growing crowd. At the very end of the row, a gypsy wagon stood off to the left side with a sign proclaiming "Fortunes Read." On the right side was the largest of the tents, where the main show was to be held.

The covered stalls offered games of skill like loop ball and throw ring. Prizes were to be given to those of exceptional skill. But one had to pay a small fee to exhibit that skill. The smaller tents across from the stalls boasted such oddities as a bearded lady, a tattooed man, a fire eater, the strongest man in the world, midgets, a fat lady, and many more. Again a fee had to be paid if one wanted to view these bizarre characters.

Children ran freely and boisterously as parents gave up trying to exercise control over them. Young women gasped and giggled and gaped at the painted displays of the unusual creatures in the freak tents. Young dandies eyed the young women with leering looks. Older men stood in clusters or headed for the large refreshment tent where ale and spirits flowed.

I spotted a couple of the maids from Cheviot Chase milling about with flirtatious gleams in their eyes. Everyone was dressed in their Sunday best, even the children, though that fact was slowly becoming unrecognizable.

"Would you like me to win a prize for you, Miss Clarke? I used to be quite handy with a ball," said Dr. Young.

"If you've a mind to."

With boyish enthusiasm, Dr. Young vigorously hurled the balls toward the stack of wooden milk bottles. Managing to knock down only one after several tries, Brian Young gave up, saying, "Sorry, Miss Clarke. I was sure I could win a prize for you. I've won before, but I guess one never does his best when he is trying to show off his skills."

"It was nice of you to try. I do believe these games are controlled somehow. After all, they are in the business of making money, not giving prizes away all the time. Shall we have a look at some of the sideshows?"

"Why not. It will help to distract me. I'm not happy about losing at simple games," he replied with humor.

Children skittered about us as we went from tent to tent. As we left the tent of the fire eater, a stout, old, garishly dressed woman began to cry, "Pancakes a penny apiece!"

We laughed and the laughter banished any formality between us. We became Janet and Brian when we addressed each other.

"Would you care to have your fortune told, Janet?" asked Brian as we stood before the gaily painted gypsy wagon.

"I don't think so. The line waiting to get in is much too long. Besides, not knowing the future is what makes life interesting."

He pulled his pocket watch from his vest, snapped it open, then casually glanced at it. "It's almost noontime. Why don't we stroll back toward the refreshment tent? You must be hungry by now."

"I am. And my throat is parched."

"I could do with a tankard of ale myself." He pulled my hand through his arm. "By the time we finish lunch, that big tent should be starting its acts."

As we neared the refreshment tent, a group of men, including a few older women, had formed a circle around something. Their shouts were vociferous and spirited. I paid little attention until the shouting died down and a male voice called out, "Only a quid, lads. Only a quid to fight his lordship himself. Now who's next, lads?"

I turned to Brian. "His Lordship? What are they about over there?" I gave a directional nod of my head.

"At every spring and fall fair, Lord Rathbone offers to fight any man for a quid," he explained.

"I wasn't aware that his lordship so needed money he'd reduce himself to public brawling."

Brian laughed. "The money is not for himself. It goes to the village church to help the needy. It has become somewhat of a tradition. You'd be surprised how many rash young men would gladly pay the pound to have a go at his lordship. The older men are more chary of their pounds."

"I thought Lord Rathbone was a good and just landlord."

"Oh, he is. They are mostly young lads who think they

125

are stronger and cleverer. Though they may be in their twenties with the stamina of youth on their side, they lack maturity and common sense. His lordship usually takes them out in a few minutes."

"Could we watch for a spell?" I asked.

"It's really not the place for young ladies," warned Brian. "It is a rough sport sometimes involving blood, a sight which gives many a woman the vapors. Also the language tends to be coarse."

"If I promise not to have an attack of the vapors and close my ears to any unsavory language, could we have a peek? After all, he is my employer. You can imagine how my curiosity would nag at me if I didn't see him fight."

He looked into my eyes long and hard. "Promise no vapors?"

"I promise." My smile was grateful and tinged with triumph.

Brian pushed his way through the circle then brought me to the forefront. Inside the circle was a large grassy area where the two combatants stood, fists raised, feet in a positioned stance. The sight of Lord Rathbone caused me to take a sharp breath. He was naked to the waist and his black breeches clung to his muscled legs. His physique was far more formidable than I had imagined.

As tentative punches were exchanged, I was mesmerized by the fluidity of Lord Rathbone's heavy sinews as they slid under the skin of his back and arms. Sweat matted down the thick hair that spread over his broad chest, the dark hair tapering down over his stomach and disappearing below his belt.

The young opponent valiantly tried to land a punch on Lord Rathbone's head, but his lordship's feet moved too quickly and his long-armed jabs kept the youth at bay. The lad's inexperience was soon made evident when Lord Rathbone landed a solid punch to the youth's jaw and knocked him down.

I melted back into the crowd. Brian, seeing my intent to leave, cupped my elbow and steered me away from the circle as the men clamored for another fight.

In the refreshment tent, a long, cloth-covered table was set to serve food and drink buffet style. Perpendicular to the buffet table, bare wooden tables and benches waited for customers.

We were early and the meat pies were still warm. I settled for a meat pie and lemonade while Brian had a large bowl of lamb stew and a tankard of ale. The table began to fill up and the noise level in the tent began to increase. Children would come in, buy a plum cake, then dash right back out to be with their chums.

Between discussing the rigors of a medical education and the scandalous wave that was gripping the French art community, especially Manet's shocking *Olympia*, we spent over an hour in the refreshment tent.

"Would you like to paint your own pictures, Janet?" asked Brian as we walked toward the main tent.

"Oh, definitely."

"Then why don't you?"

"I'm afraid my talent is mediocre. I'd never be able to make a living at it. And art materials are expensive, especially those of high quality. I've learned that painters must use the best materials if their work is to be of any consequence. I'm hoping Lord Rathbone will be so pleased with my work, he will recommend my services to others in his social circle. Have you ever wished to have a practice catering to the wealthy in London?"

"I've thought about it. It certainly would enable me to live a life of ease. But I'm sure it has its drawbacks as well. Pandering to the rich might embroil me in imaginary ailments which would limit broadening my skills. I am content where I am. Grant you, I do not live luxuriously, but I am comfortable."

We entered the already crowded main tent and

managed to find two seats with a fairly good view. Feats of daring on horseback, clowns, acrobats, and a magic show kept all amused or holding their breath at a particular daring deed. Gasps rippled through the audience when the acrobats and magician performed. When the show was over, we left the tent with visions of the show still lingering in our minds.

A woman screamed. Soon everyone was shouting for a doctor to come to the refreshment tent.

"You'll have to excuse me, Janet. I must go and see what is wrong and if I can be of help," said Brian before he sprinted off toward the refreshment tent.

With adults beginning to stream toward the refreshment tent, I decided it would be best to get out of their way before I was trampled. I ducked between the gypsy wagon and the small tent housing the tattooed man. I turned the corner too sharply and my foot caught on one of the ropes that secured the small tent to the ground. To my chagrin, I went sprawling. I lay in the grass for a few seconds berating myself for not being more careful.

Someone stooped down, and before I could look up, hands were under my arms lifting me to my feet. Once more I came face to face with Lord Rathbone. He had donned a white shirt with billowy sleeves and opened at the neck.

When he drew me up this time, it was along the length of his sinewy body. Even through my petticoats I could feel the pressure of his legs against mine. The heat of him was flowing into me with such rapidity, I hardly noticed the strong aroma of rum that clung to him.

"It seems I am forever picking you up from the ground, Miss Clarke." His speech was slightly slurred, his eyes were a little glazed, and there was an idiotic smile on his face.

"I tripped," I murmured, unable to take my eyes from his face, my head tilting far back. I wondered if he could feel my heart beating as my bosom rested against his chest.

Suddenly the smile slipped from his face, his lips becoming a grim, wide line. There was a wildness in his green eyes that startled me. His head lowered so swiftly and accurately, I had no time to think. When his lips covered mine and forced my mouth open, I didn't want to think. At first his kiss was hard and tenacious. I knew I should have pulled away, but my will had fled. Realizing I was not about to repulse him, his kiss softened and became one of tender passion. His arms went about me to press me closer to him. With my eyes closed, a kaleidoscope of colors danced on my eyelids to be interrupted occasionally by bursting stars. My arms rested limp at my sides. I had never been kissed by a man in that manner and didn't dare move lest I lose the memory of it.

When he finally pulled away, he thrust his hands into the small pockets of his breeches, his thumbs hooked over the top of them. He glared down at me and color rushed to my cheeks.

"Don't expect an apology, Miss Clarke."

For once I was mute as he turned and stalked away. I stood there shaking my head like a puppet. Not only had I been awkward in front of Lord Rathbone, but I had acted like a wanton by letting him kiss me without a struggle or protest. I was thoroughly ashamed of my behavior. Still I would never forget those moments in his arms. In fact, I had a suspicion I would come to treasure them.

With an audible sigh, I proceeded toward the refreshment tent, where the crowd was dissipating. I finally caught a glimpse of Brian Young and headed in his direction.

"What was wrong, Brian?" I asked, reaching his side.

"The young fellow over there had swallowed a farthing. Unfortunately it had lodged in his throat. He's fine now." Brian rolled down his shirtsleeves then put his jacket back on. "Would you like another glass of lemonade, Janet?"

"No, thank you. I think I'd best be getting back to Cheviot Chase." I couldn't tell him that my insides were sloshing about like half-melted suet pudding. If I ever came close to having the vapors, it was now, especially thinking about having to face his lordship at the dinner table.

"It has been a long day, hasn't it?"

The question was rhetorical to me. I made no effort to reply. We walked back to the trap, Brian giving a detailed account of the child's almost fatal mishap. He also did most of the talking on the ride back to Cheviot Chase. My thoughts drifted elsewhere.

My gaze wandered to the approaching moor. Far in the distance I spied a figure standing in the middle of nowhere, his legs apart, his arms curving to his back, and his black hair storming about his head. Though the figure was hazy, there was no mistaking Lord John Rathbone, his loose white shirt billowing in the breeze and two large mastiffs squatting at his heels.

I would have given anything to know what he was thinking.

Eight

My fingers trembled as I fumbled with the hooks of my gown. Sarah had been called down to the kitchen to settle a squabble. I could have used her help, but on the other hand, I was glad she wasn't around to witness my undue nervousness. I silently prayed Lord Rathbone had imbibed too much rum at the fair and had no memory of the scene behind the tattooed man's tent. I had thought to excuse myself with the alibi of a severe headache. Brian had told everyone I might be subject to them. It would be a logical and believable excuse. But I was not a coward. I would have to face his lordship sometime. It may as well be now.

My trepidation was for naught. Lord Rathbone barely noticed my existence, neither at the dinner table nor later in the drawing room. I idled the evening away with Jason playing draughts.

At breakfast the next morning, I regaled Sarah with detailed descriptions of the sights at the fair and traveling circus. She was enthralled to the point of emitting a gasp or two at some of my narrations. I saw no need to mention the encounter with his lordship.

"Dr. Young is a nice man and well liked in the village and countryside. I'm pleased he is showing an interest in you, Janet. He'll make a fine husband," said Sarah.

"Why, Sarah, I only went to the fair with the man. I hardly know him." In a way her comment amused me. Brian was a nice man and would make a very suitable husband for some woman. But not me. Though I enjoyed his company, there was something lacking, that spark, that excitement, that would make me swell with joy on seeing him.

"It might be to your advantage to get to know him better. He'd be a good provider and make an excellent father," Sarah added.

I couldn't keep my laughter from rising to the surface.

"Don't laugh, Janet. I'm serious. Time has a way of racing along and you're old before you can turn around. A young girl such as yourself, with no family, has got to think of her future."

"I'll think about it, Sarah. Right now I'm going to get to work."

"But it's Sunday. I'm sure his lordship wouldn't approve of you working on othe Sabbath," protested Sarah.

"I didn't do a stitch of work yesterday. I intend to make up for it today. At least I shall work for the better part of the morning."

Sarah shook her head. "Well, think about what I said, Janet. It's for your own good."

"I know, Sarah."

There was a smile on my face when I entered my workroom. I think I knew deep down Sarah was right. I really should cultivate a relationship between Brian and myself. We were of the same social background and he *would* make a fine father and husband. But I suppose I had a quixotic nature, a youthful desire to tilt at windmills and let the future take care of itself. Besides, I

132

wasn't in love with Dr. Brian Young. My fingers grazed over my lips to bring back the thrilling sensation of Lord Rathbone's kiss.

I was becoming a bit bored with the routine cleaning of the paintings and decided to vary the tasks by alternating a difficult one with an easy one.

Flipping through the stacks of the more difficult ones, I noticed something was terribly wrong. I couldn't put my finger on it right away and went through all of them again.

With hands on hips, I stood staring at the stacks somewhat bemused. At least none was missing. Then, like most puzzles, I recognized the obvious.

I picked up the canvas and there it was as blatant as the earth itself. Down in the left-hand corner, a small circle had been smeared clean down to the bare canvas. I went through all of them. The majority of them had that same bare spot in the left-hand corner. The rest of the smeared spots hadn't managed to reach the white of the canvas.

I had no clue as to why someone would do such a thing. It seemed like a prank a child would play. But there were no children at Cheviot Chase. I picked another one up and placed it on my worktable. I began the slow, painstaking process of removing the surface grime before I took on the task of removing the heavy, cracked, and discolored damar varnish. The morning dissolved like snow under a summer sun.

After lunch my eyes were still stinging and watery from the fumes of the solvents I had used on the painting. I had planned to continue my work directly after lunch. Curiosity tugged at me regarding those bare spots. But my eyes warned me to take my usual walk in the fresh air.

When I reached the paths forking off from the back lane, there was no hesitation in my step. I headed for the chalk downs and the sea. I had no desire to meet his lordship alone on the moor. Not that I feared him. No. It was a weakness in me that I feared.

Sea breezes caught and swirled my long full skirt as I approached the high cliffs of the chalk downs. I loosened the top knot on my head and let my long hair flow behind me as currents of winds from the sea increased. The sensations of the crisp salty air were cleansing and delicious.

I looked down to watch the sea slowly eroding the vulnerable chalk cliffs. The height was dizzying. I was thankful I was not subject to vertigo.

A tiny alcove had been formed by the relentless sea and it piqued my curiosity. I was soon hunting for an access down to that cove. I didn't expect to find one, but to my surprise and delight, there was a narrow, winding path that sloped down to the cove.

The descent was slow and I had to watch my footing each step of the way. Manmade steps had been hacked in to the chalky cliffs centuries ago. Constant footfalls had worn them smooth and rendered them slippery. To make matters worse, the soles of my shoes had also been worn smooth from use. But I managed to reach the small, sandy cove without mishap.

I looked back up at the cliffs and felt I had accomplished an astounding feat. I turned my gaze to the sea, the gently lapping water on the sand. Though I had seen water before, the constant, rhythmic motion of the sea had a mesmerizing effect on me. My experience with large bodies of water had been limited to the Thames or the ponds and lakes in London's parks.

I used to be fond of walking along the Victoria Embankment, stopping every so often to gaze at the Thames. I don't know why. It was a dirty river with a stench that could bring tears to one's eyes.

On the crest of an incoming wave, I spied an object I thought peculiar. I couldn't quite make it out. I sprinted forward to reach it before it moved back out to sea. As I did, I heard a resounding thud that made the sand shiver under its blow. I spun around to see a boulder had landed in the exact spot where I had been standing. I quickly lifted my gaze to the top of the cliff. Nothing. Not a soul in sight.

I immediately forgot about the object in the sea and backed up to get a fuller view of the top of the cliff. Though I could see no one up there, I had the distinct feeling that the boulder falling was not a quirk of nature. Someone had deliberately sent that rock down in an attempt to kill me. I lost all interest in exploring the cove and headed back up the chalk-carved steps to the top.

The ascent upward was no easy task. More than once I slipped and fell. My petticoats helped to cushion the blows to my knees. By the time I reached the top, my breath was coming in short gasps.

Regaining control of my lungs, I began an examination of the flat, grassy area at the top of the cliff. A large thick branch rested on the ground. But there were no trees around. The branch had to have been brought to the spot. Next to the branch the grass had been pressed down by a weighted object, which I assumed had been the rock. I also assumed the branch had been used as a lever to move the boulder and send it hurtling over the edge of the cliff. I looked down to the cove. The position of the boulder on the sand was exactly where it should be if pushed from this spot. And it hit the ground exactly where I had been standing.

But it wasn't fortune that had placed the rock on the edge of the cliff. There was a path of crushed grass that led back several feet to a bare spot on the cliff. The grassless area was the original resting spot of the boulder on the cliff. Someone had had to push that rock along till it reached the edge.

The full-blown horror of the deed suddenly overwhelmed me. Was someone trying to kill me? Perhaps the thought was too rash and my mythical attacker was only trying to frighten me into leaving Cheviot Chase. After all, the blow to the head on the moor had caused unconsciousness, not death. If someone wanted me dead, they could have continued with the blows to my head until he or she was sure I was dead. The thought made me shiver.

I pondered the events as I walked back to the mansion. I told no one of my adventure at the cove.

It was several days later when Lord Rathbone entered my workroom. He was followed by a footman whose arms were laden with packages.

"Put them down in the corner, Edwards. Miss Clarke can sort them out for herself," said Lord Rathbone.

The footman obeyed then silently left.

"Your packages of materials arrived from London this morning," he said as he came to peer over my shoulder.

"Thank you," I responded.

"How's the work coming?"

"Slow, but steady."

He strolled over to a group of canvases I had cleaned, and flipped through them. "Quite a difference, I must admit. You do have a talent for the work, Miss Clarke."

"I'm glad you approve of my work, Lord Rathbone. I hope you will be as pleased when I finish the more difficult ones." I rose and went to stand beside him. I felt it would be rude to keep on working. I lifted one of the cleaned paintings and held it up for his closer inspection. "The colors have revealed themselves to be quite vivid. For example, originally the blues had a brownish-gray tint to them. As you can see, after cleaning, the blues have become rich cerulean blues. The transparency of the Prussian blues plays nicely with the . . ." My voice trailed off when I realized he wasn't looking at the painting but at me.

His hand rose. A lean finger brushed at my cheek. "You have a paint smudge on your cheek."

"One of many, I'm sure." I don't know how I managed to speak. His touch made a heat rush over the surface of my skin. Our eyes met. There was a tenderness in the depths of his green eyes that seemed to vanish as quickly as it had come. He turned his gaze to the painting.

"Very nice. Very nice indeed," he commented.

I returned the painting to the stack. He moved down to the frames.

"I see you have also done some work on the frames, Miss Clarke."

"Yes. I thought it would be a shame to put newly cleaned paintings back in drab frames, Lord Rathbone."

"Commendable. If you would put the finished paintings back in their frames, I will have them removed from here and put in their proper place. It will give you more room. When you are ready, tell Jackson and he'll take care of it."

"Yes, your lordship."

At that he sharply turned and stared at me with a mixture of sadness and anger. He quickly affected an air of indifference.

"My purpose in coming here was twofold. Aside from delivering your materials, I want you to know I will be announcing the date of the ball at dinner this evening. I want to give you a suitable amount of time to fashion a gown for the event. You and Mrs. Herries have done an admirable job of refashioning those old gowns. They become you handsomely."

"Thank you, Lord Rathbone. Mrs. Herries's skill with a needle is far superior to mine."

"I doubt it."

"I don't want to appear ungrateful, but surely you don't mean for me to attend the ball. I'm certainly not on

137

the same social level as your friends."

"Your social standing is irrelevant, Miss Clarke. I certainly intend for you to be present at the ball even if you have to appear in your smock."

"But—"

"There are no buts, Miss Clarke. You *will* be there."

"I don't think—"

"Why do you persist in trying to thwart me, Miss Clarke?"

"I wasn't aware I was trying to foil your plans. I'm sure you'll do just as you please regardless of my objections."

"Very perceptive of you, Miss Clarke. And do keep that thought uppermost in your mind at all times. I trust you will be at dinner tonight."

"Yes. If it pleases you."

"It pleases me." He spun around and strode toward the door. As his hand rested on the knob, he turned to me and asked, "Is there anything going on between you and Jason that I should know about?"

"Certainly not, Lord Rathbone."

"Your games of draughts with him seem to have become a nightly habit, a rather chummy one at that."

"It was you who insisted I remain in the drawing room after dinner. It must be obvious to you that neither Mrs. Whitney nor Miss Lewis are desirous of my company, not to mention Sir Lewis. I find Mr. Watson an amiable companion with whom to pass the evening. If you have strong objections, I shall be most happy to retire to my rooms directly after dinner."

"That was not my intention, Miss Clarke. I do feel it is my duty to warn you about Jason, however. To be frank, Miss Clarke, Jason is a rake, especially when it comes to young women such as yourself. His intentions are not honorable, I assure you. He prides himself on his easy conquests of naive young women. His true goal in life is to find an aged and wealthy woman to marry. So be forewarned, Miss Clarke."

"The warning wasn't necessary, Lord Rathbone." I hoped he noticed the resentment glittering in my eyes. He raised one eyebrow and smiled in a peculiar manner before he left.

I sorted out the packages of new materials, put them away, then went to have lunch with Sarah.

"Oh, it's terrible! Terrible!" exclaimed Sarah.

"What?" I asked.

"The way the staff feeds on rumors. Ghosts indeed! Even Cook has become skittish of late. And I thought she had more sense."

"The East Wing again?"

"Yes. I'm surprised his lordship doesn't do something about it."

"He probably doesn't notice what is going on amid the staff. He does have business and guests to attend to." Why was I defending the man?

"Guests, indeed. I'm beginning to think they are permanent residents."

"How long have they been here?" I asked.

"Between his lordship's house in London and Cheviot Chase, almost a year," replied Sarah. "To my way of thinking, it doesn't take that long to make some minor renovations."

"Well, workmen can be notoriously slow. Perhaps the renovations were of a more serious nature than was expected at first."

"Not from what I heard. Several of the men working at Foxhill Manor live in the village. They claim the house is structurally sound. The flues needed cleaning and the interior needed painting and a touch-up here and there in the plaster. Now that doesn't sound to me like a year's work."

All I could do was shrug. I was inclined to agree with her. Several months, not a year, would be nearer the estimated time to complete the work. And Sir Percy Lewis showed no inclination to supervise the labor at Foxhill and spur the work along. He seemed perfectly content to stay at Cheviot Chase riding, hunting, and fishing as the mood struck him. I believed Daphne was of the same mind. She gloried in fussing about Cheviot Chase and radiated vivaciousness whenever Lord Rathbone was present. I wondered if it was the man she found so delightful or his money and power. I had to admonish myself. The actions and plans of the major inhabitants of Cheviot Chase were none of my concern.

"By the way, Sarah, his lordship intends to give a ball. He wishes me to attend for some obscure reason."

Sarah's eyes sparkled. "I knew that blue silk was meant for something special. The seams have all been taken apart. Now if you'll cut it to the design you want, I'll start immediately."

"I really can't thank you enough, Sarah. I don't know how I would have managed without you."

"Oh, I'm sure a smart young thing such as yourself would have managed quite well on your own." Sarah lowered her eyes and flushed red.

I spent the better part of the afternoon securing the finished paintings into their cleaned frames. With that done, I went to look for Mr. Jackson.

As I approached the downstairs library, I heard familiar voices. Mr. Jackson was speaking to Lord Rathbone. I stood my distance and waited for Mr. Jackson to come out of the library. Their voices were of a timbre that made them easily heard through the door, though I did not purposely eavesdrop.

"Something has to be done, milord," said Mr. Jackson. "The staff is becoming tense. I wouldn't be surprised if some of them left. To make matters worse, they are spreading all sorts of rumors in the village. It cannot be tolerated, milord."

"I'll try to take care of it tonight, Jackson. I should have been more thorough in the beginning."

"Begging your pardon, milord, perhaps if you had the East Wing opened and completely restored, it might stop any ugly gossip."

"I can't do that right now, Jackson. I'm sure you can see the logic behind my reasons."

"Yes, milord. But I do stress the urgency of the matter."

"I understand, Jackson. As I said before, I will do my best to take care of the matter tonight, regardless of the cost."

"Yes, milord."

I could almost hear Mr. Jackson backing out of the room. I dashed back to the staircase and pretended I was just coming down.

That night I left the drawing room earlier than usual. I felt I should spend a portion of the evening helping Sarah with the blue gown. It was late when I crawled into bed. I fell asleep immediately.

A scream shattered the night's silence. I bolted upright in bed, my open eyes staring into the darkness of the bedchamber. Had I been dreaming? As if to confirm reality, several feral screams echoed one after the other. I donned my night robe and hastened into the corridor. I wasn't the only one who had been wakened from sleep. Sarah Herries was bustling toward me. We looked at each other with puzzled expressions then scurried down the hall to the window that overlooked the courtyard gardens and the East Wing.

We gasped in unison at the sight before us. The East Wing was on fire. Down in the courtyard, men, still wearing their night caps, were rushing toward the East Wing.

"We should go and see if we can be of help," said Sarah.

I nodded absently and we made our way to the East Wing. Almost everyone was there. The Lewises, the Whitneys, Jason, Mr. Jackson, and a number of servants. Daphne Lewis was distraught beyond reason. She clung to her father and kept repeating, "What ever shall we do now, Father?"

Clara Whitney looked dazed while her husband stared blankly at the open doors to the East Wing.

The smoke that spewed out was causing my eyes to sting. The billowing, pungent clouds were forcing a cough or two from my throat. Everyone was feeling the effects. A hand came down on my shoulder. My head swiveled to find Jason by my side.

"I do believe history is repeating itself," he whispered, his head bent close to mine.

I said nothing as I looked around. Missing a familiar and dear face, I asked, "Where is Lord Rathbone?"

"I'm sure John is in there being outrageously heroic as usual," said Jason.

"He's in there? Alone?"

Jason shrugged. "It is his house. Oh, I imagine a servant or two is displaying righteous loyalty."

"You're being callous, Jason. Aren't you worried about him alone in there?"

"Hardly. John has a way of overcoming all travails in life and still managing to come out on top."

"You sound as if you dislike him." I looked straight into Jason's eyes.

"That's a rash word. But maybe you are right. Along with a hefty dose of envy thrown in."

I was surprised by his admission, but fear for Lord

Rathbone's life was uppermost in my mind. "Isn't someone going to do something?" I blurted out loudly.

"We are, Miss Clarke," said Mr. Jackson, carrying water-soaked blankets. "Mrs. Herries, please see to the securing of more wet blankets."

Sarah nodded and left.

Mr. Jackson began to pass out the blankets. Sir Lewis and Cecil each took one. Jason declined.

"I can't stand these fumes any longer. I must go to my bedchamber," cried Daphne.

"I'll go with you," said Clara, putting her arm around Daphne's shoulders.

I grabbed a blanket from Mr. Jackson, much to his surprise, and began to follow Cecil into the smoky wing.

"Miss Clarke, you can't go in there," said Mr. Jackson, grabbing my arm and trying to hold me back.

I wrenched my arm free. "You'll need every hand you can get." Seeing I was determined, he said nothing more.

The smoke bit at my eyes and lungs as I went through the room where the paintings had been stored. I went past what appeared to be a sitting room and knew we were getting close to the source of the smoke.

The fire seemed to be contained in one room. It was the master bedchamber located next to the bedchamber that had already been burned out.

I followed everyone's lead in trying to smother the flames with the wet blankets. A casement window had been opened. Leaning against it was a ladder with men stationed along the length of it. A relay brigade, consisting of men and women, had been organized. They passed pails of water from the ground source up the ladder to dump their contents on the blazing fingers of fire.

At first the heat was unbearable. But in the feverish attempt to bring the fire under control, I was soon acclimated. I grabbed a pail of water and poured it on the blanket to keep it sodden.

At one point I came face to face with Lord Rathbone. Surprise registered in his eyes, which were burdened with dark circles underneath. That surprise vanished before it fully developed. Without a word to me, he resumed the task of working on the fire.

I don't know how long we worked. But dawn was hinting its imminent arrival when the last vestiges of the fire were smothered.

Soot and sweat had taken their toll on me. I dreaded to think what I looked like. I thought an inconspicuous exit would be advisable. Outside, the ladder was being taken away while the men remaining in the burned bedchamber were assessing the damage. I lifted my robe and nightdress as I moved over the debris, making my way to the corridor, which, fortunately, was empty.

I was halfway down the hall when a hand covered my upper arm, halting my steps. I twisted my neck to look up at the soot-covered face of Lord Rathbone. His expressive green eyes were clear as they gazed into mine. Even though he did not speak, I saw the deep gratitude in his eyes. He released me and I scurried back to my rooms, where Sarah was waiting for me.

"I took the liberty of having a tub of hot water brought up for you. I knew you'd be needing it. It's a mite tepid now. But there will be a demand for tubs so I thought I'd better get you one while I could," said Sarah.

"How thoughtful of you, Sarah. I feel like I have the grime of the centuries on me."

"You shouldn't have gone in there."

"I had to do something." I certainly couldn't tell her I had to know if his lordship was all right no matter what I had to do.

"But with all those men. And working like a man,"

144

Sarah admonished.

"Maids were in and out bringing water, so I wasn't really alone, Sarah." I slipped out of my robe and nightdress. The tub felt good as I slid into it.

"Well, mark my words, there'll be gossip about it."

"Let them gossip. I did what I felt necessary. Have you found out who did the screaming? I'm sure it wasn't his lordship. Sounded more like a woman's voice."

"Rumor has it that it was the spirit of Lady Rathbone returning to finish what she had started," replied Sarah.

"Could it be the lady herself and not some spirit?" I asked.

"That would be quite a feat, seeing's how her ladyship is locked away in a hospital in London," said Sarah.

"She could have escaped."

Sarah shook her head. "Even if she slipped out of the hospital, there is no way she could get down to Cheviot Chase, especially clad in one of the hospital's special gowns. Why she'd never get out of London."

I said no more, but the thought lingered in my mind. It certainly would explain the ghostly goings-on in the East Wing. I wondered if I should relate my thoughts to Lord Rathbone.

At dinner I became bold, perhaps thinking I had earned the right.

"How severe was the damage to the East Wing, Lord Rathbone?" I asked, ignoring the surprised stares from everyone except Jason.

"The room was totally destroyed, Miss Clarke," he replied.

"How awful!" interjected Daphne in a whiny voice that had a nasal twang to it.

"Is nothing salvageable?" I continued.

145

"Not a thing. I feel fortunate the entire rear wing didn't go," said Lord Rathbone.

"Isn't it time you did something about that section of the East Wing, John?" asked Cecil.

"Yes, John," agreed Clara. "The stench has permeated our section of the wing. It's most distressing, John."

"I suppose you are right. I've neglected its restoration for far too long. In deference to our guests, I thought a number of workmen about the house would mar their visit." Lord Rathbone smiled, raised one eyebrow, and cast his gaze directly at Daphne.

"Workmen have such rude manners and a rough way of talking that I do abhor their presence," said Daphne as though she was expected to speak.

"You can always avoid them, Daphne," said Jason with a mischievous twinkle in his eyes.

Daphne looked at him disdainfully then turned her attention back to Lord Rathbone. "You must not cater to my fancies, John. Clara is right. The odors in the East Wing are quite unbearable. I expect they will be more so now."

"Perhaps you should go back to Foxhill Manor when the repairs begin here," suggested Jason, which brought a scathing look from Sir Percy.

Daphne looked at her father, whose expression had now become one of cold fury.

"You know very well, Jason, that Foxhill itself is under repairs. The smell of paint is quite detrimental to Daphne's health," fumed Sir Percy Lewis.

"I'm afraid that will soon become the case here," said Lord Rathbone.

"Are you requesting our departure, John?" asked Sir Percy.

"Not at all, Percy. You're welcome to stay as long as you wish. But I feel it is best I start repairs to the East Wing as soon as possible. I must give some consideration to my sister's wishes."

"Thank you, John," said Clara.

"Besides, I wouldn't want our guests at the ball to be assailed by foul odors," Lord Rathbone added.

"Oh, John. You've decided on a date for the ball?" gushed Daphne.

"Yes. A month from now. Work should be well under way by then, if not completed."

"How will you be able to get everything gutted and rebuilt by then?" asked Sir Percy.

"I'll make sure there are enough men to do the work. No sense in dragging it out," replied Lord Rathbone.

Sir Percy shook his head. "If I know workmen, they'll never have the work done in a month."

"We'll see," said Lord Rathbone.

"We must plan on going to London, Clara," said Daphne. "I will need a new gown and a number of other things."

Clara looked at Cecil. "Will you have the time to escort us, Cecil?"

"I believe I will. There are some documents I wish to examine at the University of London and the British Museum."

"You will come too, won't you, John?" asked Daphne, fluttering her eyelashes.

"Sorry, but I must see to the hiring of workmen and supervising the work, not to mention the running of the estate. It is spring and the crops must be seen to."

"Percy?" asked Cecil.

"I fear not. My lumbago has been acting up of late. Traveling would only exacerbate it," replied Sir Percy.

"This fire will pose extra work for you, Miss Clarke," said Lord Rathbone. "The large parlor at the rear of the East Wing has some paintings which I'm sure will be in dire need of cleaning from all the smoke and drifting soot."

He was so handsome when he smiled. I couldn't stop my heart from oscillating erratically. But my voice was steady when I said, "I shall look forward to the additional work, Lord Rathbone."

"'Lord Rathbone' makes me sound like a very pompous fellow. Do call me John and I shall call you Janet. Agreed?"

"If you wish, milord."

"John. Remember? Say it," he ordered.

"John," I said a bit weakly.

Neither Jason nor Cecil displayed an interest in the conversation. Clara raised her eyebrows. Daphne dropped her fork onto her plate. Sir Percy, keeping his eyes on his plate, frowned.

In the drawing room, Clara poured the tea and handed me a cup, saying, "As my brother has seen fit to accept you into our social circle, I feel I can do no less. And now it seems you will be with us for some time; therefore, I wish to extend the same courtesy. You may call me Clara. And you are Janet, are you not?"

"Yes." There was a coldness in Clara's voice that didn't match her offer of friendliness. I sensed she would still have as little to do with me as before.

Daphne offered no familiarity. I suspected she never would. It was clear Sir Percy did not approve of mingling out of his social class. I could see he ruled his daughter with an iron will. Daphne would think as he wanted and do as he wanted.

When the gentleman joined us in the drawing room, Jason came directly toward me. "It's a fairly balmy night. Let's take a stroll in the courtyard. I'm not up to draughts tonight."

I agreed. I wasn't up to watching Daphne openly flirt with Lord Rathbone. John . . . the name sounded sweet to me. I had used it so many times in my dreams.

French doors at the back of the drawing room opened

on the rear courtyard, where tulips now surpassed the daffodils.

When Jason cupped my elbow to steer me through the French doors, I recalled Lord Rathbone's warnings of Jason's rakish nature. I hesitated for a moment. But confidence in my ability to deter his amorous attentions returned and we walked out into the courtyard.

Nine

"It is quite warm tonight, especially for this time of year," I remarked. "Unfortunately the acrid smell of smoke still hangs in the air."

Jason hooked his hands in the pockets of his pants. "It rather does spoil the night air. Still it is far more refreshing than the atmosphere in the drawing room."

"Oh? I wasn't aware you found the air in the drawing room stifling."

"It's no secret Clara and I have no love for one another. And the way Daphne slobbers over John nauseates me. Cecil is a sneak and Sir Percy a snob. I suppose I'm no prize either. But at least I'm honest with myself. One would think John would surround himself with happier people after all the tragedies in his life. I'm surprised he offered the Lewises an unlimited option to visit."

"Perhaps he is enamored of Daphne," I suggested.

Jason snickered. "I can't imagine John having any serious thoughts about the simpering Daphne. I'll be glad when they all trot off to London."

"Will you be going with them?"

"Lord, no. I see enough of them here." Jason paused and glanced at the East Wing. "What do you think about his lordship wanting you to call him John?"

"I am shocked and surprised to say the least. Frankly, I find it embarrassing."

"John doesn't believe in artificial social barriers. He has a very liberal view of life, claiming we must have a forward-looking attitude in the seventies. Personally, I think he did it to exasperate our little group at the table. He loves to defy social proprieties, especially when Sir Percy is present. He did the same thing to me in front of titled nobility."

"But you are his cousin, aren't you?"

"So distant I doubt if any kinship still exists. I met John through Isobel, his second wife. The one caged up in London. I knew Isobel before she married John. Somewhere along the line a remote relationship between John and me was discovered and I became a frequent guest here. In the beginning there were numerous balls and social gatherings at Cheviot Chase and I hoped to find a suitable match. Money, you know. I'm still looking."

"Do you work for his lordship?" I asked.

"Work? Good Lord, no. I accept his hospitality. I have a small annuity that keeps me in farthings. I could never live in the style to which I have become accustomed on my annuity. Food and shelter would gobble up most of it, making the purchase of clothes a rare luxury. John takes care of the food and shelter and I make a bob or two gambling. I eke by. I suppose I shall have to garner my faculties and make an honest effort to find a woman of substance. Time is flickering by. And you, Janet. Why hasn't a young beauty like you been snagged as a wife?" asked Jason.

"I guess the right man hasn't come along yet."

"Perhaps you'll meet your Prince Charming at the ball. I assume John has ordered you to attend."

"How did you ever guess?"

"I know John. I told you he likes to shock people with his liberal social notions."

"I don't like being used in that manner."

"What is this about someone being used?"

The deep voice cut through the night air like a rapier through custard. Jason and I came to an abrupt halt in our walk, turned, and came face to face with Lord John Rathbone.

"Getting a spot of night air, John?" asked Jason.

"I think it is time you went into the house, Jason," said John in a tone that would brook no argument.

Jason looked at me, then at Lord Rathbone. "Perhaps you are right, John."

Jason began to walk back to the house. I started to walk with him until Lord Rathbone spoke.

"Janet. I didn't mean for you to go into the house. I wish to have a word with you."

I stood rigidly. The way he said my Christian name had a strange effect on me. A rather pleasant one. "Yes, milord?" I didn't turn around but watched Jason as he opened the French doors then closed them behind him.

"What is this 'milord' business? I thought I told you to call me John. Now say my name as though it was the most natural thing in the world."

"John," I murmured.

"Look at me and say it."

I turned, looked up at him, and said with decided emphasis, "John."

"That's better. Now perhaps you will be good enough to answer my question."

"What question was that?"

"Who is being used and what for?"

I resumed walking along the path that led to the rear of the garden. He walked with me, his hands folded behind his back. I decided to tell him the truth even if it did jeopardize my position at Cheviot Chase.

152

"I believe you are using me as an example of your indulgent disposition toward the working class. I am a person, not a flag to be waved by a libertine under the noses of nobility. I shall not be at the ball unless you physically carry me there," I declared.

"I might just do that."

"It would be like you."

"You have no idea what I am truly like."

"You are like every peer of the land. Principles, good manners, and an ethical conscience are what you expect of others, not yourself."

"You are quite vexatious tonight, Janet. Didn't Jason sufficiently flirt with you?"

I stopped, my hands going to my hips. "I'm beginning to think Jason is more of a gentleman than you. His conversation was amiable and courteous, which is more than I can say for your . . . your inquisition. I think it is time I retired."

His hand came down on my bare shoulder. My body became hotter than it was when I was helping to put out the fire.

"Wait," he said. "Please let me explain."

"You owe me no explanations, Lord Rathbone. I shall complete my work as swiftly as possible, then you'll be well rid of me. Unless you prefer to replace me and have me leave immediately." There I had said it. I had put my neck on the chopping block and could not complain if he chopped it off.

"I've listened to you without interruption. I think it is only fair that you listen to me. Shall we sit by the fountain?"

His arm slipped about my bare shoulders as he led me to the marble bench facing the fountain. With the bare flesh of his hand on my shoulder and the feel of his body next to mine, I would have followed him to the darkest recesses of Hades. Where was my rationality and

153

strength of character when I needed them? When we were seated, he removed his arm from my shoulder and I was master of myself once again.

"Regarding the ball. I realize Cheviot Chase is boring and isolated, especially for a woman of your youth. I also realize that, being inordinately proud, you would never come to the ball on a mere invitation. That is why I sound so demanding. I wouldn't want to be the cause of your drying up into an old prune of a woman. Your young soul needs and cries for some entertainment. Work is not the whole substance of life. Some divertissement will give you a fresh outlook on your work and life in general. I never dreamed that you would think I was using you as an illustration of my liberal views. I have no great passion to turn the British Empire into a classless society. I don't know how that thought ever entered your head."

"But Jason said—"

"Ah! Jason. Someday I'm going to have to do something about that fellow. I daresay envy pushes him to categorize me as something I'm not. Especially when I am growing. . . . Never mind."

"Please. I didn't mean to get Jason into any trouble," I pleaded.

"It's not you. My sister isn't too fond of him, as you know by now. And he is a constant reminder of Isobel. I should have had the fellow leave when Isobel went to the hospital."

"Why didn't you?" Any anger or irritation I might have felt earlier melted away as I listened to his soothing baritone voice.

"When my wife, Isobel, started to become ill, Jason seemed to have a steadying effect on her. As she worsened, Jason devoted himself to her welfare. I felt an obligation toward him in a way. I could offer him contacts he wouldn't be able to make on his own. It seemed small enough repayment. Perhaps at the ball he'll make that contact he has been trying for. I fear I have been boring you. I don't usually talk this much. I find you easy to talk to, Janet. And once you promise me you'll attend the ball without a fuss, I shall trouble you no further."

"You do not trouble me. I enjoy talking to you. I'll be at the ball, John." I kept my voice low. He was looking at me in a way that made the moment special. All he had to do was touch me or whisper my name and I would have thrown myself into his arms.

A piercing scream emanating from the drawing room shattered the moment. Lord Rathbone—John—was on his feet instantly and dashed toward the French doors. I lifted my skirts and ran but there was no way I could keep up with him. As I reached the French doors, I could see Daphne throwing herself into John's arms. When I entered the drawing room, I heard her convulsive sobs.

"What happened here?" asked John over Daphne's head. She clung to him like ancient ivy on a wall.

As Sir Percy and Cecil were peering out one of the front windows, a distraught and bewildered Clara spoke. "She jumped up and started to scream and pointed at the window. I have no idea what happened."

John pushed the hysterical Daphne from him and held her at arm's length. "What the devil is wrong with you, Daphne?" he asked. When her histrionics showed no sign of abating, he began to shake her. "Stop it, Daphne! Get a hold of yourself, woman." He turned to Jason. "Jason, get me a snifter of brandy for her."

Jason nodded and went to the sideboard while John led Daphne to the settee. Her hands clung to his shoulders. John forcibly removed them and made her sit.

When Jason handed him the snifter of brandy, John passed it to Daphne with the demand, "Drink this."

Daphne downed it in one gulp then extended it to John as though requesting another. John took the glass and handed it to Jason with a nod. The second brandy seemed to have a calming effect on her.

Sir Percy and Cecil had come back from the window and had taken seats as did Clara and I.

"Now," began John, his rich voice soothing. "Tell us, as best you can, what terrified you so, Daphne."

Daphne took a long gulp of air then, managing to keep her small bow lips in a pout, replied, "There was this ghastly face peeking into the drawing room. Oh, it was so horrible! I'm sure we'll all be slaughtered in our beds tonight."

"Nonsense," growled John, and marched to the fireplace. With hands braced on the mantel, he stared into the grate.

"Come, Daphne. I think it best you retire after this upsetting ordeal," said Sir Percy. "I'll tell Mrs. Herries to have one of the maids bring you some hot milk." As he took her hand, she rose and let her father lead her from the room.

"Was there anything out there, Cecil?" asked Clara.

"Nothing. At least nothing I could see. Did you see anything at the window, Clara?" asked Cecil. She shook her head. "You, Jason?"

"Not a thing. The way Daphne gulped down that brandy, perhaps she had a sip or two before we came into the drawing room," suggested Jason.

"Really, Jason. Don't ascribe any of your predilections to others. Daphne had nothing but tea," declared Clara. "Miss Clarke . . . Janet can attest to that, can't you, Janet?"

I nodded absently. My attention remained on the tall figure at the fireplace, his wide shoulders heaving as though trying to subdue a rising anger.

"My dear Clara, you'd swear Daphne drank only tea even if she was reeking of brandy," said Jason.

"Are you calling me a liar, Jason?" Clara's eyes narrowed, her lips compressed in an ugly manner.

Jason's smile was tinged with a sneer. "You're a woman of many talents."

"Well, I never. Are you just going to sit there, Cecil, and let him talk to me like that?" demanded Clara.

Cecil braced his hands on the arm of his chair and wearily pushed himself out of it. "I think it is time we followed Sir Percy's example and retired."

Clara rose. With an imperious look at Jason, she said, "You'll be sorry for being so boorish toward me, Jason. And that's a promise I'll make sure I keep." She flounced out of the room on Cecil's arm.

I had a feeling Cecil was going to get a good talking-to for not coming to his wife's defense.

"John, I'm going to take a walk outside and have a look around," said Jason. "Care to come with me, Janet?"

"No. I think I'll retire also." Before I rose from the chair, Jason was gone. "Good night, Lord . . . John."

Deep inside me I hoped he would make some move to stop me. If I could be alone with him, I had the wild expectation that we might recapture that moment by the fountain. I had felt so close to him then and I'm sure he thought me more than some inconsequential employee. But he neither spoke nor turned around. He remained mute and I left.

The next several days at Cheviot Chase proved to be most pleasant for me. The Whitneys and Daphne were off in London. Sir Percy's lumbago had him confined to bed. Lord Rathbone was busy hiring workmen for the East Wing and galloping about his estates seeing to the planting of the spring crops.

Jason and I dined alone for the most part. He was proving to be a most amiable companion. His numerous tales and gossip of the social elite were told in a humorous manner.

I missed John more than I thought possible. Still I was

more at ease on those occasions when he wasn't present. His presence engendered in me a tension, a desire, a longing, none of which I could explain satisfactorily.

My work moved along with a speed that astonished me. But it was the hand-delivered note from Dr. Brian Young that made the week truly outstanding. He offered to take me on a picnic that coming Sunday. I sent a note back stating my pleasure in accepting.

The day was lovely and I felt a sense of freedom as I sat beside Brian in the trap. The wheels rattled rhythmically as the sprightly horse pulled his burden down the lane.

"You've been quiet, Janet. Lost in thought?" asked Brian.

"In a way. I was thinking how beautiful the day is," I replied. "Where are we going?"

"There's a nice brook in the middle of a stand of trees a little farther on. I thought it would be nice to have some shade. There are a number of birds there to provide us with music."

When we arrived at the place he had chosen, I had to admit it was a charming spot. While Brian tethered the horse, I spread the linen cloth out and placed the picnic basket on it. After sitting down on the velvety grass, I peeked inside the hamper to find meat pies, cucumber pickles, scones, a jar of clotted cream, a tin of biscuits, and jars of tea. It looked delicious and the sight of it was making me hungry. Brian came back and we started on our open-air repast.

When we had finished most everything in the basket, Brian stretched out, his head resting in his folded hands, his eyes closed.

"That was a lovely meal. Did you make it?" I asked.

"No. I'm not much use in the kitchen. My housekeeper prepared it for me."

"Thank her for me. Tell her I thought it was excellent."

"She'll like that." He yawned.

"Tired?"

"I was kept on the go yesterday. I will never understand why most women have to have their babies in the middle of the night. Or why all emergencies occur in the middle of the night. I suppose I have to accept it as the fate of a country doctor," said Brian, trying to stifle another yawn.

"You rest. I'm going to take a walk down to the brook."

He gave me a half-nod, which caused me to smile sympathetically at him.

With a light heart and a full stomach, I strolled down to the brook. The water rushing over random rocks made beguiling bubbles of music. Sunlight and shadows chased each other in an unending game as a slight breeze trembled the trees.

I looked across the brook to the other side. The trees were denser and the shadows darker. The bank was crowded with delicate ferns and broad leaf fronds. Shrubbery was heavier on that side also. Suddenly I felt I was not alone. I had the sensation I was being watched.

I turned around and could see Brian in the distance exactly as I had left him. He appeared sound asleep. Even before I turned around, I knew it wasn't Brian watching me. I was under scrutiny from the other side of the brook. The shadows which I found intriguing at first now became ominous. An awareness that I was an intruder crept over me. Had we ventured into some gypsy's or animal's private domain?

Narrowing my eyes and stretching my neck, I tried to pierce the darkness on the other side. Nothing. Only an inky void. I continued to stare and was rewarded by a flash of white cloth catching on a bramble. I saw a hand tug at it and unsnarl it. Then everything was in shadows again.

My first inclination was to wake Brian, but he needed

his sleep more than assuaging my fancies about the woods. It was probably a young lad looking for fish in the brook. Still my curiosity was greater than my common sense.

I walked along the brook seeking a spot that offered stepping stones across the water to the other side. As I walked along, I had the impression whoever was on the other side was keeping up with me.

I didn't find any stepping stones. But I did find a large oblong stone that stretched across the brook. Only an inch of water flowed over it. It was an encouraging omen that gave impetus to my desire to reach the other side.

Lifting my skirt and petticoats high and gathering them in one arm, I made the crossing. The tips of my walking boots got wet, but not my cotton stockings.

"Hello. Is anyone there?" I called softly. There was no reply.

Pushing some fronds aside, I ventured farther into the woods, then stood perfectly still. I could hear the rustle of leaves and a twig or two snapping. Unmindful of the thickets lashing at my arms, I cautiously tiptoed toward the sounds.

My actions caused whoever it was to break cover and run. I caught a fleeting glimpse of the creature. A woman's form, clad in a once white flowing cape and gown, was racing away from me. She stumbled and fell. I took advantage and quickened my pace.

I was a few feet from her when she pushed herself to all fours and crouched before me like a wild animal. She snarled and growled like a feral beast about to attack its mortal enemy. There was a wildness in her eyes that was savage and not of this world. Her clothes were in tatters. Grime encrusted her face and stringy hair. I should have been terrified by her posturing. But an overwhelming pity engulfed me. Though she bore little, if any, resemblance to the portrait in the East Wing, I knew who

4 FREE BOOKS

TO GET YOUR 4 FREE BOOKS WORTH $18.00 — MAIL IN THE FREE BOOK CERTIFICATE T O D A Y

Fill in the Free Book Certificate below, and we'll send your FREE BOOKS to you as soon as we receive it.

If the certificate is missing below, write to: Zebra Home Subscription Service, Inc., P.O. Box 5214, 120 Brighton Road, Clifton, New Jersey 07015-5214.

GET
FOUR
FREE
BOOKS
(AN $18.00 VALUE)

ZEBRA HOME SUBSCRIPTION
SERVICE, INC.
P.O. BOX 5214
120 BRIGHTON ROAD
CLIFTON, NEW JERSEY 07015-5214

the woman was.

"Lady Rathbone," I began in my tenderest tone. "Let me help you." I extended my hand.

A low guttural snarl issued forth from deep in her throat. She snapped at my hand as if I had a lethal weapon.

"Please," I implored, pulling my hand back. "Let me take you to Cheviot Chase, where you'll be tended to. You must be tired and hungry."

It wasn't the right thing to say. At the mention of Cheviot Chase, she stood, her hands clenching and unclenching at her sides. Her savage eyes blazed with a Satanic fire. It was then I felt fear creeping up my spine. She appeared to be getting ready to lunge at me. But she surprised me and spoke. Her voice was coarse and cracked with venomous hatred.

"Cheviot Chase!" She spat on the ground. Saliva dribbled from the corners of her mouth. "Evil people. They all want me dead, especially him. He'll do anything to put me in my grave. Locking me up in a prison where they constantly drugged me. He is evil. The devil personified. I will kill him. I will kill all of them one by one. I've seen you there. You are plotting with him to keep me in prison. So I'll start with you."

Her nails were like talons as she reached out for me. I stepped back, then turned and ran. Uncaring about my boots and stockings, I lifted my skirt and petticoats and ran through a shallow section of the brook. Her maniacal laughter filled my ears as I reached the other side.

For some strange reason I felt the brook was a moat that would protect me from her. My hand on my bosom to ease my panting, I turned to peer across the watery barrier. The laughter had stopped and I was confronted with nothing more than the dark forest. It was as if the encounter had never taken place.

I walked back to where the remnants of our picnic

remained. My first impulse was to rouse Brian and urge him to get the trap so we could leave immediately. Then I looked down at him. He slept soundly, not a flicker of an eyelid to indicate a dream was passing in his mind. After hearing how he had been up all night, I didn't have the heart to wake him even though I was most anxious to return to Cheviot Chase and apprise John that his wife was roaming about near the moor.

I looked around. She hadn't followed me nor was there a hint that she was still in the area. I decided to let Brian sleep a few minutes longer, which would give me time to let my boots and stockings dry.

I sat there in wary vigil, ready to spring to my feet and wake Brian if the mad Lady Rathbone came bounding out of the forest across the brook.

But time passed and the forest became serene and benign once again and the birds commenced their musical efforts. I became contemplative as I reflected on my theory regarding Lady Rathbone and the so-called ghost of the East Wing.

Somehow Lady Rathbone had escaped from the hospital in London and miraculously made her way to the vicinity of Cheviot Chase. She was the ghost seen in the East Wing during the night and the one who had left the food in the burned-out bedchamber. I had a strong notion she was the one who had started the latest fire in the East Wing and John knew it. He had known all along that his wife had escaped and was stalking about Cheviot Chase.

I looked down at Brian and wondered if I should tell him of my encounter with Lady Rathbone. I decided against it. Lord Rathbone—John—was the only person who had a right to know. Why stir up people in the village? There was no telling what they might do.

Disturbing thoughts began to assail me. Was John really trying to kill his wife? Or was it the ravings of a madwoman? Could it have been Lady Rathbone who had hit me on the head with a rock and the one who had rolled the boulder off the cliff in attempts to kill me? But why?

The hypnotic gurgle of the brook was taking its toll on me. My eyelids began to feel heavy and I had to fight to keep them open.

The whinny of the tethered horse alarmed me. I blinked my eyes and visually searched the area. Seeing nothing, I looked up at the sky and noticed the sun was lowering. I looked again at Brian. He was still asleep. I put my damp boots back on. It was time to get back.

When I woke Brian, he sat up abruptly and looked around dazed. He rubbed his eyes as though to vanquish a dream then looked around again.

"I think we'd better head back, Brian," I said.

He shook his head and stood. "I'm truly sorry, Janet. I must have slept the entire afternoon away. I certainly didn't intend to do that. I had hoped to make this a pleasant afternoon for you. I am indeed sorry."

"Don't give it another thought. It was a lovely picnic and a quiet, relaxing afternoon," I said, folding the linen cloth.

"Next time I'll make sure I have a proper night's sleep before asking you to go on an outing. You must think me a dolt."

"Of course not. I was glad you could find some peace here and get the sleep you needed."

On the way back, Brian chatted at length as though trying to make up for his silence all afternoon.

As we drew closer to Cheviot Chase, I heard the heavy hoofbeats of a horse being ridden hard. I turned in my seat to see the hatless Lord Rathbone riding fast behind us, his black hair storming about his head, his blouselike shirt billowing behind him.

"Hold up," he called.

I put a hand on Brian's arm and nodded toward the horseman almost upon us. Brian reined in the horse and the trap ceased to move.

"You are needed at the Waring place immediately, Doctor," said John, his vibrant green eyes searching my face in a quizzical manner.

"What happened?" asked Brian.

"Waring was taking his bull out to service a cow. He was badly gored. We've been looking all over for you. He's a good tenant and I'd hate to lose him," replied John.

"I'll tend to him as soon as I get Janet home." He faced me. "You won't mind a fast ride in the trap, will you, Janet?"

Before I could reply, John said, "There's no time for that. I'll see that Janet gets home. She can ride with me. You know where Waring's place is, don't you, Doctor?"

Brian nodded then started to leave the trap, but I put a staying hand on his arm. "I can get out by myself. Don't waste any time. Thank you again for the nice afternoon." I swung my skirt-covered legs over the side of the trap and slid down. Brian waved as he turned the trap and horse around, then urged the animal into a gallop.

John reached down with one hand saying, "Grab my arm at the elbow, step on my foot, then give yourself a heave upward."

I did as instructed and was soon nestled in front of him, my legs lolling to one side of the horse. The animal was large and I had an inordinate fear of falling off. As if sensing my insecurity, John's arm came firmly about my waist. The sensation stimulated such an unknown pleasure in me I stiffened.

"Lean back against me. I won't let you fall off, Janet," he half whispered in my ear.

His arm tightened, pulling me back against his firm body. I could feel the steady heaving of his warm chest as he breathed. It caused my heart to beat that much faster. The top of my head came to his chin. Every once in a

164

while I could feel that clefted chin press the side of my head. I was grateful that he kept the horse at a walk. I tried to convince myself my gratitude was linked to a fear of being on the animal. But in reality, I knew the slower we went, the longer he would have his arm around me. His body against mine was exciting. I never wanted it to end. I was so filled with exhilaration that the memory of encountering Lady Rathbone faded away.

"First time on a horse, Janet?"

I nodded. I didn't trust my voice.

"It's not so bad, is it?"

I shook my head.

"Not talking today? I suppose you've talked yourself out with Dr. Young. You've acted quite foolish today, Janet. I hope it doesn't happen again."

"What are you talking about?"

"Your spending the day with Dr. Young unchaperoned and in a secluded spot. Most improper. It will set the whole village talking. You really should know better."

"This is the 1870s. I'm sure people have other things to think about than my spending an afternoon with Brian."

"Brian, is it?"

"What's wrong with that? You've insisted I call you John. I feel I know Brian better than I know you," I said.

"Well, now, we'll have to correct that, won't we, Janet?"

I didn't dare turn my head to reply. I knew he had lowered his head next to mine for I could almost feel the movements of his lips against my ear. If I did turn, his lips would touch mine. I didn't trust my reaction. I had heard how lords of the manor delighted in dallying with young women in their employ. I would not let myself be a plaything for Lord Rathbone, only to be discarded when the novelty wore off. No, I had too much pride for that. Besides, I prized my dignity and artistic professionalism

165

too much to have it destroyed by a romantic whim. Still the scent of him assailed my nostrils. The heat of his body flowed into mine, causing me to remember his soulful kiss at the fair.

Suddenly I felt the need to be back in the safe cocoon of my rooms. "It wouldn't upset me if you went a little faster."

"Is it thirst for excitement or a pressing need to leave my company that causes you to make that request?" asked John, his voice mocking and taunting.

"I only wish to relieve you of concern for my welfare. I'm sure you have urgent business that needs your attention."

"Business can wait. It is a pleasant day and I don't often allow myself many pleasures in life."

The pace was steady and a silence fell between us. It was then I abruptly remembered the encounter with Lady Rathbone. My nerves tingled and my body stiffened as I sought words to tell him of the confrontation.

"Something wrong, Janet?" he asked, his arm tightening around my waist. "I thought I felt you shudder."

"There's something I have to tell you and I don't know how to begin. It isn't pleasant."

"Start at the beginning." His tone became sullen. I could visualize that grim scowl of his.

I took a deep breath, then plunged ahead. "Brian—Dr. Young—and I were having a picnic by the brook in the woods just off the lane back there. After lunch, Brian fell asleep and I decided to explore the brook. I saw something on the other side of the brook in the thicker part of the forest. When I caught a glimpse of the shadowy figure, I recognized it was a woman." I felt every muscle in his body become taut as he pulled himself rigid in the saddle. "Well, you had best prepare yourself for a shock."

"Get on with it, woman. I've lived with disaster for so

166

long, I'm immune to being shocked. Spit it out in plain words," he ordered.

"I saw Lady Rathbone." What more could I say? That she wanted to kill everyone at Cheviot Chase? At first I thought he didn't believe me. But his body slumped and I knew he did. "You don't seem surprised."

"I'm not. You see, the last time I went to London, I learned that Isobel had escaped. I had a feeling she would head for Cheviot Chase. I never thought she would make it. I was sure they would find her before she left London. When I caught you sneaking out of the East Wing basement window and listened to your tale of someone using the place as a refuge, I knew Isobel had made it back. I thought I had blocked every entrance, but you were clever enough to find the one place I had missed. We, Jackson and I, would search the East Wing at night in the hopes of catching her before she tried to burn the place down again. I've been searching for her ever since."

"Do you think she set the last fire?"

"Yes."

"Didn't you block that bottom window?"

"Not at first. I was confident I would catch her coming in. After the fire, I had that window boarded up."

"But I saw a light in the East Wing not too long ago."

"That was Jackson. I sent him to inspect the rooms just in case she had found another way in. She hadn't. On occasion I would hear of suspicious events occurring in various parts of the estate. Thinking Isobel might be the underlying cause, I would chase down any rumor. When you received that blow on the head, I immediately thought of Isobel. I spent the rest of the day and long into the night searching the area for some sign of her. That is why my visit to your bedchamber was so late."

"Do you think Lady Rathbone was the one who struck me on the head?"

"I don't know what to think," replied John.

"That day you claimed you chased one of your dogs and fell, was that the truth?"

"I didn't think you'd believe that story. Under the circumstances it was the only story I could think of at the time. I didn't want to frighten you with the truth. As you might guess, I had caught up with Isobel. I tried to talk her into returning to Cheviot Chase with me. It was a mistake. She attacked me. She was quick and had uncommon strength. I tried to subdue her, but it was futile. Her biting, kicking, scratching, and writhing prevented me from getting a good grip on her. She picked up a stout branch and swung it at me. I fended the blow with my arm. For a minute I was stunned. She broke and ran with the fleetness of an escaping doe. I knew I would never catch her now that she was on her guard. And the pain in my arm had sapped my strength," explained John.

"What about the dogs? Why didn't they assist you?"

His smile was vague. "When it comes to Isobel, they are utter cowards. Always were. From the day I brought her to Cheviot Chase as my bride, the dogs would slink away and hide from her. In a way they had more common sense and insight than I."

"I think animals have a deeper perception of human character than we humans do."

"Perhaps you are right, Janet. I should have paid more heed to their reactions to Isobel in the beginning." He paused reflectively for a minute. "Did Dr. Young see her?"

"No. As I said, he was asleep."

"Did you tell him about seeing her?"

"No. I did try to persuade her ladyship to come back with me to Cheviot Chase. That seemed to set her off."

"Did she try to attack you? Be honest."

"Yes. But I ran and she didn't follow."

"Stay away from her, Janet. She is quite mad."

"I realize that now."

"Perhaps you can also understand why I didn't want you roaming the moor alone."

I nodded.

"Are you sure you are quite all right? She didn't get her hands on you, did she?"

I was grateful for the genuine concern in his voice. "I'm fine. She only frightened me."

"Do you mind if I spur the horse on? I should examine the area near the brook, although she is probably long gone by now."

"I don't mind at all. I understand your anxiety."

"Hold on."

His heels dug into the animal's flank and the beast sprang forward, racing toward Cheviot Chase as though all the demons of hell were after it.

Ten

John reined the horse to an abrupt halt before the front steps of Cheviot Chase. He swung off the animal, then raised his arms to help me down. I put my hands on his shoulders. His hands easily encompassed my waist. He held me close as my body slid down the length of his. For a brief second, there was a fire in his green eyes. His head lowered as he held me tight.

"Janet, I beg of you not to mention a word of this to anyone, especially what we talked about. No one," he whispered. "It's important. Promise me."

"I promise."

He released me instantly, swung back onto his horse, and galloped off in a fury.

The swift ride had left me shaken. My weakened legs trembled as I mounted the marble stairs to the front door.

When the door was opened by an unseen hand, I stepped in and was astonished to see Sir Percy standing there, his hand still on the knob.

"Where's John going?" he asked.

"He had some urgent business," I replied.

"Why did he bring you back? I thought you went out with Dr. Young."

I didn't like the way he said "you." There was an

arrogant superiority in his tone. I gritted my teeth and forced myself to be polite. "Dr. Young was called away on an emergency. John was kind enough to bring me home. How is your lumbago, Sir Lewis?"

"Hmph." He turned and trudged his way upstairs.

As I was the only female at the dinner table, talk revolved around the upcoming hunt. Not being a rider, I kept my thoughts to myself. But I kept my ears open and learned the ball would be given directly after the hunt.

I had already decided not to go to the drawing room after dinner. I would go upstairs and assist Sarah with the sewing of my gown for the ball. It was coming along nicely. The blue silk was beautiful and easy to work with a needle.

When dinner was over, I rose, as did the men.

"Janet, would you be so kind as to go to the library and wait for me? There is something I would like to discuss with you," said John Rathbone.

"If you wish." When I gave a nod of good night to Jason and Sir Percy, I noticed peculiar expressions on their faces. Jason looked worried. Sir Percy appeared to be fighting a battle between anger and distress.

I dismissed their odd looks as I was more concerned about John's request to meet him in the library. I wondered if it had anything to do with my meeting Lady Rathbone.

I was perusing the vast number of book titles when John entered, closing the door firmly behind him.

"See anything that interests you?" he asked.

"A number of them."

"Do feel free to borrow a book anytime you wish. The library is never locked."

"Thank you. What did you wish to talk to me about?"

"Sit down, Janet." He nodded to the two chairs flanking the fireplace.

When we were seated opposite each other, he braced

171

his forearms on his knees, his broad hands dangling between his spread legs.

"About this afternoon, I trust you spoke to no one."

I shook my head. "Not a soul."

"Good. What I am about to tell you is in the strictest confidence. I'm sure you will honor it."

"Of course."

"I did have Isobel in my grasp the night of the fire. She started throwing lighted oil lamps around. I had to let her go in order to fight the spreading fire. Now she is roaming free over the countryside. No telling what damage she might do. I want you to tell me if she said anything to you this afternoon, anything at all, that might give me a clue as to where she might be hiding."

"She kept vowing to kill you and everyone at Cheviot Chase, including me. She didn't say anything that might give a clue to where she would go. It seemed she only had death on her mind," I replied.

He nodded slowly. "She vowed the same thing when I took her to the hospital. She thinks I am the devil and lives under the delusion I am trying to kill her. Of course it is her insane mind at work. She had the same delusions when she was living here. The only one she even appeared to trust was Jason. She claimed my sister, Cecil, Sir Percy, and Daphne were also out to kill her."

"Were Sir Lewis and his daughter living here at the time?"

"No. But being close neighbors, they were frequent visitors."

"Is it wise to hold a hunt and a ball with Lady Rathbone somewhere on the property?" I asked.

"She is terrified of dogs. The hounds will keep her away from the hunt. I'll post men to stand guard during the night of the ball."

"May I ask a personal question?"

"There are few secrets between us now, Janet. You

172

may ask what you wish. If I don't approve of the question, I will not answer it."

"Why haven't you informed the authorities? Let them initiate a hunt for her," I suggested.

"What? And set the entire village on edge? They'd be shooting at every strange woman who walked the lanes. No. I can't be responsible for that, Janet."

"Shouldn't you at least warn those at Cheviot Chase?"

"It would serve only to unnerve them. And if I did tell them, it would be a constant topic of conversation soon overheard by the staff. If the staff knows about it, so will the entire village and trouble would brew. I appreciate your suggestions, but I fear none of them is feasible at the moment. Of course I might be forced into a position of having to alert the constabulary. I hope to be able to take care of it myself. If I can capture her and get her back to the hospital, I'll make sure they don't let her escape again. Have I explained myself sufficiently?"

"You don't owe me any explanations, John. In fact, you don't have to tell me anything."

"I realize I don't *owe* you an explanation. I feel you have unwittingly become involved in all this. I wanted to tell you everything in hopes that you would understand why I am insisting on secrecy. Besides it helps to have someone to talk to about it. Jackson isn't exactly a font of conversation. Do you mind my speaking to you about it?"

"Not at all. I only hope I can be of help or solace to you, John."

"You are. More than you know."

At that moment he looked vulnerable for so powerful a man. Though his expression was one of grim sadness, his eyes betrayed the tortured agony deep within him. I wanted to rush to him and clasp his head to my bosom in a heartfelt gesture of comfort and consolation. Not only would it have been improper of me, I lacked the courage

173

for it. He sat there staring absently at the floor. I braced my hands on the armrests of the chair and said, "I think I'd better go now."

His head snapped up. "Please don't leave just yet."

I sank back down in the chair and folded my hands in my lap and relaxed. Though he was silent, I sensed he found comfort in my presence. Elation flooded me. Though I may never be anything more to him than an employee, I thought, at least he desires my company. I waited for him to speak. He leaned his head back and closed his eyes.

"My first wife, Alice," he began, "was only seventeen when I married her. I was twenty. Her mother had died most painfully giving birth to her, a fact that her father would never let her forget. He would describe her birth in grueling detail over and over again when she was old enough to understand. It did something to her. Oh, she seemed normal in all respects until the day she learned she was with child. I became her mortal enemy. She adamantly refused to be in the same room with me, much less speak to me. She refused to eat. On occasion she would take a cup of tea but never finished it. Nightmares pursued her, causing her to wake up screaming. Though she had reduced herself to skin and bone, the babe continued to grow. It sent her into a panic.

"One day she took the path to the sea cliffs. When she had been gone for over two hours, her maid became worried and sought me out. I had my horse saddled and went looking for her. It was some weeks later when her body was washed up at Lulworth Cove. I vowed never to marry again. Then, years later, Isobel came along."

He rose and went to the fireplace, braced his hands on the mantel, and stared into the grate, a stance that had become most familiar to me.

"I met Isobel at a ball in London. She was vivacious, beautiful, headstrong, and very sure of her ability to

174

attract men. There was a sparkle in her eyes that was mischievous, yet alluring. I came back to Cheviot Chase and tried to forget her. I couldn't.

"I went back to London, where she was living life to the fullest. She was on a carousel of pleasure that whirled faster and faster. Her appetite for pleasure was insatiable. I should have known something was wrong then. But I was beguiled by her beauty and her lust for life. We married and I brought her to Cheviot Chase. She hated it on sight. In less than a month she was back in London. After several months the gossip started. I was laughed at, sneered at, and had my manhood questioned. I went to London and forcibly dragged her back. In retaliation, she refused to be a wife to me. She became sullen and introverted, thinking it was a punishment I deserved. Frankly, I no longer cared. I had no feeling left for her. Rather than endure vociferous arguments, I let her hold soirees and gala balls.

"For a while things were tolerable. But I soon learned that between parties, she had taken to drink, not port or sherry, but absinthe. When the absinthe ceased to produce the desired effect, she began adding tincture of opium. I tried to put a stop to it more often than I care to admit. But she was clever and I never could track down her source. The absinthe and tincture of opium began to distort her reason. In the end all vestiges of sanity snapped. I could do nothing with nor for her. Jason seemed to be able to reach her on occasion and did all he could to bring her back to reality. In the end, it was all for naught. I had no choice but to put her in a hospital where she couldn't do herself, or anyone else, harm." His shoulders heaved in a silent sigh. "There you have it, Janet. I often wonder if perhaps, in some way, I was the instrument that unleashed the darker side of their natures."

"I don't think you can be held responsible for what

their natures were like. They were formed long before you knew either of them. And there was no way you could ever change them. Those traits were in them from the very inception of life."

He left the fireplace and went to the window, where he stared out at the dark night. "It's the moor. The alien, foreboding moor. Its bleak, dismal countenance tears at one's soul. It forces the heart and mind to succumb to its gloom. Its barren wastelands roll to the horizon luring one in, then shrouding its victim in dense fog. Yet I am inexorably drawn to it. Perhaps there *is* an evil in me that finds kinship with the moor. An evil that engulfs those around me."

I rose and went to stand next to him. "I've been on the moor. There is no evil there. Only titmice, hares, birds, wild flowers, and probably little creatures I have never seen. The moor has a serene beauty. A place where one can contemplate the wonders of nature and the beauty of the earth."

He turned, looked at me, and smiled. Before I knew what was happening, he gathered me in his arms and held me close, his hand pressing my head to his chest. I prayed he didn't feel the wild bouncing of my heart.

"You are a comfort to me, Janet. You have a way of soothing and banishing the demons that dwell in my thoughts."

It took all the fortitude I possessed to pull away from him. To be in his arms and know nothing would, or could, ever become of it, tore at my heart. It was an unbearable torture.

"I'm sorry, Janet. I was swept up in the moment and lost my sense of propriety. Accept my apologies," said John.

"There's no need for any apology. I'm pleased and flattered that you think enough of me to take me into your confidence." I was a little breathless, but managed a smile.

He went back to staring out the window. "I have kept you far too long. Please feel free to leave, Janet."

Though I never wanted to leave him, I managed to mumble a good night, then took my leave.

True to his word, Lord Rathbone hired a substantial crew to begin the clearing and restoring of the East Wing. The acrid smell of smoke wafting through the corridors dissipated within a week. The noise at times could be irritating. But with so many men working on the project, I knew it would not last forever.

Sarah and I finally finished the blue silk gown for the ball. It was exquisite and I looked forward to wearing it.

Sarah and I decided not to pursue the remaking of gowns for a while. My fingers were sore as I'm sure were Sarah's, and I was looking forward to reading some of the books I had seen in the library. It would be a pleasant change of an evening. Playing draughts with Jason was getting tedious even though I usually won.

Almost two weeks passed before Daphne and the Whitneys returned from London. When I heard the rattle of carriage wheels in the driveway, I went to the window in my workroom and peered out. The carriage had come to a halt. A footman was assisting the ladies from the carriage. With that deed accomplished, he and the driver began to carry the many packages into the house. I could see they would have to make a number of trips as the packages were abundant. I saw Daphne stop and make a small moue at the sounds emanating from the workmen. I smiled and went back to work.

I was in Sarah's sitting parlor wondering what was keeping her. She was usually quite prompt when it came to lunch. One of the maids had brought our lunch tray but scurried off in a dither before I could question her.

When Sarah finally made an appearance, she was out of breath and her face was flushed with excitement.

"What happened?" I asked, spreading a napkin over my lap.

"You should have heard it. I've never heard of his lordship being so testy, especially with his sister," said Sarah, taking her place at the table.

"What did you hear?" Sarah had the frustrating habit of never coming directly to the point.

"Well, I didn't exactly hear it myself. It was one of the maids who overheard the argument. I can only repeat what she said. It may not be too accurate. You know how they can embellish a tale. But I'll give you the gist of it. The maid couldn't be too far off because it doesn't sound like something she would make up . . ."

"Oh, Sarah, do tell me what has you so excited."

"Oh, yes. Remember, I heard it second-hand." She took a sip of tea. "Well, it seems his lordship called his sister into the library directly after luncheon. I'll try to tell it just like the maid did.

"'What is all this?' he asks her.

"'They look like bills,' replies Mrs. Whitney. 'Why?'

"'I thought you were more prudent, Clara,' said his lordship.

"'They are not all mine, John.'

"'Then whose are they?'

"'Daphne ran a little short of money. I said it would be all right if she charged some items to your account. Sir Percy could pay you back when we came home. I see nothing wrong in that,' replied Mrs. Whitney.

"'Do you have any idea what the total is?'

"'No. I didn't watch her every purchase.'

"'It goes beyond extravagance. It is absolute squandering. How much did you spend on yourself, Clara?' his lordship asks, his voice becoming louder.

"'I believe it wasn't more than fifty pounds. You know I'm not a spendthrift, John.'

"The maid said his lordship's voice became low and menacing.

"'I have bills here totaling close to three hundred pounds. If you only spent around fifty, Daphne must have spent two hundred and fifty pounds. Good Lord, Clara. What did she buy?'

"'I know she bought a gown for the ball and the necessary items to go with it. Come to think of it, she did mention something about other gowns and frocks, but I never thought she purchased them. I thought she was talking about some she had seen. Oh, she did say something about needing a new riding habit for the hunt,' says Mrs. Whitney.

"'Don't you ever . . . ever let anyone, and that includes Daphne, charge to my account again. Do you understand me, Clara?'

"'Really, John. I don't see why you are talking to me about this. You should be talking to Sir Percy.'

"'I will in due time. In the meantime I want to make you fully aware of my wishes on the matter of the accounts or I shall limit you and Cecil to an allowance. Have I made myself clear, Clara?'

"'You always do, John.'

"The maid had to scoot away, for Mrs. Whitney was coming to the door. Can you imagine spending two hundred and fifty pounds on clothes in the course of a few days? Why, that would keep me for the rest of my life. The entire staff is talking about what they would do with that kind of money. Aside from me and Mr. Jackson, Cook gets the highest wage around here. About twenty pounds a year.

"Anyway, Mrs. Whitney whisks herself up the stairs and his lordship goes storming out of the house. A little later on, one of the footmen comes in the kitchen to ask what happened. He said his lordship was furious. He took his two mastiffs and went stalking off toward the moor. The footman said he had a mean look about him."

"Miss Lewis must have bought more than clothes for that kind of money," I said. I was appalled and agreed

179

with John. Daphne was squandering money.

Sarah shrugged. "It would seem so to me. But I can't imagine how she would spend it. Why, you can purchase a good cloak with a velvet facing for a little under seven pounds. Being an only child, I imagine Miss Lewis received everything she wanted when she wanted it. It probably gave her a lack of common sense when it came to money. Probably never handled money."

At dinner the conversation was brief and sporadic. I think everyone sensed the tension in the air. John made no attempt to conceal his foul mood. Sir Percy's face was more florid than usual, making his mutton chops appear whiter than normal. Only Daphne was oblivious to the uneasiness at the table. She tried to liven the conversation with silly comments about the shops in London compared to those in Dorchester.

John passed on the after-dinner port and went directly to his rooms. He didn't wait for the ladies to retire to the drawing room.

Seizing the opportunity, I told Jason I was not going to the drawing room and intended to get a book from the library. Jason expressed disappointment, but I sensed it was feigned. He appeared to have something else on his mind.

Midmorning, I removed my smock and went down to the library to return the book, a short novel that I had finished reading in one night. As I perused the titles for a longer novel, I could hear voices from the drawing room. There was no mistaking the voices of Clara and Cecil. They had a tendency to be loud.

"Sir Percy and Daphne are taking a picnic lunch. After lunch they are going to see how the work is progressing at

Foxhill Manor. Then they will proceed to Lady Plimpton's. Naturally, they have asked us to accompany them. It promises to be a jolly good time," said Clara.

"I couldn't possible make it, Clara."

"And why not?"

"I have sheaves of notes to transcribe and incorporate into my manuscript. It will take ages of concentrated work. Ask John to go with you. I'm sure Daphne would prefer his company to mine."

"John has already informed us he has other plans. I want you to come, especially if we are going to Lady Plimpton's for tea. She is such an old gossip. If I'm alone, she'll start tongues wagging," said Clara.

"Let her."

"Have you no consideration for me whatsoever, Cecil? All you ever think about is that silly manuscript of yours. I demand that you come with me today." Clara's voice was becoming shrill. I was sure the servants could hear it.

"Sorry. You know my work comes first. Do you think I enjoy being shut up in a stuffy room day after day, especially now that the weather is becoming pleasant?"

"You love it. You would do anything not to fulfill your husbandly duties. You shun all responsibility as though it were the deadliest of plagues," countered Clara with venom dripping on the end of each word.

"That's not true, Clara. Didn't I go to London with you and Daphne so you wouldn't be unchaperoned?"

"Hmph! You went with us all right. But once in London the only sight we had of you was at breakfast. After that you disappeared to sequester yourself in the British Museum or the library at London University. I certainly don't call that chaperoning us. For all intents and purposes you deserted us at every opportunity. I'm getting quite tired of your obsession with this book of yours. And, I might add, so is John. It is time you made some effort to contribute to the running of this household," declared Clara.

"Did John tell you to tell me that?" asked Cecil.

"He did mention something about putting us on a strict allowance."

"Hmm. Well, let him. I'm sure we could manage on my annuity."

"Manage? Only if we stopped eating, lived in the streets, and never bought another stitch of clothing."

"You are exaggerating, Clara. Besides you have enough clothes now to open your own dress shop."

"Cecil Whitney, I'm not about to give up my life here at Cheviot Chase because I have an idler for a husband."

"You won't think so harsh of me, Clara, when my history of the Romans in Britain is published."

"Published?" Her laugh was raucous. "Why, you will never get it written."

"I'm not about to stand here listening to your caterwauling, Clara. Your abusive insults will not deter me from pursuing my writing."

"Just a minute, Cecil. You haven't given me your promise to come with us today."

"I thought I made my position clear. I intend to spend the entire day sorting out the notes I took in London. There is nothing you can do or say that will dissuade me. Now I have work to do."

I heard the heavy tread of feet going up the staircase. I assumed they were those of Cecil Whitney. I selected a novel and was about to leave when John Rathbone stalked into the library.

"Janet. What are you doing here this time of day? I thought you worked all morning," he said.

"I usually do. I'm waiting for a canvas to dry before I apply another solvent. I thought I would use the time to return a book and get another one. I hope you don't mind," I explained.

"Certainly not. Jackson has rehung the paintings you

have finished and I must say they look splendid. Your father taught you well."

"Thank you. I enjoy the work."

"What else do you enjoy, Janet?"

"Someday I would like to try doing my own painting."

"Then why don't you?"

"Perhaps I will in the future." I couldn't tell him I had enough trouble trying to make a living without the added burden of purchasing oils and canvas.

His smile was enigmatic. "Did you get your book?"

"Yes."

"Then you'll excuse me. I have some paperwork to do." He went behind the desk and seated himself. "I'll see you at dinner."

I nodded and made a hasty exit.

After lunch with Sarah, I prepared for my usual walk. It was a fine day in late spring. As I padded down the corridor to the servants' staircase, I glanced out the window that encompassed a view of the rear courtyard with its lovely garden and the rear section of the East Wing. I could see workmen scurrying about the damaged rooms. I had heard the plasterers would soon finish and the painters would begin their tasks.

I was about to turn away and continued toward the back staircase when I saw Cecil emerge from the French doors of the drawing room. He had a black satchel in one hand and a burlap bag in the other. I watched him cross the courtyard and head for the lane. It seemed odd to me that he was leaving the house when I distinctly heard him tell Clara he would be working in his room all day. I continued to watch him trot down the lane. He was almost out of sight but I managed to note he took the path toward the moor. Why had he lied to his wife? Though I knew it was none of my business, curiosity impelled me to follow him.

I kept well behind him. In fact, so well behind I

sometimes lost sight of him. But I would rather lose him than have him find out I was following him.

He went to the same vicinity where I had first seen him digging. I had to duck down behind a random group of gorse when he threw his satchel and bag down, then looked around surreptitiously.

When I felt it was safe to watch his activities, I peered out from behind the bush. He was crouched down, and owing to the slope of the hill, I couldn't quite see what he was doing. I dashed to the cover of an ash tree, where I could stand and look down on him. Again he was digging a hole as if to bury something on the moor.

Suddenly I felt quite silly standing behind a tree like a spy. And like a spy, if I was caught the consequences might be serious. My work at Cheviot Chase might be in jeopardy. Knowing Cecil was fully occupied, I walked away as quickly as I could.

I was halfway back to the house when I spied a piece of cloth clinging to a thorn bush. It reminded me of the garment Lady Rathbone had worn. I wondered if she was out on the moor, hungry and miserable.

I went over and plucked the small piece of cloth from its thorny prison and looked around for a sign of her. There was a small stand of trees near the lane leading to the rear courtyard. I decided to see if she was there. Though I was frightened of her, my conscience wouldn't let me walk away if she was in trouble.

My head swiveled as I cautiously looked around while I was entering the coppice. Holding branches and bushy undergrowth aside, I walked slowly. My foot struck something. I looked down.

I had found Lady Rathbone.

Eleven

I pushed a shrub aside and my hand flew to my mouth to prevent an incipient scream from escaping. I now had a full view of Lady Rathbone.

There was no doubt in my mind she was dead. Thoroughly dead. Her throat had been ripped open as though by some wild beast. Her eyes bulged abnormally, while her tongue protruded from her mouth in a ghastly manner. Her face was spattered with blood as were her bosom and shoulders. A fetid odor swirled around her. Ravens sat patiently in a tree waiting for me to leave so they could resume picking at her throat.

I groped my way out of the coppice feeling ill. Once I reached the lane, I picked up my skirts and ran.

Reaching the manor house, I went up the front steps, pushed the front door open, and burst into the foyer. Mr. Jackson was entering the foyer from the dining room.

"Where is Lord Rathbone?" I gasped, my chest heaving from lack of breath.

"I believe he is at the stables, Miss Clarke. Is there anything I can do?" Mr. Jackson called after me as I had already dashed back toward the door.

"No." I went out the still open front door.

I found John in the stable yard kneeling to scratch

behind the ears of his mastiffs while he waited for his horse to be saddled. I came to an abrupt halt before him, my hand on my bosom as if it would stop its rising and falling. He got to his feet and stared at me in bewilderment.

"What is wrong, Janet?"

"You must come with me right away. I've found Lady Rathbone. I'm afraid she is dead." I blurted the words out.

I suppose it wasn't very considerate or compassionate of me to announce a death so curtly, especially when it was the man's wife. The shock had been so great, my mind wasn't functioning at a polite social level.

If he felt any emotion, he never showed it. His expression remained impassive. Even his eyes did not betray his feelings. The only thing I did detect on his handsome face was the throbbing of a vein at his temple.

"Where is she?" he asked.

"In a coppice. I'll take you there."

He walked over to a stable boy and said, "Never mind the horse, Jim. Get the cart ready immediately." He turned to me, cupped my elbow, and led me outside to wait for the cart. "Are you sure she is dead? Perhaps she was sleeping or ill."

"I'm quite sure, John. Her throat had been ripped open. There was blood all . . ." I started to tremble. The import of my findings had a delayed reaction on me.

"You're shaking. Perhaps you'd better stay here. I'll find it," said John.

"No. It will be quicker if I go with you. I'll be all right." I swallowed hard and forced myself to be calm. The only dead person I remember ever having seen was my father and he looked at peace with the world. The brutal death of Lady Rathbone was outside my experience.

When the cart was ready, John hoisted me up onto the

seat. Like a lithe animal, he was instantly on the same seat next to me. He snapped the reins and neither of us spoke until we were at the coppice.

"This way," I said, leading him through the fairly dense foliage.

When we reached the body, I recoiled and turned away. Not only had the rancid odor increased, but the ravens had been busy. Her throat was black with them. Two ravens had begun to peck at her bulging eyeballs while others busied themselves with nibbling away at her protruding tongue. The sight was beyond ghastly. It was ghoulish.

John went back to the cart and returned with the heavy tarpaulin he had brought to cover her body. He snapped it at the carnivorous birds. They noisily cawed their protest but he managed to disperse them away from the body. Some of the ravens sat expectantly in trees while others were brazen enough to strut around the body.

He quickly wrapped her up in the tarpaulin while I went back to the cart, fighting the rising nausea in me. I climbed up onto the seat. I closed my eyes as I heard John push the body into the rear of the cart. Again, silence ruled during our ride back to Cheviot Chase. Without a backward glance I left the stable yard. I heard John giving orders for someone to fetch the doctor and the constable.

I went directly to my bedchamber, sat at the small table near the window, and looked out. I couldn't stop the image of Lady Rathbone's body from dancing in my mind.

My thoughts tumbled over one another. I recalled how John had stalked off the other day. He had taken his mastiffs and headed for the moor. Could he have set those beasts on Lady Rathbone? Though my mind had conjured up the question, my heart refused to acknowledge or deal with it. It had to be some wild creature of the moor.

187

A notion kept tugging at the recesses of my mind. A most peculiar thought had fleetingly skittered through my brain when I first discovered Lady Rathbone. I tried to dredge it up. There was something very wrong with the scene. For the life of me, I couldn't remember what was odd about the sight of Lady Rathbone lying there.

A soft rap echoed on my door. Before I could rise to answer it, Sarah Herries came in.

"Oh, my poor dear," she said, coming to take the chair opposite me at the table. "It must have been dreadful for you. Being alone and finding the body like that. Simply awful. Can I get anything for you? Tea perhaps?"

"Maybe later. Right now I want to pull myself together. How did you find out so quickly? We just came back."

"A gust of wind lifted the tarpaulin. He told the stablemaster who, in turn, told one of the footmen. The footman told one of the maids. Well, you know how it goes, Janet. Anyway, it was said you were the one who found her ladyship's mutilated body. I thought I would come up straight away and see if there was anything I could do," said Sarah.

"Thank you, Sarah. I'm afraid there is nothing anyone can do."

"How did she die?" Sarah rested her arms on the table and leaned close, her large eyes wide with curiosity.

"I don't know. From what I could see, her throat had been torn open by some wild animals. It wasn't a pleasant sight, I assure you."

"Oh, dear me. Her throat, you say?"

I nodded. I didn't mention the ravens. Bad enough that I might have nightmares. I didn't want to pass them along to Sarah by giving her a vivid description of the scene.

"Well, I'll be blest. Was it greatly torn?"

"Quite."

Sarah shook her head dolefully. "Poor woman. Grant

188

you, before his lordship had her confined, she developed a wicked and mean streak. But to die like that. Dear me. And here we all thought she was safely tucked away in a London hospital. I wonder how long she's been roaming around here."

"I suspect she may have been the ghost that was thought to inhabit the East Wing," I said.

"Hmm." Sarah tapped her fingers on the table. "I'd better get downstairs and see that the maids attend to their duties instead of standing around gossiping. Why don't I have Annie bring up that cup of tea for you now?"

"That would be fine, Sarah."

When she left, I knew it wasn't to supervise the maids, but to tell Cook what she had learned from me. I continued to stare out the window. I hardly noticed Annie putting the tea tray on the table.

Sarah was right. The hot tea had a definite soothing effect on me. As it suffused me with its warmth, the scene in the coppice came back to me with a new clarity. I remembered what had struck me as odd at the time.

There were no marks on her arms, no scratches on her white hands. Surely if she had been attacked by wild animals, she would have fought to protect herself, at least put her arms and hands up defensively in an attempt to ward them off. It would have been a natural reflex. Yet her hands were free of any sign of defense. There should have been claw marks on both her hands and arms as she tried to free herself from the attack. And her frock should have been shredded in a life-and-death struggle. It puzzled me.

My musings were replaced by the sight of Brian Young driving his trap up to the front door. A man I had never seen before accompanied him.

An hour had passed when Annie arrived to collect the tea tray and inform me I was wanted in the drawing room.

Jason, Cecil, and the stranger stood when I entered.

John was already standing by the fireplace, his back toward it, his hands in back under his frock coat.

"Please sit down, Janet. Constable Andrews has a few questions he'd like to ask you," said John.

I took a seat, noticing the tall stature of the constable. His brow receded into brown hair which was liberally sprinkled with gray. He was clean-shaven and had a pleasant-looking face that was on the square side. Though he had the look of someone's kindly and benevolent uncle, there was a keen accusative glint in his dark brown eyes. I would have felt more at ease if Brian had been in the room. With the exception of John, the other three men had a way of looking at me as though I were a suspect, especially Cecil. With eyes narrowed, he stared at me. There was a touch of malice in his gaze, which caused me to wonder if he had seen me following him.

"Miss Clarke, I understand you were the one who discovered the body," said Constable Andrews.

"That's right, sir."

"Could you please tell me what made you go into the coppice?"

"I had seen a piece of cloth caught in a thorny bush. It looked very much like that of Lady Rathbone's frock."

"Oh? Had you seen Lady Rathbone before?"

"Yes."

"Where?"

"In a wood off the main road," I replied.

"And what were you doing in this wood?"

"I was on a picnic."

"Alone?"

"No. I was with Dr. Young."

"Did he see Lady Rathbone on that occasion?"

"No. He was asleep. I was exploring the brook when I happened upon Lady Rathbone. She was wearing a somewhat soiled white frock and cape."

"Surely there are many white frocks worn by women. What made you think that particular white scrap of cloth was that of Lady Rathbone's frock?"

"It was of a special muslin, not the type of cloth that would normally be used to make a day frock," I replied.

"I see. Why did that scrap of cloth prompt you to go into the coppice?"

"I had a feeling Lady Rathbone might be nearby and in distress. As I had a clear view of the surrounding area, I thought she might be in the coppice."

"Weren't you aware of her mental state and that she might be dangerous?"

"Yes. But I had a feeling she needed help."

"A feeling?" asked the constable.

"I don't know how to explain it, Constable Andrews. All I can say is I sensed something was wrong."

"By the way, what were you doing out on the moor in the first place?"

"I always go for a walk after lunch."

"I can vouch for that, Tom," said Lord Rathbone. "If the weather is fine, Miss Clarke takes a daily constitutional directly after lunch. She either strolls the moor or walks toward the coast."

"I see. After you discovered the body, Miss Clarke, what did you do?" asked Constable Andrews.

"I left the coppice as quickly as I could, then ran to fetch Lord Rathbone."

Constable Andrews nodded. "Lord Rathbone verifies that. He told me what happened next."

When Brian came into the drawing room, he tossed a smile at me. His countenance then became somber. He went up to John and said, "My condolences, Lord Rathbone."

John nodded, his demeanor complacent.

"Did you learn anything, Doctor?" asked Constable Andrews.

"Her ladyship was not killed by wild animals, Constable. She had been strangled with a piece of rope, then had her throat torn open." Brian turned to John. "I'm sorry, Lord Rathbone. I can only conclude your wife was murdered."

"Are you sure, Doctor?" asked the constable.

"There's no doubt in my mind. The back of her neck definitely reveals rope burns. Some rope fibers are imbedded in her skin."

"How do you explain her opened throat?"

"Some sort of instrument, I would say, did the deed," Brian replied.

"Not a wild beast?" asked the constable.

Brian shook his head. "Not a chance."

"Oh? What makes you so certain?" asked the constable, his sharp eyes narrowing.

"If it had been an animal with talons, the tearing of the flesh would have left cleaner cuts. The cuts on Lady Rathbone's neck were wide and jagged, certainly not those of sharp claws. And there were no other marks on her body. If she had defended herself against wild animals, there would have been signs of a struggle, cuts on her arms and face and so forth. Besides her face displayed the classic symptoms of strangulation," explained Brian.

"How long would you say she was dead?" asked the constable.

"Yesterday. Perhaps sometime around noon. But I can't be sure due to weather conditions. It has been unusually warm of late."

The constable turned his attention to John. "I shall need statements from everyone in the house regarding their whereabouts on the day in question."

"My sister, Sir Percy Lewis, and his daughter, Daphne, haven't returned from their sojourn at Foxhill. It will be a shock to them when they learn of my wife's brutal death. I doubt if they'll be able to collect their thoughts, Tom. I'm afraid we are all in a muddle now. Couldn't it wait until tomorrow?" asked John.

"Of course. What time tomorrow?" asked Constable Andrews.

"I shall make a point of having everyone gathered here by ten in the morning. Is that satisfactory?"

"Fine," replied the constable. "Now I would greatly appreciate it if you would take me to the coppice where the body was found, Lord Rathbone."

Constable Andrews braced his meaty hands on the arms of the chair and pushed himself out of it. He shook hands with the men and gave me a cursory nod, then followed John out of the drawing room.

"I could use a drink about now," said Jason as he went to the bell cord and pulled it. "Anyone else?"

"I'll have one," answered Cecil with a nervous frown twitching on his brow.

"Doc?" queried Jason, and received a nod. "Some sherry for you, Janet?"

"I believe I will, Jason." Even though Brian's announcement had explained my vague questions about Lady Rathbone's body, I experienced a sense of shock to learn she had been murdered.

Mr. Jackson materialized and Jason gave him the requests for drinks.

With a shaking hand, Jason made short work of his scotch and indicated to Mr. Jackson he wanted a refill. When his services were no longer required, Mr. Jackson left.

"Perhaps John's mood will lighten now," grumbled Cecil.

"Whatever do you mean, Cecil?" asked Jason. His hand was still shaking, and he had developed a slight tic at the corner of his mouth.

"He's wanted her dead for a long time. It's no secret he

wants to marry again and have an heir," said Cecil, staring at his scotch as if he wasn't quite sure what was in the glass.

"Are you insinuating John had something to do with Isobel's death?" asked Jason.

"I'm only stating the obvious. It wouldn't take much for those mastiffs of his to tear someone's throat apart. John has complete control of them," said Cecil.

"What a dastardly thing to think and say, Mr. Whitney. I thought I made it quite plain that the tears on Lady Rathbone's neck were not made by animals," said Brian.

"I don't see how you can be so sure, Dr. Young. By the time the ravens did their work, I can't imagine there would be such clear-cut evidence," retorted Cecil.

"How did you know about the ravens, Mr. Whitney?" I asked.

"John. He had to tell the constable why he moved the body," was Cecil's terse reply.

"I think your suggestion is scandalous, Cecil," said Jason.

"Who else would have a reason to see Isobel dead? You? Me? Come now, Jason. Be logical. Certainly no stranger would strangle Isobel on a lark," continued Cecil. "Murder requires motive. John is the only person with a motive. It is as simple as that."

"You seem to forget, Mr. Whitney, that Lady Rathbone was quite mad and wouldn't hesitate to attack a stranger on the slightest provocation. Someone could have been defending himself and accidentally killed her," suggested Brian.

"Really, Doctor. I doubt if you will be able to convince the constable of that," said Cecil.

"Does the constable suspect John?" I voiced my thoughts aloud unwittingly. I reddened when they all turned to look at me.

"I don't think the constable has any conclusive thoughts on the subject at this time," said Brian. His smile was reassuring.

"I do think Constable Andrews is going to start to wonder about John," said Cecil. "After all, no one really saw his first wife jump from that cliff. It could be she was pushed. Now his second wife dies under suspicious circumstances. Yes, indeed. I do believe the constable will thoroughly mull over the peculiar fatalities of John's wives." Cecil downed his scotch, then went to the sideboard to refill his glass before resuming his seat.

"After all John has done for you, Cecil, I should think you'd be more inclined to defend him," said Jason. "Instead you seem to relish the idea of condemning him as a murderer."

"John has done nothing for me except try to turn Clara against me," said Cecil.

"I think you are doing a good job of that yourself, Cecil. You can't deny he lets you live here and practically supports you," said Jason with a touch of venom.

"Clara was born here. It is as much her home as his. And it is common knowledge that I support Clara and myself on my annuity," countered Cecil.

"Perhaps that is why you are so eager to see John dragged away as a murderer. That would certainly clear the way for Clara to gain complete ownership of Cheviot Chase. Is that your intention, Cecil?" asked Jason.

"How absurd! You've always been a troublemaker, Jason. If I were you, I wouldn't be so quick to point an accusing finger at me. Without John's benevolence you would be walking the streets in rags. Ever since he married Isobel, you have been nothing more than a parasite leeching away at him," said Cecil, malice grumbling in his throat.

"Gentlemen. Please. There is a lady present,"

195

interrupted Brian.

"Janet knows what is going on around here. She is at the dinner table every night," said Jason. "If she doesn't know by now how things stand in this house, it is time she did." Jason turned to me with a silly grin. "You don't mind a little gentlemanly bickering, do you, Janet?"

I put my empty sherry glass on the low table before me and smiled. "I believe the sherry has had a relaxing effect on me. I think I need a brief rest before dinner. If you'll excuse me, gentlemen." I stood. As I was about to head for the door, Brian spoke.

"I'll go with you, Janet. It is time I got back to the village." He rose and cupped my elbow. When we reached the foyer, he said, "Walk me to my trap, will you?"

I nodded.

Outside, as we stood next to his trap, Brian said, "I hate to keep mentioning Lady Rathbone's body. It must have been horrible for you. Did you notice that only her neck bore marks?"

"Not at first. On reflection I recalled the matter."

"It was the first thing I noticed and it reinforces my belief the damage was not done by animals. Though I didn't mention it to the constable, it is my theory someone came up behind her, slipped the rope about her neck, and strangled her. It must have been done quickly for she didn't have time to put up much of a struggle. From the condition of her body, I'd say she was weakening from lack of food, which could also explain why she didn't fight her attack more vigorously. Do you believe what was said in the drawing room just now? That Lord Rathbone strangled his wife?"

"No."

"Mr. Whitney seems to think the case against Lord Rathbone is a sound and convincing one. Why do you think he didn't do it? Proof? Or instinct?"

"I suppose it is instinct. Why didn't he kill her ages ago when she was in the house and at the height of her madness? He could always say it was a matter of self-defense. But he put her out of reach in a London hospital. And how could he know she would escape? None of it makes sense to me."

"Who else would have reason to see her dead?"

I sighed. "I'm sure I don't know."

"Well, I suppose we'll have to let the constable sort it all out. When can I see you again? I promise I won't fall asleep."

"I don't know. I imagine everything will be at sixes and sevens around here for a while. Will you be at the funeral?"

"Yes. Being the family doctor, I feel it my duty," Brian replied.

"Why don't we talk about it then?"

He smiled. "All right. I hope we can get together soon."

"It's all so distressing," Clara exclaimed.

With the exception of John's announcing we were all to be in the drawing room at ten o'clock the next morning for the constable's questions, dinner had been cloaked in silence. At the sound of Clara's voice, everyone looked up as though an unexpected gong had clanged.

Clara's skin had taken on an unhealthy pallor. Her eyes were puffy as though she had been crying. I found it hard to believe Clara would cry over Lady Rathbone's demise. From what I had gathered, they hadn't been that close.

Though he presented a physical entity at the table, Cecil's mind and body seemed to be elsewhere. He appeared to be wrestling with a problem far beyond the confines of the dining room.

The tic at the corner of Jason's mouth had disappeared along with the trembling of his hands. But his troubled eyes darted about like a snared rabbit looking for an escape.

Only Sir Percy and Daphne remained unruffled.

"It is quite distressing to have a murder actually committed on the grounds of Cheviot Chase," said Sir Percy. "And now to be subjected to the inane questions of the local constable is positively humiliating to say the least. It makes us look like common criminals. I'm surprised you are going to allow it, John."

"It is routine, Sir Percy," said John. "It is a minor inconvenience, but I do believe in cooperating with the authorities. I want to see this thing cleared up and discover exactly how Isobel met her death. If it is murder, I want the murderer revealed."

"I still don't see why we should have to endure any interrogation," protested Sir Percy again. "Surely the man doesn't think any one of us is responsible for Isobel's murder."

"Sir Percy, couldn't you say death instead of murder?" asked Clara. "Murder sounds so dreadful."

"Murder is dreadful, my dear sister," said John.

"It must be such a relief for you, John, to have Isobel finally put to rest," said Daphne with a trace of a giggle in her voice.

"She was my wife and I loved her at one time," said John.

"I didn't mean . . . oh, John. I'm sorry Isobel is dead. Truly I am. But now you are free of that terrible responsibility. You won't have to worry about her anymore." Daphne's bow mouth settled into a childish pout while her eyelashes fluttered as if to implore forgiveness.

"What you mean, Daphne, is that now John is free to marry again," said Jason with a wry smile.

"You are a boor, Jason. You have all the manners of a hog digging for swill," cried Daphne, an angry heat causing her face to flush crimson.

"I wasn't aware you made a habit of watching hogs dig for swill, my dear Daphne," said Jason.

With lips still pursed in a pout, Daphne gave a shake of her blond curls and turned her attention to her father. "Father, do make him stop."

In a great grumble, Sir Percy cleared his throat. "Young man, this is not the proper time to display your insulting flippancy. I suggest you desist at once."

"And if I—" began Jason.

"Enough!" interrupted John. "I'll not tolerate asinine squabbling, especially when the occasion is a solemn one."

"Are you going to hold a funeral service for Isobel, John?" asked Clara.

"Of course. The funeral will be in three days. I'll make all the arrangements tomorrow. The sooner she is put to rest, the sooner we can put this tragedy behind us."

"Amen," said Jason, which brought stern glances from John.

Shortly after Jason's terse comment, dinner was over, much to my relief. I followed Daphne and Clara into the drawing room with the intention of having my tea then quickly departing to my rooms.

My plans were altered when Clara implored me to relate every detail about finding the body. Having my plans thwarted put me in a somewhat spiteful mood. In gruesome detail I described the scene and the grisly work of the ravens. Several times Clara winced and wrinkled her nose in horror. Daphne surprised me. The tale seemed to excite her and she listened with rapt attention. The men entered as I concluded.

*   *   *

The next morning everyone was in the drawing room well before the appointed hour. Daphne chattered incessantly about her lack of funeral attire. She moaned over the fact that it was much too late for her to go to London and purchase a proper and fashionable frock. Clara tried to soothe her by declaring she had an extra bonnet with a black veil. It did nothing to alleviate Daphne's lamentations. Mourning clothes posed no problem for me. I still had my frock and bonnet from my father's funeral.

Sir Percy kept pulling his watch from his vest and peering at the time. "Where the devil is that constable? Bad enough to have to endure his questioning, but not being prompt is adding insult to injury."

Jason was standing at the window looking out. "He is riding up now." He left the window and took a seat.

Again Cecil was quiet; his dismembered spirit roamed elsewhere. I remembered how loquacious he was the previous day when John took the constable to the coppice. I wondered why Cecil was always so taciturn in John's presence. Mr. Jackson ushered the constable in and my mental wanderings came to a halt.

The constable took a seat which faced all of us, then scrutinized each face with sharply narrowed eyes. His gaze could have wilted the hardiest of flowers.

"Shall we begin?" he asked.

Twelve

"I hope this won't take long, Constable," grumbled Sir Percy.

"I shouldn't think so," said Constable Andrews.

"I don't see how you can suspect anyone here," added Sir Percy.

"No one is above suspicion where murder is involved, Sir Percy," said the constable impatiently. "Now if we can get directly to it, I hope to conclude my questioning within the hour."

"Hmph," muttered Sir Percy.

"Mrs. Whitney, where were you on the day before yesterday?" asked the constable.

"I was in the house all day. Daphne—Miss Lewis—and I had just returned from a shopping trip in London. I was quite busy sorting everything out and putting the items away. I believe Miss Lewis was engaged in the same occupation," said Clara.

"Miss Lewis can speak for herself," rebuked the constable. "I take it you were in your rooms all day."

"Well, not all day. After breakfast I was with my brother in the drawing room. Then I went up to my bedchamber until lunch. After lunch I rested for an hour or two then went to Daphne's bedchamber to admire her purchases."

"Can anyone vouch for your presence in the house for the entire day? Your husband perhaps?"

Clara gave Cecil a scathing glance. "My husband was secluded in his workroom and becomes quite distraught if anyone disturbs him. I'm sure the servants can attest to my being in the house for the entire day."

"I see. Mr. Whitney, your wife claims you were working in your room that day. Is this true?" asked the constable.

"Yes."

"Can anyone corroborate that?"

Cecil shrugged. "I don't know."

"Did you come down for lunch?"

"No. I often have a tray left outside my room when I'm working. Interruptions can destroy one's train of thought," replied Cecil.

Constable Andrews compressed his lips, turned his large hand up, and stared at his palm as though his questions were written there. "And where were you on that day, Sir Percy?"

"I was in bed suffering from painful lumbago."

"Did you come down for lunch?"

"Sir, when one is in pain, one does not think of food. No. I did not come down for lunch."

"Did servants attend you while you were confined to your bed?"

"No. I cannot tolerate people trouncing around the room. It increases the pain."

"Miss Lewis, did you look in on your father anytime during that day?"

"No. Should I have done, Constable?" Her blue eyes opened wide as though confronted by the unthinkable.

"Weren't you concerned for your father's welfare?"

"Father doesn't like to be disturbed when he isn't feeling well. Besides I had so much to do and London had been exhausting," replied Daphne.

The constable turned back to Sir Percy. "Then no one can really verify you were confined to your bedchamber, Sir Percy."

"Sir, I take offense at your insinuation. I can verify it. My word should be sufficient," boomed Sir Percy.

Constable Andrews's eyebrows rose. A barely audible sigh of exasperation escaped his lips and he turned to Jason. "Can you account for your time, Mr. Watson?"

"Pretty much. I rode into the village and arrived at the pub shortly before noon. Played darts. Ate lunch. Then entered into a game of cards before leisurely riding back to Cheviot Chase. I'm sure the men in the pub will verify that," said Jason with a smug smile.

"I'll make it a point to talk to them. And you, Lord Rathbone?"

"After breakfast I went to the library to do some paperwork. When I heard my sister in the drawing room, I went to speak to her. Our conversation took an unpleasant turn and I left to take a walk and calm my thoughts."

"A walk where, Lord Rathbone?"

"On the moor."

"Alone?"

"Not quite. I had Romulus and Remus with me."

"Romulus and Remus?" queried the constable.

"My dogs."

"Ah, yes. The mastiffs. Did you return in time for lunch?"

"No."

"Then you have no substantial alibi."

"I wasn't aware I would need one," replied John.

"I see. And you, Miss Clarke?"

"I spent the morning working on the paintings, then—"

"Working on paintings?" interrupted the constable.

"I was hired by his lordship to clean and restore a

number of his paintings," I explained.

"I see. Do go on."

"I routinely had lunch with Mrs. Herries. I went for my usual walk after lunch for an hour or an hour and a half. I walked to the chalk downs, where I could view the sea from the cliffs. When I returned I went back to my room and work. No one saw me and I didn't see anyone," I said.

Constable Andrews nodded his head. "From what everyone has said, I conclude that Mr. Watson, Miss Lewis, and Mrs. Whitney are the only ones with credible alibis."

"What are you insinuating, sir?" asked an irate Sir Percy.

"I'm not insinuating anything, Sir Percy. I am only attempting to ascertain everyone's whereabouts and clarify the events in my mind." Constable Andrews stood abruptly. "Lord Rathbone, I would like to talk to the staff, if I may."

"Certainly." John rose and went to the bell cord. "Jackson will escort you."

"Thank you."

"Well, that wasn't so bad," proclaimed Jason, rising to his feet. "I think I'll have me a good gallop. Anyone care to join me?"

Cecil and Sir Percy rose in unison, cast a disdainful glance at Jason, then left the room.

"I have to go into the village and make the necessary arrangements," declared John. Aside from being handsome of face and form, he was an elegant man. As he walked across the drawing room, his step was agile and quick, indicating a reserve of power.

Daphne watched him go, her eyes full of lust. I really couldn't blame her. John was a very desirable man.

Without a word, I went to my workroom and directed all my efforts to cleaning a painting. I didn't want to think about the murder of Lady Rathbone. I used every facet of my mental powers to ignore what was lurking in the dark recesses of my mind. Lord John Rathbone was the only person who had a strong motive and the opportunity to murder his wife.

The slate sky promised a steady rain. As if to tease the earth, a mist hovered in the damp air. Smoke from the chimney pots of distant cottages spiraled in an upward struggle through the thick, soggy air. Nature seemed to abet the overwhelming pall already created by the impending funeral of Lady Rathbone.

The black catafalque, containing the coffin, was drawn by two black horses with black plumes adorning the tops of their heads and led the cortege to the church.

I rode in a small closed carriage with Sarah and Mr. Jackson. The carriages of the family, the Lewises, and Jason preceded us.

"I'll be glad when this day is over," said Sarah. "Perhaps the gossip will die down and everything will return to normal."

"What gossip?" I asked.

"Surely you have heard the servants twittering in the corridors. Why, their talk has been positively outrageous. Mr. Jackson has been at sea trying to stop their vicious prattle, haven't you, Mr. Jackson?"

A stiff, curt nod of the head was his reply.

Sarah went on. "I, myself, have been doing my best to bring such nonsense to a halt, especially when they talk in my presence. Goodness gracious! I've never heard such poppycock in all my life. I'd give a month's wages to know who started the wicked and idle talk. Mind you, I don't believe one word of it. Still, wherever there is water, there has to be a source."

"Sarah," I began, trying not to show my exasperation.

"Whatever are you talking about?"

"Why the rumors, of course."

"What rumors?"

"About his lordship." She looked at me as though I had initiated the topic.

"Sarah, do be precise and tell me what they are saying about his lordship."

"That he is really the mad one. That he made his wives appear mad then did them in by setting those mastiffs on them. They are saying he ordered those beasts to attack his first wife, and when she ran, he directed the dogs to chase her off the cliff. As for Lady Rathbone, he commanded the dogs to tear her throat out."

"Really, Sarah. Of all the absurd notions, that is absolutely ridiculous. Dr. Young is positive Lady Rathbone was strangled, then some instrument was used on her throat to make it appear as if the dogs had done it. You can't possibly believe for an instant that his lordship could commit such a heinous act."

Sarah looked thoughtful for a moment. "Doctors have been known to be wrong on occasion. You have to admit it is peculiar the way he stalks the moor with only his mastiffs for company. And why does he put up with the likes of those leeches?"

"Leeches?" I asked.

"Sir Percy and that puff-headed daughter of his, Jason Watson, and Cecil Whitney. Not one of them has done a lick of real work in their lives. His lordship is not a foolish man. He must realize they are taking advantage of his generosity. Why would he allow them to bleed him if he wasn't a bit—"

"Mrs. Herries!" admonished Mr. Jackson.

"Don't say it, Sarah," I said. "He is our employer. We should foster nothing but loyalty regarding his lordship." I had more than loyalty toward John Rathbone. I was becoming more in love with him as the days passed even though I realized how hopeless it was.

"You are right, Janet. I'm sorry," said Sarah with a sigh.

"After all, Cecil Whitney's wife is his lordship's sister. Sir Lewis and his daughter are neighbors and, I understand, good friends. As for Mr. Watson, I believe he was of great help to Lady Rathbone when she needed a friend. His lordship probably feels he is repaying a debt," I said in defense of John.

"I have my doubts about Mr. Watson having an altruistic nature. It has been said that he was Lady Rathbone's lover before she married his lordship. When she started acting peculiar, he turned his amorous attentions to Mrs. Whitney. He left her when Miss Lewis caught his fancy. That's why there is bad blood between Mrs. Whitney and Mr. Watson," said Sarah.

I gave a slight shake of my head and smiled. "I can see rumors abound at Cheviot Chase."

Sarah shrugged. "Rumors are not plucked from thin air, Janet. I don't think it wise for you to be alone with his lordship. He has a way of putting the ladies under his spell. Take care, Janet, and heed my words. If the hunt and the ball are still to be held, you will see for yourself the power he exerts over women."

The look on Mr. Jackson's face was one of utter disgust. I said no more as the church came into view. But I wondered what Sarah would think if she knew I was already under John Rathbone's spell.

The church services were mercifully brief. The cortege headed back to Cheviot Chase and the private cemetery some distance from the manor house. As the reverend began a concluding prayer, the sky opened its dark clouds and the rain pelted down in large drops. Great black umbrellas were snapped into position then assumed a place over the heads of the mourners.

I looked around at the visible faces of the men. I saw no

real grief on any of them. My stomach knotted when my gaze came to rest on John's face. There was a shadowy smile on his lips. For a brief instant, the thought that the gossip might have some basis in fact flickered through my mind. Was he not at all the man he appeared to be? I was thankful my face was hidden behind a veil. I was sure John would have discerned the momentary doubt in my eyes as he was looking straight at me. I quickly shifted my eyes to the lowering casket.

I caught a glimpse of Daphne when we returned to the house. During the funeral I hadn't noticed what she was wearing. Now I did. Instead of a borrowed, and perhaps out-of-date, mourning frock, she had donned a very fashionable dark blue taffeta frock with a multitude of flounces. I indulged in a small knowing smile.

While Sarah supervised the setting out of a repast for the mourners who came back to Cheviot Chase, I went up to my rooms. Lady Rathbone's funeral had reminded me of my father's funeral. I wanted to be alone.

I stood at the window in my bedchamber for several minutes. The torrential rain had spent itself, leaving uncertain droplets to find a place to rest. Dark clouds scudded before an increasing breeze. When the lowering sun finally dominated the sky and sent its shafts of light into my room, I decided to work, knowing absorption in a task would chase any sad thoughts from my mind. I studied the painting lying horizontally on the table. I had cleaned it of its surface grime and examined the extent to which the accumulated dirt had become imbedded in the varnish. Even with the surface dirt removed, the painting still presented a dark brown color to the eye. I had no choice but to remove the varnish if the painting was to have its true color restored.

I poured some alcohol and turpentine into a small china bowl, plucked a wad of cotton from my supply, then dipped it into the solution. After squeezing it until it was moist, I began to remove the varnish with small circular motions. I had to go slowly to make sure I removed only the varnish and not the paint.

I was so engrossed in my work that I barely heard the light rapping on my door. The door opened and the tread of a booted foot on the bare wooden floor caught my attention. I turned to face my visitor.

"Why aren't you downstairs enjoying the excellent food and drink?" asked Jason. "I'm sure John wouldn't approve of your working today of all days."

"Funerals depress me. It hasn't been too long since I buried my father. I find working helps," I replied.

"Well, this funeral has lightened John's mood. He's being quite jolly down there. Jolly for John, that is. That man always seems to have a demon eating away at him."

"He appears to be a patient and understanding man to me."

"It is a facade, believe me. John is a brooding, sullen man given to violent and sudden outbursts of temper. With John, I get the feeling there's a latent, but dangerous, power beneath the surface ready to erupt."

I smiled. I didn't dare defend John lest my true feelings about him emerge.

Jason sauntered toward me and, in a lowered voice, said, "I daresay you've heard the rumors about him."

"Rumors?" I feigned ignorance.

"Really, Janet. Sometimes you baffle me. You must have heard the servants talking. They think that because he so desperately wants an heir, he has gone dotty. Isobel, in her condition, was incapable of producing a child. With the care she was receiving at the hospital, she could have gone on for years. Now he is free to take a wife who will bear him children."

"You don't really believe he is capable of killing anyone, do you, Jason?" I could understand the servants indulging in idle gossip as a means of entertainment. But

209

I was stunned and disappointed that a person of Jason's ilk could believe that nonsense.

He shrugged and flipped his hand back and forth. "One never knows what another person is capable of when he is being thwarted beyond endurance. John is a powerful man and knows every facet of the moor. Frankly I don't blame him if he did kill Isobel. I might have done the same thing in his position."

"Those are terrible words to say, Jason, much less think. I'll entertain no more on the subject." I turned back to my work.

He came to stand behind me and peer over my shoulder. "Are you still only cleaning them?"

"I'm removing the varnish."

"Aren't you afraid you will remove the painting itself?"

"One has to exercise extreme caution."

"I don't see why you don't take a pail of soap and water and scrub them clean," Jason suggested.

"The canvas is sized with glue, creating a layer between the canvas and the painting. Using water on the surface of the painting, which may have fissures for the water to seep through, would tend to dissolve the glue, causing the painting to lift from the canvas. I want to restore paintings, not destroy them."

"I guess there is more to what you do than I originally thought. Have you ever removed part of the painting while removing the varnish?"

"Only when I was learning the art. Why do you ask?"

"Sheer curiosity. I see there is a little white circle down in the far corner. It looks like you reached the bare canvas there. A test or a mistake?"

"Neither. I admit it is most peculiar. I have no idea who did it. And this isn't the only canvas that has a white circle. All the others stacked against the wall there have also been defaced in that manner."

Jason walked over to the stack of paintings and gave them a cursory glance as he flipped through them. "So they have. As you said, most peculiar." He walked back to me. "Are you sure I can't persuade you to come downstairs? Food is abundant and quite tasty."

"Sorry. But I do appreciate your thinking of me."

"I'll see you later then, Janet." Jason ambled to the door, waved, then popped out, closing it quietly behind him.

I never ceased to be fascinated by the moor, especially now that spring was sliding into summer. Wild flowers opened their buds displaying species that were alien to a city-bred woman like me. I felt the demise of Lady Rathbone now made the moor safe for me to roam. John's warnings were based on his fear of his mad wife stalking about the bleak stretch of land. I was sure he would have no objection now.

I had always enjoyed the works of Ann Radcliffe and the American writer Edgar Allan Poe. As a child I voraciously read all their works I could find. I was especially fascinated by Mary Shelley's *Frankenstein*. Much to the dismay of my father, I would lie abed at night and read them. Though he didn't approve of that type of fiction, preferring I read history, he never made me desist. He believed that reading any book was better than not reading at all.

Perhaps my proclivity for reading tales of terror as a child inculcated in me a sense of the macabre, for one day, as I walked the moor, my feet began to trudge toward the coppice where I had found the body of Lady Rathbone. I tried to find some rationale for so ghoulish an act. But there was none.

Reaching the coppice, I went directly to the scene of the brutal murder. The ravens were gone. What birds were there fled at my noisy approach. I think I expected the place to be sinister or exude a sense of violence. It didn't. It was a simple coppice where nature exhibited its dominance.

I was about to make my way toward the lane leading back to Cheviot Chase when something caught my eye. I bent down to examine it. It was a black button from a man's riding coat. It is a wonder I spotted it as there was a good deal of nature's debris strewn about the ground. I suspect it was the depth of its blackness and perfectly round shape that made it stand out to my artistically trained eye. I picked it up and studied it.

The button was common to many men's riding coats and therefore held no great import. I stood and slipped it into my deep skirt pocket. A set of low growls behind me quickened the flow of blood in my veins and paralyzed me. I knew they were the mastiffs, at least I hoped they were. I could only pray John was with them.

With mincing steps and keeping my body rigid, I managed to turn around without too much movement. Romulus and Remus were in a crouched position ready to attack. Their ears were back and upper lips were raised to bare sharp, strong teeth. John was nowhere in sight.

"Good boys . . . nice boys," I said in my sweetest, calmest voice. I kept repeating the words, then garnered enough courage to extend my hand, palm up.

They eyed me warily, but their lips lowered. First one stood in a normal position, then the other. Their ears perked up as I continued to speak soothingly to them while continuing to hold my hand out.

Finally one of the dogs became bold enough to pad toward me and sniff my hand. I swallowed hard and used every bit of willpower I had to hold my hand still, even though images of it being bitten off danced in my mind.

He lifted his large black head to scan my face with his black eyes as though he was having difficulty in making up his mind to trust me.

I cautiously turned my hand over. I held my breath as I reached down to stroke the top of his head. I slowly released that breath when I saw his tail wagging. It wasn't long before the other mastiff came up to me, offering his head for an affectionate pet.

I was soon down on my haunches. Both my hands were busy as I stroked heads and both tails wagged. I talked to them in a stream of soothing words. They seemed to enjoy the sound of my voice.

Suddenly they moved back from me and sat.

"I see you have conquered the unconquerable, Janet." John's deep, rich voice reverberated through the coppice.

I stood and turned around. "They are of a mood to be friendly today."

"Why did you come here of all places?"

I shrugged. "Impulse."

"A rather morbid impulse, wouldn't you say?"

"I suppose so."

"Then why?"

I briefly explained my penchant for reading horror stories as we strolled out of the coppice back toward the lane, the dogs at our heels.

"What were you hoping to achieve?" asked John.

"I don't know. Nothing, I suppose."

"Don't tell me you have added sleuthing to your many accomplishments."

I laughed. "Hardly. I'm sure the constable has everything under control. I appreciate your comment about my having many accomplishments, but I fear you are overrating me. I lack many of the skills valued in women. Music ability, needlework, and the like."

"I'm sure you could master them if you put your mind to it. See how easily you made friends with Romulus and Remus."

"To be honest, I never thought I would be able to do that. They have always appeared ferocious whenever I saw them."

"At the time they sensed your fear of them. They are quite friendly if you give them a chance. Are you aware the East Wing is almost completed?"

"I assumed it was almost completed when I saw the painters leave. What is left to be done?"

"Cleaning some rugs and furniture. I am awaiting new items to replace the burned furniture and sundries. I have apprised the vendors of the necessity of the items reaching Cheviot Chase before the end of the month. I'll need the rooms for guests if there is to be a ball and hunt. I suppose you think it callous of me to hold such festivities so soon after my wife's death."

"It is not my place to sit in judgment of you."

"Too bad you are not a man, Janet. You would have been an asset to our diplomatic corps." He looked up at the sky as though all the sages of antiquity had written the solutions to human problems there. "My wife, Isobel, has been dead for a long, long time as far as I am concerned. Her actual death and funeral were merely delayed reality. I had been drained of all emotion some time ago regarding Isobel. There is nothing left. I thought the hunt and the ball would restore some normalcy to my life." He sighed deeply. "I seem to burden you with talk of myself whenever we are alone. What about you? How is the restoration work coming?"

"Quite well. I shouldn't be much longer in completing the work," I replied with confidence.

"There are more paintings from the East Wing. I believe their condition is fairly sound as they were painted within the last ten years. But they are rather sooty. I would appreciate your working on them immediately as I would like to put them back in the East Wing before any guests arrive. I shall have Jackson bring them to your workroom. Will it upset your schedule?"

"Not at all. Is the portrait of Lady Rathbone one of them?" I gathered my lower lip between my teeth the minute the question slipped out. I didn't mean to voice my thoughts aloud. A vein at his temple throbbed. His expression became grim and brooding. I instantly regretted asking the question. I could almost feel the drop of a barrier between us shattering the earlier mood of open friendliness.

"It was destroyed," was his terse reply.

The silence between us deepened and his pace quickened as the manor house came into view.

We were several yards from the front door when Daphne came flouncing out and down the steps. She was dressed in a fluffy frock of pale yellow tulle with white daisies embroidered on it. She clutched at her matching parasol. I had to admit she looked quite fetching, feminine, and vulnerable. I felt like a drab spinster in my gray linen skirt and starched white blouse. The minute she spied us, she lifted her skirts with one hand and came running toward us.

"Oh, John. Where have you been?" she asked, lowering her parasol and throwing herself against him, one arm clinging to his shoulder. "It is awful."

"Here, here, Daphne," soothed John, pushing her from him and holding on to her upper arms. "What has you so distraught?"

"It is father. His lumbago has taken a turn for the worse." There seemed to be a sob in her throat, but there wasn't a hint of tears in her eyes.

"Why didn't you send one of the lads for the doctor?" asked John, dropping his hands.

"I didn't think you'd want me ordering your servants about," she replied, looking wistful.

I wanted to laugh out loud. Many a time I heard Daphne give orders to the staff when John wasn't around, especially the maids. And she was less than courteous about it. However, it was not my place to revive her memory regarding her treatment of the servants.

"Let me take the dogs to the stables, then I'll see to your father," said John.

"Never mind the dogs. You must come now. I'm afraid he'll have an attack of some sort," pleaded Daphne as only she could.

"I'll take the dogs to the stables," I offered.

John looked at me with that one eyebrow raised imperiously. "Do you think you can?"

"Oh, let her, John. My father is more important than those silly old dogs of yours," said Daphne, shutting her parasol and putting a possessive arm through John's. "Please come to the house now."

"Come along, Romulus, Remus," I urged softly as I edged toward the stable yard. To my surprise they followed me as Daphne pulled John in the opposite direction.

My ego greatly inflated when the dogs followed me into the stable yard instead of racing after their master. That ego was quickly deflated when the dogs went bounding toward the crouched stablemaster.

"Come on, lads. You know where your home is, don't you?" said Thomas Irons, the stablemaster. The dogs threw themselves into his outstretched arms as he petted and fondled them. He looked up at me.

"Where is his lordship?" he asked, rising to his feet.

"Miss Lewis required his presence in the house immediately. Evidently her father has taken a turn for the worse. I seem to have developed a rapport with the dogs so I told his lordship I would take them to the stable for him," I replied.

"I'm surprised they have taken to you, Miss Clarke. They don't care for women too much. Like to keep themselves in the company of men," said Thomas Irons.

"Any particular reason?"

"Lady Rathbone hated them. She'd be taking a riding crop to them whenever they came around her. I think she was afraid of them but wouldn't admit it. Rest her soul."

"Were the dogs afraid of her?" I asked, reaching down to pat a black head as one of the mastiffs nudged my skirt.

"These dogs are afraid of no one. I'm thinking they would have liked nothing better than to tear Lady Rathbone apart. Rest her soul."

"Do you think they are capable of killing a human being?"

"Aye. That I do. If a person doesn't have a weapon, that is. Would you care to have a look at the horses, miss?"

"Yes. I think I'd like that."

glad when these days are behind us and everything is back to normal.

Thirteen

Sarah Herries was waiting for me when I entered her sitting parlor to have our lunch. She looked haggard and weary. I put on my best smile and sat down.

"The blue gown is beautiful and fits perfectly," I said. "You certainly would be a much-sought-after seamstress in London, Sarah. Not only would the aristocrats seek your services, but, I daresay, you would be summoned by royalty itself."

Her face brightened and a flush of roses spread on her cheeks. Still, tired lines remained around her mouth and eyes.

"You had a lot to do with the sewing. I still appreciate the flattery, but I hardly think royalty would be demanding my services as a seamstress, Janet."

I studied her for a moment. "What is it, Sarah? You look a might peaked. Are you ill?"

"Lord, no. Tired. That's all. Getting everything ready for the hunt, the ball, and guests has worn me sorely, especially having to deal with new chambermaids. They are not familiar with the manor house and it seems I have to be everywhere to instruct them. And Cook is having a time with the new scullery girls. She rattles on to me about her burdens, which I am of no mind to hear. But I guess she has no one else to listen to her troubles. I'll be glad when these days are behind us and everything gets back to normal. Sometimes I think I'm living in a madhouse. Of course, Mr. Jackson is of no help. He is more of a valet to his lordship than an aid in directing the staff. That burden is entirely in my hands."

"I wish there was some way I could help you, Sarah."

"You are a help by not demanding anything. Every time I have a parlor or chamber maid set about her duties, Miss Lewis countermands my orders and has the maid tend to her personal needs."

"I thought she had her own maid."

"She has, but her personal maid only tends to her hair and toilette. She orders my maids to see to her other needs. Tea and biscuits at odd hours. Personal laundry. God forbid if something isn't ironed just the way she wants it. The regular staff knows how to take care of her whims without disrupting the order of things. But she has these new girls at sixes and sevens.

"At times Sir Lewis is no better. He can be quite grumpy when the lumbago is on him. He demands food at strange hours when he is abed. Between you and me, Janet, I'll be glad when Sir Lewis and his daughter are gone from this house. I believe the entire staff feels the same way. I often wonder about his attacks of lumbago. I'll wager he won't have an attack during the hunt and ball."

"Whatever his illness is, it hasn't affected his appetite," I said. "At the dinner table last night he ate enough for three men."

"From what I hear, he does equally well at breakfast and lunch. If he didn't eat so much, perhaps he wouldn't have lumbago, or whatever it is," commented Sarah. "Out of curiosity, next time you see Dr. Young, why don't you ask him the precise nature of Sir Lewis's ailment? Do you expect to see him soon? I know he was called in to examine Sir Lewis the other day."

"I expect to see him on Sunday. There is to be a church bazaar in the village," I replied.

"How exciting."

"Would you care to come with us?"

"Good gracious, no. I'll be much too busy." In detail, she told me about all the chores that had to be done.

When lunch was over, I rose to leave, saying, "If there is anything I can do to help you, Sarah, do let me know. I'd be only too happy to assist you after all you have done for me."

She waved a hand of friendly dismissal.

As I walked down the corridor to the servants' staircase, out of habit, I looked out the window toward the East Wing. My peripheral vision caught a figure moving through the back courtyard. Cecil Whitney again, satchel in one hand, a burlap bag in the other.

I went down the staircase and opened the door that led to the rear courtyard's garden. Not in the mood for a walk, I sat on the bench facing the water fountain. I breathed deeply of the fresh air flavored with the scent of flowers. The aroma of lavender was especially robust.

My thoughts soon strayed to Cecil Whitney and his clandestine treks to the moor. He was always so adamant about not having his manuscript read, I wondered if he was burying sections of it on the moor. It seemed a silly thing to do. But then to devote one's entire life to the Romans in Britain to the exclusion of everything and everyone else wasn't the height of rationality. I began to wonder if there wasn't something in the Rathbone character that made them choose unsuitable mates. And judging from John's willingness to extend the stay of Sir Percy and his enticing daughter, I had the suspicion Lord John Rathbone was about to make another wrong decision regarding a future wife.

"Janet."

His voice had the power to churn up my insides like a

newly formed whirlpool. I turned in my seat to watch him come toward me, his stride lithe yet strong and powerful. Looking at him made me swallow hard.

"What are you doing here? I though you usually went for a walk after lunch," said Lord John Rathbone.

"I thought it would be nice to sit here for a change, smelling and looking at the beautiful flowers while the sound of trickling water in the fountain provided its special music. How did you know I was here?"

"I was supervising the furniture delivery in the East Wing and happened to look out the window. I was surprised to see you sitting here. I thought I would come down and see how you are making out with the soot-covered paintings."

"I hope to finish them soon. As you intimated, with the exception of the soot, they are in good condition."

"Let me know when you are finished. I'll send Jackson for them."

"Were there any problems with the furniture?" I asked.

"No."

"Did they bring everything you ordered?"

He smiled. "Yes. They did. Would you care for a tour of the newly refurbished East Wing?"

"I'd like that." I stood. He cupped my elbow and steered me to the French doors of the drawing room.

"Thomas Irons told me he gave you a tour of the horse stables. Did the horses frighten you?"

"At first. They are so huge. But Mr. Irons gave me some sugar lumps and showed me how to feed them to one particular horse, a chestnut mare. He had me stroke her nose. After that any fear I had disappeared," I replied.

"Would you like to learn how to ride?"

"I don't think I'm ready for that. Besides I wouldn't have much use for horseback riding in the city."

"Why not? There are a number of bridle paths in the parks of London."

"You forget, Lord—"

"John. Remember?" he interrupted.

"John. I am a working woman. I could never afford the clothes or the fees to go riding in Hyde Park."

We walked through the drawing room, into the foyer, and up the stairs to the second level of the East Wing. The other levels were undamaged.

"I think you would enjoy riding, Janet. I'll speak to Irons about giving you some lessons. Surely you can spare some time after lunch."

"It is not a question of time. I don't have the proper attire."

"What you are wearing now is suitable. One doesn't need fancy riding habits to become an accomplished horsewoman. Are you sure it is not fear that holds you back?"

I may say what I like about my courage, or lack of it, but it cut to the core of my being to have John think I was a coward. "I am not afraid."

"Then prove it by accepting my offer." His cat green eyes sparkled mischievously.

"I will."

"Good. You'll find it will give you more freedom to explore the estate once you have mastered the rudiments. It would be near impossible to see all of the estate by walking. Ah! Here we are."

The doors leading to the East Wing—which had always been locked—now stood wide open. The walls and ceiling of the long corridor were festooned with plastered curlicues and a variety of flora. The corridor was painted in white, cream, and a light tan. The sun streaming in from the row of large windows marching down the hall made one feel bathed in a dazzling light.

John escorted me from room to room. For the most

part, they were bedchambers done in light colors. As an example, one bedchamber was painted in a pale green and cream with gold gilt touching up the highlights. The furnishings in the rooms were tasteful and artful, unlike the heavy, dark, and cluttered decor that was fashionable during those Victorian times. We ended up in the drawing room, which ran the entire width of the wing. I looked around with pleased wonder at the transformation.

"Sit down, Janet, and tell me what you think," urged John, taking a seat himself.

I sat down on a cushioned sofa which was covered with a light, gaily printed chintz.

"Lovely. What more can I say?"

"Then you like what I have done with the East Wing?"

"You did it?"

"Not exactly. A designer from London selected the materials and furniture. But I did express what I desired. The dark, oppressive damask on the walls and the massive, cumbersome furniture that filled these rooms before, I found dreary, graceless, and utterly somber. I think this is far more restful and pleasing. Do you agree?"

"Yes. Certainly. It is like walking and being in a world of light where only the ethereal reigns. I find the refurbishing more than pleasing. It is . . . well, it is soothing yet cheerful at the same time."

"I know what you mean. I am thinking of doing the entire manor in this vein."

"That would be quite an undertaking, wouldn't it?"

"Yes. But I think it would be worth it. Shall we go back? I don't want to keep you from your work too long."

We rose and sauntered back along the corridor. As we came to the section that branched off to the main part of the house, Clara was coming down the corridor from the other direction. When she saw us, her jaw sagged and her eyes widened in astonishment. She looked at John then gave me an icy glare before returning a gaze laden with suspicion to John.

"I was showing Janet the East Wing, Clara," he said indifferently.

"Oh?"

Her glance was cool. I thought I saw a trace of malice in her eyes. She made me feel as though I had committed an indecent act.

"If you'll excuse me, I have work to do," I said before walking away.

"Don't forget about tomorrow. Irons will be waiting for you," John called after me.

The next afternoon, I donned my dark linen skirt, white blouse, and walking boots. It was too warm for a jacket. I trudged into the stableyard like a somnabulist approaching the hangman's rope. I was sure I would never live to see another dawn.

Mr. Irons tugged at the visor of his cap when he saw me. I nodded and forced a smile. Fear had paralyzed my vocal cords. He went into the stable and soon came out leading a chestnut mare. My heart thu.nped wildly as he brought her next to me. He put down the stepping stool he had in his free hand.

"Don't worry, miss. She is the gentlest creature in the stable."

His words did nothing to alleviate the terror building inside me. I cursed my bravado for agreeing to this nonsense of learning to ride. But I listened intensely as Mr. Irons gave me instructions for mounting the animal. Before I knew it, I was atop the horse.

Mr. Irons led the horse around the stableyard so I could get used to the feel of the saddle. Then he gave me the reins, explaining which way to pull if I wanted to go right or left.

After several paces around the yard, the pounding in my chest subsided. I began to feel quite regal atop the creature and a surge of confidence raced through me. I was seized by an urge to make the horse break into a gallop. Common sense smothered that urge. But I knew I would be back the next afternoon.

"So you are learning to ride," said Brian Young as we paced along in his trap. "How do you like it?"

"It's hard to say. I like what I am doing so far. I only lead her around the stableyard at this point. Mr. Irons said the next steps are a canter, a trot, and a gallop. Tomorrow he'll take me down the lane and begin instruction in those forms."

"Once you learn to ride, I'm sure you will enjoy it."

"Do you ride?" I asked.

He glanced at me and smiled. "In my profession it is a necessity. Most of the time I have to make a speedy call. The trap slows me down when there is an emergency. Don't give up on the horseback riding, Janet. It can be an asset in the country."

"How poorly is Sir Lewis? I know his daughter was quite frantic about his health several days ago."

"It is difficult to tell with lumbago. There is no fever and one's general health is not disturbed."

"What is it, then?"

"Pain in the back region. If a person has lumbago and bends over, it can be extremely painful for him to straighten his back. Once straightened, he may find it difficult to stoop. The pain and stiffness may disappear as quickly as the attack comes on. Mustard or belladonna plasters applied to the area sometimes ease the pain," Brian replied.

"Can it be cured?"

"Not to my knowledge. I told Sir Lewis to dress in warm clothing to protect his body against damp, chill weather, take hot water bottles, and drink large portions of hot, weak tea. If he follows my instructions, the lumbago attacks might lessen. I hope he follows them for his sake. Has he been complaining since I saw him last?"

"I don't think so. But then I am not privy to what goes on in the Lewises' suite at Cheviot Chase."

"Miss Lewis is quite beautiful. I suppose now that Lord Rathbone is free, he will consider her as a future wife. The families seem to be very close," said Brian.

"I wouldn't know." The thought of John marrying the vacuous Daphne stabbed at my heart. I couldn't bear to think about it, much less talk about it. "Have you been to a church bazaar before, Brian?"

"Many times. I try to take part in the village activities as much as my profession allows me. I'm sure you will enjoy it, Janet. You will be surprised at the skills and talent that abound in the village."

"What about those who don't have a skill or a talent?"

"They usually donate an object they have no further use for. One can purchase an item one may need and want without spending too much money."

"Do you contribute?"

"Oh, yes. I always do. Those who can't pay my fee usually give me food. But there are some elderly who don't raise anything and no longer bake. They give me an old family treasure. As I have no use for them, I donate them to the church bazaar," he explained.

"Why do you take their treasures if you have no use for them?"

"If I didn't take them, they would feel they were charity cases and their pride would be crushed."

"Don't they resent your putting them in the church bazaar?" I asked.

"I don't think so. They know it is for a good cause. And

226

in the end, the money the church receives usually goes to assist them in some way."

Colorful stalls dotted the village green. I saw the vicar moving from booth to booth, smiling broadly and briefly speaking to all the attendants.

"Where would you like to start, Janet?" asked Brian.

"Why not right here, then come down the other side," I suggested.

"All right."

Handcrafted items were expertly executed. I purchased a lovely set of handkerchiefs with delicate tatted edges for Sarah. Though I would have liked to purchase a number of the items, I didn't have too much money left from the two pounds John had given me when we were in Dorchester.

After lunch we continued to browse the tables of those who did not have a booth. At one of these tables, I saw an item that I knew I had to possess—a watercolor set complete with brushes and paper, and everything was brand new. I found it difficult to believe someone would sell the entire set for less than half its original cost as the small sign proclaimed. I questioned the man sitting behind the table.

"My wife was ill and confined to bed. She thought learning to do watercolors might be a pleasant way to pass the time. I went to Dorchester and bought the best set they had. She passed away before she got to use them."

"I'm so sorry," I said.

"Thank you, miss. She had been sick for a long time, as Dr. Young can tell you. I knew she might go any day."

"I'd like to purchase all the materials, but I am a couple of shilling shy of your asking price. Would you be willing to wait a day or two for the balance?" I asked.

"Janet, let me buy it for you," said Brian.

"No. It wouldn't be proper for you to buy me gifts."

"Then let me lend you the money," Brian insisted.

227

I was considering the loan when the man said, "Never mind the few shillings, miss. You can have it for what money you have. No one has shown any interest in it and I do want it out of the house. It only reminds me of my late wife. I'm sure she would like someone who really wanted the set to have it. Somehow I think it would please her."

"Are you sure?" I asked.

He nodded. "Please take it."

I gave him every shilling I had and was grateful to do so. I gathered up the box and paper and held them as though I had the treasures of the monarchy in my arms. I had a giddy smile on my face when I looked at Brian.

"You look pleased with yourself, Janet," he said.

"I am. I never could have afforded to buy these at regular store prices."

"This has turned out to be a doubly fine day then."

Still smiling, I nodded. My elation was quickly drained when a footman from Cheviot Chase came running up to Brian. He was breathless and looked terrified.

"Dr. Young, you must come quickly. There has been a shooting at Cheviot Chase."

I gasped one word. "John."

Brian gave me a peculiar glance, then asked, "Would you like to stay here, Janet? I'll come back for you later."

"No!" I cried sharply. "We must get to Cheviot Chase right away." I clutched my parcels to my bosom and was dashing to the trap ahead of Brian.

The thought of John being seriously hurt or dying knotted my insides and I had all I could do to hold the tears back. No longer was there the slightest doubt in my mind that I was deeply in love with the Lord of Cheviot Chase. Brian raced the horse and trap, but I wanted the trap to sprout wings and fly.

I didn't wait for assistance out of the trap when Brian brought it to a halt before the grand portico. Mr. Jackson opened the door as I ran up the marble steps. I dashed into the foyer, my face contorted with anguish. My parcels fell to the floor when Lord John Rathbone walked out of the drawing room. My smile was feeble and I couldn't stem the tears trickling over my cheeks.

"I am sorry, Janet. I know you were fond of him," said John as he placed his hands on my shoulders.

His words didn't register in my brain immediately. I was so relieved and happy to see him unharmed that nothing would have penetrated my brain. I wanted to throw my arms around him and hold tight. But I stood there with a silly grin on my face. He dropped his hands and went to greet Brian before acknowledging the presence of Constable Andrews, who had just entered the foyer.

"Gentlemen, he is on the moor. We didn't want to move him until both of you arrived," said John.

"How is he?" asked Brian.

"I fear he is dead," replied John. "Shall we go, gentlemen? My horse is outside."

After John had led the two men out, I picked up my parcels and went upstairs, still not knowing who had been shot. I put my purchases away. After a quick wash and change of clothes, I went to look for Sarah. I found her coming up the servants' staircase.

"Isn't it a terrible, terrible thing? And so soon after the murder of Lady Rathbone," said Sarah when she noticed my presence.

"Who? No one has told me yet," I declared.

"Why, Mr. Jason. He was so young. And murdered at that. Now, who would want to see Mr. Jason dead? I'll admit he had a sharp tongue at times, but one doesn't go around killing people because of it."

"When did it happen?"

"I'm sure I don't know," replied Sarah. "I've been kept bustling what with the opening of the East Wing."

"Do you think his lordship will still hold the ball? After all, there have been two murders within weeks of each other. I should think that would dampen any festive mood."

Sarah shrugged as we reached the landing. "Nobody has said a word to me about canceling anything. You must be feeling a great deal of sorrow, Janet. You and Mr. Jason got along so well."

"It has been such a shock, I haven't had time to feel anything yet. Jason was indeed always pleasant to me." I was ashamed of myself. My relief that the victim hadn't been John overwhelmed all other emotions. The full import of Jason's death would probably affect me later.

As Sarah and I proceeded down the corridor, we were approached by the somber Mr. Jackson.

"Mrs. Herries, Miss Clarke, your presence is required in the drawing room," he announced then marched off.

Sarah looked at me with those large eyes of hers. "Now what do you suppose they be wanting with us in the drawing room? They certainly don't think we had anything to do with Mr. Jason's death."

"The constable probably wants to question everyone," I offered in lieu of a more substantial reply.

Mr. Jackson, Sarah, and I were the only members of the staff present in the drawing room. No one looked particularly sad. Clara Whitney was perhaps the only person with a trace of sorrow in her eyes. Daphne was pale and vigorously fanned herself. She gave the impression she might collapse any second. John stood by the fireplace scowling. Cecil appeared to be nervous and preoccupied. Several times he put a finger in his mouth and gnawed on a fingernail. When Cecil wasn't doing that, he would place his hands on his knees and clutch at his thighs until his knuckles were white.

Sir Percy looked the picture of ill health. His face was florid and one foot was elevated on a footstool.

Occasionally he would wince and shift the position of his foot on the stool.

As I studied everyone, I could feel Brian staring at me. I glanced at him and was surprised to find him frowning at me. Though his expression baffled me, I had no time to sort it out. Constable Andrews began his interrogation.

"Dr. Young's preliminary examination shows that one Mr. Jason Watson was shot through the heart, causing his immediate death about two hours ago. Isn't that right, Doctor?"

"Yes. Mr. Watson's face and hands were cold but rigor mortis had not set in yet. Those facts made me conclude the time of death was approximately two hours ago," reaffirmed Brian.

"It is my unpleasant task to find out where everyone was approximately two hours ago," said Constable Andrews.

"Surely you are not suggesting that anyone in this house had anything to do with Jason's death," said Clara indignantly. "Why, we had no reason to kill Jason anymore than we would—" She stopped in midsentence, glanced at her brother, then clamped her mouth shut and slumped back in the settee.

"What was it you were about to say, Mrs. Whitney?" asked the constable.

"Nothing. Only no one here would want Jason dead."

"I understand you had numerous quarrels with him, Mrs. Whitney," said the constable.

Clara lifted her chin and looked down her nose at the constable. "We had our differences of opinion. But that hardly calls for murder, sir."

"For the record, Mrs. Whitney, where were you approximately two hours ago?"

"I was in my room," she replied.

"Can anyone verify that? A maid or someone?"

"I had no need of a maid's services at the time. I hardly

231

invite a bevy of guests into my bedchamber when I am trying to relax," Clara retorted.

"Did your husband see you there?"

"No. He did not."

"Where was he?"

"You had better ask him that. I do not keep track of my husband's whereabouts," said Clara with finality.

"Mr. Whitney?" asked the constable as his gaze shifted to Cecil.

"Are you speaking to me, Constable Andrews?" asked Cecil as though roused from a deep sleep.

"Yes, sir."

"What was it you wanted to know?"

"Where you were about two hours ago?"

"Where I always am. In the library doing research for my book," replied Cecil.

"Can anyone corroborate that, sir?"

"I doubt it. Everyone knows I do not wish to be disturbed when I am working."

"I see." Constable Andrews gripped his chin and stroked it. "Miss Lewis, may I know your whereabouts at the time in question?"

"How can you even think of questioning me, Constable? Surely you must realize I had nothing to do with this dreadful business. Even the sight of a gun weakens me," claimed Daphne, her eyes fluttering as fast as the fan she was waving.

"I am not accusing anyone, Miss Lewis. I am only trying to establish where everyone was at the time," said the constable with a long-suffering smile.

"If you must know, I was having an afternoon rest. I overindulged at lunch and felt the need to lie down."

"Did a maid attend you at anytime during your rest?"

"No. The lazy wench pleaded for the afternoon off as she had promised to assist at the church bazaar in the village. I couldn't stand her whining so I told her to go.

Cheeky little slattern," said Daphne.

"Do get on with it, Constable. I want to get back to my bed," grumbled Sir Percy. "Between my lumbago and now a touch of the gout, being down here is deucedly painful for me."

"Sorry, sir. I am going as quickly as I can," replied the constable. "And you, Sir Lewis, where were you?"

"Any fool can see my condition. Naturally I was in bed until you had me dragged from that haven. And don't ask if anyone saw me. No one did. As I said before, I can't abide people tromping about when I get these attacks. Now, may my daughter and I go back to our rooms? I do believe this nonsense has gone on long enough."

"You will be remaining at Cheviot Chase, I assume."

"Damn right. Where do you think I'd be going when I can hardly walk?"

"You and your daughter may be excused, Sir Lewis," said the constable.

"Why don't you ask Miss Clarke about Jason? They were quite chummy," said Daphne as she went to assist her father from the chair.

Constable Andrews remained silent as Sir Lewis hobbled from the room, leaning on his daughter.

When they were gone, Constable Andrews said, "I know you are above suspicion, Miss Clarke, as you were with Dr. Young in the village during the time in question. But would you care to comment on Miss Lewis's parting remark?"

"I really didn't know Mr. Watson as well as the others in the house. We did play draughts on occasion during the evening and he expressed an interest in my work. He was always friendly and cordial to me. I couldn't say we had a long-standing friendship. You might say we were just friendly acquaintances," I replied.

"Did he ever intimate to you that someone might have a grudge against him?" asked the constable.

233

"No. Our talks were seldom of a personal nature."

Constable Andrews nodded. "Mr. Jackson, Lord Rathbone tells me he went horseback riding directly after lunch with the intention of paying a visit or two to tenant farmers. Was this a usual practice?"

"Yes, sir. He likes to view the crops and their condition, especially this time of year.

After giving an accurate description of the area, the constable asked, "As Lord Rathbone discovered the body, would he have any reason to be riding in that particular area?"

"Yes, sir. It is a shortcut from the Mason farm to Cheviot Chase," replied Mr. Jackson.

"Were you at the Mason farm, Lord Rathbone?"

"Yes. I'm sure they will verify that," replied John.

Constable Andrews continued to question John, but I was no longer listening. The description of the area where Jason's body was found was singing a familiar song in my head. I kept trying to visualize the spot. Like a puzzle, the pieces began to come together. I remembered.

I remembered standing there trying to hide myself while I watched Cecil bury something. Had Cecil caught Jason spying on him and, to keep his secret, murdered Jason?

Fourteen

The rain poured down as though it, too, mourned the passing of a soul. We filed into the small village church. I sat with Sarah and Mr. Jackson. Besides the family and the Lewises, a number of servants attended along with a few men from the village pub who were more closely acquainted with Jason.

The service was brief. As we left, I noticed Brian sitting alone in the back pew. I wondered why he hadn't come to sit next to me in our pew. There were only the three of us with plenty of room to spare.

Not many came to the cemetery. The servants returned to the house while the village men stayed in the village. I was surprised to see Brian come to the cemetery. I soon learned he was coming back to the house to tend Sir Percy.

Throughout the eulogy, Brian avoided my gaze. I had the sensation he was angry with me, but had no idea why.

I think I was the only one who shed a tear or two. I knew John was watching me, but it didn't matter. I had genuinely liked Jason. he was the only one who had accepted me as a person without social restrictions. I was sad. Not only had Jason not found what he wanted in life, now he would never have the chance.

When we went back to the house, I joined Sarah in a light tea.

"Oh, I don't know where it will all end," lamented Sarah. "Two funerals. Two murders. And in such a short space of time. Do you think there is a connection between them, Janet?"

"It is hard to say. On the surface I would say there isn't; yet instinct tells me there is," I replied.

"I think Constable Andrews is of the same mind."

"What makes you say that?"

"Didn't you see the constable standing in the background at the cemetery?"

"I didn't notice."

"Well, Constable Andrews is no fool. He knows something is afoot at Cheviot Chase. First, Lady Rathbone. Now, Mr. Jason. I have the terrible feeling it is not going to end there."

"Oh, Sarah. Why think such a thing? Let us pray it is all over."

"Well, the constable is still working on the murder of Lady Rathbone and evidently isn't even close to solving it. With this fresh murder, it proves that a murderer is still loose at Cheviot Chase."

"Why do you say Cheviot Chase? It could be some transient who happened to come across Lady Rathbone and Jason and murdered them for reasons known only to him."

Sarah shook her head. "Constable Andrews thinks it is someone in this house doing the dastardly deeds."

"How do you know?"

"It's all over the village."

"Who would want to kill Lady Rathbone and Jason?"

"I know one person who had a strong motive for wanting them dead," declared Sarah.

"Who?"

"I'm not saying. But it should be obvious to you."

"Well, it's not. I can't imagine anyone here having the mentality of a murderer."

"Though I love him as if he was my own son and will do everything in my power to shield him, he is the only one who had good reason to do what he did. As far as Lady Rathbone goes, I don't blame him one bit. To be tied to a mad woman who could never produce an heir is a curse no man should bear."

I gasped. "Sarah! How can you think his lordship is a murderer? I'm shocked. I refused to listen to such nonsense." I got up and prepared to leave.

"Why, you're in love with him, aren't you, Janet?"

I slumped back in the chair. "How do you know?" I asked.

"Your blind belief in him can only stem from a deep love. You mustn't let that love destroy your reason, Janet."

"All right. I do love him and I know what a hopeless love it is. But even if I didn't love him, I know he is not capable of murder," I declared. "Though he might have had a reason for the demise of Lady Rathbone, there was no reason in the world for Lord Rathbone to wish Jason Watson dead. All he had to do was send Jason away to be rid of him. Jason would have left without an argument."

"Perhaps," conceded Sarah.

Wearing my peach gown, I entered the drawing room. My eyebrows arched when I saw Brian and Constable Andrews standing there. In deference to the sadness of the day, I greeted them glumly. They returned the solemnity, but I thought I saw a deeper emotion in Brian's eyes, a frigid, detached emotion directed solely at me. Though it disturbed me, I didn't have time to ponder it for Constable Andrews offered me his arm as we went into the dining room.

237

At dinner my theory about a transient being the culprit was thoroughly shattered. I had no choice but to believe the murderer was someone living at Cheviot Chase.

"Now that you have confirmed the gun used to kill Mr. Watson is one of a set of matched pistols, Lord Rathbone, do you remember when you had seen it last?" asked the constable.

"Not really. They were on view in the library. I hardly ever looked at them," replied John.

"When you say 'on view,' what do you mean?" the constable continued.

"They were housed in a glass-covered box."

"Was the box locked?"

"No. It was designed and manufactured without a lock," replied John.

"Then anyone in the house could have taken it, including the servants."

"That's right, Constable."

"What are you saying, John?" squealed Daphne. "You left pistols around for anyone to take? Oh, my, now we'll all be murdered in our beds."

"Really, Daphne. Don't become unduly alarmed," said John.

"Alarmed? I am terrified."

"Well, don't be. The constable has the gun that killed Jason and I have put its twin under lock and key," John assured her.

"With all these strange workmen wandering about and making all sorts of noise, I have every right to be wary," whined Daphne, a pout punctuating her sentence.

"Perhaps you would feel safer and more comfortable at Foxhill, Daphne," said John, smiling.

"Poor father couldn't make the trip now. Between his lumbago and the gout, he can barely move," said Daphne.

"How is Sir Percy doing, Dr. Young?" asked Cecil.

"As well as can be expected. He must learn to stay with the diet I prescribed for him and to exercise moderately," replied Brian.

"You should make your father follow the doctor's instructions, Daphne," said Clara.

"You know very well, Clara, I can't make my father do anything. He is a strong-willed man."

"Miss Clarke, Lord Rathbone tells me you talked with Mr. Watson often. Did he ever mention any enemies?" asked Constable Andrews.

"No. He always appeared to be fairly carefree to me," I replied. "By the way, Constable, where was the gun?"

"Next to Mr. Watson's body. When we showed it to Lord Rathbone, he identified it immediately and showed me where it was originally housed. Have you ever seen them in the library, Miss Clarke?"

"No."

"Have you ever been in the library?"

"Several times."

"I see."

"Does Jason's death mean the hunt and the ball will be canceled, John?" asked Daphne, a beseeching glint in her eyes.

The constable and Brian looked at her with eyebrows raised.

"With two deaths at Cheviot Chase and so close together, I don't think it would be appropriate to have any kind of festivities here, Daphne. The hunt and the ball will be postponed indefinitely."

"Oh, no, John," moaned Daphne. "I've planned on it so. I have a new gown and all the accessories. It took me ever so long to find the right gown."

"I know, Daphne." There was a sneer in John's voice.

"Please don't cancel the ball, John," she pleaded.

"I'm sorry, Daphne. My mind is made up. I intend to respect the dead. After all, Isobel was my wife and Jason, though we weren't very close, was a friend. I can't dismiss those facts from my mind."

"You were going to hold the hunt and the ball after Isobel's death. Why should Jason's death make any difference?" argued Daphne.

"I've given it some thought since then. I came to the conclusion to cancel them before Jason's tragedy. I intended to announce that fact tomorrow. Jason's demise hastened my announcement," explained John.

"Oh, John. It's not fair," mewled Daphne.

"I have an idea," said Clara. "Foxhill should be finished soon. Why don't you and your father hold the hunt and the ball?"

A momentary sparkle came into Daphne's eyes. As if remembering a stray thought, the sparkle vanished. Her voice was dull as she said, "I'll talk to father."

As customary, Clara poured the tea once we were in the drawing room.

"I think your brother is mean, Clara," said Daphne. "He makes promises then doesn't keep them."

"Under the circumstances, Daphne, I think he is right. I'll admit I wasn't fond of either Isobel or Jason, but one must respect the dead," said Clara.

"Oh pooh!" exclaimed Daphne. "Why should we mourn a crazy woman and a snide little twit like Jason? They never did anything for me."

Clara sighed. "You are so young, Daphne."

"And what is that supposed to mean?"

Before Clara could respond, the gentlemen entered.

"John, dear, I was so peeved at you for canceling the hunt and the ball. But I've decided not to hold a grudge," said Daphne, her smile sweeter than a mixture of sugar and honey.

"How decent of you, Daphne," said John, his gaze drifting to me then to Brian.

"Lord Rathbone," began Constable Andrews. "Thank

you for the excellent dinner. I must take my leave now. There is much work to do as you can well imagine. Good night, ladies."

"I think I will follow the constable's example," said Brian.

"Are you sure my father is all right?" asked Daphne.

"I will check on him before I leave, Miss Lewis. Thank you for the dinner, Lord Rathbone. Good night, ladies."

Brian didn't even glance at me when issuing his good night. I was perplexed. Perhaps on his next visit I would have a chance to talk to him alone and find out what was on his mind to have caused this sudden frostiness toward me.

With only John, Cecil, Clara, and Daphne left in the drawing room, I felt unneeded and unwanted. I stood.

"If everyone will excuse me, I think I will retire early," I said.

"Are you feeling all right, Janet?" John asked.

"Yes. The day has been a trying one. I really don't feel like conversing.

"I understand," said John. "Why don't you take tomorrow off?"

"I'll think about it. Good night."

I put my book aside and turned down the oil lamp. I snuggled down in my bed, interlaced my fingers, put them behind my head, and lay my head on the pillow. I knew I would cry if I let myself think about Jason. I forced myself to concentrate on the fact that no transient could have taken the gun from the library. The constable was right. It had to be someone from the house.

I immediately ruled out myself, Sarah, and the staff. Neither Daphne nor Clara could have committed the atrocious murder of Lady Rathbone. They wouldn't have had the stomach for it. I doubted if Cecil would either. Sir

Percy didn't seem to have the strength to subdue Lady Rathbone. If John couldn't hold her, how could a sick old man? Jason? No. Jason was not a killer. He was a rake and a user, but not capable of cold-blooded murder. My heart refused to let me think of John. That left only one person. Mr. Jackson.

Mr. Jackson's devotion to John was unquestionable. Knowing Lady Rathbone was the bane of his lordship's existence, he could have been the one to rid John of that burden. But why would he kill Jason? The whole thing was a muddle to me. I pulled the covers up to my chin, turned on my side, and spent the rest of the night dreaming about a multitude of funerals where Brian would turn his back on me every time I tried to speak to him.

The days passed without new tragedies. Although the constable came no closer to solving the murders, my abilities on horseback improved tremendously. I was able to go about on my own. As I improved, so did my confidence and daring. Though I occasionally rode to the cliffs and the sea, the moor was still my favorite haunt.

One pleasant summer afternoon I decided to ride to the village and see Brian. I knew it was bold on my part, especially since Brian hadn't made any attempt to see me since Jason's funeral. Curiosity regarding his altered attitude toward me burned like an unquenchable fire. I was unconcerned about not having a proper riding habit.

One of the stable lads was helping me mount the mare when John came into the stableyard and headed my way, a warm smile on his handsome face.

"I must commend you, Janet. I hear you have mastered the skills of riding quite handily," said John.

"I've had a good teacher and Mr. Irons has chosen a most tractable mare for me to ride."

242

"Where are you off to today?"

"I thought I would ride into the village for a change," I replied.

"Good. I'll go with you. I have some business to tend to there. Today would be a good day to take care of it. Do you have a specific purpose for going to the village?"

"I thought I'd stop in and see Dr. Young."

"Is something wrong?" asked John.

"No. I wanted to say hello. I haven't seen him in some time."

"I see." The smile vanished from his face. "Then perhaps you would like to go alone."

"Oh, no. I would enjoy your company," I said, a little too quickly.

I waited until he mounted and we began the journey, keeping the horses at a leisurely pace.

"Do you ride into the village often?" asked John.

"No. This is my first venture there. Is there any news from Constable Andrews?"

"No. It seems he is no closer to solving the deaths than he was when they occurred. I am beginning to suspect they will never be solved."

"Surely there must be some clues. It has been almost two months."

"Unfortunately the longer they go unsolved, the more difficult any resolution of the crimes. What makes it baffling for him is the different modes of death and lack of connection between the two murders. But let us not dwell on the morbid. The day is too pleasant for death and murder. How is your work coming? I imagine you have nearly finished."

"There are a few left. But they only need the soot taken off them. I have one that is in rather bad shape and then I should be done. It shouldn't take more than a month, if that long," I replied.

"Then what will you do, Janet?"

"Place another advertisement in the newspaper, I suppose, unless you know of someone who could use my services." I really didn't want to think about the future. Cheviot Chase had become home to me and I dreaded leaving it.

"I'll see what I can do. I believe Cecil has some connections at the British Museum. Now that Foxhill Manor is being refurbished, perhaps Sir Percy would like to have his paintings cleaned and restored. I'll speak to him about it."

"Is Foxhill Manor almost finished?"

"I don't know. I haven't been over there in some time and I never think to ask Sir Percy about it."

"Where is it?"

"Down the road in the opposite direction. It is the first large house past mine. Our lands abut one another."

"Is Foxhill Manor as large as Cheviot Chase?" I asked.

"About one-third the size of my estate. Why do you ask?"

"Idle curiosity."

When we entered the village, John asked, "Will you be at the doctor's long?"

"I don't know. He might not have time to see me or he might be off on an emergency call."

"Doesn't he know you are coming?"

"No. It was a sudden whim of mine."

"Perhaps we will meet and ride back together."

"That would be nice. I must leave you now."

He nodded and I veered off toward Brian's house. I tethered the mare to a post and was admitted to the house by a tall, thin woman I judged to be in her fifties. I entered the empty waiting room and took a seat.

When Brian came out of his surgery, he was preceded by a woman holding the hand of a young child. He acknowledged my presence with a nod, then saw the woman and child out before taking a seat next to me in the waiting room.

"What can I do for you, Janet?" asked Brian. "Have you been having headaches?"

"No, thank goodness. I'm here on a social call. I haven't seen you in a while and I was wondering if you were ill or just overburdened with work."

"Neither." One hand clutched the other tightly as Brian stared at them for several seconds. "I suppose I do owe you an explanation, Janet."

"You don't have to explain anything to me, Brian," I said, noting the tension in his body as he wrung his hands together.

"I think you should know I am courting a young woman in the village. I am thinking of asking her to marry me," said Brian. He looked up and gazed at me. "I'm sorry, Janet."

Even though my ego was slightly deflated, I managed to smile. "There is nothing to be sorry for. I am very happy for you, Brian."

"You'll always hold a place in my heart, Janet."

"Thank you. I treasure your friendship."

"You must know I had more than friendship in mind when I first began seeing you. But the day Jason Watson was shot made me realize you were in love with someone else. My hopes, not to mention my pride, were shattered. I couldn't bear to go on seeing you knowing your thoughts and heart lay elsewhere. Though I think your love for the man is in vain, I realize one can't direct one's heart with one's brain."

"I don't know what to say, Brian."

"Don't say anything. I prefer to let it rest at that. Talking about it won't change the facts."

"I suppose not. You are very observant, Brian. I didn't realize I was so obvious. At any rate, I shall be leaving Dorset in less than a month. My work at Cheviot Chase is almost finished." I rose and extended my hand. "I wish you the best of luck and happiness, Brian."

He took my hand and held it between his. "I wish you the same, Janet."

I smiled, but he didn't. I left without another word. I couldn't bear to see the hurt in his eyes. I walked the horse back toward Cheviot Chase, hoping John would catch up to me. My visit with Brian had been unexpectedly brief, probably too brief for John to have completed his business in the village.

Deciding it was useless to maintain a slow pace along the road, I took the shortcut across the moor. When I reached the spot where Jason had been shot, I brought the mare to a halt. Tears welled in my eyes as I remembered Jason's boyish smile and lighthearted manner. I perched there for some minutes when I suddenly felt I was being watched. I looked around.

There in the hollow was Cecil Whitney, staring up at me with spade in hand. Though I couldn't discern every nuance of his expression, I had the sensation he was scowling at me. I waved and continued my journey back to the house at a quicker pace, thinking I would work harder so I could leave Cheviot Chase all that much sooner.

As I bent over one of the sooty paintings from the East Wing, my thoughts began to dwell on Dr. Brian Young. Perhaps Sarah had been right. I should have looked on the practical side of life instead of indulging in romantic fantasies. But the heart has a tendency to be perverse and ignore practicality.

If I had encouraged and eventually married Brian, I could have been assured of my future. More importantly, I could have stayed in the village with the hope of glimpsing John now and then. But I did not have the nature to marry for practical purposes and without love.

I would have been deceiving myself and Brian. I liked him too well for that.

As I wondered what kind of woman Brian was seeing, I became careless and knocked over a solvent as I reached for a fresh wad of cotton. To my dismay and exasperation, the solvent splashed onto the painting I was working on.

Swiftly plucking wads of cotton, I began to soak up the solvent. I was horrified to see the paint coming off. Such a mishap would mean hours of extra work. I was so angry with myself, I didn't realize what was happening at first. Then it began to emerge. *There was another painting underneath. A much older painting.*

As the picture I was working on was a poorly executed landscape, I felt justified removing more of the surface paint. Besides I was curious.

The sun was lowering in the sky as I bared more of the underpainting. I lighted several oil lamps and strategically placed them around my worktable. I became excited as I cleared away more of the top paint. The underpainting was proving to be very old and perhaps valuable. I continued to work feverishly, forgetting time and place.

With three quarters of the underpainting revealed, I knew what I had. A fifteenth-century masterpiece by Hans Memling. *The Madonna of the Apple.* Though I had no idea of its exact worth, I realized it was extremely valuable, if not priceless. I went back to work.

The door to my workroom slammed shut with such force, my body jumped in the seat and a gasp echoed from my throat.

Fifteen

"What the devil do you think you're doing, Janet?" boomed Lord Rathbone as he strode across the room. "Is your work more important than putting in an appearance at dinner? You know I insist on your presence at the table. Are you so anxious to leave Cheviot Chase that you feel it necessary to work far into the night?"

His anger with me couldn't dampen my enthusiasm and excitement. I turned to face him with eyes sparkling and a broad smile.

"You are being very smug about it, Janet." His tone softened. "Are you really that anxious to leave here?"

"Not at all." I rose, went to him, and in my exhilaration, grabbed his hand and led him to the table. "Look what I have unearthed." My bold gesture seemed to startle him. He stared at me rather than the painting. I quickly released his hand and was glad the amber light of the lamps masked the crimson beginning to splotch my cheeks. "The painting. Look at the painting."

His eyes wrenched themselves from my face and scanned the painting. "So?"

I apprised him of the painting's age, the painter's genius, and the possible value of the painting. I was startled when he threw back his head and laughed in his rich baritone voice.

"This is not a laughing matter. You are the owner of a very valuable painting," I said solemnly.

He brought his laughter under control then explained his mirth.

"Before her mental faculties deteriorated, Isobel often threatened to leave me again if I did not cater to her whims. When I vowed to cut off all her funds if she left me, she would laugh, saying she had assets she could turn into cash that would last her a lifetime. I always wondered what she meant. Now, owing to your efforts, I know. I had a few suspicions regarding the paintings, but I was never sure."

"Is that why you wanted someone to clean and restore them?" I asked.

"Yes. I wanted to make sure," said John.

"Why paintings? She could have meant her jewels."

"Her jewels were always locked in the safe and taken out one set at a time when the occasion called for them. Only I had the combination. She never would have been able to get her hands on all of them at once. Besides the pawning or selling of jewels never brings their full value. But art masterpieces increase in value. Aside from her clothes, all she brought from London were some paintings."

"Why didn't you give me these paintings right away instead of having me do all of them?"

"At the time, I paid little heed to what she brought with her. Frankly, I didn't even glance at them. As time went by, I had forgotten all about the paintings and had no idea what they looked like. Occasionally she would purchase other paintings and was always changing their positions around the house. When it came to my mind that the paintings might be the assets of which she had spoken, I had no notion which might be the valuable ones."

"Did anyone else know about her paintings?" I asked.

"I don't know. Why?"

I told him about the spots of bare canvas on the preceding paintings which I had had to repaint. "I think someone else was looking for those underpaintings. Someone who didn't quite know how to go about removing surface paint."

"The only person she might have confided in was Jason," said John. "Did he ever question you about your work?"

"Quite frequently. Some evenings, over draughts, he would ask questions as though it was an inquisition. On several occasions he came here to watch me work. Do you think Jason was trying to discover the masterpieces on his own?"

"I wouldn't be surprised. I was always curious why he would stay here. He was a clever young man and could have found a way to sustain himself in London society, where he would have stood a better chance of finding a rich woman to marry. Prospects at Cheviot Chase were quite limited."

"If it was Jason, I can't understand why he waited so long. He could have asked someone at the British Museum to explain the art of restoration, or gotten a technical book on it," I said.

"For one thing, all the paintings were stored in the East Wing, which I kept locked. Evidently he didn't have your ingenuity, Janet. I doubt the thought of an open window in the basement ever entered his mind. Even if Isobel had told him of her secret assets, I don't think she told him which were the valuable ones. She was too crafty for that."

"I suppose we will never know the truth now," I said.

"It doesn't matter now that you have confirmed my suspicions."

"Do you think his murder might have had something

250

to do with the paintings?"

"It's hard to say. Now that Jason and Isobel are dead, I guess we will never know the truth of the matter."

"Shall I tell the constable about it?"

"I don't think it will have any bearing on the case," replied John. "If Jason did know about the paintings, then there were only the two of us who knew. I certainly didn't kill Jason because I suspected he had knowledge of the paintings. It is a ridiculous thought. No. I am of the opinion that Jason was killed for an entirely different reason. Why? I don't know."

I sighed and probably looked a little sad because John changed the subject.

"How was your visit to Dr. Young?" he asked.

"Brief."

"Oh? I thought the two of you would have a great deal to talk about."

I smiled. "Actually, it was more of a good-bye. I will be leaving Dorset soon and Brian's free time is now devoted to a young woman in the village. I believe he is thinking of marrying her."

"Does that bother you?"

"No. Why should it?"

He shrugged, but he also gave me a warm smile. If he had held out his arms, I would have welcomed his embrace. This time, I changed the subject.

"To remove surface paintings will take me longer and I might be here a little longer than my original estimate. Will that be a problem for you?"

"Will it for you?"

"No."

"Good. It poses no problem for me. In fact, you seem part of the household now."

Suddenly I was empty inside. Hopes and dreams flowed out of me like a river rushing to the sea. Though I had thought I had seen a warmth toward me in his eyes and smile, I was no more to him than Cook or one of the maids.

"If you don't mind, I think I'll retire now. It has been a long day and I want to get an early start," I said.

"But you've had no supper," John protested.

"I'm not hungry."

"Nonsense. I'll have a supper tray sent up to you."

"Please don't bother. If I feel hungry, I'll go down to the kitchen and get some food."

"I'll not have you eating in the kitchen like some lowly servant. A tray will be sent up. Don't argue with me, Janet."

"As you wish." I was not of a mood to argue. When hopes are shattered, one has a tendency to want to be alone.

"I'll say good night. I would appreciate it if you would tackle the rest of the paintings rather quickly. I'm curious as to how many precious paintings she had. Good night, Janet."

"Good night."

"Oh, by the way, do keep your doors locked, especially when you are not here."

"I will."

I rose earlier than usual the next morning. My enthusiasm and inquisitiveness had not abated. I practically gulped down my breakfast then dashed to my workroom. I put the unfinished Memling aside. I put the two remaining soot-covered paintings on my worktable with the intention of clearing enough of the surface painting away to ascertain if there were underpaintings. By noon I had discoverd there were indeed underpaintings. And I had cleared enough away to recognize the artist. I was so excited I bubbled over with the urge to tell someone.

Lunch with Sarah had me on edge. I had to fight to keep my composure and not let my exhilaration show. To my relief Sarah bore most of the conversation in a practically unending stream. Our tea was brought to an early halt when Sarah was summoned to the kitchen to resolve Cook's dilemma. Evidently Dr. Young had prescribed a certain diet for Sir Percy and Daphne had countermanded it, which was fortunate for me for it meant I could get away early and seek out John. I was most anxious to tell him the news about the paintings.

When Mr. Jackson told me his lordship had left the house, I went to the stable.

"Good afternoon, Miss Clarke. Shall I be saddling up the mare for you?" asked Mr. Irons.

"That depends, Mr. Irons. Do you know where Lord Rathbone went? I have some urgent news for him," I said.

"He went walking with the dogs."

"On the moor?"

"Aye. On the moor."

"Which direction did he take?"

"I'm not sure. I think he went that way." He pointed to the left.

"How long ago did he leave?" I asked.

"Oh, not more than ten minutes ago, I'd say."

I casually strolled in the direction he indicated. When I was sure I could no longer be seen from the stable, I picked up my skirts and ran, stopping every so often to scan the area.

I smiled in triumph when I spied his tall form walking briskly over the moor, the dogs scampering at his heels. He wore a loose white cotton shirt and tight black breeches covered to the knees with black boots. Once again I picked up my skirts and ran toward him.

As I came closer, I called, "Lord Rathbone."

He stopped and turned. By the time I reached him, I

253

was breathless. I put my splayed hand over my bosom and pressed as though it would enable me to speak.

"Janet. Is something wrong at the house?" he asked, placing his hands on my shoulders.

I shook my head. I still didn't have enough breath to speak.

"The paintings?" he asked.

I nodded.

"Take time to catch your breath. I'm in no hurry. Shall we walk?" He put his arm around my shoulders.

Again I nodded but not from lack of breath. His arm around me had paralyzed my vocal cords. We walked in silence for some time. When the impact of his close presence had worn off somewhat, I spoke.

"I have cleared off portions of the other paintings, enough to make an educated guess. I believe they are the work of Hans Memling and of a seventeenth-century Flemish painter, Jan van der Meer, a Dutch master known as Vermeer. If I am correct, they are extremely valuable."

He stopped and spun me around to face him. "You ran all the way out here to tell me that? Weren't you afraid to face me alone on the moor?"

"No. What reason would I have to be afraid of you?" I asked.

"You must have heard the rumors about me by now. That I am mad and unpredictable. Aren't you afraid the madness might seize me, causing me to murder you on the spot? I might even set the dogs on you."

I smiled and looked into his green eyes. "You would never do a thing like that. And I don't believe for one minute that you are mad."

"You barely know me or the life I have led."

"I know enough to form my own opinions. The rumors are unfounded as far as I am concerned. Mere gossip conjured up to amuse those who have nothing else to

254

occupy their minds."

"Don't you believe the theory that all gossip has some basis in fact?" asked John.

Not where you are concerned, I wanted to say. Instead, I replied, "I don't believe in rash generalizations."

"Are you saying you have complete faith in my innocence?"

"Yes."

He gathered me in his arms and drew me to the hard length of his body. One hand pressed my head to his chest.

"My dear, sweet, Janet. Never before have I been blest with so much faith in my character. But you are young. Your innocent eyes haven't yet been tortured with the harsh reality of the world. Your youth has not given you the time to peer into the darker passions of a man's soul. Oh, how I envy your ingenuous nature. Would I could but see the world though your guileless eyes. For the better part of my life, I have become old and jaded beyond my years. Only with you do I see there can be a kinder, more beautiful world."

His hand left my head. One lean finger crooked under my chin and tilted my head back. His lips touched mine lightly, tenderly. He pulled his head back while his eyes searched mine. In an instant his mouth covered mine and both his arms were about me, his hands pressing caresses on my back. The kiss was deep and probing. My hands crept over his back to feel sinew move against sinew so easily under his skin beneath the thin cotton of his shirt. When my blissful stay in an ethereal firmament came to an end, we walked in silence back to the house.

"I should like to see the paintings," said John as we approached the stableyard.

"They aren't finished," I said.

"Then I will watch you work on them. Will that disturb you?"

255

"No."

"I promise to be quiet."

He kept his promise as I worked at the table. He had pulled up a straight-backed wooden chair and sat next to me. At first my hand had a tendency to tremble. His nearness and the remembrance of his kiss had a disquieting affect on me and I found it difficult to concentrate. But the work soon absorbed me and I began to work as though I were alone in the room.

There was a loud knocking on my door and John went to answer it. I turned to see Mr. Jackson talking to John in a muted voice. John closed the door and came back to the table, but he did not sit down.

"Constable Andrews is downstairs," said John.

"I hope he has good news. You had better not keep him waiting."

"He wants to see both of us."

"Oh? I wonder why he wants to see me." I stood, removed my smock, then tried to smooth the loose tendrils back up the rear of my head.

"Shall we go down and find out? I told Jackson to have him wait in the library."

As we went down the corridor, Daphne was coming from the opposite direction and appeared to be heading for the main staircase also.

"John! Wherever have you been all afternoon? I was hoping you would take me into Dorchester this afternoon," said Daphne, taking possession of his arm and ignoring me.

"I had other things to occupy me, Daphne," replied John.

"That is very naughty of you. After all, I am a guest here and you should make some effort to entertain me," said Daphne as they descended the stairs with me trailing behind.

"Unfortunately I cannot be at your beck and call every

minute of the day, Daphne. I do have an estate to manage."

"Well, you seem to be free now. Let's take a walk in the garden. It is such a lovely day and we have so much to talk about," said Daphne with her usual fluttering of eyelashes.

"Do we, Daphne? I wasn't aware of it. Are your accommodations unsatisfactory here, Daphne? Is that what you wish to talk about?"

"Do be sensible, John. You know very well I adore being at Cheviot Chase. I want to talk to you on a more personal level," claimed Daphne.

I could see her squeezing John's arm and pressing the side of her body against his suggestively. As we reached the foyer, John disengaged her arm from his with irritation.

"I'm sorry, Daphne. I don't have time to walk about the garden. Constable Andrews is waiting to speak to us in the library," said John.

"Us?" queried Daphne.

"Janet and me."

"I don't see why the constable wants to talk to *her*," said Daphne without even glancing at me. "*She* is nothing more than a servant in this house, a passing one at that."

"Janet is as much a guest in this house as you are, Daphne."

"A trollop from the seamier side of London? Really, John. I thought you had more discretion than that. You certainly can't think *she* is on my social level. I am the daughter of a peer of the land. I am shocked that you would even mention *her* in the same breath with me. I am sorely disappointed in you, John, and I will expect a contrite apology before dinner." Daphne flounced into the drawing room with a suitable pout on her face.

"The only apology I feel is necessry is to you, Janet. Daphne had no right to speak of you like that. I am afraid her father has spoiled her beyond redemption. Pay no heed to her," John said.

"I won't." I knew Daphne spoke from jealousy. I didn't take her seriously. But I did resent the way she spoke about me as if I wasn't there. I wondered if I would ever be able to forgive her for that.

When we entered the library, Constable Andrews was perusing the books on the shelves. He spun around at our entrance. We all took seats.

"Have you learned anything new, Tom?" asked John.

"I think so. I've asked to speak to both of you as you are the only people in the house that didn't appear to be hostile to Jason Watson. I was afraid answers from the others would be colored with prejudice," replied the constable.

"What have you learned, Tom?" John reiterated.

"I talked to some men at the village pub. They told me Mr. Watson was bragging about a lot of money he expected to inherit. He was also buying rounds of drinks for the lads and flashing about a good deal of money. I was wondering if you knew anything about it. For example, do you know of any inheritance that might be due him? And where did his sudden increase in cash come from? The lads at the pub say he was usually frugal with his money unless he won a substantial amount in games of chance," said the constable.

"I know of no inheritance, Tom," said John. "From what little I know of Jason's background, there was no wealthy relative ready to make him an heir."

"Did he ever mention this inheritance to you, Miss Clarke?"

"No. From the way Jason talked, the only prospect he had for wealth was to marry a rich woman. That seemed to be his primary goal in life," I replied.

I thought of the three paintings sitting upstairs. John looked at me at the same instant I glanced his way. Our eyes communed. John told the constable of the paintings and our suspicions that Jason might have planned to purloin them.

"I see." The constable rubbed his chin. "When did you come to this conclusion, Lord Rathbone?"

"Yesterday when Janet discovered a valuable under-painting on one of the canvases," replied John.

"Then you didn't know about it before he was killed."

"No," said John.

"That might be the answer to the supposed inheritance. Now what of all his sudden extra cash? Has money been missing from your accounts, Lord Rathbone? Or did you give him the money?"

"All monies in the house are strictly controlled by me and all accounted for as of yesterday. As far as giving Jason cash, it would be unthinkable to me. For the sake of my late wife, I provided him with food, shelter, and the freedom of the stables. I felt that was enough," said John.

"And you, Miss Clarke. From the other members of the household, I gather you were rather chummy with Mr. Watson. Had you been giving money to him?"

I almost laughed aloud. "Hardly, Constable Andrews. And I wouldn't say we were exactly chummy. We were on casual but friendly terms as I told you before."

"May I explain for Janet, Tom?" asked John.

"Certainly."

"So far I have only paid Miss Clarke two pounds of her due wages. And that was a while ago. I'm sure it is quite gone by now."

"I see. Did you have a sizable amount of cash when you came to Cheviot Chase, Miss Clarke?"

"No. I used my last shilling to hire one Mr. Sullivan to bring me here from the railroad station. There is no way I could have supplied Mr. Watson with any sum of money," I declared.

"Well, then." The constable put his hands on his

knees as if to rise. "That clarifies my original theory."

"And what is that, Tom?" asked John.

"That Mr. Watson was blackmailing someone. Blackmail is usually the source of sudden money when one does not see any other explanation. I talked to the men in the pub regarding Mr. Watson's character. They seemed to be of the opinion that Mr. Watson was indeed capable of blackmail. What is your assessment of his character, Lord Rathbone? In your mind, would he be capable of such a thing?"

John hesitated for what seemed like a long time. "Tom, though I hate to say it, I believe Jason was capable of any unscrupulous scheme if enough money was involved. Money was his god and, I sometimes think, his only reason for living."

"Miss Clarke? May I have your estimate of the man's character?"

"I tend to agree with Lord Rathbone."

"Do you think Mr. Watson capable of murder?"

"No." My reply was emphatic.

"Lord Rathbone?"

"No. Jason was capable of being devious, exploitative, fraudulent, and downright crooked. But murder? No. He would never have taken a human life."

"I see. Now the question is who was he blackmailing and why," said Constable Andrews. "Do you have any ideas? Either of you?"

"I haven't the foggiest, Tom. I know it wasn't me. Jason knew I would laugh at any attempt at blackmail and probably would have ousted him from Cheviot Chase. He was too smart to bite the hand that feeds him."

The constable looked at me with the same question in his eyes.

"I was not privy to Jason's private plots or schemes. I have no idea who his victim might have been. And there is nothing in my background that would initiate blackmail."

"Though your answers haven't shed any great light on the case, at least I know a little more than I did before. Thank you both," said the constable, rising from the chair.

"Do you think you will be able to substantiate your blackmail theory?" asked John getting to his feet.

"In time, Lord Rathbone. In time. When someone has a dark secret in his past, or present, sooner or later someone else learns of it and the cycle of blackmail begins again. Good day to you, milord. Miss Clarke."

As John saw the constable to the door of the library, I left my seat and prepared to leave. But John shut the door as I approached.

"Janet, I would appreciate it if you'd keep our conversation with the constable between us. I don't want anyone else in the house to know blackmail is involved. If the culprit is indeed someone in this house, the more he, or she, is kept in the dark, the safer he will feel and might show his hand. Will you do that for me?"

"Of course. I won't speak of it to Mrs. Herries even though I know she will barrage me with questions regarding the constable's visit here today, especially when he requested to speak to me," I replied.

"I am sure you can manage a convincing story if she becomes too inquisitive." He smiled.

"I'll do my best."

"Why don't you have a rest before you change for dinner?"

I picked up the watch pinned to my bodice. "I think I will work for a couple of hours. There will be plenty of time to dress for dinner."

"As you wish."

He opened the door for me and stepped aside. He closed the door behind me and remained in the library.

By the time we filed into the dining room, I was

261

ravenous. The escalloped oysters were followed by a light and tasty beef barley soup. Still I filled my plate with slices from a saddle of mutton, boiled potatoes, fresh baby beets, and mounds of last winter's turnips. An ample supply of fresh-baked biscuits and breads were already on the table along with freshly churned butter. Sated, I thought I could never eat another thing, yet I managed to consume a dish of raspberry cream.

Sir Percy had hobbled down to eat at the dinner table. I thought my appetite was huge, but his proved to be enormous. Daphne did me one better by ordering another raspberry cream from the kitchen. Clara picked at her food while Cecil ate mechanically. Every now and then I caught Cecil casting furtive glances my way throughout dinner.

"What did the constable want to see you about, John?" asked Clara.

"He wanted a little background on Jason," John replied.

"Is he any closer to solving these murders?" asked Sir Percy.

"I don't think so," said John.

"The constabulary is not very gifted. I'm surprised the Yard hasn't been called in. Did the constable give you any indication he might do that and get this mess cleared up once and for all?" asked Sir Percy.

"Thomas Andrews is a capable man, Sir Percy," said John. "I am sure if a solution eludes him much longer, he might consider calling in the Yard."

"What good will the Yard do then?" asked Clara. "Any or all clues will have been lost by then."

"Please!" cried Daphne, digging into her second raspberry cream. "Couldn't we talk about something else? This is all so depressing, especially at the dinner table. It takes one's appetite away."

"What did the constable want to see you about,

Janet?" asked Clara, ignoring Daphne's plea.

"Essentially the same thing. He seemed to think Jason might have confided in me. Of course he never did." I was a little surprised that Clara had directed a question at me. I was usually ignored at the dinner table.

"John, won't you reconsider about holding the hunt and the ball? It would be ever so gay," said Daphne.

"My daughter is right, John," said Sir Percy. "A good hunt and a festive ball would take our minds off all these grisly events. We need some cheering up. I haven't been on a jolly good hunt in ages. Be good for my lumbago and gout. A good ride to the hounds is what we all need."

"It would be in poor taste with the pall of murders hanging over Cheviot Chase. Perhaps I will reconsider when everything is cleared up," said John.

"Would anyone care to accompany me to Dorchester tomorrow morning?" asked Cecil, causing everyone to stare at him.

"Are you actually offering to take me somewhere, Cecil?" asked Clara.

"If you wish to view it that way, yes, Clara," said Cecil.

"Well, I'm not about to pass up the opportunity. Why are you going to Dorchester, Cecil?"

"I am running low on paper and ink. I need supplies," Cecil replied. "Would you care to come, Sir Percy?"

"No. I don't think so. I can feel my foot starting to throb. I suspect by morning I will be bedridden."

"I'll go," said Daphne brightly and eagerly. "Dorchester isn't London, but it is better than being stuck here."

"Then it is settled. I would like to leave early in the morning," said Cecil.

"Can we make a day of it?" asked Clara.

"Perhaps."

That night as I lay in bed, the word *blackmail* haunted me. Ideas were beginning to form in my brain, but I was having a hard time trying to string them together. I decided to give it up and go to sleep. As I started to doze, my ideas crystallized. I was now wide awake. Why is the obvious always so obscure?

The fierce look Cecil gave me when he saw me watching him bury objects on the moor should have given me a clue. All the other times he had furtively left the house to ply his secret diggings on the moor came back to me in a rush. Perhaps Jason had found out what Cecil was burying on the moor and it was so heinous that an opportunity for blackmail presented itself. The place where Jason's body was found—the same place where I had hidden behind a tree to watch Cecil—might have been the payment rendezvous. Cecil was probably tired of being drained of his money and shot Jason. The theory seemed feasible to me. But it all hinged on what Cecil was burying. If the items were of no consequence, then there would be no basis for blackmail. Though I probably should have told the constable of my theory, I didn't think he would take me seriously without concrete evidence. Besides, I didn't want to implicate anyone in the family until I was sure of myself. I would look like a fool making wild guesses without being able to substantiate them.

Before I went to sleep, I made up my mind to investigate that section of the moor before voicing my thoughts to anyone. As Cecil would be in Dorchester for the day, I would carry out my search tomorrow during my usual after-lunch walk. Doing it that way wouldn't arouse undue suspicions.

Early in the morning I went to the stables to tell Mr. Irons I wouldn't be riding after lunch. I found him in the stableyard readying the carriage for the trip to Dorchester.

"But I was planning to introduce you to the art of jumping. You are progressing with such speed, jumping is the next step," said Mr. Irons.

"We'll have to make it another time. Perhaps in a day or so," I said. "Where are the dogs?"

He gave a low whistle and the dogs came out of the stables. I crouched down to play with them.

"I'll keep the day after tomorrow open in the afternoon for you, Miss Clarke. Will you be able to make it then?" asked Mr. Irons.

"I'm sure I will. I will be looking forward to it."

Mr. Irons went back to the carriage. I played with the dogs for a few minutes longer then went back into the house.

I was passing through the butler's pantry when I heard the voices of John and Daphne in the dining room. I slowed my pace and perked my ears.

"Why aren't you dressed for traveling, Daphne? Aren't you going to Dorchester with my sister?" asked John.

"No."

"Why not? I thought you were looking forward to it."

"I changed my mind."

"Why?"

"With father in bed, I thought it best I stay here. Besides I suddenly realized you would be here all alone. I thought it would be nice if I kept you company," said Daphne.

"I thought you wanted nothing to do with me until I apologized to you for the other day," said John with a wry smile.

"Oh, John. You didn't take me seriously, did you? You know I could never be truly angry with you. I thought we could spend the day together. Perhaps go on a picnic near the shore. We haven't been in ever so long. I have told Cook to prepare a nice basket for us. Mr. Jackson is going to select the wine. It will be such fun," declared Daphne with a girlish giggle bouncing in her throat.

"I'm sorry you went to all that trouble, Daphne. I intend to spend the morning visiting some of my tenant farmers. Then I will be having lunch with some gentlemen in the village. I'll probably spend the afternoon with them. You had better tell Clara you have changed your mind again and are going with them. I'm sure they will wait for you," said John.

"Really, John. Why can't you stay here with me?" asked Daphne.

"I just explained it to you. Now hurry and tell Clara."

"No. I am staying here. You might change your mind and I want to be here if you do."

"Suit yourself, Daphne."

I hurried along in case Mr. Jackson came into the pantry. I didn't want him to know I had been eavesdropping. I smiled as I climbed the rear stairs. I knew why Daphne decided to stay and not go to Dorchester. She didn't want me to be alone with John. The thought amused me, and at the same time, I thought it flattering.

The more I cleaned the painting I was working on, the more positive I was that it was indeed a Vermeer. The colors and light were fabulous.

I would have loved to talk to Sarah about the paintings as we ate our lunch. But I had promised John I wouldn't tell anyone. I had never broken my word before, and I was not about to do so now. Besides I had more pressing thoughts on my mind.

After lunch I went to the gardener's shed. No one was there. I picked up the small hand trowel and slipped it into the pocket of my skirt. Then I left for the moor.

As I approached the designated area, the sky darkened as if in warning. I made my way down the knoll to the flat land where I'd seen Cecil. I began a slow search for fresh signs of digging. It took me a while but I finally found some.

I dropped to my haunches and began to dig with the trowel. Nothing. I dug farther down and still there was nothing. When the earth became hard-packed, I knew it hadn't been disturbed. Cecil had not gone that far down. I gave up on that spot, pushed the dirt back in, and searched for another fresh dig.

When I found it, I proceeded as before with no results. After five more empty holes, I realized to continue would be fruitless.

I stood there, discouragement and failure creeping into my bones. My clever little theory was totally misdirected. I felt like a fool. There was nothing to do but go back to the house and leave the sleuthing to Constable Andrews.

I was about to leave when I remembered the trowel. I had left it on the ground. I dropped to my haunches again. As I did, a shot rang up and dirt spit up inches from me. Foolishly, I stood and looked around in fear. Another shot rang out. This time the puff of dirt was closer. I started to run from the direction of the sound as shot after shot rang out. Then I fell to the ground.

It was terrible. Daphne. Absolutely horrible. He shouldn't do such a scene with us. I specially had time to look in a shop window he time Gail arrived we return to

Sixteen

I hadn't been shot, but I thought the ruse might make whoever was shooting at me think the bullet had found its mark. I don't know how long I lay there perfectly still, but the minute I hit the ground, the shots ceased. I could only pray the person wouldn't come to see if his shot was accurate. I waited and waited until I thought a suitable time had elapsed, then stood.

As a mist began to settle on the land, not too far in the distance I saw smoke curling upward in the damp air. I ran toward the rising smoke until a cottage came into view. When I reached it, I practically battered down the door with my persistent knocking.

A stout woman opened the door. Her mouth fell agape when she saw me. I was disheveled and filthy. I quickly explained I was from Cheviot Chase and had gotten lost on the moor. I saw no reason to mention the fact that someone had tried to kill me. There had been enough trouble and rumors at Cheviot Chase without my adding to the unsavory gossip. By then her husband had come to the door. He agreed to take me back.

I was still shaking when I entered the gracious marble foyer of the manor house. My anxiety was diverted by Clara's raised voice coming from the drawing room.

"It was terrible, Daphne. Absolutely horrible. Be thankful you didn't come with us. I barely had time to look in a shop window before Cecil insisted we return to Cheviot Chase. I told him I expected to spend the morning in Dorchester and have lunch there at least. He claimed he had spent all his money on paper and ink. Really, Daphne. Can you believe it? He said if I wanted lunch, we had best hurry back here. The man is impossible."

"Why didn't you stay in Dorchester and have him send the carriage back for you?" asked Daphne.

"I was too outraged to argue or to think of an alternative. I am seriously thinking of divorcing the beastly man."

"Really, Clara?"

"I am going to talk to John about it," declared Clara. "Where is he, anyway?"

"He said something about staying in the village for the afternoon. But whether or not he is really there, I wouldn't know," said Daphne.

"If John said he was going to the village, then that is where he is. What makes you doubt him?"

"The way he was carrying on with that slut from London. I wouldn't be the least bit surprised if he went to meet her in some secluded spot where he could have her. She's been gone for a good part of the afternoon," spewed Daphne.

"Daphne! You had better not let John hear you talk like that. He wouldn't take kindly to it. I don't think *I* like it. My brother isn't the sort of man to go around taking advantage of young ladies, especially someone under his own roof," said Clara.

"Lady? Really, Clara, you don't put *her* in the category of being a lady."

"She has shown decorum at the dinner table and when we have our tea in the drawing room."

269

"It is all an act. She is a conniving little trollop, that's what she is. Make no mistake about it. Look how long she has managed to stay here pretending to be hard at work when she spends so much of her time strolling about the estate and inveigling John into having Irons teach her to ride. Then ingratiating herself with John by helping to put out the fire in the East Wing. I wouldn't be surprised if she killed Jason because he found out about her past life in London," said Daphne.

"Don't be absurd, Daphne. I don't think I like the way you are talking."

"Well, it is possible. She had as much access to the pistol in the library as anyone else and she is forever walking the moor."

"We all had access to the gun. Oh, I don't want to talk about it. My day has been trying enough without thinking about John and Miss Clarke. I'm going up to my room and rest," said Clara.

I raced up the stairs. I didn't want to be caught listening to their conversation. Eavesdropping seemed to have become a habit with me.

Could Daphne hate me enough to try and kill me? I pushed the thought aside. Words were Daphne's weapons, not guns. Instinct told me to finish my work and leave Cheviot Chase as soon as possible, no matter how it would break my heart never to see Lord John Rathbone again.

As I walked into the drawing room shortly before dinner, I scanned everyone's face. If the fact I was still alive surprised anyone, no one registered shock. I was completely bewildered.

As Daphne floated toward John to claim him as an escort into dinner, he walked past her and offered me his arm. Daphne's face reddened. Whether from embarrassment or anger, I couldn't tell. I was in a state of euphoria as I took his arm. Daphne went to her father to be escorted.

An abnormal silence reigned during dinner. Even Sir Percy, who usually expounded his political philosophy at the dinner table, remained quiet. Only the rattle of dishes being cleared, placed, or served made one aware that there was life swirling about. I was glad when the unsettling evening was over.

Though there was a trace of fear in me, I was looking forward to the afternoon. Mr. Irons was to instruct me in the art of jumping a horse.

As I came into the stableyard, Daphne was there pacing back and forth, her riding crop slapping against the skirts of her blue velvet riding habit. She would have looked lovely if her face hadn't been screwed up in an expression of angry impatience.

When Mr. Irons led my mare into the yard, Daphne called to him. "Will you see what has happened to his lordship, Irons? He was supposed to meet me here at one sharp."

"It is only a few minutes after one, Miss Lewis. I'm sure he will be with you shortly," he replied.

Mr. Irons put the steps down for me and I mounted the mare. He handed me the reins and began to head for the stables to retrieve his own horse.

"Didn't you hear me, Irons? I'm not accustomed to being ignored," cried Daphne.

"I'm sorry, Miss Lewis. My orders are to take Miss Clarke out for her riding lesson," said Mr. Irons.

"Since when does an employee take precedence over me? My father is a peer of this land. Now do as I say, Irons, or you'll have his lordship to answer to," warned Daphne.

271

"I'll send one of the lads to speak to Mr. Jackson."

"I don't want one of the lads to go. I want you to go. Understand me?" Her voice had become strident.

Mr. Irons looked at me with raised eyebrows and a shrug of his shoulders. "I'll be with you shortly, Miss Clarke."

"That's all right. I'll walk the mare down the lane a bit and wait for you there," I said.

I veered the horse to the side, walked her a short way down the lane, and patiently sat there while the mare nibbled at the summer grass. Some minutes passed before Mr. Irons came riding up.

"I'm sorry, miss. I know you don't allot yourself much time for these lessons," he said.

"I don't mind. I don't know what use riding will be to me once I leave Cheviot Chase. But I do enjoy it," I said as we cantered toward the open fields lined with hedges and stone walls.

"That Miss Lewis is a strong-willed woman, she is. I fear her father spoils her."

"Did you find Lord Rathbone for her?" I asked.

"I gave the message to Mr. Jackson. I'm not about to go tromping through the house with manure on my boots. Mrs. Herries would have my head, she would."

I smiled. I knew Sarah could raise a right temper if she was of a mind. "Where are we going for our lesson?"

"That field over there," he replied, raising his arm to point. "The stone walls and hedges aren't too high there. Do you remember what I told you?"

"Yes."

"Getting a good start is important. The mare is a good jumper. Just give her her head." When we reached the field, he said, "Shall we start?"

I nodded and urged the horse to go faster. She breezed over the first hurdle of hedges and I felt exhilarated. Soaring in the air with a powerful animal beneath me was an experience I would never forget. Mr. Irons smiled and nodded to me then indicated the next hurdle, a stone wall. I prodded the mare on. Her front legs curled back and I was in the air once more, but not on the mare's back. I had been thrown to the ground with a nasty thud.

For several seconds I was stunned and my view of the earth was arcing in circles. Mr. Irons's face wavered before me.

"Are you all right, miss?" he asked.

"I think so." My body ached but I didn't think I had broken any bones.

I took Mr. Irons's outstretched hand and tried to stand. My leg crumpled. I almost fell, but Mr. Irons caught me.

"Perhaps you'd best stay here, miss, while I fetch someone from the house to bring a carriage for you," said Mr. Irons, rubbing his chin thoughtfully. "You might have a broken leg. Frankly, it's a wonder you didn't break your neck after a fall like that."

"I'm sure it's only my ankle. If you could help me up and get me on the horse, I will be able to get back to the house," I said.

Mr. Irons went over to the mare and picked up the reins. He looked at the saddle, which was askew. He lifted his cap and scratched his head, then examined the saddle closely.

"You had better ride my horse back to the stable," he advised.

"Why?"

"This girth has been cut. No wonder you fell off."

"Cut?"

"Aye. A sharp instrument like a razor."

"Who would do a thing like that?" I asked.

"Don't rightly know, miss. I do know we had better get back to the house. His lordship should know about this

273

right away. He don't take kindly to anyone doing damage to either his horses or equipment, especially when it might endanger someone's life."

He lifted me onto his horse and I followed as he led my mare back to the house. Two footmen carried me into the house and up to my bedchamber with an anxious Sarah following behind them.

"What happened, Janet?" she asked once the footmen had left.

"I fell off over a jump," I said, looking sheepish. It sounded so ridiculous.

"Oh, dear me. I'll have someone fetch the doctor right away."

"Mr. Irons already sent for the doctor." I lifted my skirts and leg up then peered down at my ankle, which was fast swelling.

"Oh, my," exclaimed Sarah as she stared at my foot. She knelt down and removed my boots and cotton stockings. "We'd better get you into your nightdress and into bed."

"Look, Sarah. I want to be dressed when Dr. Young gets here."

"That ankle of yours looks nasty. How did the accident happen? I thought you were doing quite well on the horse."

I decided to tell her exactly what happened. It would soon be all over anyway. "It wasn't an accident, Sarah. Someone deliberately cut the girth on my horse. The more I rode, the looser the saddle became. On the second jump, the saddle slid to the side and off I went."

"Oh, dear me. You mean someone was out to harm you?"

"Yes. If not kill me." I thought about the shots on the moor and now this. No doubt was left in my mind that someone wanted me dead. But who? That was the burning question.

"Kill you? Oh, good Lord! Does his lordship know about this?"

"I don't know. I'm sure he will hear about it though."

"It certainly won't improve his mood. He has been cross with everyone this afternoon," said Sarah.

"Why?"

"It has something to do with Miss Lewis. I haven't found out exactly what it is, but I'm sure I'll know by the end of the day." Sarah got a footstool and put it under my foot. "I'll go downstairs and get you a nice hot cup of tea. I'll be right back."

I nodded. My ankle was starting to throb. Brian entered on the heels of Sarah.

"Can I get you some tea, Doctor?" asked Sarah.

"No, thank you, Mrs. Herries." He turned to me. "Let's have a look at that ankle."

I raised my foot a couple of inches as he knelt down before me. "This may hurt a little, Janet. I'll try to go easy."

He probed and poked all around my ankle. And it did indeed hurt. I winced several times and bit my lower lip rather than cry out.

He stood. "I'm happy to say nothing is broken. But you have given it a bad twist. Do you hurt anywhere else?"

"No. At least nothing more than an aching bruise or two. Otherwise, I feel fairly normal."

"Well, I'll tape your ankle. You will have to stay off it for at least a week. After that, I'll have another look. Mrs. Herries?"

"Yes, Doctor."

"Come watch me tape her ankle. It should have a salt bath in the morning and evening, then be retaped. Do you think you'll be able to manage, Mrs. Herries?"

"Of course, doctor." She sounded wounded at the suggestion she wasn't a capable nurse.

"I'll see you in a week, Janet. If it becomes abnormally painful, send for me at once."

He picked up his bag and left. I was disappointed by his cool, abrupt manner, but not surprised. I think I hurt him when he saw my love for another man in my voice and eyes. Sarah and I had our tea.

Evening was approaching when Lord Rathbone came to my room.

"Irons told me what happened," he said. "I talked to Dr. Young. He said it is a very bad sprain and you must keep off it. Does it hurt much?"

"A bit."

He walked over to the window, in front of which rested my small table. He stared out with his hands clasped behind his back. "I am embarrassed and irate that someone in this household could have done such a horrendous thing. I used to pride myself in the integrity so highly valued at Cheviot Chase. Now it has become a place of murder and mayhem. And I feel helpless in the face of it." He turned to face me. "Please accept my humblest apology, Janet, for placing you in danger."

"There is no need to apologize, John."

He came and took a seat next to me then took my hand in his. "I feel responsible for your safety. Perhaps it would be best if you left."

I was stunned. Where would I go? And how would my heart survive not seeing him every day?

"What about the paintings?" I asked, trying desperately to hide my feelings.

"I'll get someone else to finish them. As soon as you are able to walk, I'll make arrangements for you to return to London. I have some influence at several London museums. I believe they might be able to use an excellent restoration artist. Meanwhile, I think it best you confine yourself to your rooms."

"With my ankle the way it is, I don't think I'll be

dashing about for the next few days. But I can still work. Brian never said I couldn't hobble. I can't sit around for the next several days doing nothing. Also, I feel I must earn my keep," I declared.

"You have more than earned your keep, Janet. Having you here has been one of the bright spots in my life. Do you have any idea who would want to harm you?"

"I've been trying to think of someone ever since the shooting."

"Shooting? What shooting?" His grip on my hand tightened. "Maybe you should start at the beginning, Janet. I have always had the feeling Isobel wasn't the one who hit you on the head with a rock. She would have been more inclined toward a direct attack. Tell me everything. Perhaps we can get to the bottom of all this."

I started from the very beginning, telling him about the boulder at the beach being shoved over the cliff to where I had been standing. The shots being fired at me on the moor and how I pretended to be dead.

"I think you are omitting a key point. You must have seen or done something to cause these attacks. Think, Janet," said John.

I hesitated. I didn't want to inform on or point a finger at Cecil. After all, he was John's brother-in-law. As John's cat green eyes continued to search my eyes, I lowered my gaze to stare at my bandaged ankle.

"You are holding something back, aren't you, Janet? Tell me. I promise you it will go no farther than this room."

"I don't want to implicate anyone. Besides I have no proof."

"Janet, you must tell me before there is another tragedy here. My reputation and that of Cheviot Chase are fast deteriorating. I beg of you, tell me."

I looked into his eyes once again. Between the anguish in his eyes and the plea in his voice, I could hold nothing

277

back. I told him about Cecil's furtive escapades on the moor and how I was searching the holes he had dug when the shots were fired at me. I also told him how the spot where Jason was killed overlooked that particular section of the moor. John released my hand and stood. He began to pace the room.

"Think hard, Janet. Were you hit on the head before or after you discovered Cecil's secret diggings on the moor?" asked John.

"After."

"Are you sure?"

"Positive."

"Perhaps Jason knew what Cecil was doing, blackmailed him, and got killed for it. What do you think?" asked John.

"I hate to admit it, but that was the first thought that entered my mind. But Jason talked about a large inheritance due soon. Does Cecil have that kind of money?"

"No. But my sister will. Next month she comes into a large inheritance left by our maternal grandmother. I received mine three years ago."

"Did Jason know about it?" I asked.

"Everyone here knew about it." He sat back down, steepled his forefingers, and gently tapped his lips. "Did you ever see what Cecil was burying?"

"No."

He sighed, stood, and resumed pacing. After several minutes, he said, "If you didn't find anything in holes Cecil dug, it may be he wasn't burying anything at all. Perhaps he was unearthing objects."

"I never thought of that. It could be," I responded.

"I think I shall make it my business to see exactly what Cecil is up to."

"Please don't confront him with what I have told you. I wouldn't want to accuse anyone without substantial proof."

"Don't worry. I am not going to mention it to Cecil until I have caught him at it myself. I am afraid if I say anything now it might put your life in further jeopardy. I do wish you had told me all this sooner."

"You had enough troubles to contend with, John. I didn't want to add to them."

He smiled and kissed me on the forehead. "You are very sweet, Janet. I'll go now and leave you to rest. I'll see to it your supper is sent up."

"Thank you."

With remorse in my heart, I watched him leave. It was only a matter of weeks before I would be leaving. And the kiss on the forehead made me feel like a good child who deserved a sop. I tried to console myself with the thought of a comfortable position at one of London's prestigious museums even though I dreaded the thought of living in the city again. I had come to love the moor and the freedom it offered. I loved being near the sea, where the smell of salt air refreshed my lungs. And most of all, I loved the Lord of Cheviot Chase. I would never love like this again.

Sarah had supper with me in my bedchamber. I was grateful for the company and actually enjoyed listening to her tales of the staff or family.

"I hear things aren't the same at the dinner table now that you and Mr. Watson are no longer there," said Sarah the next evening. "It is like a graveyard, they say. Mr. and Mrs. Whitney don't speak to each other and Sir Lewis gets grumpier every day. I suspect his lumbago is bothering him. Miss Lewis tries to make cheery conversation, if you can call her complaining and whining cheery. But it all seems to fall on deaf ears. When no one pays attention to her, she becomes sullen and broods. So much unhappiness! I thought his lordship's burdens would be lifted when Lady Rathbone passed on. But they seem to have become heavier. He seldom smiles. I wish I knew what was deviling the man.

I'll be sorry indeed when you leave, Janet. You have been marvelous company for me. I will truly miss you. It won't be long before you leave, will it?"

"No. Only a matter of weeks, I'm afraid."

"That is what his lordship says."

"Oh? I didn't know he had mentioned it," I said.

"He told me and Mr. Jackson. I hear he also announced it at the dinner table the day you were thrown from the horse."

He is anxious for me to leave, I thought. Perhaps he thinks my absence will stop the troubles at Cheviot Chase. After all, they seemed to start with my arrival. Still, I was determined not to leave until I had finished my work.

"Sarah, is there a cane around the house somewhere?" I asked.

"Whatever for?"

"I want to be able to hobble between here and my workroom."

"The doctor said for you to keep off your foot," she said in an admonishing tone.

"I will. I'll hold that foot off the ground and use the cane as if it were my foot. I am tired of sitting around doing nothing but reading. I want to go back to work."

"Well, I . . ."

"Please, Sarah," I pleaded.

"Oh, all right. I'll bring you one tomorrow morning. There are plenty of them lying around. Sir Lewis has been using one of them. Right now it is time to bathe your foot in the salt bath and retape it." She stood and picked up the tray. "I'll take these down to the kitchen and bring up your hot water bath."

"I'll take the bandage off. Do you think Annie could help me get dressed in the morning?"

"I'll see to it," said Sarah. "Has she done a good job in preparing you for bed?"

"She does an excellent job. She is a kind and considerate girl."

Washed, dressed, and with cane in hand, I reached my work table without undue difficulty. It felt good to be doing something useful again. Besides, my ankle was no longer painful. Several times I was tempted to put my weight on it, but common sense told me to wait a few more days. I was afraid I would do more damage by using it too soon.

The only thing that dampened my elation at being back at work was the sight of John and Daphne riding out of Cheviot Chase every afternoon. The heartbreaking part was that John seemed to enjoy it.

True to his word, Dr. Brian Young came at the end of the week. With my foot propped on a stool, he unwrapped my ankle, then examined it.

"The swelling has disappeared and everything seems to be back to normal. Does this hurt?" he asked as he moved my foot around.

"Not at all," I replied.

"Well, I guess it is time you tried putting some weight on it. Do you think you are up to it?"

"Very much." I got out of the chair and gingerly put my foot on the floor. I took a deep breath then put my weight on it. I sighed and smiled at the same time, then walked around the room. "You are right, Brian. My ankle is back to normal. Not even a twinge of pain. It feels like nothing at all had ever happened to it."

"Good. I'm glad there was no permanent damage. Well, I guess I had better get back to the village. If you have any trouble with the ankle, send for me."

"I don't think I shall be bothering you again, Brian. I will be leaving Cheviot Chase in a week or so. My work here is almost finished," I informed him.

"Oh? I didn't know you were leaving so soon. Where will you go?"

"Back to London, I imagine."

"I wish you the best, Janet."

"Thank you. And I wish you every happiness, Brian."

"I see our invalid is back on her feet," said John, who had entered so quietly we hadn't noticed his presence at once. We turned at the sound of his voice.

"She has been a good patient, Lord Rathbone," said Brian with a smile.

"She has had a good doctor," said John. He seemed in an exceptionally jolly mood.

"If all my patients did exactly what I told them, my rate of cures would go up."

"Can she resume her normal activities, Doctor?" asked John.

"I don't see why not. I wouldn't recommend sprinting in a foot race at this point, however. Perhaps in another week," replied Brian.

"Would you mind taking a look at Sir Lewis? He heard you were here and feels the need of your services," said John.

"Certainly. Good day to you all." Brian left, his black bag in hand.

John turned to me. "I suspect the first thing you would like to do is get some fresh air. Are you up to a walk outside?"

"I hope to resume my usual walk after lunch. Right now I want to get back to work."

"The devil with your work. You need some sunshine. You are as pale as a ghost. Besides, I enjoy talking to you. Shall we go to the rear courtyard? I think that is far enough for the first day," said John.

The gardens in the rear courtyard were bursting forth in their summer glory. The attar of fully bloomed roses permeated the air while pink and yellow snapdragons nodded their appreciation to the warm breeze. We sat down on the marble bench facing the water fountain.

"I really should be working, John. There is a chance I can complete my work before the end of the week, at which time I shall leave and be out of your way," I said.

"What makes you think I want you out of my way, as you put it?"

I shrugged. "I have been here some time. It is time I moved on. I have appreciated your generous hospitality."

"And what makes you think you'll be leaving by the end of the week?" he asked.

"I understand you told Mrs. Herries and announced the fact at the dinner table."

"Pay no heed to that. I thought if I spread the word that you were leaving, it would put you out of harm's way. Contrary to what I said and what you heard, I expect you to complete your work at your leisure."

"By the way, the pictures are Vermeers. You are the owner of some very valuable paintings. It shouldn't be more than a week before I am truly finished. Will you really speak on my behalf to Cecil about the British Museum?"

"We will talk about that when the time comes, Janet. Besides, if your suspicions about Cecil are correct, I don't think he will be of a mood to aid you in any way."

"I see."

"Don't look so glum. I do have connections of my own. I know a few of the peers on the boards of trustees at the Tate and National Galleries. I certainly won't leave your fate up in the air," John assured me.

"Thank you. But you aren't obligated to concern yourself with my future."

"I have put your life in jeopardy. I feel I *am* obligated to you. But let us not speak of it now."

"About Cecil. Have you discovered what it is he is

283

doing on the moor?"

"No. He hasn't left his rooms except for meals. It is as if he knows he is suspect and is being overly cautious. I certainly can't prod him to go to the moor. But something is afoot that might force him to go," said John.

"What?"

"What I tell you will be strictly between the two of us. Promise?"

"Of course."

"My sister is planning to divorce Cecil once she receives her money from the trust next month. Divorce can be a costly procedure, especially for a woman."

"Does Cecil know?"

"No. We want it kept quiet until she receives her legacy. If our suspicions about Cecil are correct, my sister might be in danger."

I thought about it for a second, then decided I had to tell him about the conversation I overheard between Daphne and Clara even if it did make me appear the snoop.

"One day I was in the foyer and heard your sister tell Daphne she was thinking of divorcing Cecil."

"Damn! I can only hope it doesn't get back to Cecil. Daphne isn't exactly closed mouth about things."

"Do you really think Miss Lewis will tell him?" I asked.

"I hope not. The thing I fear most is that she might let it slip out at the dinner table. Usually she has very little to say or to do with Cecil. She is much too concerned with her own desires."

His statement about Daphne surprised me. "I thought you and Miss Lewis . . . well . . . were on a more than a neighborly footing."

His laugh was sonorous. "Dear Janet, you must give me some credit for recognizing character traits. I have learned much from the past. I think my prior experiences with women have given me a greater insight where the fair sex is concerned, if you'll excuse my bluntness."

"I'm sorry to have intimated a different relationship. I saw you riding with Miss Lewis on several occasions and you seemed to be enchanted with her company," I said, little red spots dancing on my cheeks.

"I find her amusing in a comical way. Her obvious attempts at playing the seductress are clumsy and ludicrous. She is a shallow, greedy woman whose only concerns in life are her own ease and comfort. But I didn't bring you here to talk about Cecil and Daphne, Janet. I want to know if you—"

"Lord Rathbone," called Brian Young from the French doors. "May I see you alone for a few minutes?"

"Excuse me, Janet."

I nodded.

John rose and went to see Brian, who did most of the talking. John seemed to be getting angrier and angrier. Though they were speaking so softly I couldn't hear them, John seemed to make a terse comment to Brian, then stalked into the house. Brian stood there looking baffled. My curiosity was stirred. I left the bench and walked toward Brian. He saw me coming his way and appeared to be about to flee. But he didn't.

"I see the ankle is bearing up well," said Brian when I reached his side.

"Quite well. What happened to make his lordship so angry?" I asked with a troubled mind.

"I am afraid that is privileged information, Janet. As a doctor, I cannot discuss my cases with anyone."

"I'm sorry. I shouldn't have asked."

"That's all right." He smiled. "I know of your concern for Lord Rathbone. It is only natural you should wonder what news I imparted to upset him."

I returned his smile. "We are friends, aren't we, Brian?"

"For as long as you want, Janet."

"How is your young lady in the village?" I asked as we strolled into the house and proceeded toward the foyer.

"We are to be married in the early spring," he announced with a boyish grin.

"How wonderful for you!" I exclaimed. "I sincerely wish every happiness for both of you."

"Thank you."

We said good-bye and I went upstairs and back to work, wondering what John had intended to ask me in the garden. And curiosity about John's sudden anger nagged at me.

For as long as a could stand there
How is your sister, Jack? to the vehicle, I asked. I asked it
At least into the house and measured toward you to you

Seventeen

After being off my feet for long stretches at a time for the week, the insignificant trek to the garden had tired me more than I realized at first. Dressing to have dinner downstairs was an ordeal I didn't have the strength to execute even if Annie helped me. Besides, I wasn't of a mood to be in the company of the Lewises and the Whitneys. I informed Sarah I would be taking my dinner with her.

"I hear you had a walk in the garden today, Janet," said Sarah, pouring gravy onto her mashed potatoes then slicing into the rounds of lamb on her plate.

"Yes. It seems like ages since I had a walk in the fresh air and sun," I replied.

"Well, it has done you good. The roses are back in your cheeks. I heard Lord Rathbone was with you." She smiled with a knowing gleam in her eyes.

"He insisted on taking me into the garden."

"I think he is growing fond of you."

"Oh, Sarah. He is just being kind. I am still only an employee like the rest of you. Besides, I won't be here much longer."

"Be that as it may, I know for a fact he smiles more often when he is in your company."

"He wasn't smiling this afternoon. I think Dr. Young gave him some bad news," I said.

"You mean you haven't heard?" asked Sarah.

"Heard what?"

"Oh, there has been quite a row, there has." Sarah's large eyes glittered with excitement.

"Between whom?"

"His lordship and Sir Lewis. Lord Rathbone usually keeps his temper in check and his voice low. But when Sir Lewis started to bellow, his lordship lost his temper and bellowed back. A real shocker. The front of the East Wing echoed with their voices. His lordship made no secret of his displeasure," said Sarah with a firm nod of her head.

"What did they argue about, Sarah?" I tensed. I had the foolish notion Sir Percy had overheard what John said about Daphne. But if he was abed with his lumbago and gout, it would have been impossible for him to hear what John said in the garden.

"I didn't get the story word for word, only the general idea of it. You know how stories are never exactly right when the tale passes from mouth to mouth. Sometimes I wish I was right on the spot when these things happen. *I* know I would get the story straight," declared Sarah.

"Sarah. Please come to the point and tell me about the argument," I said, doubting if she would ever change. Her preambles to a tale seemed to get longer and longer.

"Well, the way I heard it, Dr. Young must have said something to his lordship about the bill for services rendered at Cheviot Chase. They weren't being paid and they were getting sizable," began Sarah.

"Oh, no," I interrupted. "I never thought about it. I had better ask his lordship for enough of an advance on my wages to pay the doctor bill. How foolish of me not to think about paying the doctor. I don't know how it slipped my mind."

"It has nothing to do with you, Janet. I know for a fact that his lordship paid your medical bills. Oh, no, not you at all, dear child. It is Sir Lewis's bills that haven't been paid. From what I heard, Sir Lewis charged all his medical bills to Lord Rathbone's account. Oh, his lordship is furious. I guess he told Sir Lewis he was giving them room and board as a neighborly gesture and that he wasn't about to pay for the doctor's visits and medicine used by Sir Lewis. He gave Sir Lewis a right talking-to, he did."

"What did Sir Lewis say?" I asked.

"Well, at first, he appeared to be contrite, saying it was a misunderstanding. He said he would take care of the bills as soon as he could. That Dr. Young must have misunderstood him and put the costs on Lord Rathbone's account. Can you imagine? Putting the blame on Dr. Young like that? I think it was quite underhanded of Sir Lewis, don't you, Janet?"

"It might have been an honest mistake. Sir Lewis is old and ill. He might not remember what he told Dr. Young exactly," I suggested.

"To my mind, he is not that old nor that sick," declared Sarah.

"From what you have told me, I don't see any basis for an all-out argument, especially when Sir Lewis seemed so amenable. What was the shouting about?"

"I guess Lord Rathbone decided to mention a few other things when he saw Sir Lewis in a receptive mood. He brought up Miss Lewis's extravagant purchases in London. That is when Sir Lewis started to get testy. Among other things he accused his lordship of being parsimonious. Well, that set his lordship off and he accused Sir Lewis of taking advantage of his hospitality. He said Sir Lewis was using him as though he was the Bank of England.

"Sir Lewis shouted he would pay back every farthing

and as soon as Foxhill Manor was habitable he and his daughter would leave Cheviot Chase. There was more shouting, but the maid was afraid his lordship would come bursting out of the room at any minute. She fled. I don't know if anything more was said. I was wondering when his lordship would come to his senses and realize how those people were taking advantage of his generosity."

"Do you think the Lewises will leave, Sarah?"

"Sir Lewis said they would. I don't see any reason for them to stay if the renovations at Foxhill Manor are completed," she replied.

"What if the workers haven't finished?"

Sarah shrugged. "Hard to say. For all his bluster, his lordship has a soft heart. I can't picture him turning them out, especially if they have no place to go."

"Don't they have a townhouse in London like Lord Rathbone?" I asked.

"I'm not sure, Janet. I do remember they did at one time. I think they sold it over ten years ago when Sir Lewis's wife died. Miss Lewis was a slip of a girl then. Perhaps twelve or thirteen. It was so long ago. I do know they have resided at Foxhill Manor now for the last ten years. They seldom go to London unless it is with Lord Rathbone or the Whitneys."

"I wonder how near completion Foxhill Manor is?" I said, voicing my thoughts aloud.

"To my way of thinking, it should have been done ages ago. Look how quickly the East Wing was restored. And there was certainly a lot more work done on it than just a little painting and plastering. Why, it practically had to be rebuilt," declared Sarah.

The next afternoon I made up my mind to visit Foxhill

Manor against John's wishes that I stay close to the house and not venture out alone. I knew he was thinking of my safety, but I felt I would have the advantage of a swift horse if anyone tried to attack me. After lunch I headed for the stables.

"Glad to see you up and about, Miss Clarke. How is the ankle?" asked Mr. Irons.

"Fine. The doctor said it is as good as new," I replied.

"Are you going riding today, Miss Clarke?"

"Yes. It is a fine day for it. Frankly, I have missed riding."

"I'll have one of the stable lads ride with you. His lordship doesn't want you riding alone."

"That won't be necessary, Mr. Irons. I intend to stay close to Cheviot Chase." I didn't want anyone to know I was going on a spying mission.

"I have my orders, miss."

"Really, Mr. Irons, I would prefer to be alone."

"If anything happened to you, it would be my job."

"I'll take full responsibility. I promise you nothing is going to happen to me. I won't be out for more than an hour. I'm sure Lord Rathbone will understand my need for solitude."

He lifted his cap and scratched his head. "Well, I suppose it won't hurt this once if you stay within calling distance. If you get into any trouble, you can call and someone here will hear you and come to your aid."

"Thank you, Mr. Irons."

"You're not afraid to get back on a horse, are you?"

"Not in the least. But do make sure the girth is properly fastened."

"That I will, miss. I'll saddle her myself and bring her directly to you," Mr. Irons said, then lumbered toward the stables.

It felt good to be back on a horse again. I even told

myself if I got a good position in London, I would occasionally treat myself to a ride in Hyde Park's Rotton Row.

I cantered the horse down the road in the direction of Foxhill Manor. I had to see for myself the state of repair, or disrepair, of Foxhill Manor house.

I slowed the mare to a walk as we went up the long graveled driveway, which was beginning to spawn weeds among the pebbles. The place appeared deserted. I had expected to see workmen about the place with their carts cluttering up the driveway. But there were no carts or signs of anyone about. For a minute I thought they might be inside the large and imposing edifice, but there wasn't a horse or a vehicle to mark their presence. The place had an eerie aura. I was seized with a sudden urge to turn back and not meddle in other people's affairs. But I dismounted and tethered the mare. I walked up the steps to the front door and soundly rapped the brass door knocker.

I patiently waited for the door to open. A place like Foxhill Manor couldn't be left totally unattended, I thought. The door finally opened to reveal a burly man dressed in shabby, ill-fitting pants and a soiled, torn sweater. He stood there and stared at me with narrowed eyes full of suspicion. When he seemed disinclined to greet me, I spoke.

"Are you the caretaker here?" I asked.

"Who wants to know?"

"I am Janet Clarke. I am doing some work for Lord Rathbone at Cheviot Chase."

"So?"

"I was wondering if there are any paintings that might be in need of restoration. I understand the manor house is being refurbished."

"You'll have to talk to the owner."

"May I see him?" Something was wrong, but I couldn't put my finger on it.

"He's not here." He started to close the door, but I put a staying hand on it.

"Please, sir. Is there someone I can talk to other than yourself? Perhaps one of the staff."

"Ain't no staff."

"Then perhaps the overseer of the work crew," I suggested.

"They all left over a month ago. I'm the only one here and I've got me work to do. I can't stand around blathering with a snip of a girl all day. Speak to the owner if you want any more information."

He started to close the door. I let him and went back to my horse.

I rode back to Cheviot Chase in a stupor. Why was Sir Percy keeping up the pretense of work being done at Foxhill? Where was his staff? Why was a caretaker the only one in charge of so large an estate? The questions nagged at me like a swarm of hungry flies over rotten fruit. But my greatest dilemma was whether or not to tell John.

I felt he should know, but I didn't want to be the one to tell him. I had burdened him enough with my suspicions about Cecil. I didn't want to be bringing more coals to Newcastle. All he had to do was ride to Foxhill himself. After the argument with Sir Percy, I had a feeling he would be doing just that and soon.

My stomach tightened when I saw a figure on horseback riding hard in my direction. Had I been too confident in my ability to elude an attacker? I smiled with relief when I recognized John. He reined in his horse so sharply that the animal pawed at the air and whinnied. He didn't say anything until our horses were pacing side by side.

"What do you mean by riding off alone like this? I gave strict orders that you shouldn't ride alone. Someone had to accompany you." His voice was gruff.

"I'm sorry. Please don't blame Mr. Irons. I talked him into it."

"Where did you go that was so secretive?" asked John.

"Nowhere in particular. I just wanted to be alone."

"Don't you realize you might have put your life in jeopardy? Even if you are on the main road, the moors that flank it are bleak and desolate, making you an excellent target. I didn't think you were that foolhardy, Janet."

"As I will be leaving soon, I wanted to see as much of the countryside as possible. You did say I needed fresh air and sunshine. I assure you it will be my last venture. I will stay in the house until I finish my work."

"If you do get the urge to gad about, let me know and, if possible, I will accompany you."

His words stirred a longing in me, an ache at the thought of leaving him. I changed the subject. "Did you know Dr. Young will be getting married next spring?"

"No, I didn't."

"A young lady from the village."

"I suppose it came as a shock to you. It must have hurt you deeply when he told you."

"On the contrary. I am very happy for him."

"There was a time when I believed you and Dr. Young would be taking the marriage vows. He would have made a find husband for you. Are you disappointed?"

I laughed lightly. "He is a good friend and has never been anything more to me."

"That brings me to the question I intended to ask you the other day in the garden," began John. Just then Mr. Irons came galloping toward us in a swirl of dust. "What the devil has happened now?"

Mr. Irons reined in his horse so quickly the three of us

were enveloped in dust.

"The constable wants to see you right away, Lord Rathbone. He said it was urgent. Something about some papers he has discovered and thought you should see them," said Mr. Irons.

"Where is he?" asked John.

"In the village, milord. He sent a lad out to fetch you. Sounds very important."

"You will have to excuse me, Janet. I had better see what he wants. Perhaps he now has evidence that reveals the murderer. I certainly hope so. Irons, see that Miss Clarke gets back to the house safely."

"Aye, milord."

I watched John gallop off in a fury toward the village. When he was out of sight, I turned to Mr. Irons and asked, "Did the lad say anything else?"

"No, miss. But he was very agitated as though the constable had impressed upon him the urgency of his task. I think the constable has discovered very important evidence."

Mr. Irons went on about the weather and the condition of the horses in his charge as we paced slowly back to the house. I half listened. I wished Mr. Irons had delivered his message a few minutes later. I was curious about the question John was about to ask me."

When we arrived at the house, I went directly to my workroom. I put on my smock and sat down at the table to put the finishing touches on the Vermeers. I prepared my solvents and put the bowl in its usual place.

I pushed all other thoughts from my mind and concentrated on the paintings. I calculated I would finish my work in a short time.

After an hour or so, I leaned back in the chair to study the painting before me. As I did, a cord looped over my head to circle my throat. The cord began to tighten. I clutched at it, but it was so tight against my flesh, I couldn't get my fingers between the lethal cord and my throat. I was beginning to swim toward darkness. There was a gurgling sound deep in my throat as my lungs screamed for air. I knew I had to do something quickly as strength and life began to drain from my body. What could I do? The room was getting darker.

Eighteen

Though my vision was impaired and my arms felt like leaden weights, I reached out. I knew exactly where I had placed each item on the table so I moved swiftly. I reached for my bowl of solvents. Even though my strength was fast ebbing, I managed to toss the contents over my shoulder in what I hoped was the direction of my assailant's face.

My hopes were fulfilled. A male voice groaned and sputtered in agony. Air rushed into my lungs and I gulped it down greedily. At the same time, I jumped out of the chair and raced toward the door. Though his hands were over his face, I knew my attacker.

I raced down the corridor to the servants' staircase, then bounded down the stairs like a frightened hare leaping over the moor. I practically crashed into the kitchen, causing its occupants to gape at me in wonder. My hand circled my throat as I continued to gasp for air. To my relief, Mr. Jackson was in the kitchen. I addressed myself to him in a raspy voice.

"Mr. Jackson, please send someone to the village immediately to fetch the constable and Lord Rathbone. Then please go up to my workroom and hold that man there even if you have to do it at gunpoint. He tried to strange me."

He stared at me with a quizzical expression. For a minute, I thought he was going to ignore my orders and rebuke me for overstepping my authority in the house. But suddenly his eyes betrayed a respect for me I never knew he harbored. Without a word, he turned on his heel, gave the order to a footman just entering the kitchen, then went upstairs faster than I have ever seen him move.

"Whatever happened, Miss Clarke?" asked Cook, wiping her hands on her apron and looking startled.

"I was attacked." I removed my hand from my throat to reveal the deep red welt the cord had left.

"Eeh my!" exclaimed Cook as the scullery girls gasped and twirled their aprons into a spiral. "Go fetch Mrs. Herries," ordered Cook, nodding to one of the girls before turning back to me. "You sit yourself at the table, Miss Clarke. I'll be getting you a good hot cup of tea with a healthy dash of brandy in it. I always keep a bottle in the kitchen for medicinal purposes. Now sit you down."

I meekly obeyed. My legs were getting too shaky to stand on. "Thank you," I said hoarsely.

"Now don't you be trying to talk. Your throat is neither looking nor sounding too good," said Cook as she poured a hefty dash of brandy into the tea then pushed the cup toward me.

More people sauntered into the kitchen to stand around the table and stare at me. I was oblivious of their steady gaze as I sipped the hot, refreshing tea. The brandy had a relaxing and soothing effect on my throat.

Some time had gone by and I began to wonder where Sarah was. Usually, she was on the spot when there was trouble in the house. When she finally arrived, she looked sick and nervous.

"Oh, my poor, dear, Janet. How horrible for you. Let me see your throat, child." When she had examined it, she shook her head and made clucking sounds with her tongue against the roof of her mouth. "Mr. Jackson told me what happened. Thank God you are all right. They have sent me to bring you up to the drawing room straight away."

"They?"

"Lord Rathbone and Constable Andrews," she replied, wringing her hands.

"Are they here already? They were sent for only minutes ago," I said, rising from the chair after draining the brandied tea from the cup.

"They were returning to Cheviot Chase when Mr. Irons caught up to them and told them what happened," Sarah informed me as we mounted the stairs. "They raced all the way back."

Sarah remained in the foyer while I headed for the drawing room. When I entered, my knees buckled at the sight of my assailant sitting there, his eyes red, his face flushed. The solvent had done its work, for which I was grateful.

Seeing me teeter, John was instantly at my side, his strong, steadying arm around my shoulders as he led me to the settee. His arm remained around my shoulders as we sat down together. I nodded an acknowledgment to Constable Andrews. Mr. Jackson stood in the background.

"Jackson, get Miss Clarke a snifter of brandy," said John.

In seconds Mr. Jackson handed me the brandy then went back to being unobtrusive in a corner of the drawing room.

I took several sips of the brandy.

"Better?" asked John.

"Yes." My voice was improving.

John lightly traced a finger over the red welt around my throat, then turned to the man sitting in a straight

299

chair across from us.

"I could kill you for this, Percy," said John.

"Here . . . here. Please let us have no more talk of killing," said Constable Andrews, ensconced in a comfortably padded chair. "Now, Sir Lewis, would you care to tell us why you tried to strangle Miss Clarke?"

Sir Percy remained mute as he stared straight ahead with red, watery eyes, his hands clasped tightly together in his lap.

"Come now, Sir Lewis," the constable continued. "We will get the story one way or the other. We have found out about Foxhill Manor."

Sir Lewis shot him a look of raw anger, glanced at John imperiously, then stared into space again.

The constable's shoulders heaved in a silent sigh. "We know you are no longer in possesson of Foxhill Manor. We also know you lost the entire estate to one Mr. Harold King of London in a game of chance. And that he is the person who initiated the renovations at Foxhill. You have been living off the good graces of Lord Rathbone. Do you have anything to say in your own defense?"

Sir Lewis remained mute.

"Do you have any suggestions, Lord Rathbone?" asked the constable after a sigh of irritated disgust.

"Perhaps if we brought his daughter down here, she might be able to shed some light on the attempted murder of Miss Clarke," said John.

"Possibly," agreed the constable.

"Jackson, please tell Miss Lewis her presence is required in the drawing room," said John.

"Yes, milord."

"No! Wait!" cried Sir Lewis. "I don't want my daughter implicated in this. I will tell you what you want to know. Ask your questions, Constable."

Constable Andrews arched his eyebrows. "Let us begin with the attempt to take Miss Clarke's life."

"May I have a whiskey first?" asked Sir Lewis.

The constable looked at John, who turned and nodded to Mr. Jackson. With the glass in hand, Sir Lewis took a long pull on the whiskey before he spoke.

"John was showing undue interest in Miss Clarke. She is not of our class and I thought it unfitting of him, especially with my daughter in the house. She was diverting John's attentions away from my daughter. I thought if she was out of the way, John would come to his senses and realize my daughter would make a suitable wife. That's all."

"That's all? That's all?" cried John, his tone menacing. "Snuff out a human life as though it was no more than a speck of dust on your frock coat? How could I have harbored such a fiend under my roof?"

"I believe Lord Rathbone informed everyone that Miss Clarke was to leave Cheviot Chase shortly," said the constable. "Why did you still attempt to kill her? She would have been away from here soon."

"Out of sight is not always out of mind," said Sir Lewis. "We all presumed she would be going back to London. John has a townhouse in London. I believe the best way to rid oneself of the competition is to eliminate it."

"And is that why you killed Lady Rathbone? To get rid of the competition and make sure Lord Rathbone was free to marry again?" queried the constable.

Sir Lewis's mouth fell agape as he stared at the constable in terrified wonder. "How did you know?"

"Actually, it was a guess. Lady Rathbone was strangled with a cord. The same method used on Miss Clarke. I felt it was too similar to be a coincidence. I think you owe us an explanation, Sir Lewis."

Sir Lewis emitted either a moan or a groan. I was happily sipping the brandy, feeling euphoric with John's arm around me.

"Lady Rathbone was hopelessly insane," began Sir Lewis. "She could have lived a long time. My time was running out. What little money I had left was dripping away. I had to get John to marry Daphne quickly if I was to maintain our position in life. While Lady Rathbone was in the hospital, it was next to impossible to dispose of her. Fate stepped in to help me. She escaped. When I saw her sneaking through a basement window in the East Wing, I knew an opportunity would soon present itself. When the East Wing became closed to her, I discovered she was living on the moor, her favorite place being the coppice. She was weak and in a deep sleep when I put the cord about her neck."

"Why and how did you rip her throat open?" asked the constable.

"I used the hand rake from the gardener's shed. I wanted everyone to think the dogs or some wild beast did it," said Sir Lewis tonelessly.

"I see." The constable got up, walked behind his chair, and braced his hands on the back of it. "Let us return to Miss Clarke. Lord Rathbone tells me she was assaulted twice when she first came to Cheviot Chase. First with a rock on her head, then a near-miss with a boulder falling on the beach. Were you instrumental in those attacks, Sir Lewis?"

Sir Lewis took a swallow of the whiskey, then nodded. "I only wanted to scare her away at first. She didn't appear to be a threat in the beginning, but she was young and slightly pretty. I did not want any young woman around competing with my daughter. Later, when John insisted she dine with us and wearing her fancy gowns, I saw her as a definite threat." He spoke and looked like a man who was more than beaten; he was totally vanquished and had resigned himself to his ignoble fate.

There was a gleam of confidence in the constable's eyes as he plunged ahead. "Why did you kill Jason Watson?"

"He had seen me come out of the coppice with the bloodied rake in my hand. He started blackmailing me. Jason didn't know I had lost everything to gambling. He saw me as an unending well of money. As I was running out of money, I had no choice but to kill him. When I saw him coming up the knoll for his payment, I shot him before he came close enough to see the gun."

"I see." Constable Andrews stroked his chin. "And what did you use to weaken the girth on Miss Clarke's saddle?"

"I don't remember."

"Surely you must know what you used, Sir Lewis. You held it in your hand."

"I was under a great strain. I don't remember," Sir Lewis insisted.

"I see." Constable Andrews scratched his head. "I understand you suffer from lumbago and the gout. Is that correct, Sir Lewis?"

Sir Lewis nodded.

"Then tell me how you managed to carry out your nefarious deeds when suffering from these painful ailments. I should think they would have impeded your attacks," said the constable.

"I faked them to give me an alibi when needed."

"You must be an excellent actor to have duped a man of Dr. Young's abilities."

"My father had lumbago and gout. I learned the symptoms from him and I learned them well."

"Are you willing to sign a statement that reiterates all you have told us here this afternoon?" asked the constable.

"Yes." Sir Lewis drained the whiskey from his glass.

Constable Andrews turned to John. "Lord Rathbone, would you mind if I had Sir Lewis confined to his room until my men arrive?"

"Only if he is removed before nightfall," replied John.

"My men should be here shortly. I will have him out of

303

here long before dinner, I assure you, Lord Rathbone."

"Jackson," called John. "See Sir Lewis to his room. Take the shotgun with you and stand guard at his door."

"Yes, milord." Mr. Jackson took Sir Lewis by the arm and pulled him from his chair as though he were a limp puppet.

When they had left, Constable Andrews said, "It is not knitting together, Lord Rathbone."

"What do you mean, Tom?" asked John.

"For one thing, Jason Watson was shot at very close range, not from several feet away as Sir Lewis claims. Another thing, it isn't plausible that Sir Lewis remembers everything except what instrument he used to cut the cinch. His story doesn't quite hang together. Instinct tells me he doesn't know what instrument was used to cut the cinch. In short, Lord Rathbone, I believe Sir Lewis had an accomplice. I wonder if you would be so kind as to have Miss Lewis join us in the drawing room."

"Surely you don't think she is involved in all this, Tom."

"I have a few questions for her, Lord Rathbone. She might be able to clarify a few points."

John removed his arm from my shoulders and went to pull the bell cord. I was still sipping at the brandy, feeling warmer and more at ease with each passing minute. After listening to the horrendous tale told my Sir Lewis, I felt foolish when I realized there was a smile on my face. I quickly erased it when Sarah came into the room. After speaking with John, she vanished and he resumed his seat beside me. This time he did not put his arm around my shoulders.

I sat a little straighter and perked up when Daphne floated into the drawing room. Her smile was sweet and sparkling, while her golden curls bounced around her head. Her blue eyes were wide with innocence.

"Did you want to see me, John?" she asked as she came

directly to the settee and prepared to sit down.

"Constable Andrews would like to speak to you, Daphne," said John.

The sweet smile on her face disappeared as she spun around to see Constable Andrews standing behind the Queen Anne chair.

"Please have a seat, Miss Lewis." The constable came around the chair and, with an opened hand, gestured for her to be seated in the Queen Anne.

"What is this all about, John? I thought *you* wanted to see me," said Daphne as she demurely sat down, arranging her full skirt in pleasing folds.

"I believe this is your show, Tom," said John.

"Miss Lewis, your father has just made a full confession. Once I have him in the village, he is prepared to sign a full disclosure statement regarding the murder of Lady Rathbone and the attempt on Miss Clarke's life."

"I don't know what you are talking about, Constable." Daphne glanced at John with a fluttering of eyelashes. Her gaze returned to Constable Andrews when he resumed speaking.

"A little over an hour ago, your father tried to strangle Miss Clarke. Her quick thinking not only prevented him, but caught him in the act. He has made a complete confession. We had already found out, through court papers, that he had gambled away his estate, Foxhill Manor, and was almost out of money."

"I know nothing about it. My father doesn't confide in me." Her jaw had a stubborn set to it.

"Did you know Jason Watson was blackmailing your father?" asked the constable, trying to control his growing irritation with the young woman.

"No. Why would Jason blackmail my father?"

"Jason Watson knew your father killed Lady Rathbone."

"This is ridiculous. I'll not sit here and let you defame my father's good name." Daphne put her hands on the arms of the chair as if to rise.

"Please stay seated, Miss Lewis. I am not finished," declared the constable.

"John, aren't you going to do something? You can't sit there and let this man accuse my father of such heinous crimes," said Daphne.

"Please let Constable Andrews continue, Daphne. I am sure you will be interested in what he has to say," said John.

"Constable, you must realize my father is a peer of the land and can very well boot you out of your job," Daphne warned. All the soft coquettishness had left her face. That seductive sparkle in her eyes had become a hard, bitter glare.

"Your father is an impoverished peer, Miss Lewis, not to mention he will get the gallows for murder and attempted murder," said the constable.

"I don't believe one word of this. I want to talk to my father. He must be in a state of shock with those vile accusations you have heaped upon him." Daphne folded her arms over her bosom resolutely.

"Lord Rathbone, do you think you can convince Miss Lewis of my veracity?" asked the constable, casting a pleading look at John.

"Daphne," John began gently. "Constable Andrews is telling you the truth. I was seated right here when your father told us everything about the murders and the attempt on Janet's life. Please cooperate with Constable Andrews or it will go poorly for both you and your father."

"Me? I have nothing to do with all this," cried Daphne.

I peered at Daphne through narrowed eyes. Her expression hadn't changed when John verified the constable's words. She seemed to have transformed herself from the fluffy, inane seductress to a ruthless, calculating woman. Her bow mouth curved down in a harsh, implacable manner. She looked far more dangerous than her father. A shiver tickled my spine and I took another sip of the brandy.

Daphne took a deep breath. "If this is all true, I had better go up to my father. He will need me now. I presume he is still in the house."

"Yes. Jackson took him up to his room and is guarding it until the constable's men come for him," John informed her.

"Just a few more questions, Miss Lewis," said the constable.

"Please make them brief, Constable. My father is not a well man."

"Of course." The same glint of confidence came into the constable's eyes, as if he hoped another long shot would pay off. "Tell me, Miss Lewis, why did you shoot Jason Watson?"

Daphne's hands gripped the chair's arms and all color drained from her face. Her complacent expression turned to one of fear. She stared at the constable as though he was an intolerable mythical beast intent on victory.

"Come, come, Miss Lewis," said the constable. "I told you your father has confessed all. Surely you realize the game is over. All the plots are now in the open."

"The old fool! He botched everything up with his damn soul baring. He never did have any strength of character," spewed Daphne. "You have no proof, no proof at all. You only could have gotten him on attempted murder if he hadn't opened his stupid mouth. Stupid old man! I told him to make sure he had a clear field before coming out of the coppice. But no! In his hurry to get away, he let that weasel Jason see him. I had everything planned so carefully."

There was a trace of surprise on Constable Andrews's face as though he had opened Pandora's box and was startled at the contents. He quickly masked the expression.

"You haven't answered my question, Miss Lewis. Why did *you* kill Jason Watson?"

"Jason was younger and stronger than father. My father was afraid he wouldn't be able to garrote Jason as easily as a woman. Frankly, I think the old bugger was afraid of Jason. And Jason was always on his guard whenever he met with father. I decided I had to be the one to stop Jason's blackmailing. Jason always expressed an interest in me. I played on it and encouraged him. When I met him on the knoll, he wasn't the least suspicious. When he came to embrace me, I shot him," said Daphne with the coolness of a detached observer.

"Where did you get the gun?"

"Guns were the only articles my father hadn't gambled away."

"And the attempts on Miss Clarke's life on the moor and the cut cinch of her saddle?" The constable smiled with the confidence of a hunter who had trapped his quarry.

"So he told you about that, too. What a bloody informer he turned out to be. My own father betraying his daughter. Vile old man!" She glared at me. "Everything would have gone smoothly if *she* hadn't shown up. I even had a plan to do away with Isobel while she was in the hospital. Her escape made it easier if that idiot father of mine hadn't bungled it. I would have been Lady Rathbone by now if the ubiquitous Miss Clarke hadn't ingratiated herself at Cheviot Chase. I really thought I had gotten the little strumpet when she was digging on the moor. I should have remembered father's guns never were too accurate at a distance. When I learned she was still alive, I had to goad the old man into doing away with her by reminding him this was our only chance to live the way in which we had become accustomed. We certainly didn't have enough money to set ourselves up in London where I might have captured a wealthier husband. Now the old fool has ruined everything." Daphne's face was red with anger.

Sarah Herries came bustling into the drawing room with the announcement, "Your men are here, Constable Andrews."

"Thank you. Please show them to Sir Lewis's room and tell them to take him into custody. And before they leave, please have them stop in here for Miss Lewis," said the constable.

"Yes, sir," said Sarah, looking stunned and bewildered as she glanced at Daphne.

"You must give me time to pack my clothes and personal articles," said Daphne.

"I'm afraid you won't be needing them, Miss Lewis."

The silence reigning in the drawing room was unbearable. Daphne stared into space while Constable Andrews kept an eye on her. I, too, was looking at her, but with a critical eye. How could such evil lurk under all that beauty? I asked myself. I was relieved when Sir Lewis and Daphne were taken away.

Constable Andrews remained to have a whiskey with John. I was still nursing my brandy.

"I was shocked by Daphne's revelations," said John. "I never thought her capable of murder. She had me completely fooled. She always appeared to be out of touch with the real world. Her mind seemed to be consumed with clothes and glittering socials. What made you suspect her, Tom?"

"I didn't believe Sir Lewis shot Jason Watson nor did I believe he cut the cinch. I had an intuitive feeling another person was involved. I wasn't sure who it was until I mentioned the loss of Foxhill Manor. If she had been telling the truth that she knew nothing of her father's business, she would have reacted to the news quite differently. Perhaps shock or hysterics. To learn of the loss of one's home would greatly upset anyone. Miss Lewis didn't bat an eyelash. I knew then she was lying. She knew a lot more than she was telling me. I cast the bait and she took it. I thought she was involved, but when she revealed she was the one behind the murderous conspiracy, I was stunned. A real shocker."

"I agree with you, Tom. Daphne's well-constructed facade certainly hides the rotting debris inside. What will become of them?" asked John.

"The gallows, I suspect."

"Even Daphne?"

"Possibly. Especially as she confessed to being the instigator, pushing her father to execute the dastardly deeds. I don't think a jury will take kindly to that. You'll all have to testify at the trial."

"I realize that, even though I don't relish reliving the horror of it all."

"Thank you for the drink, Lord Rathbone. I'd best be getting back to make sure the prisoners are secure until I can take them to a proper jail in Dorchester. The sooner I have their confessions on paper, the happier I will be."

After John saw the constable to the door, he came back and took his seat on the settee again. I drained the rest of the brandy and gingerly put the delicate glass down on the table before me. I could feel a numbness settling in my limbs. Even my eyelids were becoming heavy. I vaguely heard John say, "Now for that question I have been trying to ask you . . ." My eyes closed and I heard no more.

been telling the truth that she knew nothing of her
father's activities who would have turned to the news
quite differently. Perhaps shock or hysterics. To learn of
the loss of ...

Nineteen

Sarah's voice seeped into my brain as some distant creeping fog.

"Wake up. Wake up, Janet," Sarah urged as she shook my shoulder.

"Where am I?" I asked as I sat up and shook my groggy head.

"In your bed."

"How did I get here? The last thing I remember was sitting in the drawing room."

"His lordship said you fell asleep on the settee. He brought you up here and I put you to bed."

"It must have been the brandy. I am not used to drinking strong spirits," I said, putting my hand to my head.

"I have a hot tub ready for you. A good soak will make you feel better. His lordship wants you down to dinner this evening. Which gown will you wear?" asked Sarah.

"I may as well wear the new blue one. I will be leaving here tomorrow afternoon and I won't have much use for it after that."

"Tomorrow? Why so soon?"

"An hour's work in the morning will end my services here. There is no reason for me to stay any longer."

"Oh, dear. I will sorely miss you, Janet. Things won't be the same without you."

Once in the tub with Sarah washing my hair and the warm water soothing my body, Sarah asked, "Now tell me everything that was said in the drawing room. Mr. Jackson won't let out a peep."

"I don't know if I should, Sarah."

"Oh, Janet. Don't be silly. I know Sir Lewis tried to kill you and that Constable Andrews took both Sir Lewis and his daughter away. Gossip will be spreading all over the village like a rampant fire. Lord knows what they will be saying about all this. I want to be able to tell the staff the truth and not have them listening to distorted tales from the village."

Her argument made sense and I began to relate the events of the afternoon in as much detail as I could remember. I was dressed and my hair fashionably coiffed by the time I had finished the tale.

"I never did like Miss Lewis, but I didn't think she was capable of murder. She seemed so empty-headed and frivolous, innocent in a brainless way. Who would ever think of her being capable of plotting murders. Poor Mr. Watson. He wasn't a mean or really cruel man," commented Sarah.

"But he was a blackmailer. Money had blinded him to the dangerous route he had taken. He should have reported what he had seen to the police right away. It might have saved his life and everyone else a lot of grief." With that said, I headed downstairs.

During dinner John told Clara and Cecil all that had transpired in the afternoon. For once Cecil listened with rapt attention. Incredulity widened his eyes behind his glasses. Clara looked horrified.

"And to think I went to London and spent so much time alone with a murderess. It is all so hard to believe.

312

Sir Percy appeared to be a benign old man. And Daphne seemed so sweet and innocent," said Clara.

"I believe she had all of us fooled," said John.

"Janet. I wish to apologize to you. With Daphne's righteous talk about keeping class distinctions lest we lose our superior place in life, I let her influence my attitude toward you. It is obvious you have more morality and human decency in you than Daphne could ever conceive of or harbor. If Sir Percy and Daphne are examples of a superior class, then I am inclined to become a libertarian like my brother," said Clara, giving me a warm, friendly smile.

"There is no need to apologize, Clara. As John said, Daphne Lewis had fooled everyone." I returned her smile.

"Still, I should have exercised more independence of thought and given you a chance. I should have known John's judgment of character is seldom wrong. I should have accepted you as readily as he did," said Clara.

John laughed. "I wouldn't put much stock in my knowledge of character after this. My judgment of Sir Percy and Daphne was certainly lacking."

"We harbored murderers under this roof and they lived in our wing of the house," said Cecil as if the realization of what John told them had just struck him.

"Well, the brilliant historian has finally faced today's reality," chided Clara.

"I think we shall escort the ladies into the drawing room and have our port there. I wish to discuss something with everyone present. Are you agreeable, Cecil?" asked John as he rose from the table. John pulled my chair back and offered me his arm. "Have I told you how beautiful you look this evening?"

I blushed and thanked him.

As we settled ourselves in the drawing room, Clara

313

poured and handed me a cup of tea in a most friendly manner. John and Cecil were seated with glasses of port in their hands. It saddened me to think by tomorrow afternoon I would no longer be a part of it.

"I think you should know, John, that Cecil and I have come to an understanding. He is moving to Chester just south of Liverpool. I am to divorce him on the grounds of desertion. I will have his full cooperation in the matter. As for myself, I intend to move into our London town house and start a new life for myself," said Clara. "It is quite amicable."

Cecil brightened and became animated as he said, "Chester should hold a wealth of information on the early Romans. The city is surrounded by ancient walls and was a depot for the Twentieth Roman Legion. I am most anxious to start my exploration of it."

"I see," said John, not at all surprised by his sister's decision. There was a glitter in his eyes and a sardonic smile on his lips that indicated he was about to unleash unpleasant tidings. "Tell me, Cecil, what have you done with the objects you have stolen from me?" he asked, using Constable Andrews's direct approach.

Cecil almost dropped his glass of port as his hand began to shake. "What?" he cried.

"I believe you heard me, Cecil."

"I don't know what you mean, John."

"What possible objects could Cecil steal from you, John? Nothing is missing from the house," said Clara, causing Cecil to cast a surreptitious glance at her.

"Cecil knows what I mean, Clara. As long as you intend to leave Cheviot Chase, Cecil, I will not bring charges against you. But I want my curiosity satisfied."

Clara looked at her husband. "What is this all about, Cecil?"

"It is a small matter of no consequence, Clara,"

said Cecil.

"No consequence? Really, Cecil, you understate the situation. I think it is of great consequence when one's property is being robbed of hundreds, perhaps thousands, of pounds," said John.

Cecil stared at the glass in his hand and remained silent.

Clara looked astonished as she glared at her husband. "Whatever have you been up to, Cecil?"

"You may as well disclose your little game, Cecil. You see I did some digging of my own on the moor," said John with a smile of triumph.

Cecil couldn't meet the gaze directed at him. His eyes remained fixed on his glass when he finally spoke.

"A year or so ago I happened to find an ancient Roman artifact that rains had washed clear of its earthen grave. I took it to the British Museum to have it authenticated. They offered me a handsome price for it. It encouraged me to begin a systematic search of that section of the moor. I learned it abounded in Roman artifacts, most of them gold with precious gems. The museum continued to pay me for them and I banked the money in London. I set myself a monetary goal. When I had attained that goal, I intended to explore all of England for signs of Roman habitation. When Clara told me of her intention to divorce me, I decided to start that exploration immediately. Besides, I have almost accumulated enough money."

"Why, you are nothing more than a thief, Cecil," declared Clara. "Taking valuable objects off my brother's property without notifying him, then being so parsimonious that you let my brother practically support us, is more than I can tolerate. You have shamed me, Cecil. I am sorry I ever met you, much less married you. You thoroughly disgust me. I am going to my room and make preparations for my move to London. My doors shall be locked. I never want to see you again, Cecil." Clara rose and stalked out of the room, her head held high, her back rigid.

"The money I received from the museum is all in the bank," murmured Cecil. "I haven't touched a farthing of it. I will withdraw all of it and give it to you, John."

"That won't be necessary. I will be satisfied if you are out of Cheviot Chase first thing in the morning. Please be gone before we come down to breakfast," said John.

Cecil nodded. "I had better go pack." With his head bowed, he walked limply from the room.

"Well, that clears up the mysterious diggings on the moor," said John.

"Will you continue to dig for artifacts?" I asked.

"I have given it some thought and decided to hire a professional to dig for them. After expenses, I will use the money to have a clinic erected in the village. Dorchester is a long way to travel when a life-threatening emergency occurs."

"And the painting? What do you intend to do with those three masterpieces?"

"I thought I would see about putting them in the National Gallery or the Tate. I think it would be rather nice to see them hanging there with a small plaque stating 'On loan from the Rathbone collection.' What do you think, Janet?"

"It would be a lovely gesture."

"It has been a harrowing day. I suspect you are tired, Janet."

I put my hand to my throat. It finally struck me I could be dead now. Suddenly a weariness overtook me. "I think I will retire. I want to get up early and finish things up."

"I take it you will be leaving tomorrow afternoon," said John.

316

I nodded.

"I shall see you before you leave, Janet."

Early the next morning, I finished the paintings and had them back in their frames in a little over an hour. I decided to take one last walk on the moor. I would leave the packing until I returned. Besides, there wasn't much to pack.

I left by the servants' door. I didn't want to see anyone. I wanted to spend the rest of the morning alone with my thoughts.

I strolled the moor, which rolled inexorably to the cliffs high above the swirling sea. As I stood on the high precipice and gazed at the sea, my eyes became misted with incipient tears. I was prevented from giving way to outright sobbing by the feel of animals rubbing against my legs. I looked down to see the black mastiffs at my feet. I knelt down to give them a final petting.

Strong hands gripped my shoulders and pulled me up. I was turned around to look directly at the dear face of Lord John Rathbone.

"I thought I would find you here," said John, keeping a steady hold on my shoulders. "I don't think we will be interrupted again. Perhaps now I can ask you that question."

"I am sorry I have been so preoccupied." There was a quiver in my voice. His close presence had that kind of effect on me.

"Janet, you must know how much I have come to love you. I think I knew I would fall deeply in love with you that first day when you came into the library. What I want to know is do you think you could ever come to care for me?"

My mouth fell foolishly agape as I gazed at him in awe.

All kinds of words tumbled in my brain, but I couldn't seem to find the right ones to express my feelings.

"You don't have to answer me right this minute, but I would like an answer before you leave," said John.

When I saw the warm sincerity in his green eyes, the words poured forth. "Care for you, John? Can't you see the love in my eyes? Didn't you notice how I trembled with joy every time you touched me? And when you kissed me, didn't you recognize the love and desire as I returned that kiss? Care for you? Oh, John, I love you."

He gathered me in his arms and held me tight. "My dear, sweet, Janet. Knowing you and having you at Cheviot Chase has been the only pleasure I have known for years. I can't bear to think of life without you. Will you marry me, Janet?"

"Oh, yes, John. With all my heart and soul, I will marry you."

His mouth came down on mine with passionate determination. My head swirled in bliss.

"I will still have to leave Cheviot Chase," I said when the kiss ended. "I couldn't possibly stay here as an unchaperoned bride-to-be."

"I have it all arranged. You will go to London with my sister, where she will assist you in selecting a wedding gown and trousseau. All the proper attire for the future Lady Rathbone. I will post the banns immediately. After two weeks in London, Clara will escort you back for the wedding. In two weeks hence, you will be my wife, love."

"How does Clara feel about it? Have you asked her?"

"She is delighted and is looking forward to leading you through all the fine dress shops in London." He hugged me tighter.

"Isn't it a bit soon after Isobel's death?" I asked. "There might be talk."

"I don't give a damn. Let them talk. I want you as my wife—in my arms and in my bed—as soon as possible.

318

Will talk bother you?"

I smiled. "With your arms around me, nothing bothers me."

His head bent low to whisper in my ear. "My arms will be around you every possible moment. I will teach you how blissful a real heaven can be. Oh, my love, my love."

His lips nipped at my ear before trailing over my cheek, his mouth settling over mine to give me a taste of that promised heaven.